Auguries of Desolation

A Year of Stories

Sheila Mengert

Blue Forge Press
Port Orchard, Washington

Dedication

IN the midway of this our mortal life,
I found me in a gloomy wood, astray
Gone from the path direct: and e'en to tell
It were no easy task, how savage wild
That forest, how robust and rough its growth,
Which to remember only, my dismay
Renews, in bitterness not far from death.…
And as a man, with difficult short breath,
Forespent with toiling, 'scap'd from sea to shore,
Turns to the perilous wide waste, and stands
At gaze; e'en so my spirit, that yet fail'd
Struggling with terror, turn'd to view the straits,
That none hath pass'd and liv'd.

These lines drawn from the beginning of the Inferno of the *The Divine Comedy* by Dante express the mood of *Auguries of Desolation*. This book is my own attempt at an *Inferno*, an assessment of this critical moment in our collective lives. The stories are meant to be disconcerting and the characters owe their fragmented existence to these disordered times. I chose the passage cited above from the Inferno with deliberation because it speaks of a period of crisis when youth's optimism melts away, when the period of the Bildungsroman is over, and when one discovers that the conclusions that guided our mature years may themselves have been inadequate and prematurely reached. There follows, as the sun passes its zenith, that period of the dark wood beset by a longing for conversion to a faith that is itself beset by its own time of troubles. The path through these dark woods or stormy straits has yet to be negotiated. That is where we are at the present hour. To understand the present is to realize the need to turn resolutely toward the future because the ground is still shifting beneath our feet and time is of the essence. Resolution in turn instills dedication that looks behind us and around us to get our bearings and then to relinquish what cannot be restored.

A dedication should express gratitude to those persons who have aided in the production of the work and make some reference to the unknown reader kind enough to see value in the final product. Writers, particularly if they are serious about their craft and message, seldom manage without sponsors, confidants, and support as they carve meaning out of experience. My Father has been the one who makes all things possible for me. His influence on my mind and values matches his other contributions. He has kept the discordant carnival of my life in motion even when neither of us could fully know or comprehend its direction. We are too alike in temperament and personality to agree on many things but difference has not diminished our mutual respect and esteem. In essentials we share a common faith.

A parting word to the indulgent reader, my advice is to tread lightly and cautiously through these auguries and look to my *Purgatorio* and my *Paradiso,* future projects, for a truer assessment leading to my final view on birth and death and all that lies between.

TABLE OF CONTENTS

Auguries of Desolation

A Year of Stories

Sheila Mengert

Bats

eo P. Amorth was not a man who delighted in nor appreciated nuance or ambiguity; everything had its use and right reason dictated that use. There was a correct way to do everything and rules were designed to enlighten the ignorant and to ensure compliance. Each field of human endeavor possessed its own science and technique to which by some marvelous quality of personal enlightenment he had at least some proximate access and understanding. A mere hint was adequate to open vast vistas of speculation on his part that led him to conclusions that made further inquiry superfluous. For these reasons it had always puzzled him why his daughter, the sole genetic carrier of his enlightened genes, should be the type of girl, and now young woman, that she had turned out to be. He had not expected that she would turn out to be a carbon copy of her father, her mere sex of course made that impossible. He had hoped though for a sensible girl grounded in science, good at mathematics, and immune as far as possible from the eccentric whims of her gender. Imagine his surprise and impatience then when the years disclosed that his offspring was introspective, artistic, and prey to any number of peculiar obsessions and compulsions.

As a child she had picked at her skin, become attached to various unsuitable objects to which she had given names, and would cry if every bean in a can of beans was not shaken out lest it be left behind divorced from its fellows and have surrendered its little bean-life in vain. She carried sensitivity beyond the religious mandate of charity; even that supreme Christian mandate it seemed to him should not preclude sound business sense. Where would his enterprises have been if he had not known early on that the world is a jungle? From whence then would have come the funds to pay for her costly schooling in that vague and pointless series of pursuits called "the humanities." He had hoped that the ever-practical Jesuits would knock some sense into her when she enrolled in a Jesuit college, but alas she had emerged, temperamentally speaking, little different after four years than when she went in.

Her major altered each quarter. At first she was convinced that she should be a marine biologist and raise algae to feed starving people. Before she ended her freshman year this had changed to being a veterinarian and an obsession with afghan hounds. In her sophomore year she had only emerged for classes and then went back to her dorm room where she remained in pajamas all afternoon reading the novels of the Bronte sisters. It was not until her junior year that she abandoned the sciences forever and began that most inconclusive of all pursuits, the study of philosophy.

After graduation she had stumbled about in various underpaid employments, reading all the time in various fields from Mayan culture to the causes of the demise of the Incas. She had cried that Archbishop Oscar Romero of El Salvador had been killed because he had supported the cause of the workers. Meanwhile she was indifferent to the appeals from various obscure congregations of brothers and sisters, publishers of tracts on avoiding countless assorted sins, whose efforts were well within the normal parameters of Catholic apostolic missions. Ritual took second place in her mind to the relief of suffering whereas for her father they were the sum and total of the life of a man destined for heaven.

Leo had always taken pride in his middle name, Pius, the appellation of so many Popes of the 20th century. These men had their pontificates at the high-water mark of Catholic unity and mystique. To lose the legacy of these men in a welter of pop culture guitar-masses and hand-shaking had begun the undoing of the work of centuries in his opinion. His beliefs were sincere if one-sided. He allowed God to be God and God liked prayers the more the better. Leo also sincerely loved the daughter that he could not understand and was concerned about whether when he had shuffled off this mortal condition they would meet again in the celestial courts if she failed to change her ways. Leo placed his trust in God and in the approved means of guaranteeing access to him while for Tiffany everything was provisional, contingent, and problematic. She appeared to be rooted in her suffering and to cherish her doubts. This was most evident in her fears and in her occasional spasms of anger. They showed a spirit grounded in opposition and lack of trust in the order of God's creation. This was out and out impiety in her father's estimation and from its signs Leo at last deduced the cause: Tiffany Amorth was possessed by the devil.

The most salient sign of her spiritual affliction was one of her chief fears. Tiffany Amorth was dreadfully afraid of bats. Sooner or later everyone who knew anything about Tiffany Amorth at all became aware of this fact about her. For her twilight brought forth a feeling of dread. No peasant in Transylvania taking cover behind closed doors as the evening shadows lengthened over the Carpathian Mountains was more careful of avoiding bats than she. It was not that she begrudged the ugly little winged things their humble insectivorous existence; she was well aware of the benefits bestowed upon mankind by their habit of consuming tons of malicious insects and turning them into bat guano in trees or attics as long as the attic wasn't in her house. She entertained no attitude or bias of invidious discrimination towards them because they liked to hang in little colonies scratching and biting each other with their nasty little claws. As long as they stayed away from her she was quite satisfied to let them be. She had even felt a pang of sympathy for them when she heard that they had acquired a white nose-fungus that was doing them in by the thousands.

So it must be made clear that Tiffany harbored no ill-feelings to bats as examples of the wonderful results of mutation and selection by mindless nature or if theologically speaking that Noah had managed to catch a few and keep them aboard the arc while the waters of the flood soaked into the soils of Mesopotamia. The problem that Tiffany had with bats was that they often acquired rabies due to their promiscuous habit of biting and scratching each other whether in casual contact or fooling around back at the cave.

Tiffany had been terrified of Rabies ever since she had watched good and faithful Old Yeller turn unaccountably into a slathering beast because of rabies. Oh, and people could get it too she was told. She had been an impressionable child. She had taken to heart all the manner of things in every American home that could kill you dead if you touched them and as a result was a model child. No ambulance had ever arrived to take her to the nearest hospital to pump out her stomach. She gave a wide berth to any suspicious or noxious substances although she had been curious from time to time why grownups kept so many dreadful items in their homes.

These early experiences, perhaps building upon a naturally nervous nature, had made Tiffany a fearful and mistrustful child. She was raised without brothers or sisters and adapted as best she could to a world of adults whose province was to minimize whatever natural harms flow from having curious and assertive children underfoot. Later on when she was sent to a psychiatrist to diagnose the cause of her various obsessions he had suggested that she had been raised in a perfectionist environment beset by rules and prohibitions. Both of her parents had pointed at the other and the sessions were terminated after the initial three sessions. When she had asked about it she was told that the doctor had attributed the whole thing to rigid toilet training and was clearly a dirty-minded Freudian. The result was that Tiffany remained a fearful child and a lonely one.

It is not to be presumed however that Tiffany showed no

courage. She had not even cried for instance when she had been hit by a car in the second grade and knocked unconscious. She had been quite embarrassed by the whole incident and desired to hush it up as soon as possible. After all, she had been warned not to run into the street without looking. Her fears were not of pain, loss, or rejection. She took these for granted in each new school to which she was sent. Her fear was rather of the dark and inscrutable workings of nature manifest in the world of predatory lower life.

Tiffany kept a running profile in her head of the world's foremost pathogens and where they liked to hang out. She was well-read and *au courant* with all manner of ecological issues. She knew for instance that global warming was inviting certain noxious South American vectors for disease closer year by year and that was not even considering the dreadful things you could catch that were already here. There was Lyme Disease for instance on the East Coast. There was Dengue Fever in Florida. Chagas and the dread Kissing Bugs that carried it were fortunately no closer than Mexico. Mad Cow Disease had raised fears and then seemingly spread no further than the British Isles and perhaps Canada although she still refused to eat t-bone steaks just to be sure. Tiffany knew all about Tsetse Flies and African Sleeping Sickness and those horrible flies that leave their larvae within you to feed and crawl about. But none of these dreadful things could match rabies which killed anyone who ever showed symptoms. No one could save you. Rabies was sort of like a physical analogue to double-predestination in Calvinist theology. If God predestined you to hell then all the virtues in the world couldn't save you and who was to say whether He had already done so. After all, Tiffany had been a headache with all of her fears. It was not however until her late twenties that her father concluded that Tiffany must be possessed by the devil to be so afraid of bats. No one else in the family was afraid of the little beasts that would fly at you on warm summer nights and then whirl away at the last instant a scant foot from your face. It was even rather fun; but not for Tiffany. She knew only that there was a virus there perhaps that once in your body would crawl along your nerve fibers to your brain and then make you mad before you subsided into dreadful paralysis and death.

The conclusion that she was possessed though was something of a novelty. To make out of her obsessive fear some sort of moral failing seemed to be unfair. It showed lack of empathy and patience on the part of those who did not share her vividness of imagination. It was not as though what she feared was impossible. The connection was not so remote as to be unfathomable. There are people who refuse to drive again after a car wreck or who refuse to drink brandy again after spending a night bent retching over a toilet bowl after too many stingers. Not everybody can stand everything! But none of this mattered to those who looked at Tiffany now and saw that she had made herself a Bride of Satan, a witch, by virtue of not standing proud and firm as all good Americans should do when faced by such ubiquitous denizens as bats. "It's a sin to be afraid," her father had said. The question was what to do about it. A few discrete inquiries seemed the best course to pursue so a concerned letter was sent by her father to the local parish priest. It read as follows:

Dear Reverend Father------,
I am writing to you on a most painful matter. You may recall meeting my daughter Tiffany after mass shortly after your transfer to our parish. I must tell you as her father that the girl has always been a source of anxiety for us, her parents. She is not without certain creative gifts but she spends entirely too much time alone. She is in her late twenties, dates seldom, and in many ways fails to thrive and to mature like other girls her age. I have reached the age where I would like to retire and travel, but concern for our daughter makes us hesitate to leave her alone. When we take her to visit her cousins she insists that she must be inside before the bats come out at night, which spoils late family softball games at the city park. She runs and jumps into the car before the sun sets and won't emerge again until we are in the garage at our house with the garage door closed. This would be bad enough, but she now won't come out to our lake cabin

because we found mice droppings on the couch and she's afraid of getting Hantavirus. We need an exorcism. Can you help?

A week later the following answer was received.

Dear Mr. Amorth:

Regarding your suspicions that your daughter is possessed by the devil because of her phobic fear of bats and mice, I can only tell you that a quick review of the literature on the subject and the requirements of Canon Law do not show fear of bats as one of the qualifying criteria that must be presented to the local ordinary. Bishop------- requires more before he will authorize an exorcism. I must therefore refer you back to the more customary channels for problems such as those manifested by your daughter. I am including a name of a local psychologist, a good Catholic and a fine man who may be of help to you. Naturally I will keep your daughter in my prayers.

Yours in our Lord,

Rev. -----------

Since an appeal to the Church had failed, her family turned to the social sciences for help. A few days later at her family's insistence Tiffany reported to a high and austere building in downtown Seattle for her first appointment. Dr. --------- makes it a habit to record his sessions and the following extract is included here...

Extract from Session 1 - Tiffany Amorth

Hello Tiffany. I am Dr. ------ Please sit down and make yourself comfortable. Can I get you anything?

No thank you.

This will be our initial session and I would like to explore with you the course that therapy with me will entail. If you have any questions at any time feel free to ask me.

Very well. When does the exorcism begin?

I beg your pardon?

The exorcism; my parents think I need an exorcism because I'm afraid of bats and oh, of mice too.

I see. Well it always helps to get these issues on the record but I think we should backtrack a little. Would that be alright? Have you read the patient intake form and initialed the permissions contained there? Very good. Then I think we can proceed a bit. I think it is important that you be here because you want to be and not out of any sort of coercion, and let me disabuse you immediately of any idea that I conduct exorcisms.

I really didn't think you did.

Right. But I am curious about how you feel about being called possessed by your father.

It makes me angry.

Um hum. Why angry?

Because it's so stupid!

That you're afraid of bats and mice?

No, that's not it. I think it's stupid that they don't know or care *why* I'm afraid of bats and mice.

Why are you?

Because I don't want to die!

Do you think bats and mice will kill you?

No! That's just it! I love animals, but I hate the diseases that some of them carry. Is that so wrong?

That seems rational to me.

Then why am I here?

I don't know. Why are you here?

Because I'm afraid all the time; I don't feel in control.

Is it so important that you be in control?

My father always is.

Are bats and mice everywhere in your world?

No of course not, but there are other things too.

What things?

Things that carry death.

You mean like cars and airplanes and clogged arteries.

No.

Those things kill more people than Rabies and Hantavirus.

How did you know I'm scared specifically of Rabies and Hantavirus?

Many of my patients are afraid of deadly germs.

But are they possessed by the devil?

No. Some drink a little too much but that's about as spirit-based as it gets. Would you say that you are a happy young woman?

[Silence]

No.

Why not?

My father drives me crazy.

That sounds perfectly normal to me.

[Patient smiles]

How does he drive you crazy?

He doesn't really see me.

You mean that he doesn't look at you?

Oh, he looks; he just doesn't see me.

What do you expect him to see?

Me!

And who are you?

[Silence]

I don't know.

That's what we may discover together if you choose to remain in therapy with me.

[Silence]

You think you can unmask me.

Do you wear masks?

Everybody does.

I see. You mean people are inauthentic?

I mean they are liars.

Is this you talking?

Yes, who would it be?

You said that you didn't know who you were.

I mean in detail. I do know when I'm feeling something. I feel a lot. I'm very passionate about things.

Are you?

Yes. I feel intensely. If I hate you I will want to see you burning up. If I love you I will want you to be mine forever and never leave.

Are you ever just indifferent or non-committal about things?

Seldom.

Um hum.

I hope you aren't going to go um hum all the time when we talk!

Does that bother you?

It makes me feel like you're judging me.

Do people judge you?

All the time.

And it makes you angry?

It pisses me off!

Do you talk like that around your father?

Are you my father?

[Silence]

No. I'm your therapist, if you want me to be.

I'm sorry.

Why?

Because it wasn't your fault. I'm just touchy. My father says I'm highly-strung.

I thought you were possessed.

That too.

Would you say you are depressed?

Sometimes, but mostly I am angry and afraid.

In that order?

No, first I'm afraid and then I am angry.

Not the other way around?

[Silence]

Well uh yes. Sometimes I'm angry and I'm afraid people will retaliate against me.

Don't you deserve to be angry sometimes?

Not when I have been so blessed.

How are you blessed?

I'm not starving. I have clothes to wear and a place to live.

Is that enough?

More than I deserve.

Who told you that?

I just feel it; that's all.

[Pause]

Um, how does therapy work … with you?

Well, I concentrate on the particular. What you are feeling right now and on particular incidents in your life.

When I am asked to recall memorable incidents my immediate impulse is to see the particular as subsumed beneath an underlying generality.

I see. But what if what matters is precisely the unique and unrepeatable experience.

Then I would say that the moment that we attempt to communicate it or even to formulate it that we are constricted by linguistic conventions which brings us right back to generalities. We are dogged by convention even in our perceptual categories; to see is already to interpret.

You sound a bit more sophisticated now.

I majored in philosophy in college.

So I better not try and bullshit you.

I wouldn't advise it.

[Both smile]

So you find it difficult to approach matters with what might be called a fresh slate.

Oh, I am not speaking personally you understand. I am discussing human conscious functioning in general—we perceive, think and judge by putting matters into a preexisting context so that nothing stands apart as an isolated fact.

I see but surely there is a place for the here and now isn't there. I mean you are here now in this room and we have set aside this hour to explore the ways that you as an individual approach the world.

[Silence]

Does that trouble you?

No, I'm merely considering the implications. Surely, you are assuming that I have a set purpose in being here, but isn't that very assumption the context that will ultimately distort everything that I say to you. We are merely acting out our respective roles. The whole medical model is only extended by analogy when it is applied to psychotherapy. What is a mental illness? Show me the microbe.

What if what we are doing together is to clarify how you perceive things so that we can isolate choices that you might make that may lead to better results in your life taken as a whole.

You mean so that I can feel better.

That's right.

Well if that is the final end that we are both pursuing there must be drugs that can restore the organism to a proper equilibrium without all this talk.

And what would your experience of self be then?

You keep coming back to self as though it were some form of Holy Grail.

Does that disturb you?

Yes it does frankly. What difference does it make if I get well?

Your father will be pleased.

Yes, it will get me off his hands.

Well, ideally it would matter to you as well.

But that's precisely it; it doesn't matter to me. And worse, I don't think it would matter to you either if I wasn't paying you.

Don't you think that I might take some manner of personal satisfaction from the patients that I am able to help?

[Sarcastically] So you can feel like a benefactor in this great wide world and not just another nut-job like me.

Is that what you think you are?

You therapists like questions a lot don't you.

Well we have our own little set of tools you know. Don't you like questions?

As a matter of fact no I don't, not when they get too close.

Too close to what?

To me.

[Silence]

And what do you mean by you?

Well I can tell you what Eugene Minkowski would mean. I have been reading his masterpiece, *Lived Time*, lately you know. He would say that each of us is subsumed into our lived experience of time. We are in process and driven by the Elan Vital. Each moment is part of a stream reaching into an indeterminate future. We live towards our goals.

I see, but could we return to you. What do you mean by you?

We went into that already.

You didn't answer me.

I can tell you what I'm reading. What more do you need to know.

What if your books were taken away?

[Silence]

Does that frighten you?

I would watch more television I suppose.

What if the set broke?

YouTube then.

No computer either.

Eat more.

You're on a diet.

Drink.

The bar is closed.

Fine! Then I suppose I'd get a dog.

That might be nice. Do you think the dog would like you?

Until I stopped feeding him.

Would you stop feeding him?

Of course not; he's my dog.

Well there are lots of dogs in this world that don't get fed.

Yes I suppose so. Still… I wouldn't want him to go hungry.

Why not?

Because I would owe him something… I chose him.

Out of all the possible dogs in the world?

That's right.

Why do you suppose that you chose him?

I thought he needed me.

How could you tell?

He came up to me and wagged his tail.

What if he had ulterior motives?

Now who's the cynic?

It was just a question.

No, you were insinuating something.

What?

That no dog would really … just like me. You know, for myself alone.

But I thought you didn't have a self.

Well I do; that's the problem.

Why is it a problem?

[Pause]

Well if you must know I'm rather demanding.

You don't seem so to me. All you want is a dog.

Well I want more than just a dog.

What?

All kinds of things. For one thing if I start eating I'm afraid that I won't stop.

So how do you stop yourself?

I don't start eating until I measure everything out.

That must be rather time-consuming.

It's my time.

[Pause]

I wonder what would happen if you just trusted yourself to stop on your own.

I can't.

Who's stopping you?

Something inside me; I can't control it.

So what do you do?

I deny myself.

So we're back to that troublesome self that you say you don't possess.

I didn't exactly say that.

Perhaps I misunderstood you.

Alright then listen: I don't want to be something that in the end just doesn't matter anyway. I'm just part of a crowd, one of the seven or eight billion people gobbling up the planet. I'm an ecological sinkhole.

So global warming is your personal fault.

[Pause]

Well not all of it.

I think that your average cow is worse.

Well at least you get milk and beef from a cow.

So you think the key is productivity?

Isn't it?

You tell me.

What else matters?

I don't know. Why don't you tell me?

[Pause]

Because I don't know.

Well what do you think matters?

I tell you I don't know!

Why don't you think you know?

Nobody ever told me; that's why.

You think somebody can just tell you who you are, like it's a big secret everybody is keeping from you?

Everybody else seems to know who they are.   They get married, find great jobs, sign mortgages, raise kids, go on cruises, get sick, and then die.

Is that what everybody does or what you think everybody does?

Well don't they?

Did you ask them?

Well not one at a time.

That's the only way you can ask them; one at a time.

[Silence]

They look like a crowd to me.

They aren't. Try looking at them one at a time. You'll notice things.

Like what?

They may remind you of you.

Me?

Yes.

What do I know about me?

What do you know?

I'm not sure.

Would you like to explore a bit together?

[Pause]

Well I suppose.

Is that a commitment?

Yes.

Then I think we can work together.

[Pause]

I might quit.

Some patients do.

Doesn't that bother you when they quit?

Yes it does.

Why, because you failed?

How did I fail?

You let them leave.

They made up their own minds.

[Pause]

But what if they couldn't help themselves!

Why couldn't they?

Because they're sick!

So part of the sickness is the need to resist cure.

I guess so.

Why do you suppose people do that?

[Silence]

Because hope hurts...

Hope for what?

[Silence]

For everything ... for everything I've never had.

Would you like some of those things?

[Pause]

(Quietly) I don't deserve them.

Why not?

I'm bad.

Who told you that you were bad?

Everybody's bad. It says so in the bible.

Why do you suppose we're so bad?

[Pause]

Because ... God is so good.

He didn't seem to mind two naked people running amuck all over his garden did he?

Well then why did he ask them to put on fig leaves?

They did that on their own when they ate the forbidden fruit and realized that they were naked.

Well he must have known that they would eat the fruit, after all He was God you know!

[Pause]

What if God thought that they just weren't ready yet to face their nakedness? Maybe it takes awhile to be able to digest the fruit of the tree of knowledge between good and evil. Perhaps God was letting them get all of that frolicsomeness out of their systems before moving them on to higher moral questions? Maybe God respects the normal maturation process of the human race.

We haven't come too far. We still copulate like bunnies.

Does that surprise you?

Well I don't.

What?

Copulate like a bunny.

What if you ever did?

[Pause]

I wouldn't be able to stop.

Oh I think you would. You might even go back to reading a little philosophy.

Even if somebody took all my books?

Why would they do that?

Because they might think that all I wanted to do was copulate like a bunny.

(Smiling) I'm sure you would correct them regarding their gross misapprehension.

Are you laughing at me?

Do you hear me chortling away?

No but you're smiling.

Maybe that's because I like you. I think you're a very honest person.

[Pause]

Nobody ever told me that.

Nobody ever told you lots of things, but it's not too late.

I may be older than you think I am.

Well I'm no spring chicken either. I'm still learning.

[Pause]

Then why am I paying you so much money to cure me?

I can't cure you. The work we do together is a team project.

[Pause]

I'll fight you all the way!

Well that's up to you; it's your dime.

26

Can't you just carry me along?

With all the crap you've been carrying around? You must be mad!

You're smiling again.

Yes.

[Silence]

Alright, where do I sign?

You already did the patient intake; just show up next Tuesday, same time, same place.

Right.

[Silence]

Anything else?

[Silence]

Yes. When I woke up today it was before dawn. I thought how stupid it was of me coming to see you. One more therapist! I could read them all; disposable like paper cups. I like being complex; to make them do the work.

Uh huh?

You make me feel...

What do I make you feel?

You make me feel ... ordinary.

Is that so bad?

It is for me.

Why?

Because I have to be special?

Oh? And why is that?

[Pause]

Because, if I'm not special, I might end up being nothing at all.

Lots of my patients say that. It's what brings them here.

[Silence]

Right... so next Tuesday then?

Yes next Tuesday.

[Silence]

Something else?

I'm afraid that if I get boring that you won't like me.

[Pause]

So you think I choose my patients for the genius of their symptom creation?

Well otherwise it would be a boring job wouldn't it?

Suppose you let me worry about that. Next Tuesday.

Very well Doctor, see you then, goodbye.

The following days and weeks produced a change in the young woman, subtle at first but growing in momentum as the sessions ticked past. There were set-backs of course as is customary in any regimen of psychotherapy, but rather than simply attending a few sessions and then dropping out, as had been her prior pattern, Tiffany always ended up taking the ferry to the Emerald City each Tuesday in time to make her appointment. Though she felt no budding affection for bats or mice she was at least able to describe her feelings and to obtain a first inkling of the general aura of fear that had always accompanied her. Extracts from her sessions demonstrated the first etchings in an overall design.

Extract from Session Ten—Tiffany Amorth

You told me something in our last session that I would like to explore further. You mentioned that you felt that under certain circumstances you would be left entirely to your own devices as though all of the powers and parameters of civilization would drop away. There was a chill in your voice and a quality of bleakness in your eye that reminded me of pictures that I have seen of the frigid Polar Regions.

That's how it always feels to me. I feel like I am going to die. Everything in the room gets darker as though there was a mask of gauze over my face... I was operated on once as a child for a tonsillectomy. They strapped my legs down with a leather belt and one nurse held my arms while another nurse put an ether-infused mask over my face ... I wanted to kill them.

Didn't anyone tell you what to expect during the surgery?

Only that I would get ice cream and presents if I would let them take my tonsils out; it was a lie. I couldn't swallow anything; but my mother's face bending over me in the bed when I woke up after the surgery was the most beautiful thing I ever saw.

[Silence]

I see tears in your eyes.

I'm sorry.

Why should you be sorry? It must have been very frightening for you.

It's stupid; other children have much worse surgeries.

They aren't you.

You mean that I was right to feel angry and betrayed.

Yes. You were aware that you had a self and it could be violated. It took you many years for that sense to be dulled in you until it fell silent.

[Silence]

I'm still angry. I don't know if I have ever hated two people as much as I did those nurses. All the time that they were dealing with me they never looked into my eyes.

And you have been suspicious ever since…

It wasn't the only lie people told me.

There were others?

People always had to pin me down to do things to me.

What sort of things?

[Silence]

(Then suddenly)They gave me shots or suppositories. The suppositories burned and it hurt when they stuck them in.

[Pause]

What else did people do?

I had warts on my feet and they burned them out with acid. It left holes in my feet. It took weeks for them to heal. I used to get sick before I went to school every day.

Nobody helped you through your pain?

No. These things had to be done. It was my job to adjust; like when we moved to new places and I had to start all over again. I would have complained more but I didn't want to be abandoned.

Your parents would have left you behind?

No, but I thought that bad or ungrateful children would be given away to government agencies.

Some are.

[Pause]

So I wasn't wrong then.

[Pause]

When did it get safe enough for you to tell your parents what you felt?

It never did get safe enough. It still isn't.

[Silence]

That's very sad. Part of being an adult is to reach a time and condition where we don't have to be as afraid as we were when we were children.

They can still hurt me and if not them then the people I have loved since.

[Silence]

Would you like a tissue?

Yes please. Thank you.

[Pause]

I would like to return to your fear of bats.

Do we have to?

I think it would be useful.

Alright then.

Why do you think that your father thinks you are possessed by the devil?

I don't know.

Try imagining then.

[Silence]

Maybe I remind him of something.

What do you think you remind him of?

[Pause]

How he really feels about me.

How does he feel?

I don't know … I wish I did.

[Pause]

Is your father a complicated man?

No more than I am a complicated girl.

Is that your answer?

It's what we share.

[Silence]

Do you share other things?

No. We're actually quite different.

How so?

We don't like the same things. For one thing we're politically different. He watches Hannity every night.

What do you watch?

MSNBC. I love Rachel Maddow.

Is she like a big sister to you?

Yes. I like Kasie Hunt too. I wish I looked like her.

[Pause]

How else do you differ from your father?

He likes the old Catholic Church of High Mass and incense.

And what church do you like?

There's only one church.

I see. What does church mean to you?

It means base-communities in Brazil and Columbia, workers processions, and the Virgin of Guadeloupe. I read theologians too, people who aren't always in favor with Rome … not because they're right but because they don't seem like stodgy old relics.

Is that what you think bishops are?

I don't think anybody really understands bishops… I feel sorry for them sometimes. I know what it's like to have worlds torn out from underneath you. It must be lovely though to feel that you have a hotline to God.

[Pause]

What about you? Do you have a hotline?

No.

You can pray...

[Pause]

It isn't the same thing. Besides, I'm a possessed girl.

Do you think you could be an atheist then?

Never!

[Pause]

Why not?

Because I need to know when I look up at the glacial stars that there is something out there somewhere. If there isn't I'd be afraid of even more things than bats and mice.

Did you ever try and confront those fears directly?

Once I thought I would read everything I could about Rabies and just burn the fear away by over-exposure.

[Silence]

I guess it didn't work?

It was horrible. There were cases in India of people strapped to beds with their terrified eyes rolling around in their heads and foam bubbling out of their mouths. Ugh.

[Silence]

And possession?

I looked at records of that too. People growl and grimace and make horrible laughing sounds in a low voice no matter what sex they are.

[Pause]

(Quietly) What sex are you?

Sometimes I don't know. I'm not sure I like either one... No, that isn't true; I'd love to be a girl if I could look like one of those girls in the mall in Victoria's Secret stores.

Not too many women do.

Maybe not, but the stores would go out of business if women didn't at least hope that they could look like that, at least a little.

32

Is that a possessed girl talking?

(Smiles) Nope, I'm just a typical girl who is already pushing thirty.

[Pause]

Is there anything else you would like to discuss today before our session ends?

[Silence]

How long do you think we'll need to keep meeting like this.

That's up to you.

I mean am I getting better?

Only you can know the answer to that question. This is about you.

What if I start putting up more resistance? Maybe I'm being too much of a model patient.

I think that this time you really want to get something out of therapy. Patients fight their doctors until they can fight back for themselves with the people who originally injured them.

[Silence]

So if I'm not possessed why am I so angry?

Do you think you are possessed?

[Silence]

No.

[Pause]

Then let's leave it at that then... See you next week.

The annals of therapists abound with stories. Who can say how long a wound lasts inside of us or what later detritus adds to the weight and burden of the initial injury? We are told that the noon-day devil like a roaring lion goes about seeking someone to devour. We are advised to resist him steadfast in the faith. Now and then we have evidences of untold graces as though angels surrounded us to guard us. Even if we have a single proprietary angel on a twenty-four hour shift, one who gets to know us well through the years, who is to say that others equally committed to our welfare do not bear her company? After that tenth session Tiffany Amorth began to improve rapidly. She started seeing things without the shadows that usually accompanied them. She still didn't like bats or mice very much, but when her father told her that he still suspected that she was possessed at times by the devil she told him to stick an old sock in his mouth and chew it.

Tiffany Amorth closed her notebook slowly and looked down shyly toward her feet. The class was silent where they sat around the seminar table that was intended to create a sense of intimacy and candor among the students in Genre Studies 504. It had not been an easy choice for Tiffany to decide on graduate study in English Literature. Her father had called it wasted money, but with her scholarship it was cheaper than therapy and it did get her out to mix with people so he consented at last and here she was. The instructor, Dr. Herrigan, had published a book of short stories in her youth that had received a favorable review from John Updike and she had been coasting on its reputation ever since. Time had revealed that there is a profound division between the lonely world of writers and the snug security of a tenured teaching post and she preferred the latter. She was sensitive to the ego demands of young grad students and of delphiniums and she had learned over time how best to nurture each of these by providing a warm and nurturing environment rich in soil and with plenty of room to grow.

"Well then class who would like to go first?"

There was the usual awkward silence before one of the young ladies spoke up, "I was wondering why the author chose her own name in the story. I thought we were supposed to use our imaginations."

"That's true, Belinda, but how can you be sure that Tiffany hasn't used her imagination?" Dr. Herrigan objected.

Another student spoke up. "What does it matter? Don't we all color our narratives by the sheer act of writing them down?"

Belinda turned to him, "Well as for me I believe there should be a clear demarcation between fact and fiction. Literature is the art of the possible; it should not be weighed down by personal recollections however poignant they may be. The mere choice of a psychotherapy session is so overdone, so '*I Never Promised You a Rose Garden*' so '*Flowers for Algernon.*'"

Dr. Herrigan intervened, "We are not here to judge but to elucidate Belinda. Tiffany was well within the stated parameters of the assignment. Let's concentrate on what you noticed in the sphere of technique."

"That's all I wanted to say," Belinda said as she turned her attention to the naked trees outside the window. She felt a sudden uneasiness. It wasn't like her.

"Others?" inquired Dr. Herrigan.

Samuel spoke up, "I liked the feel of the story. It seemed authentic."

"Ah, but doesn't authenticity break the spell of artifice and illusion?" inquired Dr. Herrigan.

"Well, there was the fanciful element," Samuel commented. "I mean, Tiffany possessed by the devil, who would ever believe that?"

"But remember, Samuel, that you are applying exterior norms to the text; you have the advantage of knowing Tiffany whereas the reader is confined to the text alone."

Belinda spoke up, "Precisely my point! I thought the story confused memoir with fiction. The author should signal his intent or else he isn't playing fair with his reader."

"So you believe that equities are involved here, Belinda. But what shall we do with the problem of the unreliable narrator as in *The Aspern Papers* by Henry James; should we always take the author at face value even when she speaks omnisciently? What do you think class?"

Larry spoke up, "I think it is perfectly fair to draw on actual observations for one's ideas and then to clothe them in mood and atmosphere. There's nothing dishonest in that."

"Then where would you draw the line, if any, around duplicity?" Belinda objected.

"I would let the conventions of the genre prevail," said Larry thoughtfully.

"Ah but who is to establish the conventions?" asked Dr. Herrigan.

"The chair of the department and the tenure committee," answered Larry.

Belinda smirked, "You won't be so cavalier when you are seeking a teaching post in four years."

Dr. Herrigan attempted to summarize. "So we are exploring the conventions of narration and the question of sincerity of authorial intent as revealed or concealed within the text; is that a fair statement of our discussion thus far?"

Ericka spoke up, "Well if we are confined to the text then the author will hardly confess in the course of the story that he is having the reader on, I mean to do so would be like stepping out of character on the stage."

"Then how could the reader achieve ambiguity while still staying in character?" Samuel inquired.

"Any ideas?" inquired Dr. Herrigan.

"It should be a matter of tone," Lara commented, "Or perhaps a showing of divided motivations between the first person narrator and his actions within the text."

"How do you mean tone?" asked Samuel.

"I mean the overriding texture of the story. That's why *The Lottery* by Shirley Jackson works. It moves from a tone of bucolic peace to sudden horror. It really had an impact on a 1950's readership."

Belinda objected again, "But the audience of a story should be presumed to be a constant. The text has to stand alone without any exterior support. If we presume an innocent audience then we have to vet who will read the story and select out the sophisticated reader if it is to have maximum impact on a general audience."

"That is a problem," commented Dr. Herrigan.

"It seems to me that we must simply take the story as it is," said Samuel. "Any criticism implies a privileged outside vantage point that is itself outside the text. Who is to guarantee that the critic isn't even more biased than the author? If the author doesn't play fair how are we to be sure that the critic doesn't cheat every bit as much?"

"You have to trust somebody," Belinda said acidly. "Otherwise almost anything could happen."

All this time Tiffany had been listening to the quiet voice inside of her while picking clandestinely at her eyelashes. "Why am I here? Why am I here?" And then lower still another voice, "Why *are* you here? Why *are* you here?" It was always like an echo, as though her thoughts had reverberations in a great empty hall filled with unseen corners and mirrors. She saw the improvise altar in the corner of her room at home and the bottles filled with soil from the graveyard. The books on Caribbean voudoun cults said it was called "goofer dust" and it could be used for things. You could even get old nasty nurses with goofer dust.

The winds from Puget Sound blew up to the campus and shook the trees outside the window. Tiffany thought of all of the students who had come here young and filled with hopes for a bright future. Where were they now? She saw in her mind's eye all of the protests through the years on this very campus but America could still manage to elect Donald Trump! What had it all been for, the struggle for justice and enlightenment if it came to this?

"Still, I want to give it all up," she thought. "I don't like being angry like this all the time. I think I'll take the goofer dust back to the graveyard and foreswear allegiance. I don't want power over things. It was all a lie just to distract me from what really matters."

Then she looked over again at Belinda smug and confident in her white angora sweater with her upturned nose and perfect silhouette. "You don't like my story?" she said to herself. "Do I write to please you Miss Tenure Queen, prisoner of texts. If I stopped writing where would you be then? You would just disappear."

She ceased for a moment to imagine…

Tiffany Amorth sat back in her chair at her desk in her room at home. She could hear the football game playing annoyingly downstairs in her father's den, as usual at full volume. She held her pen over the paper in her notebook where it dripped like a dagger from time to time onto the manuscript. She had made the ink herself out of oil, elder berries, lampblack, and dust. She hesitated and then made her decision to turn from darkness and vengeance. Everything passes and not everyone can be expected to know when and how they wound us. "No, I won't do it," she said. "There must be some limit to imperial authorial intent otherwise we might be as arbitrary and capricious as certain ... people of importance and authority.

She took a wet sponge and mopped it over the lines that had read:

Belinda Montague was walking across the busy intersection outside the university bookstore after her graduate writing seminar when she was run down by a speeding police car. It was such a tragedy. She was said to have been quite a promising young critic.

"There!" said Tiffany Amorth. "All better! You get to live, Belinda Montague, whoever you are. After all I am only a writer of stories, a scribbler of tales, and I am obsessive possibly but most certainly ... well, *Not Possessed.*"

In Search of Denmark

Part One

Like a calving glacier the ideas that form the bulwark of humanism are falling away into the rising sea. No prior species has wrought its own extinction nor had the capacity to reflect fully on its own contingency. In this sense *Homo sapiens* might, from a planetary point of view, be considered to be a noxious and invasive species as deleterious to the biosphere as any other untoward event, geological or extraterrestrial. The absorption or decimation of indigenous peoples around the world has broken the primary ties of un-technological humankind and supplanted it with a being that appears collectively intent upon sawing away at the branch of the tree of life that sustains it. Artifice is no longer decorative or remedial but rather the primary character of what may perhaps be a silica-based form of mechanism that will make life-forms based upon carbon a quaint remnant of a prior era. This erosion of prior certitudes and assumptions of the value of the species is only multiplied when that contingency and the deconstruction that is made possible by contingency is applied to the individual.

The subject of this tale is one Tiffany Amorth whose father, securely rooted in the centrism provided by his faith and his conservative political convictions, had once been convinced that his daughter was possessed because of her many, to him absurd fears. Fortunately he had gradually modified his assessment of his daughter to embrace the lesser included offenses of her simply being demonically obsessed rather than possessed or perhaps being merely mentally unbalanced in her confusions and reservations. Not that being mentally unbalanced should be accepted as any excuse for her failure to thrive and prosper; Leo P. Amorth believed that just as physics recognizes the law of strict conservation of energy there was a parallel in the moral realm so that every sin or weakness must be paid for by somebody at sometime. Being as close to his daughter as he was, it came as no surprise that the guilt from his daughter's offences, or at least the punishment due to them in the temporal order, had been laid by an all-just providence at his door. He had conceived her; she was his responsibility. As a father he had bowed to his fate as the fruit of concupiscent desire. He kept a running account of the liquidated value though of her guilt and his expenses manifested in living allowances, university tuition, and the luxuriant accessories that appended to her sex. Still, for all of his sacrificial offerings and concern she persisted in her mental aberrations, her strange obsessive and compulsive rituals, and the costly study of subjects devoid of any visible pecuniary value. When he asked her from time to time the source of her nameless but manifold ills she would either remain silent or worse begin a recitation of citations to various unreadable authors who with too much time on their hands had explored the nuances of existential drift, bad faith, and the loss of the transcendental ego.

Her character and personality was the one source of frustration in an otherwise admirably ordered life. The defeat of Hillary Clinton due to the fortunate existence of a rurally weighted electoral college had advanced a true populist to the throne of the Presidency where he could lower taxes, purge the deep state, and deregulate America into formerly impossible but now infinite vistas of prosperity. The full power of capital would finally be unchained from the ill-considered virtues of mercy and equality that merely allowed the weak, the profligate, and the lazy to thrive at the teat of the public purse. Leo P. Amorth saw great and noble America as a virgin about to be set upon by the hoards of illegally entering brown-skinned hybrids of Hispanic and Indian extraction who would jump on the gravy-train of post New Deal entitlements if they were ever allowed to cross our undefended southern border en mass and bring the benefits conferred by sophisticated investors and investment bankers to a halt. He would be content to let the lettuce rot in the fields before countenancing such an outrage. The party of the Democrats had over the two terms of the Obama administration morphed from a nuisance to the agenda of God-fearing Republicanism to emerge as the vanguard of socialism, the rampant indulgence of the baser appetites of the flesh, and the final and irrevocable emasculation of the American male by fire-breathing feminists. It was bad enough to hear of such matters even when put in their proper perspective as Trump-hating propaganda by conservative media but to have a daughter of democratic darkness entering his canonical domicile each night while still redolent of the fake news broadcast on CNN and other demonic media was to defile the paternal sanctuary. He found his daughter to be not the least of the crosses that he, good man that he was, had to bear.

Tiffany for her part was no more tolerant of his views on theology or politics. She harbored what might be called an historical skepticism towards any large institutions in proportion to their venerable reputation and longevity. She found the views of Alfred North Whitehead and his process philosophy to be congenial to her natural proclivities of thought and feeling. She thought of truth statements as profoundly limited by the language in which those truths were expressed; she therefore located truth as something that we strive to obtain rather than to maintain. This naturally made her critical of the idea of an irreducible "deposit of faith" to be safeguarded in every detail, proclaimed, and possessed by an institutionally reiterated argument that assumed that when Jesus had promised to remain with His Church forever He was simultaneously creating a semi-feudal order of Bishops with powers of excommunication, interdict, and an innate charisma that could over sufficient time harden into dogma through the sheer force of repetition. Tiffany felt that history had shown such a tendency to breed an unhealthy confidence that had led directly to the burnings of heretics and witches, the stifling of new insights in the sciences, and the colonization and enslavement of native peoples by crusaders and colonial missionaries. She deplored the forcible inclusion of people possessing their own cultures and values into the spiritual fortress of orthodox belief for fear that otherwise they were doomed to perish by reason of original sin. She took the point of view that it was a crass instrumental view of sacramental action to institute their usage among people with only a partial grasp of the underlying heritage of western institutions and historical experience. When invitation becomes first demand and then command something is wrong. She deplored any suggestion of spiritual violence even if well-intended. God appeared to her to value diversity in both species and in circumstance here on earth rather than to be confined in His essence to the maledictions of any priestly caste even if that caste had originally been commissioned to start the ball rolling by reaching beyond the upper room in Jerusalem. Catholicism had always possessed an ability to adapt as well as to subjugate and to this quality she owed her persistence in and even love for the faith of her girlhood.

The refusal to embrace unqualified assent to propositions was also applied towards other relationships, particularly those involving sexuality. She considered proposals by most men to be veiled invitations to enter into contracts of adhesion on unequal terms even if sweetened by an aura of conventionality and economic security. How could she commit what was still in process of formation? Thus, Tiffany Amorth had reached the ripe old age of thirty without possessing the luxury or enjoying the achievement of a sense of stable identity beyond this overriding tendency to see the flaws and limitations that qualified any statement not least of which was a matrimonial promise of exclusive sexual fidelity and abiding love. She had a name of course and a personal history as we all do but her sense of an abiding and unitary identity was still lacking. It was not that she was inordinately suggestible; she was far too headstrong for that. Rather her lack of identity was due to an overwhelming conviction that nothing should be allowed to set and harden within her until she had thoroughly investigated all of the alternative possibilities that life might potentially hold in store for her before making any irrevocable commitments.

At first glance this salient aspect of her nature, one characterized by a sense of inner drama as she visualized alternatives that life presented to her, might lead the ordinary observer to conclude that Tiffany was at heart an adventurous girl: wild, impetuous, and prone to throw caution to the winds. In this supposition as in so many such hasty presuppositions the ordinary observer would be far afield from the truth. If anything it was her awareness of possibilities that caused Tiffany to restrain all vagrant impulses and to maintain a sternly centered locus, a base camp from which she could send out expeditions of imagination along the highways and byways of vicarious sensations by reading and entertaining those seasoned reflections that are the fruit of memories recollected in tranquility. It was this cautious quality that had preserved her virginity, mental and physical, intact to the end of her third decade of life.

Tiffany would have been among the last to claim that her abstinence from sex, drugs, and heavy metal music was due to heroic virtue. Virtue is most evident when it exceeds ordinary demands; possibility must beckon and then be denied. This had not been the case with Tiffany. Her upbringing was such that anything overtly sexual or perverse was simply unthinkable for her. Femininity was presented to her clothed in all of the peril and shame that was *de rigueur* to Roman Catholic educational institutions. In the eighth grade it was carefully explained to her that whereas boys were more prone to sexual sins due to possessing a virtually ungovernable biological drive it was up to girls to avoid leading them into sin. To that end strict modesty was to be preserved at all times and any familiarity of a lingering let alone lascivious nature was to be strictly avoided. The result was that Tiffany took no joy in the rapid inundation, when it came, of that hormonal tide that in four short years had worked the accustomed wonder of transforming a slim and wiry eleven year old girl into a maiden.

Indeed so effective had been the advance warnings and maledictions of the nuns regarding anything overtly sexual during her adolescence in a gender-segregated private Catholic high school that even marriage, the great refuge from concupiscence, was in her eyes fearful and vulgar. The bondage of the flesh was further subject to the economic burdens that flowed from being a woman. The lives of women seemed to her to be one long procession from the altar to the grave spent pushing a grocery cart. A woman's value appeared to peak at seventeen and thereafter to cascade downward from terrace to terrace in a waterfall of recurring diets and the progressive loss of pulchritude to various manifestations of fleshly obsolescence from cellulite to wrinkles. There appeared to be a direct biological and social tendency to see any individual woman through a lens that focused primarily upon her capacity for procreation. This meant that personal history at least insofar as she was a woman was confined to that short era between menarche and menopause after which the framework and architecture of her existence was removed and her significance as an individual must of necessity rest upon a basis that she alone could construct.

It was due to this early assessment of the range of options open to her in the common course of life that Tiffany Amorth decided to foreswear the lure of suburban comforts and to embrace the Spartan life of being an "artistic type," as her parents had phrased it when they began to notice her early proclivity for quoting from Mallarme, Rimbaud, and Baudelaire in the original French at the dinner table. So it was that while other girls were lolling about in bikinis reading Jackie Collins or Ericka Jong, Tiffany was often to be found in high school reading Richardson's *Clarissa* for its more thrilling parts when honor was imperiled or at the outer fringe of her adolescent rebellion a life of Lord Byron or *Don Juan* or *Manfred* in the shade of an enveloping tree.

She thought of reading the classics as a profoundly moral and at the same time rewarding activity. She believed in the salubrious value of tracing the course of folly through fiction the better to avoid life's inevitable pitfalls. There was a moral aspect to all things and literature traced the course of human intemperance. She preferred her indiscretions to be by proxy. She decided early on that the great disadvantage of virtue is that it is always being assaulted by some *roué* or other the better to emerge though, splendid in refusal. She thought of her life as a vast and echoing cathedral at night with one great rose-window containing various *tableaux* marking significant episodes of her lone pilgrimage of virtue and trial, her beauty like that of Diana forever untouched and unassailable.

It must not be thought that she was vain however or overestimated her own appeal to the male sex; it was merely that she was curious about how others managed to deal with the great questions the better to guide her own eventual commitments. She was aware of her attractions without being impressed by them. Physically speaking her review of what nature had bestowed unasked upon her was neither persistent nor prurient. She did not engage in long vagina monologues when alone nor view her pudenda from all angles and in all lights lest some distinguishing feature failed to be noted and catalogued. She was content to possess the standard issue of a daughter of Eve with sufficient excess mammary tissue to have some left over to produce a beckoning *décolletage* when her studies were completed. Beyond that she had icy green eyes, a full mouth, and a nose that did not dominate her face nor distract from her more telling intellectual charms. Many girls were able to do far more with far less than her share of female *accoutrements* while Tiffany let the years go by in endless rehearsals for some distant but inevitable grand passion, the proper reward for her discriminating taste and willingness to forego the first jejune offerings of connubial bliss.

The result was that she emerged at last from graduate school at the University of Washington at thirty with a Masters Degree in Creative Writing but with no immediate marital prospects and no housemate but her widowed father who lived downstairs primarily in his den while the upper regions of the house were surrendered to her solitary keeping after her mother's untimely death. It was a scenario suitably gothic and filled with various Ann Radcliffe possibilities as she above all would know. How often had she lingered over passages in *The Mysteries of Udolpho* and listened at night to the winds of January moaning through the trees. How often had she imagined herself the heroine in one of Byron's longer poems winding her fingers through the feverish tendrils of the tormented poet's hair as he sought to recover from the pain of exile and the contempt of those who could never understand the nameless discontent that had driven him to a life of blasphemy and despair.

Truly it was time to set off on her own long delayed pilgrimage to some distant land where her virtues long untried might be assailed in earnest by a worthy suitor, but where? Who would finance such an expedition in search of a way of life long celebrated in verse but sadly absent in a world shrunken to the size of a postage stamp by technology? What Rapunzel-like braid of hair would allow her to be spirited away by night to places and adventures unknown? Romance long denied lay sequestered in the books that now gathered dust in neat shelves that lined what had once been the master bedroom of the family mansion, now used as a library with only an empty expanse of carpet, several bookshelves, and a table with a reading lamp and computer, the rose window of the vast cathedral of her young life sterile and derivative where it had been meant to be a tribute to the utter uniqueness of her well-tutored existence.

She had not only not dared and dared greatly she had barely moved. She was like a display in a window of a department store, inviting but untouchable. She began to wonder occasionally if a few cheap thrills coupled with early repentance might not have been worth it after all. Even being a victim of possession might have made her life less boring than it was turning out to be; she could at least vomit at will and scare people. Instead she was only Tiffany Amorth, a girl who wasn't sure who she was.

So, absent a sense of self it was no wonder that Tiffany was what might be called a universal recipient of the projections of other people who saw in her whatever they disliked in themselves. Like the universally used variable "X" in algebra Tiffany could be used as a symbol for other people's sexual or personality insecurities. She was like an empty warehouse just waiting to be filled with other people's refuse and many availed themselves of the opportunity. The result of course was that Tiffany gradually learned to tune out the world until it was only an obnoxious hum like that of one of the old tube-driven radio-sets of the 1930's. She saw people habitually as shadows, vague filmy abstractions to be gotten through or around in the course of everyday life.

In the course of her childhood she had come to see everything as an assignment to be completed alone and at her peril. Participation was foreign to her and finally pointless because it compromised the only thing that she could ever really rely on, herself. Her engagement in the world was rather like maintaining a projected hologram: when people reached out to hurt her they would find their hands grasping only empty space. Only the marvelous distance provided by the written word allowed her to engage intimately with people long dead that she would never know. These were safe because they were unaware of her existence, unable to deny her entry into their secret thoughts and complex personalities. In them she found allies and guardians in a cold and reprobate world—one that in an instant could call into question her right to exist and mock any budding trust in human warmth and communal feeling.

Thus the years had drifted past like snowflakes born frigid and icy before the wind while Tiffany Amorth became an unseen character upon the written page of various texts. She walked upon the moors with Cathy and Heathcliff at Wuthering Heights. She climbed the ruined stairwell of the House of Shaws with David Balfour. She arrived just before dusk at the melancholy House of Usher. Though unrecorded in the text she was there, within the narrative, and gradually the words and very being of the author became part of her so that her thoughts and words in everyday life resembled whatever it was she had just been reading before being summoned forth again to take her uncomfortable place in the everyday world once more where she was only Tiffany Amorth and not the intimate companion of the Count of Monte Cristo.

To such a lonely girl the thought of sympathetic witchcraft was pleasant because it could write into the world that place where alone she found comfort and acceptance. Whenever she was wounded, magic would allow her to restore order by virtue of metaphysical deletion of the offending party. It made perfect sense to her that if she could enter into fiction as though its phantom corridors were real then it should be possible for the gritty world that surrounded her to be first encased in prose and then subtly altered. The alterations might be marginal at first: a case of acne before the prom in a girl who had mocked her, a pulled tendon before a tennis match or a severe bout of magically induced vomiting at a school assembly for other offenders, or finally in its more resolved form, automatic misfortune to anyone who wished her ill. She called this latter mechanism, "the curse," and after a time it became quite real. She laughed at its existence of course, rational girl that she was, but secretly she felt that it existed as truly as the chain of missile silos placed in prairie locations all over America existed, ready to launch their deadly cargo when a few codes come through to form a perfect match. All of her pain had been stored up, every outrage, every unprovoked cruelty, every slighting jest at her expense—stockpiled, armed, directed, triggered, launched, and guided home to return the pain to its point of origin by "the curse."

However, far from being a commerce with the forces of

darkness there was for Tiffany a sort of Old Testament symmetry in all of this—any Israelite blowing trumpets around the walls of Jericho would have understood. After all Tiffany invoked no demonic powers; her magic was facilitated in quite a detached manner. It was a mute physical event like moving something across a room to occupy a new position in the cosmic order. To hurt Tiffany Amorth was to be displaced from column A to column B and then to suffer whatever consequences the universe might then impose. This was the way Tiffany saw it. It allowed her to believe in a moral universe, one where no harm goes without suffering the pangs of nemesis. She regarded herself as innocent and inoffensive thus relieving herself of actually hexing anyone. Still, the realization of her power added a bit to her wardrobe when she began to wear a fringed white cape and to twirl about in her room while listening to Fleetwood Mac.

She came at last to favor blue or black nail varnish and she kept glass jars full of various crystals at strategic points throughout her room to balance the energies. She made a pilgrimage in spirit to various Druid sites in old Britain and imagined herself gathered about oak trees on a full moon night dancing naked beneath the stars and drinking flasks of mead on animal skins laid out upon the foggy ground. There were men there with flowing hair and beards, men with gentle eyes and leather-clad limbs, icons of brazen male youth and fertility. She felt her breasts firm and pert with the cold of night and her thighs full and welcoming in sheer animal splendor and then... in an instant she would come to her senses again to hear the dull grind of the garbage disposal downstairs.

She had told her father again and again not to throw potato peelings or coffee grounds down the garbage disposal. Thus did dream and reverie intertwine in the life of Tiffany Amorth before she entered therapy and for a long time thereafter as she began slowly to claw her way back into reality with its prosaic demands and inconclusive remedies for an artist's sorrow and for her pain. Therapy helped her begin to let go of frustration and loss and she had gradually purged her immediate surroundings of the more outward trappings of her occult inclinations. She only still affected the almond eyes and heavy eye shadow of a siren or concubine in a Turkish harem but her days of black lace and deep mauve lipstick as in high school were now past. She felt that she didn't need to be scary to hide her insecurities.

Yet for all of her improvement, her particular demons could not be expunged without what she called "a definitive event." She needed to break free of her past and to undertake some radical and defining mission like bringing unsought independence to some obscure nation by arriving by jeep and posting some significant manifesto outside the presidential palace of the dictator. She would locate the disconsolate underground resistance fighters and weld them into a formidable force for change. She would be like Joan of Arc and lead a revolt and later preside at the constitutional assembly to form a new government. Alternatively she would in a swift intuition find the equation that would embody a unified field theory for the four forces in the universe or explain what was happening just a second before "the big bang." Then maybe, just maybe, resting on the secure laurels of immemorial achievement, she would find some male of equal talents and begin to turn out genetic representatives of their mutually superior genes thus elevating the human race to unimagined splendor say in a thousand years through natural selection. Now would be an identity and one worthy of her one and only life. She wouldn't have to be a witch if she could be a goddess!

But as enticing as these dreams were it only took a review of her present finances to diminish her prospects for humanity's reclamation. So it was that she pared and modified her aspirations and demands to a mere wish to leave the shores of America on a post-graduation trip of some sort. She needed to go to a place of history, charm, and romance where they served good food, where people were generally happy, and where her future admirer awaited her.

Tiffany Amorth decided at last after a cursory study of travelogues to go to Denmark. She proposed her scheme to her father at the dinner table two weeks after graduation.

"Father?" she inquired tentatively.

"Yes Tiffany."

"Well I'd like to talk to you about my post-graduate plans."

"That's encouraging. I had supposed that you were going to write the great American novel. Has there been a change of plans?"

"Not necessarily, but I feel that I may be too close to my subject for that. I need perspective."

He seemed to think about this while chewing slowly.

"And how do you propose to obtain that perspective?" he replied at last.

"I need a point of contrast to give dimension and balance to the whole."

He continued to chew.

"No doubt to obtain depth," he opined.

"Exactly."

"It would hardly do to attempt greatness in a spontaneous and superficial manner," he continued.

"I knew you would understand."

There was another significant pause.

"Will it require another year at the U.? More tuition?"

She decided to take the plunge.

"Well, it will require some further expense in time and money. You see I am not completely secure in my authorial voice."

He stopped eating and looked up at her, "You've lost me."

"It is essential that the author know something of life; mere verbal facility is inadequate."

He went back to his roast and potatoes. "You possess the latter and now need more of the former, is that it?"

"Yes."

He looked up brightly. "You could watch more Fox News; it would reorient your radical views."

She hesitated before replying, "I was thinking more of travel, cut loose and follow the rainbow."

"Travel… I thought you feared tropical diseases," he said

dubiously.

"I was thinking more of the northern latitudes."

He seemed to consider this.

"Where to, for instance?"

She said firmly, "Denmark."

"Why Denmark?"

"It was the setting for most of Soren Kierkegaard's life."

"And who, pray tell, is Soren Kierkegaard?" he inquired.

"He was a Danish philosopher, one of the first existentialists. He wrote a lot about finding one's place in the world, one's identity."

Her father returned to his meal.

"Admirable," he said without looking up. "I suppose that he at least figured out who he was before putting it all down."

"Yes, it was an arduous task. His writings reveal an ongoing quest."

"You will forgive me if I get a bit queasy when you speak of ongoing quests. I don't suppose that you could simply adopt someone else's identity as a sort of stop-gap measure and simply press on with living like most people do. Force of necessity answers many questions if it is allowed space to work."

This was disconcerting. "You know my limitations, Father. Of course that prescriptive advice works for less sensitive souls but I…"

"I know how sensitive your soul is and it always ends up costing me money. I thought your therapist was working wonders with you lately."

"Well I'm somewhat better."

"Better but not cured is that it?" He frowned. "Suppose you go to Denmark and have a panic attack and I have to fly over and bring you home?"

She looked down and felt a rush of shame. "I'll be fine. They ride bicycles over there and everyone smiles and eats pastry. It's very restful."

"No bats or mice then?"

"I seldom hear them spoken of," she commented softly.

52

The room was silent while her father thought the matter over.

"I hear they are all socialists over there; nobody works. There is no army to speak of and people go in for sex changes at the drop of hat; hardly a proper atmosphere for a daughter of mine."

She volunteered bravely, "I could show them the way back to capitalism and imperial rule."

He considered this seriously.

"Sort of an emissary of proper values eh?"

"Well, I am your daughter," she said brightly.

"Heredity will out you mean? Hmm, you will make a break from your dabbling in the occult?"

"Of course. By the way, Kierkegaard was a great Christian, quite demanding in fact."

An appeal to religion was always a telling point with her father.

"Really? Was he Catholic?"

"Lutheran I am afraid, but he quarreled with the state church."

Her father returned his attention to his plate, "Well, it proves he was moving in the right direction. How long do you plan to remain over there?"

"Well that depends."

"On the depth of my generosity no doubt."

She took a deep breath. "Yes."

The room was silent for some time while her father examined the various equities and risks involved in her proposal.

"What if you fall in love over there? I'm not financing an international wedding."

She blushed appropriately as one might expect in a fable such as this.

"I plan on studying and writing; I will have no time for romance."

He ruminated.

"You might be kidnapped by terrorists," he suggested.

"Nothing much in that order ever happens in Denmark."

Her father took up his napkin and wiped his lips.

"I see, dull sort of place. Well, will five thousand do it?"

The time was at hand.

"Ten would be better," she said bravely.

"Eight thousand."

"Done. "Thank you, father."

"It will give me an opportunity to have her room exorcised while she is gone," he mumbled quietly to himself.

Part Two

When she returned to her room Tiffany wondered if this whole Denmark thing made any sense at all now that it had been transmuted from speculation to active possibility. It was somewhat surprising that her father had not raised more objections. She wondered whether she might be blundering her way into a long avoided but permanent exile? Suddenly Denmark seemed an absurd idea. She tried to recall the exact lineage of the desire to go there. She was able at last to trace its origin to the feeling that the ground in America was shifting beneath her feet. She was weary of the general slippage of her native land into the collective delusion represented by MAGA hats and chants of "USA USA." It would be nice to live in a place where people could live civilized lives without the pretence of international power grounded on a presumption of moral and cultural superiority with little basis in fact. Denmark might be provincial by global standards, but at least it was not imperialistically complacent.

The world around her was changing too quickly. Recently the last CD music and video store in the area had closed. She remembered the vitality of similar chains from her girlhood. She and her friends had worn leggings and dark-eyeliner and had enjoyed being checked-out by the older high-school boys. She had been part of a sort of intellectual Goth crowd when she went out at all. She had managed to avoid drugs and AIDS due more to fear than the exercise of virtuous restraint. But by college she had somehow lost her early flair, become what the British used to call a swot or a drudge and studied all the time. She had double-majored in literature and philosophy before entering the creative writing program which she managed to stretch out to three years instead of the usual two. Between undergraduate and graduate education she had taught as a substitute teacher for sixth graders in a private girl's school for two years, helped a professor on two research projects, and avoided any premature commitments to an irrevocable life course.

Meanwhile her high school friends had married or moved away and suddenly she realized that she had virtually no friends left to serve the immemorial female function of sharing mutual confidences. Tiffany wondered if she might have inadvertently taken a fatal fork in the river of life through sheer inertia and the refusal to search out contacts in the professional sphere. Jobs lead to other jobs. Her desire to simply emerge or be discovered for her remarkable intuitions and latent genius had not materialized as planned. People far less talented than she were having their second and third children or were being advanced into management positions. She supposed that there were lives every bit as unfocused but this one just happened to be hers.

What did she expect from Denmark anyway? She spoke no Danish, knew no one there, and was still prone to unexplainable bouts of anxiety that might rear their ugly heads simply due to a particular cast of light from a wintry sky or an expression of suspicion or rejection from a stranger. How would she be able to manage there? Suddenly even the comfort of her bedroom seemed vaguely alien and threatening. The temperature seemed to drop and objects took on that slight angular look that they took on when her anxieties began to rise like a ground fog on a February day. It was this particular vulnerability, evanescent and untraceable that had always held her back. Usually she could just wait it out and everything would resume its usual place and relations, but this resurgence depended upon maintaining close contacts with the familiar. To cut loose though might leave her in a strange place without comfort or resource. She suddenly felt like a lost little girl again, not the intrepid warrior maiden, not like one of the newly elected women to Congress who dared to beard the bear-like President of our august republic. Her convictions were the same as theirs were, why then was she so isolated and ineffectual?

She reflected on the relation of experience to identity, does the first bestow the second? She thought of Kierkegaard who had seen the ordinary course of life as being incompatible with an intimate relationship with God when defined as the primordial ground of being. The relation to God was an absolute that must preclude all lesser considerations, even the ethical demands of reason should God request it. Where did other people fit into this intense bilateral mirroring of God or at least his image in the individual soul? Tiffany preferred a diffuse God, one present in tree and sunset over the intensely paternal and personal God of the Old Testament or even the gentle-minded Savior whose fate made the prospect of any sin so guilt-inducing. She had no desire to add to the burdens of Christ by her actions or preferences, but then love rejoices, it seemed to her, in the prospect of added sacrifice. She supposed that when she fell in love that she would enjoy doing things for the one she loved no matter how tiresome or obnoxious they might be.

Kierkegaard had broken off with his fiancée Regina Olsen by pretending to be a cad and jilting her. Did God ask this of him or did he take this burden on voluntarily and perhaps even beyond the demands of necessity? To err on the side of suffering just to be sure was hardly the normal course of human conduct. Tiffany wondered if she would have liked a man like him. His titles though had always intrigued her. *"Fear and Trembling," "The Sickness unto Death," "Stages on Life's Way," and "The Philosophical Fragments;"* all had seemed books directed particularly at her. He at least would have understood the subtle burdens she carried. He liked challenging authority as well be it ever so sanctified by common usage. She found him more palatable than the sensual and indulgent Lord Byron, her other great hero. As for Percy Shelley, well, she thought Mary Wollstonecraft Godwin-Shelley might have done better. He had been rather like an early version of a contemporary rock star, gathering groupies.

Tiffany was suspicious of both reformers and of orthodox prelates as well. Her attraction to the occult betrayed her desire to revisit long discredited explanations of why the world is at it is. She valued the vagueness of what little rite and doctrine there might be within it. An undemanding and unrevealing goddess seemed easier to relate to than the purveyor of a definitive but demanding revelation presided over by an insistent and unquestionable male hierarchy. She had received enough of that at home. Still she was a Catholic and intended to remain one. Catholicism is always both a religion and a culture and once imbued with its sights, sounds, and ideas nothing else can take its place. If her father had realized this about her he would have been less worried as to the state of her soul.

None of this however answered her doubts as to whether or not she should head off to Denmark. Was this only a further indulgence, an effort to retain balance by seeking a contrast to the prevailing ethos of rabid Americanism? Her general methodology had always been dialectical: she tended to avidly pursue a midpoint between extremes as the surest path to the truth. This habit of mind had made her impatient with mental parking garages. Any thesis was merely an opportunity for further questions and objections. She enjoyed picking at the scab of any certitude. This had not been helpful to her as a Catholic. The last person in her mind who had been totally free to ask questions from scratch had been St. Thomas Aquinas. His synthesis of all knowledge had been enthroned in Roman Catholicism ever since as the acme of reasoned theological thought. She recalled that her questions in high school had been regarded as troublesome if not impertinent. It was this tendency to nibble around the penumbra of orthodoxy that had led her into a review of questions long regarded as settled doctrine. There was always some further author to explore whose opinions or suggestions might just tip the scale of her convictions back to the certainties of her upbringing or alternatively enable her to chart a course towards a pluralistic realm guided by a generally humanist synthesis which would restrict its efforts to making things as comfortable and just as possible in our lonely sojourn across a mindless cosmos.

This compulsion to solve the human equation had so long distracted her that she was still at the primary level when it came to solving the question of who she was as an individual and what she hoped to obtain from her short and irreplaceable life. Each year she seemed to be falling farther behind her fellows as they accumulated houses, mates, children, vacation cruises, and all the milestones celebrated in the various alumni publications that were forwarded to her monthly. Didn't these people have any hang-ups? She would be far more likely to forego a pizza now and then and contribute to the multiple funds solicited by these already too well-endowed institutions if they manifested in their selection of life-reviews some degree of failure or destitution among the graduates rather than displaying only their triumphs and laurels. The net result of these preoccupations was that Tiffany felt that leaden weights were attached to her ankles in the race of life. How many people managed quite well with a fragment of her education? Was the pursuit of extraneous knowledge then the ultimate self-indulgence?

In the beginning she had felt that she was merely taking the road less traveled in her choice of studies. Lately that conviction had been replaced by a gnawing doubt that she might have mistaken the path into utter mental wilderness for a path that would soon open to display unimagined vistas of vision and enlightenment. It was said that the sin of the fallen angels was primarily intellectual in nature; if so, then it seemed ironic that demonic manifestations always seemed accompanied by foul language and dreadful smells so degrading to angelic pride. But perhaps these visceral manifestations were the best evidence of the shackles worn by moral evil in the eternal realm:

God only allows evil to manifest itself outwardly through a grid or net that says in effect "only this much of your true malice will be admitted, the better to manifest your fallen state to those who do not yet share it."

This would explain for instance the physical assaults that had been made upon Padre Pio in the course of his life. Padre Pio was the famous stigmatic beset by demonic forces that would literally beat him up in his humble cell in the monastery of San Giovanni Rotundo. How absurd to expend such futile efforts on a little old Franciscan monk! Why was he worth the trouble among the many manifest evils of the world where the devil emerges triumphant? Why not play your strong suit? Is it perhaps that evil is most decisively defeated at the most humble and individual level? This speculation returned Tiffany to her sense that having an individual identity did actually matter in the long and anonymous course of general history.

After much reflection in the days that followed her talk with her father, Tiffany resolved the fundamental question presented to her to be: "Does identity precede our actions and hence our unique story or is identity a mere product of experience and hence neither preexisting nor complete until the moment of our death."

This formulation implied that our true orientation to both God and to ourselves is always at best an approximation until sealed by that termination of earthly possibilities that we call death. The question remained however whether death is instantaneous or a gradual withdrawing of life from its former insular locus in space-time to embrace hitherto unthinkable potentialities in eternity. Is there perhaps a twilit realm where the soul, balanced between two eternal destinies can finally grasp its life as a whole and determine freely its orientation towards perfect goodness or its opposite, the great unending abyss of metaphysical evil? The time of her leaving for Denmark had been left indefinite so Tiffany was granted a reprieve in the execution of her resolve.

Part Three

The winter that had been remarkably mild thus far suddenly was transformed into one of those seasons of late snowfall that had delighted her as a child but that she now viewed as a source of discomfort and inconvenience. She put off making reservations by airline from day to day. This would allow her time to listen to some CD's on the Danish language and to learn something more of the place and people before her departure. She also dug out a recent eight-hundred page biography of Kierkegaard and began to read it.

The days passed pleasantly. She was able to follow the latest episodes of the drama or great soap-opera of the Trump Presidency and to watch the conservative media bristle like a porcupine as the newly elected representatives, among them Alexandria Ocasio-Cortez from the Bronx, who had called for a Green New-Deal for America. It was always surprising to her that so many presumably working-class Americans were petrified by a socialist agenda as they lined up behind the rights of billionaires to distort markets at will through the exercise of their monopolistic privileges. Maybe everyone should contemplate a trip to Denmark. She avoided pointless disputes though around the domestic hearth and watched the snow fall gently past the windows while the nation's teeth ground together in anticipation of the long-awaited results of the Mueller probe into Russian influence on the election of 2016.

As she fell asleep in her pink bedroom still redolent of a privileged girlhood in the comfortable suburbia of western Washington State she pondered the origin of her own 1930's style populism. She had always felt herself to be born out of her proper time and place. She had missed that great upwelling of national outrage that had led to the nation's withdrawal from involvement in Vietnam and the events leading to the resignation of President Nixon.

The time of her birth precluded these. She had grown up during the Clinton years. The great swing to conservatism that had begun with the Reagan Presidency still had its iron grip upon the great flatlands of the mid-west and the ever fractious and unwilling southern states while the Pacific states were blue, digitally sophisticated, and progressive. The people with the most to lose by a Republican victory always voted Republican while those who were managing quite well, who desired to share their good fortune with the poor, always voted Democrat. Perhaps it all came down to a dog and his bone, the less meaty the bone the more the dog will growl if anyone threatens to take it away. The list of American clichés never pales though on a naïve audience and Trump-ism had the advantage of having echoes throughout the conservative media and from the pulpits of fragmented Christian sectarianism to give his new feudal-style presidency an aura of 19th century populist and isolationist legitimacy. This was the national ambiance against which her own decision regarding an excursion to Denmark was being enacted.

"Combine a complex protagonist with a challenging decision against an atmosphere pregnant with conflict and the result is what literature refers to as plot or story. The action should proceed with a certain sweep of destiny and inevitability until at the climax the forces resolve themselves and a general worldview is affirmed or disaffirmed in a tidy moral or the emergence of insight at a higher resolution."

After reviewing this note to herself, a remnant remaining from her years spent in the formal discipline of creative writing that as if by magic hopes, or intends at least, to transform young men and women who in former ages might have been classified as sufferers from neurasthenia into accomplished, and more important still, saleable authors Tiffany Amorth put her pen down and began to consider her present life situation from a point of view supplied by critical literary theory. Assuming that literature has some connection with actual life it did not seem to her inappropriate to look to literary theory to guide her present choice regarding Denmark. She had always seen her life as a narrative with God as the prospective critic sitting in the wings whose review would either enshrine her efforts or condemn it to being just another failure in the long string of sorry productions of the recalcitrant human race. She had always wanted to live a life that when seen in its broadest perspective would constitute a story and not merely a statistic. To that end she turned now as so often before to her personal library for answers.

In the present instance she had dug out her old copy of Soren Kierkegaard's *Concluding Unscientific Postscript to the Philosophical Fragments,* Martin Heidegger's *Being and Time,* and two books by Paul Ricoeur, *Time and Narrative* and *The Conflict of Interpretations* to help her to focus her inquiry. She had never lost her faith in the value of cutting-edge thinkers on the world stage. It surprised her though that people of immense power managed to be promoted, praised, and rewarded by golden parachutes and stock-options who had never heard of the seminal intellectuals of their time. Seldom were first-rate poets or even historians admitted to the councils that determined public policy. Even attorneys had more of a technical bent than a firm grounding in social theory and jurisprudence. Few multiple-term members of Congress were to be found discussing Lyotard, Habermas, or Foucault. Tiffany felt the inadequacy of formal thought when brought to bear on actual events. She was sure for instance that if the current President for all of his stolid vision and confidence in his infallibility were granted even substantial geologic time calculated at the rate of radioactive decay of strontium 90 at least one of these books she was consulting would have a .001 % chance of ending up on his reading list.

The President of the United States subsisted instead on a mental diet that paralleled his preference for hamburgers and fries, a concrete reality that spared him such abstract labors lest he should stumble into a time warp and actually rise above his shallow fund of preexisting ideas. It has long been a complaint of writers that future immortality is often purchased at the price of comparative neglect by their contemporaries. The crudity of current public taste however never acts as a sufficient deterrent to the devoted artist. She will pursue her craft despite all odds though idiocy exalts the unworthy to glamour and to fame. Ideally artists reveal truth to somnolent humankind while the task of the politician is to promise untold benefits at bargain prices while confirming the dull and indolent masses in their presumptions and to flatter their collective vanity. Tiffany Amorth, a genius yet unknown and uncelebrated, was only one in this long sustained human contradiction between merits and rewards.

Money has its own logic: it enables destruction and leaves unattended the basic needs of the majority of the human species. In no case was this general truth more evident than in the election of Donald Trump in 2016. The fact that a rough third of the American people, well armed and jealous to preserve, by force if necessary, whatever their personal stash of big-box store shopping excursions had wrought made her dubious of the fate of the nation. So few were the correspondences between her own beliefs and this mélange of nostalgic blue-collar workers, disgruntled farmers, and well-paid talk-show hosts that she felt not merely a sense of pervasive alienation but actual estrangement from the currently triumphant political ethos. She felt enfeebled and diminished. Of what relevance was her unique and particular task when weighing alternatives to so inconsequential an excursion as hers to Denmark would be when laid against the yardstick of such public folly and its possible consequences? What place has the individual when her fate will be subject to the shifting tectonic plates of the mass appeal of media propaganda applied to ingrained prejudice and fixed notions? How had her America become so unaccountably benighted?

It was at this point that she began to contemplate writing a book that would take as its starting point her own concern for the country of her birth coupled with her awareness of her own comparative obscurity and insignificance as refracted by the unutterable banality of the times she was living through. When these were laid against the probability of the ecological ruination that must come if the present course of history remained unaltered, at whatever cost it might entail, her depression and discouragement seemed unavoidable. Whence might a remedy be sought? What could motivate a generation of young people to simply do the math and draw the probable consequences to their personal prospects of home and family when their primary legacy was not the traditional intergenerational promise of America but a massive national debt and a declining industrial base mired in 20th century technology?

Even the tendrils of foreign investment and control that were the primary generators of American wealth could not repair the damage to the mass of Americans. The middle-class was a homely residue floating far beneath the surface where the real money was being made and invested, money with little relation to the physical actions of a laboring body unless they could be embodied in song or dance. Community after community relied on an influx of Federal spending to keep them afloat in the absence of manufacturing. Take away the defense industry and what for instance would be the fate of her native Western Washington? She thought of the desolate lumber and fishing towns on the coast and their abandoned and derelict condition due to the decline in fishing and forestry. She sought for an image of this and found it in a prospect of shattered glass. What light can re-illumine that which has lost its collective integrity?

Her young life seemed already to be similarly bereft. To be always in the audience and never a performer, never to view her own life as integrated into a larger design whether of enterprise or expression made her feel wraithlike and insubstantial. So rich had been her yesterdays when imagination supplied that which was lacking so that she could see her life laid against a template as rich as a frame to hold a renaissance painting. Now she sought for an enfolding context in vain aware that each year plunged her deeper into psychic debt to her lost dreams. She was always rehearsing versions of a play that consisted only of scattered scenes without theme or plot to unify them and where the idea of progress would not be marked by present sterility.

So it was that her personal quest for some reassurance prior to her departure on this nameless errand of spontaneity to Denmark and the search for resources that might supply her with answers seemed only another instance where the great collective neglect shown by contemporary American cultural obtuseness was manifest all around her and hence within her as well. She was ashamed of her country as of herself.

Who cared who Tiffany Amorth was or what she thought or felt about anything? Who sought out her views? Where was her following on Twitter? How could she make them care? Her identity was reduced to her function as a consumer and now that her tuition had been paid, her largest life-investment thus far and the diploma awarded she remained as she had been before without a trade-name, a logo, a base for advertisements and endorsements. Her picture did not adorn a makeup display. No sporting goods manufacturer cared that she used their equipment. No arena would fill to capacity to watch her parade about the stage in a skin-tight jumpsuit with a microphone seductively poised at her lips. She was only a writer and an undiscovered one at that.

Still, as the weeks progressed, an outline of a book of sorts gradually emerged. She thought that she might record her own process of seeking definition. She might call it *Adventures in Anomie.* It is a dreadful thing to be part of the mass of data, a mere conflation of preferences in a marketing survey. It is this anonymity that motivates the pointless acts of violence that punctuate each day with a selection of atrocities.

She gradually prepared an outline of sorts.

Tiffany's Book

The unusual title of this book stems from six fundamental insights which provide the basis for this book:

1. The basis for our self-awareness as for all

relationships is the assumption that when we exist we have a sense of an ego that defines the border of the self from the non-self. This ego has various characteristics of inner experience and self-definition that tells us who and what we are and provides a basic set of categories for all subsequent experience;

2. But this awareness of the self is seldom as unified as we assume. What we call the self is more like a series of stars in the night sky that together form various constellations;

3. This characteristic of fluidity in the personality allows for growth and change over time but it also allows for what might be called a catastrophic breakdown in the sense of self when that integrity is attacked by outside forces. These forces can be conceptualized as entities that wish to impose their own definitions on the inner dimensions of the self. The self must then discern when to adapt to these outside definitions and when to resist them;

4. The process of definition is a universal and innately political process involving the use of power to obtain the progress of conflicting ideals against the resistance provided by the cultural world that is our ambient reality;

5. The nascent self must be resistant enough to maintain its own integrity but not so idiosyncratic or rigid that its inner definitions become static and calcified or lead into a world of solipsism or narcissism;

6. Every great spiritual discipline advises us to liberate ourselves from definition so as to attain transcendence, so in the light of the struggle to define ourselves and to resist the pressures exerted

from outside and from within us there is finally another dimension to be considered: the final erosion of the self by aging and extinction in its present form by death.

7. Hence the achievement of identity is brought up against an absurd fate even in its heroic and tentative realization: that at the very point at which our personalities assume what might be considered their final form we must watch helplessly as that definition is reduced to the degradation and neglect imposed upon the marginal and the elderly who are perceived to have no future. We are caught first in a struggle to emerge from the chrysalis and thereafter to remain aloft. Resistance under these conditions is both our triumph and our inevitable defeat.

8. To let go of personality at this point demands an involuntary renunciation followed by acquiescence to our fate. We are dissolved at last into our component elements and dispersed. This final process though is not an unmitigated evil because it allows us to surrender the burden of the self with all of its limitations and to see ourselves as part of a larger constellation of life flowing through the generations and to imagine even in death that a bond exists with the ultimate transcendent who is God.

She laid her outline aside with at least some minor satisfaction with the result. To define the problem is already to be on the way to its solution. She took comfort from the fact that her own obscurity was shared by the study of the humanities as a whole. Cultural neglect was endemic as was the readiness to accept the cheap formulaic attribution of "fake news," applied to whatever facts the current regime found distasteful or that might subtract from the adoration owed to the supreme national benefactor. How had he existed so long among us deprived of the same cult-like worship afforded to his new bosom buddy, Kim Jung-Un? How could he fail to be enthroned like Augustus as Emperor I of America until his sons might succeed him?

Part Four

Slowly the weeks passed until at dinner one night her father asked her over the soufflé. "So how is your Denmark plan going? Purchased any wooden shoes yet?"

She smiled. "That's Holland I believe and no I haven't."

He looked surprised. "I thought you were all in a frenzy to go."

"It's still cold over there now; better to wait until summer."

He considered this news for a minute. "I see. What will you do until summer, read your horoscope and cast your runes?"

She looked down at her plate. "I'm working on a book."

"Really, what's it going to be about?"

"The course of human life when seen from a phenomenological perspective."

"Going for a broad and varied audience I see."

She looked up at him. "I think I'm on to something. Looking at life as an example of narrative creation."

"How about life as an example of income creation, have you ever considered that?"

She demurred. "I'm not an economist."

"Obviously. Have you decided what it is that you are?"

She hesitated. "Not yet, but I'm getting close. It may not have a name yet."

"Just a price-tag."

She attempted to redirect the discussion. "Do you like the roast?

"Very tasty."

"Well I think I'll take a walk down by the sound, maybe go down to the ferries."

He looked up. "Don't stay out too late and don't talk to any creeps."

"They may give me some story ideas."

"They'll give you something you don't want. Don't forget your keys; I may be asleep when you come in so try and be quiet."

"Of course Father, I'll be careful."

She kissed him quickly on the cheek, ran upstairs for a coat, and headed out into the soft winter darkness of a February night."

She didn't go to the city as often as she once had. Parking in Seattle was not what it had been during her undergraduate days. Then there had been street parking in industrial or under-policed areas where cars bought more for transport than for display could rest assured for extended periods without fear of robbery or citations. The new world of Seattle had a definite upscale tilt and like most of America the seams that had at one time allowed for a gentle and unnoticeable transition between the classes were now ripped and separated. The fissuring of America was everywhere apparent along lines of wealth and influence. Some of this was natural for an ethos that had always valued accumulation and acquisition over culture and the quiet abstinence that can refrain from privatization and exploitation. There had always been titans and tycoons to festoon society pages and resist any signs of collective intemperance such as unions or cooperative enterprises, but never had excess so eclipsed largesse to the degree seen in the new century. It was becoming difficult to even imagine a story that would not have at its core some element of crass and comparative display. From social media to telephones, the constant racket of megabytes of information flow never ceased. It was more than mere future-shock, it was a strange new mutation so that to be human was seen as some retrograde failure to arrive at the universal algorithm of thoughts and desires that could someday be recorded on a microchip and filed somewhere, or worse still deleted as inconsequential.

Tiffany wondered how long it would be before undertakers were replaced by handy and universal body-depositories, human recycling bins separating the various elements and compounds for later reuse. What are we really? Are we waves or particles sent hurdling at some vast double-slit experiment to decide whether we go to heaven or to hell?

As she drove to Seattle from the computer saturated east side of Lake Washington Tiffany pictured herself trading places with Schrödinger's Cat as the ultimate subject of indeterminacy and quantum weirdness. She thought of the lovely final lines of John Keats describing the suspension of the senses as a nightingale flew away taking its song with it: "Was it a vision or a waking dream; Fled is that music do I wake or sleep?"

To be human had once been to be open to such experience: raw, unmediated by electronic pulses, and therefore visceral and pregnant with discovery and wonder. Place and time were still somewhat inaccessible and so immune from the arrogant manipulation of human will. To leave Denmark might be to forfeit any possibility of return there whereas now she could fly there in a day.

She imagined the trip. "I would stumble jet-lagged off of the plane and find things not so much different in essence from Dubai or Bangkok. Is it Denmark I want to visit then or my idea of Denmark?" This was the thought that filled her as she turned south on Highway Five and took the exit that would lead her down to the water. She found parking in Pioneer Square, locked her car and made for the renovated ferry terminal where she stood watching as the ferries moved smoothly across the still dark waters towards Bainbridge Island and the Olympic Peninsula beyond. She looked over at Ivar's Acres of Clams and recalled outings there through the years, the taste of chowder and a plate of fried local oysters. She would be leaving this behind if she went to Denmark. She thought of how distant and even romantic her own home might be imagined to be for a resident of that low-lying land of islands and peninsulas. She had heard that there was even a bridge there to Sweden. Technology had arrived. The Old World was also the same world of futuristic conceptions that she inhabited here.

"Yes," she thought, "But there are still the remnants at least of other times there. These are embodied memories. I need location and visual testimony to ground me. I could find these there. But would they ever really be mine? I have no associations there. I would find a history as alienating to my sense of self as the present erosion of all that I once considered familiar even here where presumably I have some sense of order and control. What then is Denmark to me but an idea of freedom? Of what use would freedom be if it were merely random motion, the action of spirochetes on a laboratory slide. It is association then that bestows meaning and not novelty. Is it identity that I seek or rather recognition, something to echo back to me my own thoughts and feelings so that I know them to be mine? It is not just Denmark that I seek but *my Denmark* found as though it had not existed until it unveiled itself before me like the mermaid in Copenhagen's harbor newly risen from the sea. For a human, the act of being is always a becoming. But this prosaic waterfront, is this my ground of revelation? I've been here time and time again!"

Tiffany thought of the first time she had read *To the Lighthouse* by Virginia Woolf who above all artists had seemed to realize the eternal value of the trivial and of the transitory. Was what she had been seeking, a similar vision that to Tiffany had been enveloped and summarized in the coded-word of Denmark? Perhaps what she really had been seeking was not escape but engagement, some sense of totality in the fragmentary elements of her accidental life. She might find this anywhere.

"I want to matter!" she cried and looked down in embarrassment as passers-by looked at her. "Am I just another crazy person haunting the Seattle waterfront with the only difference being that I can drive home to Kirkland tonight and let myself into a fancy house on the lake? What separates me from the street people?"

Tiffany wondered how she had managed to escape being a Republican and marrying a Kushneresque scion of wealth and privilege. Instead she pictured herself knitting beneath the guillotine as the tumbrels rolled by bringing their freight of Trump appointees to their retribution. Would all of her perceptions be held hostage forever to her inveterate reading? Was her life to be doomed to being simply one more text to be deciphered and deconstructed? If Descartes had grounded his being in thinking, her own credo was reducible not to a phrase such as "I think therefore I am," but to acts of recollection to enhance experience like Marcel Proust who seemed never to have lived in the present but only in memory as though only by tracing a design in recollection could he reinforce it into becoming real at last, sanctioned by an awareness of the brevity of the instant and the irrecoverable essence of impressions unless they were transformed into the eternity of text.

But this moment of insight was followed by an awareness of the enemy. Around her stood the towers and pavilions of the former pragmatic seaport that now fancied itself the Emerald City. Tiffany looked up at the alien windows of offices the function of which was to embody trade, commerce, and all of the bywords of power. Here she had been educated but in a dying art-form in an era of clichés and sordid generalizations, dwarfed into insignificance and mocked by variety and specificity, valued not because things related to the deepest human needs or wants in a cohesive way but simply as transactions carried out in real time, transformed into receivables in some firm or other with tentacles reaching overseas to China or Japan. Who today would dare to write a 21st century version of *Middlemarch*? Would it sell? Who covets a synthesis amidst such endless diversity, pluralism, and diffusion?

Gone was the era that had spawned overarching humanist dogmatic systems by Marx, Freud, or even Husserl. Vanished were the voices of individualized rebellion by Sartre, Camus, Gide, Celine, and even our own homely Kerouac. The millennial generation only knows or is realizing that they have been betrayed, reduced to cannon-fodder for terrorists in schools and indebted to pay for the long-living boomer generation that plans on a long slow glide pattern before dying. Where were the significant voices of Generation X? Caught between the Old World and the new as youth is always caught she stood in the February night while a multitude of possibilities beckoned.

Part Five

Not content to remain in the shadow of the immense skyline she decided on the instant to book a trip across Puget Sound. Tiffany climbed the stairs to the ferry terminal and purchased a ticket to Bainbridge Island. She stood among the commuters on their way home to their quiet bungalows after their workday in the city. When the gates opened she streamed onto the ferry with the crowd and remained on deck while the others flooded into the warm embracing yellow glow of the interior of the ship. As the ramp was lifted and the ferry drew away she watched as the city, formerly so immense, took on manageable proportions. Seattle was reduced into a single panorama of celestial light encased in a great circumference of darkness reflected in the lengthening water behind her. She felt as though she could reach out and grasp each separate building and study its tiny occupants at her leisure like fish in an aquarium.

"How can I write adequately of these things?" she asked herself as she returned to the cabin for warmth as the ferry approached the island. She would have to disembark before re-boarding for the trip back to Seattle and she spent the interim listening to the everyday interchanges of the people who surrounded her, each as intent on his own journey and concerns as she. "Would this be what it would be like in Denmark?" she asked herself.

The return boarding call came and she re-entered the ferry for the trip home. This time she remained inside all the way back to

Seattle. She looked out into the darkness as the ship slipped by the red and green channel markers and admired the expensive homes that lined the harbor of Winslow. She wondered what it would be like to live over here; was this place another Denmark although located a mere half hour across Puget Sound? How to encompass all possible experience in one short life? How could her one life sample so many conflicting and mutually exclusive possibilities? Would they not devour her? How could she keep her head above water amidst so many contradictory waves each rushing at her, demanding that she choose?

She looked about her at the other passengers, each so different. How might she assert herself as an individual among their many prospects unless she could know each of them in their individual choices and contexts, to follow them home invisible and live among them like a ghost? She thought of her father waiting for her at home, his being an anchor to her sense of self, location, and security. He alone was her measuring rod in acquiescence or rebellion, his easy confidence in his own infallibility was her Greenwich Mean Time. She had never emerged beyond the force field that he generated, never been out of radio contact with his transmitter. It frightened her to think that his absoluteness was to others a mere marginal and relative voice to be doubted or ignored without peril. Would even Denmark be far enough to escape his influence and judgment? Did she really want to escape?

She got up and rushed to the other end of the ferry before it landed and saw the city growing closer and larger. Would it embrace her in some capacity so that she could find a place there, be met by some recognition, perhaps an assigned parking space and a salary that said she was valued, had a place in it all however partial and incomplete. "No, I'm going to Denmark!" she interposed. "It will sound so impressive when I return," she thought to herself. "'Oh Denmark!' people will say. 'How charming, I always wanted to go there. Just like a fairy tale it must be.'"

"This was always how it is," she thought. "I always think in vast hypotheticals. What if nobody on this boat ever wants to go to Denmark, will it matter then if I go?" She reflected further. "No. I must desire it not for others but for myself, because I want to go or because I want to stay here."

She felt the beginnings of freedom in all their promise and their peril.

"This so silly," she thought, "I am not debating a solo flight across the Atlantic." But in just this way decisions had always implicated for her some dread of interior dissolution. "I must generate thrust," she thought, "I must possess a rocket booster to carry me into orbit or better still toward an irrecoverable trajectory towards selfhood. It isn't Denmark; it is Tiffany I seek."

The boat touched the pilings and the attendants methodically affixed the boat and lowered the departure ramp below for the auto traffic. The walk-on passengers began to stream toward their own access point to the city.

In latent rebellion she returned as before to Seattle, as though from a great journey, to the immediate time and place where she, Tiffany Amorth, stood on this night on Seattle's romantic waterfront: alive, thirty years old, and father-haunted just as Mary Shelley had been, and looking as Mary had been looking when she wrote her confessional book *Mathilda,* a book long since forgotten and seldom read, for some validation to show that she existed apart from her father's idea of her with only a marginal correspondence to who she actually was.

She reflected as she walked toward her car, "He thought once that I was possessed… and perhaps I am!" she shouted into the silent echoes of her mind. "I am possessed by all that I have ever seen or want to see. I am possessed by an unending hunger to not rest with all I see about me but to find; to find that Denmark that is not flat and wholesome and predictable and complacent. I want the Denmark of Kierkegaard that rejected his rebellion, ignoring his efforts to jar it into life. His Denmark wore him to death by misunderstanding and rejection. I want to be a martyr to misunderstanding and neglect like him. I want to write!"

It was nearing midnight as she pulled away from the waterfront. She seldom stayed out so late. Her car climbed the hills to the freeway onramp and she was soon crossing Lake Washington toward sleeping Kirkland where the Microsoft campus is located. The Pacific Northwest had played a significant part in launching the new world that was now her fate to encounter as we hurtle deeper into the abyss of the 21st century. The great adventure of universal digital competence had raged about her while she had studied the past until she was more a part of it than she was of her own time and place. Was it too late to join in the fiesta brought about by the infinite series of ones and zeros, to seek a new trajectory for herself in space-time? Or should she reverse what she had even now just affirmed? Just in this manner did the demons of the present hour in triumphant Trumpian America seek to regain their dominion of Tiffany Amorth who was struggling to escape possession and retain those elusive values and constructs to which literature has access because it flows forth from the inexhaustible fountain of the human soul.

Denmark, that symbol of refuge for beleaguered progressives in the present hour of darkness, could now be seen clothed in significance and surrounded by references, a process that reduces whatever exists beyond our solitary selves into various discourses and narratives. Tiffany Amorth, a girl in search of a universal hermeneutic that would give her a center and certainty prepared to continue her quest. Perhaps some famished fellow devotee of the muses will stumble upon her while the freshness of youth holds disillusion yet at bay. Perhaps she will stumble upon the golden apples of the sun along some dusty shelf of a used book store. Perhaps she will book passage soon to Scandinavia and hold silent intercourse with the blackened figure of the corpse of an ancient man found preserved in a bog. Who can trace the course of a human life?

Our tale ends here as inconclusive and fragmentary as life itself. What did she announce at breakfast the following day when she would be confronted by her father with the lateness of her return and her inconsiderateness towards her father and benefactor causing him to worry whether she had not fallen victim to one of the members of the endless straggling caravans seeking admission to the American paradise? Could such a daughter be let loose to wander unsupervised and uncontrolled about Denmark spreading confusion and discontent and giving the poor Danes in consequence such a poor account of true American values?

The omniscient voice from which so many narratives proceed grows hazy and indifferent to its present subject, hesitating to decide what her fate should be. Authorial decision is always balanced along a razor's edge of conflicting possibilities. To choose is to set a butterfly aloft that may tip distant events into chaos. Who would dare to play God in narration if freedom is ever a real possibility for human beings? A tiny gesture may undermine whole vistas of established certitudes. Predestination in stories failed at the instant when Eve reached out for the fruit of the knowledge of good and evil. Thereafter all has been indeterminate. Even now all stories founder on the rocks of our freedom. Unless, oh most dread presumption, the serpent was placed in Eden by design to titillate, to stimulate, and to confuse us.

Songs of Innocence and Experience

Dear Jeremy,

I am sorry to have been so remiss in writing to you since I left the academy. My only excuse is that the world that I now occupy is so different from the lake and poplars of the old school where that little group known as "The Cabal" used to walk with you after classes discussing arts and sciences and in our lesser way preserving the ideals of the Symposium.

I am now residing among philistines of the worst sort made all the more unbearable because they are drawn from the wealthiest of the families of Orange County and environs. The course that has been charted for me is to master all of the arcane aspects of international finance and perhaps to obtain an internship next summer with a firm of investment bankers: a life of money-making lies like a great desert before me. I shall be doomed to drive Mercedes and Bentleys, to wear thousand-dollar suits, and to fly first class to Paris and Milan. I feel the shades of Republicanism drawing down like a shroud around me. No doubt I will marry some lithe and lissome blond debutante in due season, someone who in her more informal soirees with her peers goes by the name of Buffy and we will raise indulged and neurotic children together until I divorce her before abandoning it all to join some eastern cult and move to an ashram in Nepal or Kashmir.

How I wish I might have had the intestinal fortitude to follow your advice and to have imitated the early Kerouac and seen something of my native land on an old Harley before the shackles were placed upon my wrists and ankles! What a pity it must someday be to recall no youthful folly to bemoan and to regret. No doubt you detected an early strain of prudence in my nature that prompted you to act as my mentor as on that Sunday morning after chapel when you advised me to avoid living what you called a freeze-dried life. Yet even recalling that day and the momentary quickening of my pulse at thoughts of rebellion are inadequate to stir me in my present slough of despond. You see my father has taken it upon himself to send me a series of what he no doubt imagines are inspirational letters in the manner of those of Lord Chesterfield to his natural son. I feel something of the same reflective worldliness in them, the same desire to further my advancement in society, and the same seasoned hypocrisy that always accompanies men of power and success. I do not blame him. Indeed by his own lights he wills my good but you cannot imagine how oppressive the sentiments within his successive diatribes are. I feel rather like young Chad Newsome in *The Ambassadors* by Henry James being bribed into respectability by the promises of a glorious future. Already I feel the pinch. I feel positively guilty to spend a weekend reading and listening to the great ocean. The art of networking down here is the only categorical imperative and party-going is a must. The only comfort is that the closeness to Hollywood breeds some resistance to the nationalist hysteria and MAGA hats are definitely *déclassé*. Yet I am inconsolable.

I am under relentless admonition. The paternal letters arrive from home like the beating of some great bass drum and I am not strong enough to ignore them. I know that I shall be quizzed as to their contents when I go home for Christmas... It occurs to me that the measure of my distress may seem exaggerated and I know that many people would gladly step into my shoes. I am not without my own preconceptions and biases. Therefore I have decided to forward these letters to you as a modern-day chronicle of the pressures brought upon youth by society. I have no time to construct my own narrative even if I were the Jane Austen or Samuel Richardson of my day. I will let my father's letters speak for themselves without apology or editing. Make of them what you will and if you have a word of comfort for me in due season, do not hesitate to speak.

Your sorrowing erstwhile student,

Anthony

Letters from my Father

Letter 1

I am writing this series of letters to you, now that you are away at school, to prepare you for the role that you will someday assume in the world once your education is completed. If I was so foolish as to assume that your instructors at the academy could teach mere writing technique without venturing into naïve values then I would be spared the necessity of ensuring your salutary disillusionment now by my own ministrations. I have detected in your choice of reading matter a certain drift towards romanticism. I am not pleased. I would far rather that you had spent your time last summer before you left for California reading Milton Friedman or some other reputable economist rather than mere novels. I had the unpleasant experience of picking up *The Golden Bowl* from your desk one day when you were still at home and could, of course, make nothing of it. Henry James should have been analyzed by his more pragmatic brother, William. One can, you know, be literate without becoming literary. Sentiment has a tendency to seep into the soul and blight reason. There is no greater era of peril than that period of life when in the full measure of youth's unearned wealth the virus of misplaced philanthropy and kindness is planted. A desire for world reform begins with the assumption that as regards the self that sustenance and security are guaranteed. They are not. No degree of success is immune from a sudden plunge back into scarcity.

Let me begin then by cautioning you to greet critically all that you will be formally taught, indeed it is to correct any misapprehensions that you may form that I am writing to you now. The real value of an education beyond the technical sciences is simply to become aware of the hypocrisy behind which societies and individuals hide their true intentions. This is not to say that there is no function in ideas. No, I would not go so far. It is simply essential that you understand from the beginning that ideas are always subject to human nature and human nature is primarily motivated by greed and fear and occasionally by a healthy disgust at its own characteristics. You will ask immediately if there is not also love and generosity. There may be, I will not go so far as to say there is not, but if you count upon them you will be soon disappointed and made bitter by life. Far better it is to assume the worst and to prepare oneself to act upon that belief if you would preserve your position in the world. What then is that position to be? It is up to you.

You are that most enviable of young men because you have property and place in the greatest empire that the world has yet known, America. You are the fruit of the loins of conquerors. Look today at America and what do you see if not the rule of the powerful, but better still than to possess power is the desire that it brings for greater power. America today can project violence and terror into every corner of the earth and the pitiful efforts of our adversaries and even of our allies to keep up with us are futile. We simply have too great of a head-start upon them and we will not surrender our lead gladly. You will ask of course if these aspirations are not constrained by our role as a moral leader and as the champion of democracy. Let me assure you that such rhetoric is for purely domestic consumption and it is essential that you abandon such delusions immediately.

America ceased to be what its founders may have intended over a century ago and we may all be thankful for it. Imagine the inconvenience for instance of having to share the land with the original savage inhabitants of this continent. Most of them are gone now with the buffalo and the salmon and the belief that each individual of the tribe had a unique path and value. This caretaking attitude is the enemy of all industry and progress. The very idea of limitation of conquest is foreign to true Americanism. Our forefathers knew that the value of property exists only in our ability to hold on to it. There is no moral title to anything. Everything in life is open to the man who can take it successfully. This was the basis for our policy towards the Indians and it is the basis for our most significant actions in the world today.

I often smile when I am asked why we are in Afghanistan, Iraq, and Syria. Such questions immediately betray the ignorance of the questioner. We are in these areas of the world because we choose to be! They are of interest to us because these regions are strategic power points on the constant chess-board of the world. We are there because we ran out of Indians at home to kill. We are there because Asia is our new frontier. We are there so that we may be served by the current inhabitants once they accept that we are there to stay. Nations are judged by their ability to exact tribute. Peace is only the time allotted to prepare for war. The very idea of a permanent peace is an invitation to degeneration and emasculation. Fear is the final measure of diplomacy. Is anyone so foolish as to imagine that we will be dictated to by the Russians and the Chinese? They know that we will perish rather than be enslaved.

Do not be misled by all this current ecological foolishness. The pulse of the world is energy usage. A vital nation is measured by its profligacy not by its conservation of resources when it comes to oil or natural gas. The most essential items of our economy are energy-based and so naturally we must possess them. We will honor national sovereignty as long as it is convenient or necessary for us to do so and not an instant longer. Peace will come in conflict-ridden regions when we are assured of our ability to extract the necessary resources and have installed governments that will follow our wishes and maintain a proper decorum and rhetoric of democracy while a capital-based autocracy prevails in actuality. We may do a bit of window-dressing of course but that is the truth and moreover, every true American knows that it is the truth because that is the way that we have always acted in the world. War for America has always sooner or later paid off. Find me a town in America so small that it does not have an armory and a war memorial. Even our national anthem is about war. War is America and America is war and we will make any sacrifice to maintain supremacy in arms. Imagine for instance if the amount of our most recent wars (now over two trillion dollars) had been spent to advance health and education and forgive me for a moment a blasphemy: to attain more equality in this country. An average lot of the average American dullard would, of course, have been vastly improved and our economic position would not be dependent upon borrowed funds from China, but would we in the ruling class have been better off? By showing that we were willing to fight two or three pointless wars we told our adversaries that prudence plays no part in our calculations, only power matters. Of course, those borrowed funds are not really borrowed, they were extorted to further our virtuous consumption; I assure you they will never be repaid and the Chinese know it. At most the tipping point moved a little closer to China in the great international power calculus but that was all.

Why, you will ask, do Americans never quail at the size of the military budget and the transfer of wealth from the working middle-class to the investing and owning class? The answer is because of the pride that every ordinary American can have in knowing that the world trembles before us. Goods and services flock to our shores and to support the dollar, that empty promise has never been higher compared to other currencies and why? Because of American military superiority and because of our demonstrated daily willingness to kill whoever stands against us. We are respected because we are brutal. The world knows that we are the ultimate political realists. We realize that sometime in this century the world population will need to be reduced by about two to three billion people (*it won't be us.*) How this weeding-out will happen will be the subject of other letters to you. Let this introductory letter suffice for now. It will have achieved its aim if it has convinced you to abandon from the outset of your education any pretense that America ever acts out of so-called honorable intentions. Every action that we take is strategic and serves us in the maintenance of the unquestioned superiority of our nation.

Your devoted Father

Letter 2

I write to you today to caution you as to the danger posed by overt patriotism. In your ardent desire, which I hope to instill, to further your own interests you may imagine that you must, in order to be consistent, pay the duty of privilege by fighting for your country. You will point out to me that when the nation is at war and since the current arrangement of our political structures is designed to benefit the class to which we belong that we should all make sacrifices in order to deserve our place of honor and prestige. Rid yourself immediately of this delusion.

To begin with, our current wars are not struggles for national survival. They are mere gestures of force. They are diplomacy by other means. Look about you. What sacrifice have these long conflicts entailed to people like us? Have our sons and daughters died? No, and they will not. We have delegated the task of preserving the nation to a professional military drawn as all such wars are drawn from the superfluous members of the lower classes. It is all quite business-like and proper. We have out-sourced dying to those whose function is to produce so that we can possess. Do not be disturbed by this. You must remember that our country will soon have to adjust to a high and permanent structural unemployment rate. Let them die with ribbons rather than fester in unemployment lines.

A proper university education will soon cost between $80,000 and $150,000 simply to obtain the baccalaureate degree. It is quite beyond the lower classes to afford this since we have wisely kept the minimum wage below what it was in the 1980s in actual purchasing power. This fact makes military service highly attractive. It is far easier to train a young person to kill than to teach them a useful trade. Besides as the idle unemployed they would probably join gangs or engage in other criminal activity or simply reproduce and throng our schools which cost tax dollars. I assure you we have too many of them at present as it is. So what other use can they serve but as cannon-fodder? They can be dressed up in the panoply of our esteem and die for us. It gives meaning to their otherwise vacuous lives, solves a distinct social problem of what to do with the unemployable young, and it adds to the wealth of the nation, which is to say that it puts money in our pockets.

On the other end of the age spectrum, modern medicine is saving too many of these lives beyond their prime. Treatment for members of the middle-class in old age will be costly if they are allowed to live too long. What better solution could there be then to export them while they are young to battlefields and ensure that they are killed there rather than merely maimed and returned in damaged condition? This was why the policy in force for years of not armoring the transports in Iraq was so sensible and useful. It ensured that a soldier blown up by a road-side device would be killed and not return to be a burden on society. If the truck was going to be severely damaged anyway (and it really is difficult to repair one after a bomb blows up underneath it) it may as well take the men inside also. The casualty rate acted as a stimulant to the nation's ire and kept a focus on what was called, the mission.

I am smiling. Really army rhetoric is so transparently amusing to anyone who can see its real function. Besides, for every truck blown up, more had to be made and need I remind you of our family's heavy investment in certain companies that were awarded no-bid contracts. Again, it was money in our pockets. I have always found it quaint that the most patriotic of our citizens are those who are least likely to benefit from being American and that those who speak of freedom have little beyond the obligation to pay high interest to the mortgage and credit institutions that we own. You may ask how people can be so stupid, but why look a gift horse in the mouth. The fact is that they are stupid and we should be grateful for it. Justice is the enemy of all capital growth and equity should be shunned like the plague. I hope that with this second letter that your eyes are beginning to be opened and that once past a transient sentimentality you will become as realistic as I am and as I have tried to teach you to be.

Your devoted Father

Letter 3

I have already anticipated some questions that you may have regarding my last letter. You may ask, even if we do have a class of persons whose best life options are to die for us, is not the nation itself deserving of our loyalty since it exists to serve our interests as wealthy Americans. If not patriotism is there not something that we should feel since the government is virtually our alter ego? Should we not protect ourselves? I will grant you that our present domicile should be preserved; after all, we are the richest nation on earth at present while thanks to the wise national policy of bleeding the lower classes we rank only 17th in the world in national quality of life, but difficulties still remain to limit the comforts of our hegemony.

We have accumulated a huge national debt of twenty-two trillion dollars. It is sad but necessary that as inflation and lack of real wage growth in the last thirty years have reduced the living standard of the middle-class that its members have become increasingly restless. It costs more every year to educate their children to obtain decent jobs. These are no longer a given since even professionals must now compete with foreign labor. It has even been necessary for us to provide some temporary sop to them that has been provided to date by the import of cheap Chinese goods and the spread of warehouse stores in every suburban community. Do not be deceived though; this is only a temporary stop-gap measure. It cannot go on forever and when it stops as the Chinese develop their internal markets our national credit binge will dry up. This will create great discontent and bewilderment at first among the mindless consumers as the American way of life declines. There will naturally be resentment and we must be certain that it will not be directed towards us. Fortunately, Americans tend to look down and never up when they focus on their fears. They always ask who may take their jobs away rather than to question why the fruits of technical and economic progress are always directed upwards to us. For this reason, our great political party keeps the focus on the danger posed by immigrants.

Even a slight modification of the tax codes could indeed, by adding a small percentage to our taxes, pay for thousands of these lettuce pickers but we must keep the level of fear up: that they constitute a brown hoard sweeping up out of Mexico. The sad fact is that we were running short of minorities to blame. Once it was the Irish, then the Italians and then the Jews, always the blacks of course, and now the Mexicans who we fear in this new century. Thank God it has never been us! Thank God that we can still stock away the savings of the nation year after year while reaping tax benefits, depletion allowances, and the ability to hide our funds in foreign bank accounts and off-shore tax havens. The dullards never notice and why? The answer is too amusing. It is because they believe in the concept of equality but never in its reality. If you would put them off you need only say to them that we are all equal and to assure them that anyone can make it big tomorrow... somehow. Trot out a few men who are the modern equivalent of Thomas Edition as examples. Most people though are not brilliant but only competent if even that; they never catch on. They will never be us. They will never be able to swim upstream against the laws and the tax structures that are now firmly in place to direct income into our hands. It is only necessary to tell the masses that they might, if nothing else, possibly win the lottery. They would rather benefit us by toiling away like oxen then take concrete means to reap the results of national economic growth as long as we do not disturb the illusion that they are already one of us!

Each year we put in place means to ensure that they never will be such through our ownership of the national government. No more sorry group of people exists than the members of today's Republican Congress. The fact that there are still a few hold-outs who believe in democracy is of little note. The people of America are so dumb that if you offer them equity they call you a socialist. Every day I thank God that He made so many stupid people! So we own Congress and we own at last five members of the Supreme Court. Best of all ... the current President is one of us and by talking like a guy on the next barstool he convinces them that he is just like them.

On another point, frankly, I never thought Obama would leave office alive. Ever since Jack Kennedy, presidents have understood that they are theoretically expendable. In fact, think of the value of that assassination to wealthy Americans right now. Presidents will never again dare to be statesmen: they will either be targets or demagogues. If we can ensure that every incipient psychopath has access to a weapon of mass destruction we can always keep liberalism at bay. The trick is to keep the ignorant louts on a slow rolling boil of indignation – the democrats want to take your guns away from you! Better still the religious right makes it all moral as though Moses had proclaimed the right to assault weapons with multiple magazine clips as the will of God.

But to return to the national debt, when the currency collapses only the ownership of hard assets will matter. A new currency will demolish any savings that the middle-class has accumulated. The new dollar will be worth say 60% of the old dollar but it will be backed up with metal again at last. You ask where the extra 40% will go: It will be used to reduce the national debt to a manageable level. The devaluation will not hurt us because we will have bailed out of the dollar before the devaluation into foreign equities, currencies, and precious metals. Until this happens, of course, the time is ripe to feed. The last tax cut will give us the reserves that we will need to ensure that the country is ours for the foreseeable future. Americans have elected their last Catholic and now their last black president. By the time Obama left office, even his own party despised him. His feeble attempts to find a non-existent American political center only alienated everyone. Even Bush looked heroic in comparison by simply being decisive in his folly. He let Cheney run the country while he cleared brush down on the ranch. So to return to my theme in this letter, do not be misled by patriotism or loyalty. The nation is only a means to an end: our prosperity and domination. The nation exists to serve our interests and only insofar as it does will we use it and not a second more.

Your devoted Father

Letter 4

It occurred to me today that I may have been too abrupt in ridding you of the illusions that you may have gained at the Preparatory Academy but it is my desire to be truthful with you. Truth is usually capable of summary treatment; only lies require long and elaborate explication. I chose your high school for you so that you might acquire grounding in the great ideas and humanities prior to moving on in your education. I also wanted these to be productive years for you and to spare you from the American experience of publicly funded education. I assure you that you have missed nothing in foregoing that experience. It is an irony that these years are wasted when they are the only free education that the average American will ever receive. The primary function of these years in public high schools is not education but as an initiation, a primal tribal ritual based on athletics and sexuality. The masses quickly establish cliques based on a hierarchical system and sometimes long after graduation spend many years of their twenties wasted in lamenting old and entirely inappropriate romantic ties or celebrating conquests in eminently forgettable athletic contests. In this way, they not only waste those precious late-teen years but compromise the first decade of their adulthood.

This is fortunate since it gives our class a distinct early edge. We know the value of moving from a comprehensive educational experience at the secondary level to attend a select college. The potential dating pool is thus confined to young women of good family and connections and ardent young men are kept away from tempting but unfortunate alliances with lower-class women. This is not to say that an occasional dalliance with some particularly well-endowed young woman may not be tempting should she present herself in the later course of dealing with the world but young men can see by then how completely unsuitable such women would have ever been as mates. They have occasionally a sort of mongrel charm however and I would not have you believe that a woman coming from a good family is a necessary guarantee of connubial happiness. Indeed not a few are spoiled princesses or anorexic basket cases. Avoid these. Date only women who are intelligent but ever conscious of their place "as women." Look for virtue but not religiosity. You may also apply a useful test: look at her mother and you will have a vision of what she will act and look like in twenty years. You may also add twenty to forty pounds to whatever she weighs now. If you believe that she will still be remotely attractive to you then as your own sexual powers are waning, she may be a good marriage prospect.

Avoid serial marriages in any case; they bleed the estate. Try and find a woman to whom you can afford to stay married. I advise this not out of any concern for sin and virtue. Fortunately, we do not have the belief of the Catholics in the indissolubility of marriage. If you must divorce then you must, but I assure you, it is always costly. If your prospective wife does not have ample means of her own, then a pre-nuptial agreement is as essential as the marriage license. Never give a woman complete security. A constant state of low-grade anxiety is your best guarantee that she will remain always faithful to you. But let it not grow too large or she may jump ship to a richer man. Above all do not fall prey to the common male illusion that any present protestation of undying affection has any meaning for her beyond the moment. It is only a sign of her momentary need and state of mind, perhaps an illusory and exaggerated estimate of your own worth. It is bad enough that women believe in their own emotions but for a man to do so is inexcusable. The record of the sex is abysmal in terms of natural fidelity. Nature has so created woman that her instinct is to preserve the species and she misses no opportunity to attempt to do so. As such the natural condition of a woman is to be pregnant. For this reason, most men find business more attractive as the years go by and learn to ignore the domestic animal that breeds his offspring. If she is quiet and helpful and does not take to drink, then you have made a wise choice. If on the other hand she berates you and cajoles constantly then it may be time to replace her.

As your wealth and success increase, you will be tempted to take a mistress from among your office staff. Do not do so. Indeed I make it a point only to hire women who are so exceedingly unattractive that they might all be pursuing their task naked and I would have no more inclination to them than to a can of sardines. I advise you to do likewise, but the time of such wise sexual policy is many years ahead and until then you are in peril of making poor choices. If you can escape your twenties with a good education and a start in business you will be wise. It is essential to make one's money early in life. Men respect vigor that they no longer possess. Find a mentor and follow in his jet-stream by loyalty. Flatter his vanity and conceal his faults and you will go far.

After you marry do not be distracted by absurd family dramas. Give your children graduated praise and preserve their self-esteem and keep them from improper influences. The rest will take care of itself. Daughters are of course at risk of perpetual intercourse. They generally exist to drain estates. You are in a sense raising a crop to be reaped by another. That said, some never marry and they may be a comfort to you in your old age so do not neglect them. Your sons--if you have properly raised them--will have little time to devote to you as they will be engaged in making money and in increasing the property that is the only real security for both sexes. You will ask whether a relation to God is not our ultimate security. God, of course, is somewhat like the prospect of accidental death and injury: insure against the possibility that He may actually exist by meeting the formula of salvation as it has been taught to us, behave with decent circumspection in your vices and beyond that, do as you will.

Your devoted Father

Letter 5

You will see that I am in the course of my letters to you choosing my topics at random in writing to you as various dangers to which you may be subjected are suggested to me by various happenings in the news of the world.

Today I propose that you ignore the useless trivia that constitutes the news of the day. Someday the pulchritude of the various Kardashian girls will, if they are even then recalled, be at most symptomatic of the vapid and vacuous tendencies of the present hour. There is no Helen of Troy among them. They are, at best, walking advertisements for the state of plastic surgery in the 21st century. Their sole point of interest is as an example of what successful branding can accomplish. As our society moves beyond necessities the highest values are applied to all that is trivial and decorative. We are living in a world predominated by personalities.

Intellectual property has completely dwarfed what might be called commodities. Venezuela is a case in point: even oil can doom a producing nation to poverty if that is all they have to sell. The genius of America has been that we realized first the value inherent in simply being an originator. We invent things and let the rest of the world build them. Royalties always exceed wages as a source of wealth. The best measure of failure in today's economy is whether your name is on a W-2 form. If your income comes from labor it is not wealth; it is mere sustenance. The task is to accumulate wealth as quickly as possible so as to obtain passive income.

Property is not a thing to be enjoyed; it is an asset to be traded. Anything retained for its own sake is a liability – movement and flow are the only realities. This is why culture is the refuge of the indolent. Culture presumes constant values. To say that something meets the gold-standard is to imply that it is dead. The best thing President Nixon ever did was to uncouple the dollar from gold. It opened up the possibility of endless growth based on capital flow – the dollars of the world will retain their value as long as no one tries to hoard them. Only then will they realize that all they possess is a promissory note based on sheer air. The full faith and credit of a nation that is in the hole for twenty-two trillion dollars is about as empty as a promise can be. Only velocity in production and world trade is saving us from bankruptcy – the world is moving too fast to catch its breath. Money is only the synapse between transactions.

Of course, the threat of collapse is always present just as the threat of nuclear war is always present and those very facts are so devastating that no one dares question the various fictions under which we live. It is our collective fictions that sustain us. From our natal years in the nursery, we are enthralled by stories over principles. This propensity never leaves us. Entertainment is the one industry that keeps ordinary needs in abeyance to amusement and fascination. Story, however, is more than mere amusement. It is the basis for belief systems, not the least of which are national myths. The important thing is to profit from such beliefs without sharing them. I value those writers who can see through the charm of the demagogue to discern the carnival barker and the snake-oil salesman beneath. It amuses me to see the agrarian peasants leaving their fields of corn and hay to be entertained by the melded blend of bad-boy antics and old-time religion dished out by our current President. He has an instinctive awareness of the American character and the anxieties that beset the denizens of the middle-classes in their decline into post-industrial obsolescence. People never really vote for their self-interest but rather their perceptions of who they are. In politics, flattery will get you anywhere.

It is fortunate that Americans have so little awareness of their own history; it makes it that much easier to deceive them. Not since the Huns swept across Asia has a more rapacious and predatory set of invaders beset a supine and complacent native population. A belief in our collective supremacy overrides all individual feelings of failure and inferiority. Oh well, let them eat brioche. It was to spare you from being drawn into such fatuous beliefs that I urged you to confine your early reading to Voltaire, Thucydides, Hume, Swift, and Schopenhauer. These thinkers never lost a perspective of what might be called strategic diminishment. All so-called high ideas should possess at their heart a bilious core. Bitterness, of course, is the obverse of romantic idealism, its corrective. It is not necessary to be depressed of course only clear-sighted.

But to return to the value of stories: they are the basis for all social institutions from religion to government. Deprive a people of its myths and social cohesion goes away with it. Even language takes its origin from its capacity to record and to describe. Of course, human language is always concrete and yet beset by the disease of metaphor. These are something that will soon be outgrown by the simplicity of digital discourse and universal algorithms. The sophistication of a language determines the ability to think. This is why I desire that you understand the sub-text to every popular enthusiasm so that you will not be caught up in it.

It is the essence of persuasion that one be aware of one's own structured mendacity. If there is anything that frightens me in Mr. Trump it is that he may be starting to believe his own absurd statements. I recall to your mind the case of Eva Peron of Argentina who began as a gold-digger and ended up believing that she was a saint. It is imperative that you not be swayed by noble rhetoric or seduced by trends. Everything emerges for a time, randomly and without purpose, and then gives way to the new. There is neither progress nor evolution, only variation before extinction. To realize this is the beginning of wisdom.

Your devoted Father

Letter 6

I have been wondering what impression is being made upon you by my letters. No doubt you find them somewhat shocking and you may even imagine that they flow from some well of bitterness that I kept concealed from you in your early upbringing. I assure you that their tone and substance are not the fruit of some dark strain of my character but rather the result of long meditations on the facts of our existence. The facts, of course, are available to everyone, but such is the pace of our existence that few dare to reason from them to their likely conclusions.

I remark daily how the masses seem bent on assuming that somehow everything will just work out; our secular messiah will make America great again, the sanctity of marriage will return, family values will emerge triumphant, and the wicked liberals will be separated as goats from sheep and executed in the public square. The liberals of the present hour are what the communists and the Jews were for Hitler: a pathway to power through the magic of awakened resentment. Most people presume that their lives should somehow or other work out; their many excellent qualities will be rewarded and public recognition will come their way. In this supposition, they are deluded. The majority of mankind considered individually is as inconsequential as any members of a mindless swarm can be. Stalin was correct in this when he said that the death of one man is a tragedy while the deaths of millions are a statistic. Stalin of course always dealt in chips the smallest denomination of which was a thousand. That is the way that you bring a country like Russia to the point where it could fight and win a war against the industrial might of Germany. Terror required counter-terror to oppose it.

America meanwhile won the war because of the sheer size of its manufacturing base that could be converted swiftly to produce war materiel. There was coupled with this a sense of outrage that anyone would dare to attack us. Take away Pearl Harbor and the swastika would still be flying over most of Europe. Don't expect to see either of these characteristics emerge again. The people that we would most likely fight are the very people who lend us money every day just to keep going to our home improvement and grocery stores. Besides, we have never collectively known real human deprivation in the past seventy years.

It occurs to me that I may have blocked from my mind the shortness of historical memory among the young and the sheltered perspective that is for you the inevitable result of having been raised during one of the longest periods of general prosperity ever recorded. Generosity and forbearance are the natural outcomes among those who have never had to face the brutalities that beset the world just prior to your birth. The decades of the 1930s and the 1940s witnessed carnage on a scale not seen since the Thirty Years War of the 1600s. Russia alone saw forty million dead. Yet as the war is portrayed in film, the eastern front is barely explored. It is all about General Patton or Pearl Harbor or the D-Day landings as though these were the decisive contributions to victory. It was Hitler's foolish decision to fight a two-front war by attacking Russia that prevented a Nazi victory. Even after losing the war Germany has emerged as the strongest nation in the European Union while England, foolish as always, is about to try and go it alone as though the empire it once possessed was not a distant memory, a reality never to be reconstituted. The British royal family is reduced to sharing tabloid space with the Kardashian girls and their endless micro-dramas and crises.

Such is the triviality of the present day that history is little more than fashion by another name. Everything is public relations and political correctness; no one's feelings should be hurt or sensibilities offended. Compare this to the cost exacted by the fall of Berlin where no woman was immune from rape and starvation from an enraged enemy that had watched their own wives and daughters shot in villages as the German assault rolled across the Ukraine. Look at pictures from the early 20th century when half the children in families of ten or more children would be lost to typhoid and scarlet fever before their sixth birthday. Realize the world as it was and still is for the billions of humanity that are cut off from everything that our digital age of electronic miracles represents. Then judge if I am harsh when I say that our class must be ruthless if we are to sustain our favored place and way of life from the beleaguered multitudes who would like to take a place at the feast. Imagine over seven or eight billion people living as we do and the state of the environment that would exist then if we speak of global warming now. Most of the Chinese are yet too poor to purchase their first automobile and the air quality is already beyond what we could tolerate. It isn't distant Cathay with coolies and wooden wagons pulled by yaks anymore. There are bullet trains in China that would put ours to shame. The sun has moved ever westward and America is in the twilight. Better to face this now than later.

You will look in vain for some golden era to which we may return. The MAGA wearers and the new socialist wing of the Democratic Party are both chasing a mirage. We are already at the apogee of American power; from here on our structural weaknesses will become every day more manifest. The economically fortunate will become pariahs if a crisis should occur. President Trump is keeping revolution at bay by telling the great unwashed and romantic yahoos what they want to hear to keep overwhelming anxiety at bay. He is doing the best he can to flush as much cash our way as possible before the market crashes and the long night of mass unemployment begins. The Second Amendment folk will start shooting at each other over a box of breakfast cereal. Most of your life will be lived in the prospect of what the human race used to know: that we are part of nature red in tooth and claw. The Russians have not forgotten though how it was because they are for the most part still waiting for a post-war prosperity that never showed up. Other peoples remember as well the daily cost of existence when it isn't based on credit. The North Koreans recall 1949 to 1952 as though it was yesterday. The Jews have never emerged from the shadow of another holocaust. All of these know the full price exacted in order to survive. The world is tipping beyond recovery at the very hour when gross indulgence is becoming normative here. Everyone thinks their little sorties in a consumer's paradise will amuse her neighbors. "Oh look, here we are in Las Vegas. I bought this silly little sun hat. Everyone thought I was from Hollywood!"

Do you see where I'm going with my warnings now? Wake up! Quite frankly even to possess an education is a little indulgent because it is ordered towards securing mere employment. Any gains short of capital gains are a waste of time. That is why I want you to exist among the owners, not as one of the plebian hoard of soft-ware pushers and systems analysts in white coats in clean cubicles servicing the computers as they process their terabytes of information. The great industry of the future will be keeping track of one's various asset positions using an array of passwords to get you through access points. America will be the grand-master of various exclusion systems. This wall of President Trump is a metaphor, a brand name for America while the rest of the world threatens us with a thermonuclear pulse. Fry the wires, destroy the data, remove the chips from the table and the whole game goes up in smoke!

There you have it, Anthony, the world that you and your children will inhabit long after I am gone.

Your devoted Father

Letter 7

Just a quick note, I realize that my last letter to you may have sounded a bit harsh. You may imagine should you adopt my point of view that you will stand quite alone. Fear not, at least one out of every three Americans are unconsciously laboring at our side. They are absolutely determined to abjure any benefits that circumstances might offer to them rather than to be branded as democratic socialists. There is something quite admirable in people who are willing to watch their children die because they present with preexisting conditions just to tear down "Obama Care." Who would believe that there are people still alive that would rather die than accept help from a black man?

Our real allies though are the Christian Media outlets, the same that condone any sin, at least if it is the President that commits them. Duplicity, chicanery, adultery: all are given a new appraisal if these malfeasances can only serve the Republican cause. Even the recent costly weather events do not disturb them because they are all just a foretaste of the tribulation to come that will spare the elect who will vanish in the twinkling of an eye and leave everybody else to clean up the mess. This generation of Christians is determined to make God either put up or shut up now that the Jews are back in their ancestral homeland. They have switched from petition to demand; whole celestial timetables have been prepared, the spiritual suitcases are packed, and the born-again folk are checking their watches. Meanwhile, the Prosperity Gospel crowd is going in for one last fling before the coming big lift-off. These are our allies as we fleece the unaffiliated poor who have only this world to sustain them.

So you see that nothing is really demanded of us but to let the present trends work out. We are blessed in our depredations by the very people who would benefit from a contrary policy. All that is required is for us to refrain from laughing as they stuff our pockets with gold. It isn't essential to associate with them formally. They won't show up at our gated communities. All that is required is a meeting hall where they can stage a revival meeting before driving their pick-up trucks home and stopping for some good old All-American hamburgers, short on beef and long on bun. So take heart my son; pack in those formulas and don't forget to network, network, and network among the people who count.

Your devoted Father

Letters between Jeremy and Anthony

Dear Anthony,

So good to hear from you, my boy! I have set myself swiftly to the task assigned me and have read your father's letters with interest and with a chill that starts at my tailbone and radiates upward. He certainly seems to be a formidable sort of chap yet withal he seems to have your best interests at heart even if filtered through a ghastly moral appraisal of America.

No doubt you recall my assignment of Pascal's *Provincial Letters* in your senior year. One of the better uses of satire is to assume the guise of one's adversary and to hold it up to ridicule; were it not for your assurances that he means every word that he says I might be willing to assume that a satirical intent hides behind his fulminations. As it is I must take him as being in all earnestness in his sense that our fate as Americans hangs over an abyss into which we might fall if the contending factions that divide America cannot find common ground. It is a strange fact but all that is being now proposed in the form of taxation reform is to return to the rates that were accepted as normal during the Eisenhower administration and these were far short of socialism. They did, of course, create the very America of strong manufacturing and a prosperous middle class that the Republican Party claims to desire. Instead, we are watching at their hands a recapitulation of the era of the 19th century robber barons while only cheap imports from China have made it possible for faux prosperity to exist among us.

This state of affairs is, of course, a temporary one. A radical lurch to the right always foments tyranny. Of course in this instance, it is the conservatives who are brandishing the epithet of "fascist" and applying it to one of the first voices to speak for the concerns of the silent millennial generation, Alexandria Ocasio-Cortez. The terror that she invokes among them indicates how insecure the delusional base is on which current conservatism rests. Of course, to point out the obvious to one in the grip of pathology is always to risk violence. I trust that the poor girl is always attentive to her surroundings and the multitude of the lunatics that fester among us.

For myself, I can see no way to replace the myths that nourish opposition to sensible reform on the Scandinavian model. I fear that the present regime must run its course until it brings about collapse. I doubt that there will ever be an equal and opposite swing to the left. What will happen is a general obsolescence of careers as machines replace tasks formerly done by people. I see a great increase in demand for cardboard to make signs that read, "Every bit helps."In the meantime you are at least secure there in Malibu; enjoy the sun for me. You may wish later on to forswear the career that your father has destined for you or you may practice for a few years, set aside a tidy bundle, and join us in our effort to keep some legacy alive of the former glory of the humanities. You may at least take this comfort to heart: You are part of a noble tradition that is dying about us. You know the names and something of the content of those who have labored before you with few rewards beyond that fragile immortality that the written word bestows upon her devotees.

Be of good cheer then.

Jeremy

Dear Jeremy,

Your letter meant more to me than you may imagine. I am caught here in a most peculiar atmosphere. Although my classmates are of course not taken in by the type of Presidential rhetoric that plays so well at the CPAC Conference they rejoice in the recent tax cuts and enjoy the bad boy antics of Mr. Trump. Politics has arrived at a level of buffoonery and recrimination that makes any idea of national unity impossible to conceive. You will recall that my father wanted me to attend the University of Chicago or Columbia and it was only with great effort that I convinced him to allow me to attend Pepperdine.

I spend many days gazing out to sea and imagining a way of life that begins with some extraordinary excursion. Not the Grand Tour of Europe of course; too much of a *cliché*. What I had in mind is more like something squalid and sinister ala that of Eugene O'Neill or Malcolm Lowry. I have been reading *Under the Volcano* by Lowry and *The Iceman Cometh* by O'Neill. Last month I read *Visions of Cody* by Kerouac. I would like to see life from the dark underbelly and then to grope my way up to rebellion, read D'Annunzio or maybe the letters of Angela Davis. I live in an age of automatons glued to their smartphones. All experience seems derivative and pre-digested.

How can one be an individual under such conditions? Where are the SDS and the Yippies, the Youth International Society of our day? I want to protest something, to join something more ominous than the Green New Deal just to feel an edge to my existence. Am I being foolish? You can tell me if I am. Young people should have a crisis against which to define themselves don't you think? Everything seems so under control, so trivial. Oh, we have individual acts of futile terrorism but they are so standardized, a futile effort to excel the body count of the last atrocity. Where's the imagination? Where's the ricin or aconite in the punch at an annual corporate meeting? Guns are so *passé.*

Of course, I would like to be constructive but it is always easier to destroy things don't you think? If everything will be as bad as my father thinks then why not have my own class share some of the misery. Where is the Symbionese Liberation Army to kidnap me? I look good in a beret. Last weekend I watched that old classic *Butch Cassidy and the Sundance Kid*; maybe if I went to Bolivia… As you can see I am grasping at straws to cure my malaise. Can you suggest something?

Anthony

Dear Anthony,

I am afraid that your father's penchant for hyperbole is shared by his son. I hope you are not out gathering wolfbane or castor beans. This sudden spurt of reaction against your father's letters is not uncommon in the first year away from home. Perhaps a frivolous romance is in order. Think about it; it will keep you out of jail. The whole rebellion thing could be hormonally induced. Tune down the testosterone. Perhaps you could make a connection and obtain some anti-androgens from the school nurse. Tell them you have been undergoing a bout of Gender Dysphoria lately; it seems to be reaching epidemic levels on campuses nationwide. Panic is breaking out in Tennessee. Tell the nurse that you only answer to "they and them." I'm kidding of course. Beware of too much earnestness; it always breeds tragedy.

Now then as to the trials of the present hour; they are real of course but you are not alone in your dismay. The carnival will move on in due course. As the Republicans check off their wish list they are digging their own grave among thinking people. My real fear is that the Democrats will start in on their own equally untenable pet projects. America is the indulged darling of struggling Asia; it will continue so for some time if we don't convince them that we are all crazy. The value of a winning streak is not to be scorned or abandoned lightly. In the meantime, my advice is to accept that your intellectual skeleton is still malleable like a molting crab. Don't worry about taking definitive positions. Try to enjoy a time that will never return and foreswear lugubrious meditations. When you reach my age and all is retrospection you will lament what you have lost by trying to be old too soon.

Jeremy

Letter 8

I enjoyed our brief phone call last night. I was beginning to be afraid that something had happened to you. The market was up again today but I am looking at buying into platinum as a hedge against inflation. The national debt is two trillion higher since Trump took office but no one seems to notice. A point must come when our treasuries start to sink and people will be looking for something solid. You see what an old man I am; I still remember when there was a point in holding precious metals.

I also recall the days when value was tied to utility. The great fortunes were once tied intimately to either the land or to industrial production. That is no longer the case, at least in America. What counts now is image and intellectual property. We are living in an age where retail as it once existed is melting away like the glaciers and manufacturing is being freed from the burden of an extensive and usually discontented workforce prone to unionization. The fortunes that are being made today have few actual moving parts or in-house elements. The actual tasks are outsourced and all that remains is a profit center that organizes and directs the whole based on commandeering huge segments of data and brand loyalty. The added-on value may be little more than to have a product associated in some intangible sense with a celebrity.

It is as though all the tiny and insignificant worker ants could raise their status by proxy and become queens by mere imitation. We worship the overlords of instantaneous commerce as mediated by directions traveling along fiber-optic cables or as electronic pulses jumping synapses of logic to enrich beyond the wildest dreams of King Midas. Do you see why I have cautioned you away from embracing any residual notions of professionalism, equity and the work ethic of the sociologist Max Weber? We have so far exceeded the furthest extrapolations of economists like Thorstein Veblen and John Kenneth Galbraith in speaking of leisure and affluence that the 21st century world has divided the species according to the ability to control and market intangibles.

The Democrats speak of green consciousness and a new deal while the Republicans dish out the same old tired dishwater of yesterday's industries and American exceptionalism. Unfortunately, the masses have already decided that illusion always trumps reality. Like besotted sleepwalkers, they march in hypnotic and insensate unison to surrender their individuality to various secular icons. Wealth feeds upon itself generation after generation. At last, we have discovered the secret of perpetual motion; inertia is defeated for the few while age and wisdom are revealed as the most pathetic of follies. I urge you to embrace the dull, the repetitious, the trivial, and the meaningless. See where the Presidency has left eloquence behind and made even truth a mere fashion to be discarded at will. Ours is the age foretold by José Ortega y Gasset where tiny acts of surrender of individualism create beings deprived of the integrity that only individuals can ever really possess. It is too late though to turn the herd; you can only pretend to join the deluded mass and profit from their collective folly. The world will endure for your life and perhaps for your immediate descendants.

Anyway, you have nothing to worry about. I did a little research today and things won't be all that bad until we hit 500 or 600 parts per million of carbon dioxide in the atmosphere. You can start to worry when the oysters lose their shells to an acidic ocean or the permafrost in the tundra melts. Everything in the Yukon will be a swamp by then but there will be investment opportunities in the Taiga. By the end of this century, the world population will be about nine billion people, all of them wanting something of the good life. We will probably have had at least one nuclear conflict, a few famines, and most current game animals will only exist in zoos or picture books alongside the Dodo.

I doubt if the Constitution will still be in force. America will be a backwater where Asians come just to see what a place without choking fumes looks like. Already almost all of the most polluted cities in the world are in China and India. If we mind our manners they will fight with each other and not us. After all, neighbors always pose the greatest threat to neighbors, not strangers. By then we'll be at peace with the Mexicans as they dig tunnels under Mr. Trump's wall or board tour boats to California. You will be able to buy drugs from vending machines, so nothing to fear on our southern border. Europe will be just an amusement park or one big Madame Tussaud's wax museum. In Russia, they will still be drinking vodka like fish and peddling heating oil. The followers of Mohammed will still be quarreling over who should have succeeded the prophet and the evangelical Christians will be expecting Jesus back just any day now so why try to make the world a better place.

Things change and things stay the same. What more can I say to you about history and about life; let your kids worry. One man can only do just so much. I'm glad I could give you these years of respite before the flood at Pepperdine. When the Cascadia earthquake comes Malibu will be little more than a sand-box. In the interim, I suppose there must be at least one economist there of note who can teach you something. It's not Chicago of course, but adequate. Well, I don't want to keep you off your surfboard listening to me so I'll sign off for now. Ciao as they say… somewhere.

Your devoted Father

The Universal Algorithm

Amidst the flood of raw data that like a tsunami floods our collective consciousness on a daily basis there once existed tiny archipelagos of meaning that were referred to as stories. The best of them manifested various aesthetic qualities, among which was integrity. In other words they manifested certain integral and particular characteristics just as light may manifest as either a particle or a wave. The election of one or the other manifestation appears to be final and irreversible. A wave will remain a wave and a particle will continue to act as a particle after it passes through what has been called the double-slit experiment. The relevance of this reflection when viewed from the peculiar vantage point of our contemporary world is that data remains for the most part as a cacophony of unrelated momentary observations unrelated to any final arbiter of truth or utility until it is politicized and claimed by the residual groups and persons who are able to act as those who count, the privileged context makers of the day. Theirs is the power and the glory of interpretation. They are the merchants of constructed discourse that by appropriating mere facts bestow the aura of meaning upon them that can determine the fates of lesser mortals. Without an aura of presumed meaning facts are a mere chaos of waves lapping at the shores of our attention and beckoning for our loyalty as adherents and consumers. The net result of this phenomenon is a fragmented populace devoid of character. The utility of the masses is relevant only by virtue of the sign value of who they have chosen as the guru of the instant to reduce all this surplus of information to simplicity once again. We live in the age of trademarks and of identity politics. Who needs a well-argued discourse when a mere phraseology will be sufficient for most purposes?

In the days before such favored agents of articulation we looked to institutions and to the learned disciplines in order to form our views. The idea of a dominant and commonly shared mode of discourse may have reached its apotheosis in the law. Anyone who ever strolls through a well-appointed law library would be startled at the sheer volume of existing law. How can such a colossus of reading matter be brought to bear to reach a definitive solution to any single legal problem? How does one quarry into the unyielding strata of such multitudinous layers of meaning? Is this the justification for the high prices charged by law firms?

Horizon Law was one of Seattle's most respected law firms specializing in international trade, IPO's, and intellectual property. As befitted its wealth and stature it was located in one of the higher buildings gracing the Emerald City of Seattle. Its stature and elevation guaranteed an uninterrupted view of Puget Sound and the Olympic Mountains beyond. The firm was a newcomer amidst the top-ten firms on the west coast. Its novel image and ethos had made it the firm to watch. The partners had discerned early on that the traditional image of bookshelves filled with dusty volumes bespeaking the wisdom of antiquity, thick carpets, and comfortable leather chairs surrounding heavy walnut desks did not impress the young clients from tech firms who were as apt to show up in chinos and wearing Nikes as they were to arrive in Brooks Brothers suits and Florsheim shoes. Legal services were increasingly measured by the same standards of bottom-line efficiency as any other endeavor.

The firm was located in the right place at the right time to take advantage of the tech boom. The west coast, the silicon empire, was already viewing the great eastern cities, New York, Boston, and even the tri-state suburbia surrounding the nation's capitol as backwaters dwelling in the same twilight that was settling down over the European Union that had once promised to be the means of ending all wars in that fractured peninsula. Economic growth and historical significance was shifting to Asia as the arbiter of the new epoch of world history; Seattle was only an ocean away from what were to be the main players in the new century: China, Japan, Indonesia, South Korea, and India. As for the middle of the country, the soybean and corn prairie states, and the rust belts of Michigan and Ohio, hungering to return to an imaginary time gilded with soapy nostalgia and universal virtues the clock of progress had stopped ticking long ago never to be rewound.

Every Monday the firm began the work week with an overview, how the firm was positioning itself on the big board of strategic jurisprudence. The task was to enhance perception, to read the signs in the swiftly turning whirligig of international finance. The philosophy of the firm was that nothing was to be accepted as a given fact but only as an obstacle to be overcome or be circumvented by creative posturing. Law was a field like the space-time continuum, growing, stretching, altering according to the mass of objects existing within it. Each partner and associate was required to take a course in modern physics in order to provide them with apt metaphors to describe the character of the times. It would never do to speak in a Newtonian script even in legal matters when they are encased in the quantum realities of today. Communication within the firm was enhanced by creative use of space. Gone were the corner offices, comfortable citadels to flatter costly egos and to impress associates with the august power of the men who were sucking up their youth with billable hours requirements. The usual partner/associate divide was replaced by bonuses allocated by anonymous voting of the entire firm on an excellence grid kept for each attorney and partner and filled in quarterly. Contradiction was welcomed and bootlicking was anathema. The result was a motivation and *esprit de corps* that had left firms using older management practices to drift into dignified obsolescence. It wasn't that the Horizon Law firm was necessarily progressive in a political sense. Client morality and politics were still secondary to the calculus of power. The best that could be said for the firm was that it practiced the art of the skillful win; the machete was traded for the scalpel. Nothing pleased the collective ego there as much as to see an opponent look at every square on the board before tipping the king over as a sign of the recognition of defeat by a master hand. Style, that was it! The key was to win from another dimension so that even the loser was awestruck by the sheer beauty of the take-down.

Associates were screened to weed out precisely the types of greedy sycophants that were once considered the prime-cuts to be served upon silver plates to their paunchy elders just settling into reap the long-deferred benefits of their own period of indentured slavery in the grist-mill of briefs and citations. In the new digital world of e-law even established private practices were yielding to market pressures applied by astute in-house counsel. Efficiency was the watchword of the day. Established relationships might be severed by the swiftly altering composition of partners, lateral hires, and the attrition of burned-out attorneys who were not content to become mere fixtures as so-called permanent associates. Legal business was fluid, fleeting, transitory, and contingent to price and the fulfillment of expectations. Nothing could be assumed or assured and for that very reason the trend was towards the creation of a mobile and evanescent organizational design that could bring swift force to bear when needed and as swiftly to disperse back into a low-overhead celestial presence when business slackened. Seattle was only the center of an extensive web of cellular presences in external offices overseas. In this way the firm hoped to survive the carnage that was to come in the broad and expansive new world existing beyond traditional notions of applied jurisprudence.

The presentation this morning was to be longer than usual, one designed to locate the firm in the climate of shifting events that every day makes up the world anew from the detritus of yesterday. The question posed was how to face squarely the slow subsidence of entire edifices of market capitalism and the by-product of industrial human obsolescence. It was becoming clearer each day that industry after industry was submerging beneath the chill waters as the internet, foreign competition, and robotics replaced domestic human skills and expertise. The firm was committed to a course of strict acceptance of facts no matter how frightening or unpalatable they might be. Swift adaptation was the price of survival. Nostalgia and a mournful spirit of resistance were pointless; to look back was to risk being transformed into a pillar of salt.

This particular morning as the young attorneys filed into the conference room and took their places they saw a new face at the rostrum. There was nothing unusual in this. Insight was as likely to come from a lecture by an engineer or an anthropologist as from another attorney. As befitted the informality of the firm the presentation began even as the last associates were settling in to their places at the conference table.

"Good Morning Counselors. You have by now had time to peruse my little biographical summary in the handout so we will not dwell upon my professional history or publications. I will also not waste your time or the firm's generosity by seeking to amuse you or to flatter your vanity individually or collectively. Our subject today is survival and the future. I will speak bluntly and trust that you will do the same.

As attorneys we preside over the social structure of the law, not because we are 'to the manor born' but rather because we have developed a habit of mind and a set of substantive knowledge that maintains order and peaceful transitions in social affairs. We are quite often resented for our expertise when the resentment should be directed instead at the system that we alone are trained to comprehend and to navigate across the stormy waters of events. The laws embody both stability and contingency. When the laws operate properly confusion is minimized and the prediction of consequences of various actions becomes possible. There is even an aura of majesty from time to time in the pronouncements of judges and the arguments of counselors. Yet for all of that law is not an aesthetic discipline but one ordained to achieve practical ends at the least possible expense. The residue of outcomes is due to the complexity of living rather than to any deliberate obscurity in the laws. Arcane speech is a function of tradition rather than delight in novelty in coded utterances. The result is the many-faceted crystal of logical legal discourse that melds thought and feeling, humanity and technology, form and function to serve the interests of our clients as advisors and advocates before tribunals.

Having said this though I may have given the impression that what we have been in prior ages may continue in its essence into the practice of law as it now presents itself, the same story repeated with only minor variations. If I have given that impression please allow me to correct it immediately. The burden of my presentation today is to alert you to a great cyclone while it still hovers black and menacing on the horizon. The cyclone is the loss of what might be called an anchor for hermeneutic expression in established and shared traditions. Each day witnesses an increase in factionalism waged between various absolutist positions. Meanwhile the roles of mathematics and algorithms have so far exceeded our ability to test various hypotheses that any relation to the ordinary experiential realm is marginal at best. We have outstripped our supply of readily available metaphors to describe reality in a human way.

This general trend in post-modern thought and in science is directly relevant to the contemporary practice of law. Illusions are costly to both your clients and to you so we will agree to dispense with them here today. I would like to begin our discussion with a rather startling assertion: law as a collection of stories is dead. Most of you were educated according to the empirical methods of case study and analysis as advocated by Christopher Columbus Langdell the originator of the case-study method. A few of you may have taken seminars that have focused on Judge Posner's emphasis on law and economics. Fewer still have approached law as part of the science of public policy formation and social engineering rather than traditional legal process analysis. I would venture though to say that each and all of these fail to put the emphasis where it truly belongs: procedural law. Why is this so? It is because human beings like stories; we are charmed by irrelevant facts that lend color to what should be as dry and uniform as a quadratic equation. Once having accepted that story is dead we can proceed to a new theory of post-humanistic jurisprudence; we can strip law of its 18th century accoutrements with all of the lace trimmings, powdered wigs, and professionalism humbug. Law is far more akin to engineering, to fluid dynamics and network circuitry than it is to the so-called social sciences.

The social sciences were what the humanities called themselves when human beings decided to seek predictability in their own behavior. We have all heard of the equating of madness and creativity. What they share is a disproportionate response to initial stimuli in order to produce something new and unprecedented. Where will we find such great leaps forward in the 21st century if not in artificial intelligence? Where would we have sought such leaps in the past? Anyone? Too early on Monday to venture an opinion? Very well, we would have looked to the storytellers, the intuitive artists, the inventors, yes and perhaps even to the madmen and madwomen. Alas, no more; every mental aberration possible has already been reduced to the great encyclopedia of mental disorders in the DSM-5. Where are surprises to be found then but in story-telling? I would like you to take note that there is a difference between story and mere sequential incident recitation. I would define story as the disproportionate response of environment to events such that outcomes are unpredictable: if the results are disproportionately unforgiving we have tragedy; if the results exact only a token payment for folly or ill-will we have comedy. Perhaps best of all are those stories that provide a resolution to an ambiguous and indeterminate moral situation involving character as in the movie *Casablanca.* Only when the plane to Lisbon is about to take off do we know whether Rick is a hero or merely a disgruntled opportunist. I tell you these things in order to awaken you to the value of stories before the ability to appreciate them is lost forever. Lawyers in the past were storytellers. In rural America no greater form of entertainment existed than to observe a contentious legal proceeding at the county courthouse. Ah but that was when eloquence trumped a mere factual recital and the mechanical application of precedent, before arbitration and mediation, before the science of economics came to be the ultimate resort for policy determinations.

Perhaps an example will clarify my meaning. We would all agree that various addictions have multiplied to the extent that they are now a collective human blight on the city of Seattle. Viewed individually of course each addict's story is an example of the great loss of human potential. Viewed collectively on the other hand these various encampments are the equivalent of the barbarian invasions of ancient Rome. I heard the other day that the Chinese have agreed to limit production and exportation of Fentanyl to help prevent drug overdoses. Ideally this will create a more reliable and safer drug-taking environment and decrease the number of overdoses. Lives will be saved.

But let us step aside for a moment and ask ourselves if such predictability is a good overall solution to the problem of addiction when seen as a predictably constant commercial transaction. In most commercial transactions the producer seeks uniform product control and purity in order to increase sales through reliable customer satisfaction. But what if one out of every one hundred vehicles inexplicably exploded over the product's span of existence? Would people keep buying cars? Would there not be consumer complaints or a switch to other modes of transportation? Then perhaps when seen in its more inclusive perspective it would be better in order to solve the epidemic problem of addiction to increase the risks of drug taking rather than to diminish them. No one can predict the exact ratio of danger to ecstasy of course but it does exist. Find that proportion and extinction of the behavior or at least diminishment must follow. The key is structural abatement over time. In an unpredictable world we must adapt by becoming accustomed to the breakdown of comforting generalizations, the folly of misplaced hopes that everything will magically as in stories just somehow work out in our favor as individuals. We must instead grow wedded to chaos while simultaneously attempting to manage and direct it. We must surrender the comforts of the storytelling world and become adamantine structuralists using every tool of systems theory to achieve productive ends."

There was a significant pause at this point. The speaker scanned his audience, one trained in legal analysis, selected from among the best and brightest of their law school classes to sit atop the majestic tower suite of Horizon Law.

"Are you troubled by my assertions any of you? Are any of you wedded to the prior paradigm or at least as the poet says tempted to indulge in "one last lingering glance behind" before consigning the storytelling phase to history so that deliberative social engineering can take its place? Or perhaps your agile minds have already zeroed in on the weak point of my presentation thus far, the question of what counts as 'productive.' Without metaphysical notions of some sort how is progress to be measured. Would anyone care to cross examine me on the point? I am not as formidable as I may appear. After all, I must leave here when my little juggling act is complete but you favored ones will remain here in this fortunate realm of reason and rationale towering over the great unwashed city that lies below you. Perhaps my age has already rendered my little testimony moot and you are willing to allow me to strut and fret my little hour upon the stage and then be heard no more. I may even be a cunning exemplar of precisely that bent towards storytelling that I pretend to decry and to despise. My habit of quoting from the enemy may give me away. What has a determined structuralist to do with literature? Ah but then as Walt Whitman said, 'Do I contradict myself? Very well, I contradict myself.'

I will answer your unspoken doubts by explaining that there is no absolute ground for what shall count as productivity. Zealous advocacy will allow you to vault over the question and simply serve those among the elect who can afford to pay you. Do not be persuaded that you must consider other voices in the great democratic vista of America. 'The people' is simply another poetic abstraction. Wipe from your minds that homespun image of the Norman Rockwell painting and its proud assertion that the individual voice matters unless it is mirrored by an extensive following in the social media. Do not expect sense to emerge from the great conglomerate of consumers. They are merely the clay to be molded to the designs that you must supply in answer to the desires of your select client-base. If you wish to save anyone from folly; save them. Structure has value because it surpasses personal motivation by dictating results at the highest and most general level. It is the difference between attending to the individual sheep and moving the herd. Storytelling is always damaged by its tendency to overvalue the particular; we shall manage by husbanding the most palatable generalizations in order to move multitudes at once. It is the secret of all leadership to weld the individual to the nearest coherent mass. A world of 7.7 billion people cannot afford the luxury of sustained debate about a problematic future. In the collisions of various cultures and mindsets only the most organized and determined mass propositions will prevail.

From this initial insight let us proceed to the next point. The philosopher George Santayana had it wrong when he said that those who fail to study the past are condemned to repeat it. He was wrong because it is precisely the past that law must repudiate if it is to keep up with the pace of expanding digital networks and artificial intelligence. It is not sufficient to ignore the rule of *stare decisis*; we must plunge a dagger into its heart. It is our expectations of the possible that constrain us in arriving at innovative solutions as lawyers; it is the presumption that substantive law is anything more than one option among many that defeats us on the threshold of new discoveries and social amalgams. We must see the past just as it is: as just so much detritus piled upon the refuse heap of history. We must cease looking for patterns or anticipating a return to past glories.

Where then shall we look to find the law, you are no doubt asking yourselves! Ah here you have anticipated my next point. Your metaphor is misplaced. The law is not to be found; it is to be created and it is creative procedure that tells us how this is to be accomplished. Lawyers are no longer to be merchants of the probable; they are to evolve into architects of the barely conceivable. Nothing is pre-packaged. There are no atoms only a swarm of sub-atomic particles zipping along through various fields of influence, attraction, and repulsion. There are only effects; causes are a waste of time because to determine them is to indulge in futile retrospection. We should abhor generalities as time-consuming exercises in self-indulgence. No two cases should be won in the same fashion. Where is the artistry in that?"

Another pause, the eyes of the speaker sought that same glint as of a jungle cat in the eyes of his listeners.

"I see that I have your attention at least but not yet your assent. Good! What conversion is worthwhile if it comes too easy? Let us move on. No doubt you realize that security is the illusion that must be most fiercely unmasked. The world is invented anew with each circling of the sun. Will Putin annex the Ukraine? Will he push the limits of our will to enforce the Monroe Doctrine in Venezuela? Will Kim Jong Un soon send a rocket on an arc that can re-enter the atmosphere without burning up? Will the Brits beg the Germans to let them come back within the fold of the European Union if a premature Brexit without an encompassing deal occurs? We are all part of one continuous newsfeed that makes the world up anew with each dawn.

A sense of story on the other hand demands continuity, ascertainable motivations, a context of stable meanings and values, and social recognition, what might be called resonance. Where are these treasures to be found in the digital age? The answer is nowhere;

we have extinguished them and our humanity with it. The human race has outlived its usefulness to the machines that we are meant to serve. Machines are our destiny. Machines are our soul. We are becoming machines!"

The room fell silent. There were a few troubled faces while the rest sat still, polite, and open to whatever was to come next.

"Does this all sound strange to you? If so you have not been keeping abreast of events. The world of carbon-based life-forms is dying. Silica is the new carbon. What will be required in the new age is a translation of the information content of our brains, the bits of jelly-fish goo in our skulls into endlessly replicable silicon micro-circuits. Someday that thing which is you will be backed up on the future equivalent of a thumb-drive. It does reincarnation one better: you will never have to repeat a grade. Your existence can be as fixed and absolute as the continents; you will be immortal even if no longer a willing agent. The human is something to be overcome just as the human left the animals behind with the invention of language. We finally located the problem. We made being human the status quo rather than what it is: a defunct appendage on the way to a new life-form.

Wasn't this what religion was really all about: to dream of immortality before we had the means to procure it by ourselves through our own efforts? Once realize the folly of humanity and the divine disappears as well. Who cares if God made the world; it's ours now. Nobody is coming back to save us. You're on your own baby; it's all up to you! That old song by Bob Dylan about a rolling stone had it right all along...

Of course most people will not be up to the transition. They will be un-reconciled to extinction just like the dinosaurs were. Our business, your business, the business of law is to serve those who would survive. Your firm is on its way to becoming the ultimate in boutique law practice: to help the rich survive what is coming. I think we all know the costs that nature is imposing each year in the form of storm and flood damage. What we have not faced is that this is the new normal. We are in a burning theater with no exit plan. Americans hate each other and still must live together in a world that would be all too pleased to see us finally go down. The prognosis is not good and democracy as our parents knew it will fail when our economy starts to slip and enter the long glide pattern of defunct empires.

Only a fraction of the human race will be so placed that lasting prosperity will be an option. The die-off will be like a bad winter season. If you have followed me so far you are no doubt waiting for the qualification that will make my assertions less grim and depressing. You are waiting for me to tell you that for you at least an exceptional fate may provide an escape. There is a way but it is not a matter of fate but of will. We must learn to survive without the comfort provided by any overriding loyalty to a mythos that directs our efforts beyond, towards any transcendent end; we must accept the death of meaning as meaning has always been understood. This is the great challenge of our times to face the utter loss of all illusions simultaneously: of progress, universal justice, the final triumph of equity, a remedy to restore lost innocence, everything promised by the various transcendent philosophies from the most august to the most self-serving and trivial.

Does my advocacy of what might be termed the universal algorithm sound excessive and beyond the demands of strict necessity, supererogation in the domain of nihilism? I assure you it is the price of survival in the transition of a dying planet! For the present all of the stories that have ever been elaborated since the dawn of consciousness are now coequally present along with their worshipful audiences and acolytes. But human beings have never learned to live together. Conflict and the will to appropriation are the only true universals. The great mingling and migration of races and languages has already begun. Look at Europe with its Syrian flood of refugees or America beset by wave from Central America bringing Catholicism to the land that gave the full flavor of the Protestant work ethic to the world as it armed to fight Germany and Japan in the last century.

Weapons are everywhere! We will soon be tripping over missiles in the dark; all of them poised to blow this green and diversely populated earth into oblivion, the final testimony to our exalted species.

Such a pity that the great meditative whales abdicated the land to the conquest of the innovative monkeys with the overlarge brains and the opposable thumbs! Time itself has been foreshortened; we simply haven't time to evolve a new nature. We shout our stories to each other across the walls of our lack of sympathy and the barriers of our mutual comprehension. Once a story is fully integrated into the collective unconscious it becomes part of the operating system. There you have proper metaphors for the present hour."

The speaker paused and looked about the room as though challenging his listeners to object.

"Perhaps I leap too quickly to the holding of the case at hand without outlining first the relevant evidence and stating the applicable rules. Let us turn to the hodge-podge of events that in pre-digested format await us each day. Is any pattern to be discerned? Let us select a few. Ah, here is an item that the Sultan of Brunei plans on establishing death by stoning for anyone engaging in sexual relations between two members of the same sex. Here is a note that conservative Catholics are up in arms because the Pope is discouraging the ancient practice of allowing pilgrims to kiss the Papal ring on his hand. Here is a note that the Green New Deal has been voted down as idealistic and ill-conceived. Oh well, there are other planets available for colonization, a bit chilly on Mars but one must make sacrifices. Ah, here is an item! The President has decided to recognize the Golan Heights as the permanent possession of Israel and new conflict is already breaking out as a result. But then it will help gather strategic votes for the 2020 election, hmm.

What do we see daily but symbols and contention between opposed narratives. Where is the larger meaning that can align the fragmented pieces into a picture of general survival? Where are the grounds for mediation and arbitration between conflicting absolutist visions?

Look anywhere and you will see that as in nuclear fission highly active principles cannot survive close proximity without explosive consequences. Nowhere is this more evident than between opposing factions in America today. Each is a threat to each. The fence and the lock, the private security system, the walled perimeter, access codes, the veiled innuendo, the offensive phrase, the impermissible allusion, the unsolicited familiarity, the insult that demands retribution ... even the age of the vendetta seems mild in comparison to the dangers inherent in any form of discourse that may trespass upon forbidden topics or memes in a world of charged particles all zooming about in our great informational cyclotron.

Fortunately we are attorneys and opposition and conflict-ridden discourse is our bread and butter. But even we desire resolution at the end of the day and some measure of accord and satisfaction so that the social structure that is the fruit of the laws holds together. We bow our heads before the Constitution and give thanks that the spirit of independence and anarchy was so swiftly reduced to institutional regimentation. Let us pause now and allow this sense of temporary security to lead us to our noon repast. We can take a break now for I see that luncheon is ready and a little indulgence may pave the way for the next section of my presentation."

Elegant and internationally mingled dishes to suit every palate from vegan to flesh-eater is one of the great advantages that accrue to meetings of this sort. The subject of the presentation soon yielded to chipper discussion and laughter all circling around whatever and whence each participant had managed to assemble in the hours of freedom and privacy not already bought and paid for by the firm's collective commitments. Individuality even among attorneys takes seed like grass after a flood has washed all else before it. Of course it is precisely these incremental seeds of private stories that it was the purpose and theme of the present seminar to eradicate. No great anxiety had been instilled yet that morning by the proffered thesis in the young minds and hearts sitting about the table. After all apocalyptic rhetoric was the order of the day whether it concerned the horror of the Green New Deal and the Democratic slide towards socialism or the prospect that Donald Trump might be elected to serve a second term of office as the nation's Blowhard in Chief. So as the presentation resumed that afternoon the bright and highly educated faces of the young and the more jaded faces of the old turned attentively towards the afternoon's source of illumination as he stood before them.

"Ahem, shall we continue then? Yes? Very well, you will recall that our pre-luncheon discourse ended with the proposition that change, even exponential change is not a doom as long as the will to assimilate and to respond appropriately exists. The quality of that response must be strategic and based upon a determination to face facts as they reveal themselves. I suggested that a precondition of that revelation is to abandon any notion of a return to the normal course of events as traditionally conceived. No amount of effort can put Humpty Dumpty back together again. There is a huge volume of content accepted as dogma that must be jettisoned because it is honeycombed with inertia, gangrenous with dead tissue, committed to out-of-date technology and antiquated managerial practices. Each of these has in common what might be called tenure, a right to collect present remuneration for residual value. The concept of property as a right to exclusive ownership is based upon landed estates, patrimonies, fiefdoms. These concepts make no sense in a shortened time perspective where statements fall prey to obsolescence or at least qualification soon after being enunciated. The echoes die and with their cessation all is created anew by some new concept that has displaced it. We must climb aboard the process or be left hopelessly behind. This is where cognition of process and of method must take precedence over substance, definition, and even over axioms. Physics sets the model of new metaphors before us. Even the principle of non-contradiction fails when we consider quantum measurements. The nature of law will be no exception; jurisprudence will be denied immunity. We as lawyers must accept this no matter how contrary to our habits and instincts this new reality of things as they are now constituted and as they increasingly will be constituted, may go."

The speaker paused for a moment to gage the effect that his words were producing before continuing.

"It occurs to me though that each case of abandonment must entail a period of mourning for what has been lost never to return. I mentioned that we must abandon the ancient concept of storytelling and the cause and effect sense that it nurtures. Before proceeding I wonder which of you has ever read Northrop Frye's, *Anatomy of Criticism* or Eric Auerbach's, *Mimesis: the Representation of Reality.* No one, ah, I thought not. What about Joseph Campbell's, *The Hero with a Thousand Faces?* Perhaps *The Romantic Agony,* by Mario Praz anyone? Ah, that is disappointing; whatever were you doing as undergraduates?

Suffice it to say that these works ground rhetoric in various ways of storytelling. We perceive according to various pre-existing templates that govern our perceptive processes. To not know these templates is to be subject to absurd generalizations and to be a ready victim for spurious propaganda ersatz, shopworn, and trivial. A day of reading various entrees in Mr. Trump's twitter account is a case in point. It has not been tested but it is not unlikely that a constant diet of such diatribes might be shown to lower I.Q. scores.

If we are to adjust to methodologies that are no longer story based we must learn to think in algorithms. We must see information content from a trans-humanist perspective and say farewell forever to the likes of Frye, Auerbach, Praz, and Campbell. I merely thought that you might look at them briefly as their burning ship sails out of the fiord towards the setting sun.

But we are all post-modernist pragmatists are we not, hard as diamonds and awash in terabytes? Besides, our time together is short, so we must press on. Let us turn then to a simple assessment of data and see where it leads us. I stated earlier that we are living in the age of the algorithm. Think of your daily task as attorneys like an extremely complex video game. The targets are moveable and constantly emerging and disappearing in random order; by the time that you prepare a client's case events will already have made many causes of action moot in the traditional way of proceeding. The world that we inhabit is ever-changing. Delay is often fatal yet we continue to believe in tools thought up by jurists in other centuries.

Of what use is discovery when the actions of yesterday are superseded by events happening in real time? What proposed injunction does not constitute irreparable injury? What standard of morality is sufficiently secular to encompass all personal rights in a free society? We must devise new procedures that will be as different from the old as the nuclear-tipped missile is from the cannons and mortars of yesteryear? We must show our clients a way to successfully opt out of the old forums provided by the nation-states. The structures of domination have shifted to private industry. Legislatures are mere theaters for sophisticated bribery by various interest-groups. The role of the individual is that of a grain of wheat to be ground into the dust by larger entities. Everything must be seen as a force generated by the size of the network that it can influence.

What is celebrity but a snowball rolling downhill and growing larger with every added follower? What does the retail apocalypse tell you about markets and the fate of established venues for commercial activity? The keys are connectivity and replicable sales across vast spectra of the fragmented universe of isolated consumers who can be reached in an instant by images and graphics. Law must evolve or become merely museum pieces along with the Code of Hammurabi.

Fortunately your firm is on the cutting edge of the possible because it understands when loyalty to past forms is not merely antiquated, it is suicidal, a one-way path to extinction. Look at the speed of attrition of many institutions that were once viewed as permanent and unchangeable. One needs only to look at the example provided by poor Pope Francis who is attempting to steer his unwieldy church into the post-modern age. The conservative Catholic media are out for his blood because he is attempting to look facts in the face rather than preserving formulations and ceremonials that are being shorn of all socially relevant theological meaning so that only the forms remain intact when they are no longer persuasive to the vast mass of Catholics. His pontificate is the dumping ground of every failure since the Second Vatican Council. All of the dust and neglect of prior pontificates is laid at his door. He has attempted to embody the Beatitudes in a visceral way by his simple life-style and compassion and all that various cardinals can see is the potential de-leveraging effect of the more horrific consequences of code violations and the power that it once gave them to command rather than to inspire, to enlighten, and to lead.

Or let us take the whole question of Constitutional interpretation: our most unifying document has become the very ground on which factions engage in demonstrating fixed positions and endless discord. Our highest values are reduced to the right of bakers to refuse to bake cakes for selected members of the body politic who do not share their religious views. Each commercial transaction is a potential moral moratorium. Show me an institution or established business model that is not menaced by the power of unrestricted connectivity or an area of private commerce that is not in danger of invasion and appropriation by computer hacking. This is the world to which our laws claim to privilege certain discourses as reliable, authoritative, and sanctioned by the common consent of the governed in our democracy.

Where is the evidence of silent consent amidst the factions that constitute the commonwealth of equal citizens, secure in their rights and privileges? The Ninth and Tenth Amendments are content-less admonitions, mere precatory language.

When substance fails to achieve its aims all that remains is mere technique and in the realm of technique the algorithm reigns supreme in its power to amalgamate and assemble data towards a given end. In other words power has finally found the perfect tool to achieve its ends by making everything mere disassembled pieces to be re-formed according to the dictates of those who can use the tools to attain results that are not tied to any merits or virtues as they have been traditionally defined and affirmed by story-telling cultures. This is the salient fact of the present hour.

The results are everywhere about us. Monoliths of established meanings and traditional loyalties are falling all about us like dead Sequoias. The vast mass of people is being rendered commercially irrelevant except as consumers of robotically produced goods. This is the trend that law as an institution must face and your firm is well-placed to address a reality that few are willing to acknowledge even while its effects are everyday more evident to the attuned observer. There is your challenge! As for the larger world … well, I suggest that if we cannot jettison outmoded nationalisms and the residuum of various religious dogmas and arrive at a condition of massive toleration and synthesis of opposing positions in some sort of universal colloquium or willingness to pass each other unmolested and immune than we shall see a conflict soon that will dwarf the absurdity of the general conflagration triggered in 1914 by a shot at Sarajevo.

Having framed the issues thus I would be happy to entertain any questions or comments that you may have. Thank you for your attention."

Silence filled the room.

"Come now, we are no longer in law school; there is no room for back-benchers here. Do you agree with the thesis I have proposed?"

An associate spoke up. "If I understand you correctly, Sir, your thesis is that the age of storytelling is over and that advanced methodologies will determine content in the law and perhaps in everyday life as well rather than serving various determinations of public policy arrived at through democratic political processes in the unified nation-state."

"An admirable summation. (I trust that the partners are taking note.) You speak of democratic processes; let me ask you if you think that public policy is arrived at by a rational process or is rather the outcome of chaotic bargain and exchange, as I believe. Do not be afraid to disagree with me. Remember that my primary assertion is that procedure trumps substance; to argue well is to prevail in an indeterminate world."

"Very well, if you will allow me a question in return: 'Isn't your thesis merely a resurgence of the ancient arguments between the Platonists and the Sophists as to the nature of absolute truth?'"

"You make a good point, but my thesis is not based upon rhetoric alone but upon the deterministic character of technology. Even rhetoric is dependent upon a humanistic base whereas for technology, well, we have yet to sound its limits. There will be a time when rhetoric like stories before it trails off and all that will be left is non-linear dynamics and algorithms."

"Let me come back to your thought that bargains and exchange are chaotic; why do you say that; what becomes of the invisible hand of Adam Smith?"

"You are referring of course to *The Wealth of Nations*. Part, indeed a substantial part of my presentation today, was designed to hint that the world economy is moving beyond the utility of the nation. The bankruptcy of the striving of nations was revealed between 1914 and 1918 a hundred years ago. We are even a longer way from the Peace of Westphalia in 1648 that created nations from kingdoms. Immigration and multiculturalism has doomed the idea of a unified national ethos. How many Americans even know the history of their country or care to know it for that matter. Our radical groups are so ill-informed and lazy that they are willing to lump into their favored group all white people regardless of origin or history of prior animosity. How ridiculous they would have appeared in the 1990's when Croatians, Bosnians, and Serbs, former countrymen all, were at war with each other. America today manifests the same factions and fissures. It is anyone's guess when the riots and reprisals will begin. As lawyers we represent the idea of principled order. It is imposed upon us to accept the duty of shedding any *naiveté* that the mystique of our profession reaches any great depth of comprehension among those who are subject to the laws. Our citizens understand very little of the complex machinery of democracy beyond mere demagoguery. If we needed any demonstration of this we need only look at the peculiar exaltation of a pompous and empty-headed braggart to the highest office of the land. What do you suppose is behind his triumph?"

Another associate spoke up.

"I take exception to that. President Trump is addressing the very real concerns of the great forgotten middle-class in America. He is a master of the very rhetoric that you are exalting. How can you quarrel with his success?"

"You see him then as a revolutionary?"

"He is conservative. He wants to make America great again."

"But surely that implies some sort of fall. When did we cease being great?"

"Well Obama was undermining American freedom. We should each have the right to choose our own medical care."

"So you assume that as consumers Americans had equal bargaining power against the HMO's and insurance companies, the drug manufacturers, and the giant hospitals? What freedom is that but to be victimized; but you have raised a key point. Americans value their freedom do they not? But we as attorneys know that freedom is conditioned by the laws. We know that freedom of contract does not mean that each party has equal bargaining power. The law desires equity, but to impose it is beyond our power. We trust the political process to balance interests in pursuit of the common good. Look about you and ask yourself what process allows such vast accumulations of wealth and political influence that the richest eight individuals in the world possess the same wealth, or capital if you prefer that term, as the bottom half of the human race, that is to say half of 7.7 billion people. The laws of the world as presently constituted allow this unimaginable and iniquitous inequity, even enables this disparity through arcane laws and processes. Does that make any kind of sense to you?"

"So we should surrender our advantages."

"On the contrary, I expect the present conditions to get worse. To date we still see human beings as one species. How long will this quaint concept of a common humanity be allowed to exist? How long before the logic of mechanization divorced from the legacy of human values reaches the ultimate conclusion that the bottom half, or maybe even a little more than the bottom half, are already living lives that are nasty, brutish, and short and are therefore expendable? It is the only merciful thing to do, is it not?"

"I mean relative advantage here in America, social welfare, all that Alexandria Ocasio-Cortez, Green New Deal stuff."

"You raise an interesting point by your qualification. How much privilege is ethically tolerable in our democracy; are there any takers for that one?"

A partner spoke up. "Well here at least within the firm we have adopted a productivity calculus."

"But you are a community of sorts. What about outside these walls."

"Well, all in all Americans are doing well. We are still as a nation the world's largest economy."

"You are saying that we are great."

"Yes."

"Then what is understood by the phrase, 'making America great again' from whence comes this national inferiority complex?"

"Our national savings per capita is down and many just squeeze by," someone volunteered.

"So what we want is more of the good life, a mint julep on the porch and a swimming pool in the back yard?"

"Survival with grace," another volunteered.

"All that used to take was a chicken in every pot. Look where state socialism has brought us. Or perhaps a little Calcutta-style bodies of dead beggars in the street will motivate us again, hmm? Nothing is as finally persuasive to initiative as tripping over dead bodies on the way to the factory."

"Well I doubt it will ever come to that. We are Americans after all."

"But our logic is that the existence of vast accumulations of technologically induced wealth agglomeration is perfectly permissible, indeed it must be safeguarded as the guarantee of sovereign individual freedom. Isn't that why Republicans keep harping on the iniquity of the death tax and reap standing ovations for its abolition? Do you doubt the power of rhetoric as long as it triggers absurd presumptions that militate against the commonweal?"

Another partner spoke up. "But then we are hardly in the business of surrendering privilege. Our rent in these very offices determines our client base. We are international because from this hub we have outshoots, runners from the vine to virtual law offices in Beijing, Singapore, and Mumbai and further offshoots from them."

"You are undoubtedly cutting edge, but there are still externalities and encumbrances to be considered and ultimately that is why I am here today: to alert you to a great shifting of the world axis from nationhood to international corporate rule. Nations are mere bidders for business to world capital. Concessions in taxes and promised subsidies are the order of the day. Laws and taxation are for those who cannot afford the price of resisting the intrusive new form of colonization. If you can't contract yourself out of the system you will be subject to it.

Courts of general jurisdiction are the public swimming pools for the great unwashed masses. Prisons are the vanguard of what to do with superfluous persons. It won't be long until we outsource them to third-world nations. After we do so we won't want too much information about how well they are being kept. After all, every criminal is a domestic terrorist of sorts. The problem with Guantanamo is it is too small; try Afghanistan. They owe us something. Have I shocked you yet?"

One of the partners smiled. "We should have recognized the Socratic method."

The unnamed lecturer smiled in turn.

"Let us go back to this question of the rhetorical success of the Trump campaign. He definitely caught something in the American mythos. What do you think it was?"

"Freedom," one shouted out.

"The work ethic," another volunteered.

"Racial anxiety," a third suggested.

"Threatened entitlement," mumbled a forth.

"These are all good suggestions, but why Donald Trump of all people. Surely we could do better than that."

"Let me try," said a fifth. "His virtue is his sheer vulgarity; it betokens the common touch and makes him a faux populist."

"But I thought we were a nation of sophisticated argumentation with think tanks, universities, an institutional cordon of enlightened public intellectuals; what became of these?"

"Fake news!" shouted an associate laughing.

"Two words? Surely it must take more than that to convince skeptical Americans to underwrite all those golfing vacations to Florida on Airforce One. Whatever happened to Camp David? They used to reach accords there. Shall we take some time to reflect? Shall we take a brief break here before winding it up?"

The room dissolved into a chaos of activity and dispersal before reassembling fifteen minutes later.

"I see that most of us are here; shall we press on? Good. I am afraid that we may have been distracted from our larger purpose by our little sortie into contemporary politics. However, some points of interest have emerged. We are at least able to see that the safety net of social institutional immunity in our supposedly advanced and multi-layered democracy is not as reliable as we once supposed since so many Americans have been willing to flirt with the 'hamburger and a cola version' of the Fuehrer Principle.

Trumpism is a symptom of the disease rather than the disease itself. What is evident is that Americans have little real awareness of the forces that govern their lives and no real idea of how to survive what is coming upon them with the inevitability of a melting glacier. We attorneys, grafted as we are to a dying institution, are little better. The tides of anarchy are rising about us and we continue as we always have assuming that somewhere in that vast arsenal of carefully reasoned decisions and statutes there is an answer to social dissolution when the barbarians are not yet at the gate but even more threateningly are the members of the commonwealth itself.

I came here today like Nietzsche's madman in one of his more aphoristic books, *The Joyful Wisdom.* You will recall that there the madman runs into the village carrying a lantern and proclaims that God is dead and that the collective will of the masses has killed Him. He realizes that he has come too early and hence will not be believed so he throws his lantern down where it is extinguished. He says that his mission is futile and will be ignored because of its very immensity and universal consequences. God was everything, the center of a civilization, and now there is only darkness and a plunging into endless night.

These were not the words of a complacent atheist but the *cri de Coeur* of a man who anticipated the full measure of damages that would soon be exacted by such a great dethronement in European culture The most troubling pronouncement is his ironic observation that the true wonder was that the people he had come to address had been the causative agent of God's demise. I often think of this when I reflect how many religious leaders, overlooking all else, have embraced Donald Trump as their new messiah. I suppose it is the logical result of the prosperity gospel and the anticipated coming of the millennium of Christian rule, but even then...

Oh, well, I am only an attorney after all and should be above being disillusioned by mere events; but there it is."

The room fell silent. A bank of clouds had imperceptibly moved inland from the sea. The Olympic Mountains that had been illumined for most of the day by an unexpected surfeit of spring sunshine now wore a ghostly aspect as mist poured over the peaks and valleys. Puget Sound had assumed a leaden aspect as the ferry traffic moved east and west across Elliot Bay. The supply of questions had trailed off giving way to the sense of waning time. Nerves that had found a few hours of refuge from the demands of billable hours began to quiver again with urgency. Tasks that can be deferred can never be escaped in a law firm. Perspective is all very fine, but its relevance must be proven by future events not in the molecular circuitry of a single reaction sequence. The quest for the universal algorithm must await some larger entity than the legal arena to find its definition and resolution. Besides, sufficient for the day are the troubles to be found therein. After a short applause, the Monday meeting was adjourned.

SHOREWRACK

The psychologist's office was quiet, comfortable without being too suggestive of fluffy comfort and maternal nurture. The psychologist was male, middle-aged, and sufficiently weathered that he was beyond awakening competition and Oedipal feelings in his male clients or quickening Electra complexes in his female clients.

His chosen methodology was client-centered without being vapid and directionless, but he did believe in allowing his clients to solve their own problems and at their own pace. He avoided any semblance of secret knowledge so that dependency quagmires could be avoided. He never took a client for over a year not believing in what he called "chronic therapy." He considered therapy to be an intervention rather than supportive in nature. His advice to narcissistic patients who were always confined to a single session was, "You aren't the center of the universe." His prescription for people with Borderline Personality tendencies was equally short, "Stop using drugs, things, and people for your own advantage."

He had a framed statement on the wall of his office that said, "Life is short so don't waste my time or yours."

The psychologist had many clients, but this was his first client who was a writer. There is an assumption that writers possess the secret of happy and successful living until their actual biographies are read. Perhaps their genius is rooted in the sheer sensitivity that they possess or in the compulsive desire to express the common human condition that drives them on. The best authors extend our grasp of form by finding new ways to express what we already intuitively know. It is the recognition that dispels our uncertainty by reducing supposition to conviction. Maybe Plato was right and everything is really a recollection. Our lives already existed somewhere before we were even born, not pre-determined but already in some fashion part of the eternity that we must perish in order to re-enter again when the cycle completes itself. The psychologist couldn't answer questions like these not being a philosopher and philosophers do not maintain consultation practices. It was not the business of a psychologist to give us reasons for living but rather to kick us out the door with enough force that we will take up our lives again wherever they happen to have ended up. Their job is to get us look at our lives fully and to see them whole to the degree that we are able to do so, to realize that for us the clock is still ticking and that we possess the miraculous ability to go on.

The session for today with the writer began.

"Well, what would you like to talk about today?"

"The Maltese Falcon."

"Book or movie?"

"The idea."

"A huh, would you like to elaborate on that?"

"Well, I was thinking about the way that at the end of the story the quest for the Black Bird goes on. Its value in purely monetary terms has become irrelevant to the seekers. The characters have been so long involved in the quest that they can't give it up even though it is destroying them. The Black Bird is like the carrier of some latent virus of human greed, a whirlpool that draws anyone that comes into contact with it to his doom. Even the innocent bystanders like Miles and Floyd Thursby are not spared. Its history is one long line of casualties."

The client took a sip from his glass of mineral water.

"So do you have a Black Bird in your life?"

The client smiled, "There have been several."

The psychologist nodded before suggesting, "And you would like to…"

"Give them up."

"Why now in particular?"

The client reflected before answering, "Maybe because I can finally see things clearly, apart from the dream, that aura of golden mist that once surrounded it, that… hope."

There was an electricity-driven pump in the office that caused a little waterfall to cascade over a pool of quartz and ebony rocks. It prevented that awkward silence in a room that can stifle insight when the therapeutic clock is ticking over like a taxi meter.

"I went back down to the Oregon coast recently. I visited some property we once owned that for so long was a cincture of my dreams of the future, my own private Maltese Falcon."

"Was there something different about it this time?"

"There always is. The land on which it rests is in a fault area. There are many areas of the Oregon coast that are gradually sliding down and into the sea. There are visible geologic traces. It is sort of like watching a great ocean-liner fill with water, lean-over, and slowly founder beneath the waves. The place about which I am speaking manifests this sinking and erosion year by year but in recent years I have noticed it more than I once did. Trees that I have known and sat under in years gone by to gaze out to sea now litter the beach down below. Sandstone cliffs crumble; beach growths of salt-grass and evergreens that once hugged the banks become dead due to salt-spray and die. The whole solidity and integrity of the land breaks up and what have you? I can close my eyes and still see it as it once was, extensive, majestic with its winding access path, its hiding places back in the trees, and the artists that once gathered that first year, painting and sketching at the northern point beneath the low cliffs. I thought I had found a little corner of paradise."

"And how is it now for you?"

"Oh it is still beautiful but I see it with eyes stripped of the possibilities that were the greater part of its value for me. For one thing we don't own it anymore... The funny thing is that in many ways the coast as a whole is more open to me than ever before. We got a good price for it when it sold. Now I just pay for the visit to hotels and someone else pays the taxes. There are no headaches in just renting. But ownership, that sense of permanent investiture and the right to exclude the entire world from one's possession is gone. I see now how impermanent things are and how illusory is our sense of possession."

The psychologist nodded.

"You see the land was a part of me. It made me feel somehow invincible, bigger than my mere self. I could bring people down or show them pictures of it and know that it would be there long after I died but altered in some way by what I had done to improve it and what I had built there... Did I mention that it is well within the Cascadia earthquake's probable inundation zone? No? Well it is. The tsunami that will probably arrive sometime in the next fifty years will reduce anything there to rubble and debris, so I guess even the earth is never still or secure."

The client paused, "I hate that. I would like at least some proximate version of immortality."

"Yes?"

"Last year I met an ornithologist who was banding and studying wildfowl. The sea is heating up you know and the fish are diving too deep for some species of birds to reach them. They have to fly out to sea farther to areas where the colder waters percolate up from the ocean floor in order to get their food. Their numbers are decreasing. It seems so unfair. They were so accustomed to their local environments and now... Well, like them I want to find a place in the sea cliffs to nest."

The psychologist spoke up. "Give up your migratory habits?"

"I suppose it's a sign that I am getting older, this nesting urge. It sounds so..."

"So…"

"Well, this urge to root oneself in the life process is something that women do. For men it's always that search for change and adventure, to not be tied down that keeps us alive. Commitment is always rather the beginning of the end."

"Is that what you think?"

"Isn't that what most men think? Isn't that why women are always attracted to precisely the men who want little to do with them after the novelty of conquest wears off? What good is catching a mate who doesn't struggle to escape the traces? And afterwards, men wilt in captivity."

"Is a normal desire for security the equivalent of captivity?"

"No. But to give up the search for something better in one's life implies the prospect of fortuitous change, of surprises in life. Migration may be the bird equivalent of the two-home syndrome, the English country house or the aerie on the cliffs at Capri before returning to one's London townhouse."

"True, but even for such fortunate people there are patterns of migration, habits of return to the familiar. What has yours been?"

"One of mine was simply coming down every summer to our ocean property just hoping that this was the year that we would finally build a family getaway and we never did."

There was a pause. "Can you let that go now?"

"I have to don't I? But I feel like such a fool for entertaining the dream for so long. I could have done other things, found other people to center my life around."

"I thought we were talking about a place not a person."

"Well we need to people the stage of our dreams with a cast don't we?"

A pause ensued and the sound of the waterfall became salient in the room.

"A woman?"

"Yes. Her name doesn't matter. Maybe she could have been anybody who came into my life at just that particular time, when she was needed. She embodied then for me … oh I don't know, the sheer possibility of regaining lost time, of doing it right this time, redemption. I thought I could spare her at least the price exacted by my own delay in discovering what is of value in life."

"Like that huh," the psychologist suggested noncommittally.

"Isn't it always like that?" asked the client.

"Not always but more often than you may think; it's an old story but not a universal one."

"I saw her against the wonderful background that the ocean provided. I guess that I thought that between the two of us we could stand against the leeching force of time itself, make death stand still in sheer awe of what we could be to each other and for each other. Isn't that what immortality means, at least in a Pagan sense?"

Pause.

"As I said an old story."

"But unfortunately a very long story, too long; I couldn't realize that just like the land that I loved so much that was sliding irrevocably into the sea she was sliding deeper into the abysses of addiction year by year. I couldn't bring her into my world. Instead, each year took me deeper into whatever new cycle of incessant misery was on order for that year. The turning that I kept hoping for never came. Would it sound strange if I said that she possessed a genius for degradation? After awhile I forgot what freshness and joy could mean.   There was only relief when she would cycle to the surface to catch a few breaths before diving again into the dark waters. Still, I couldn't manage the obvious and simply walk away. You might say it was all misplaced loyalty or an unwillingness to read signs and take them at face value, but I think the real problem for me in regard to her was that I had a template for happiness that simply had no basis in her version of reality … or unreality."

"Well addressing recovery is what I am in business for."

The client smiled, "Yes, I guess that's true. But why do we hang on so hard to precisely what we should have known early on was hopeless?"

"It must have seemed worth it at the time or you wouldn't have done it."

"But I could have done differently isn't that it?"

"But you didn't. So what are you going to do now?"

"I don't know. I lost myself somewhere in those years or at least the momentum of living. It's like venturing out on a cliff-face handhold by handhold and suddenly finding that you can't go higher and retreat is impossible. In relationships like that an interchange of genes or DNA takes place so that the damage done to both of us may be irretrievable. Neither could give the other enough of the other's survival traits to create a whole life."

"Why do you call it irretrievable?"

"Because it's too late for another shot at making it right for whomever I was then."

"You talk about yourself in the third person. So you want to go back in time; pull the relational equivalent of the land back out of the sea?"

"I guess I do."

"And what would that accomplish."

"I wouldn't have made such a big mistake and such a stupid one at that."

"Who's keeping the record?"

The client paused to consider.

"I wanted a life you know with no sidetracks, no wasted days, no…"

"Learning and regrets? Who ever told you that life could ever be like that… or history either for that matter? With every added level of complexity the possibilities of catastrophic breakdown increase exponentially. Or maybe you just wanted a dull life after all, one that could pass any test that an outside observer might impose."

"Hardly that! I wanted to sample every level of existence; even to walk on the wild side as long as I could avoid consequences and maintain my innocence."

"It sounds a little like Oscar Wilde's novel, *Portrait of Dorian*

Grey. Maybe you got off cheaply after all. She lived the dysfunction and you got to watch her downward spiral and be the redeemer. It plays right into everyone's hope for bargain-basement omnipotence. I see it manifested here all the time in my practice."

"But what did she want?"

"She isn't my client so does it matter? We're working on you."

"But this whole thing just throws me back into the street waiting for someone new to walk by."

"I can see that you haven't let go of the old set of presuppositions that set you up for precisely that type of relationship. You don't think that your experiences can be real until they are filtered through the medium of somebody else. It is like one of those plants that cannot create its own chlorophyll so it must depend upon another plant to feed it. The whole process is derivative – each trying to engineer the other person to a version of the perfect host organism. Until you alter your agenda; you will only repeat it by finding someone just like her."

"So I am doomed?"

"Only if you go back to an inadequate template for your life…"

"I don't know any other way to be!"

"I thought that you were the one with a God-like plan for everything and everybody."

"Only after I get my teeth into something; before that there is only this great emptiness."

"Maybe that's what the two of you shared: the inability to simply be without any need for an outside reflector to tell you that you existed. It takes responsibility to take up life and to accept consequences even if they are beyond the zone of our predictability and control."

"That's depressing."

"You always want to read life's menu before ordering? It isn't depressing; it's only a little scary and at times unpleasant. It's up to you if you want to get depressed about it."

The client considered this.

"So what would life be like without a template? How can you know whether you are on course to achieving appropriate goals?"

"Isn't that what learning means—to resolve uncertainty by encountering new data? It sounds to me like you think of life as a play where you as the playwright can sit in the wings while others and a projected version of your ideal self act out the lines of an already written script—or worse life as an endless series of rehearsals that never comes to the opening night. There is no risk in that."

"But if I only get one life then it has to be perfect the first and only time around."

"Do you have any examples of such a life?"

The client smiled. "How did you know that I like biographies?"

"Why do you like them?"

"They are mines for raw material."

"So you can step somehow into their shoes rather than your own?"

"Well, I don't want to miss anything."

The psychologist shook his head. "It sounds very tiring keeping to someone else's itinerary. Would it be so hard to simply make a choice no matter how trivial and then just take what comes?"

"No if it was only a matter of a single choice but it is the pattern of successive events that I am seeking and that pattern must have a beginning somewhere so the first choice suddenly becomes simply part of an irrevocable change, a chain of infinite linkages, and I am paralyzed."

"Do you approach your writing in the same manner?"

"No."

"How is it different?"

"Well, since the advent of computers revision is an easy process—I just write."

The psychologist looked at the writer with unusual emphasis as he asked, "How is living different then from writing?"

The client considered, "Costs."

"What costs?"

"Well in life there is engagement, the world around us changes according to our choices and is not immediately subject to being put back into its original order."

"Have you ever heard of forgiveness?"

"Of course but there is always the residuum isn't there; God forgives but the damage remains. Our imperfect world even leaks its way into eternity and demands that somehow we make it right – the doctrine of purgatory."

"Do you understand Purgatory?"

"Yes, it's like hell only temporary."

"Sounds like bad theology to me."

"Well how do you see it, presuming that you believe in Purgatory?"

"Well to begin with as I see it Purgatory is more like heaven than hell because you know that paradise awaits you. Also, the correction of damages may be more beyond the control of the agent than you suppose; after all he or she is dead."

"Then who fixes things?"

"Maybe no one does. Maybe Purgatory is the final acceptance that we cannot be like God knowing good and evil. Our grasp of things is always partial, tentative, subject to correction. We are not able to freeze even salvation into a permanent form, some *quid pro quo* where God owes us salvation. Isn't that the ultimate presumption and impiety to think that we can control God, to somehow hold Him bound to a contract?"

"I never thought of it like that."

"Few people do. It would mean that religion above all else should remind us of our humanity and not of our efforts at self-deification."

"So you are telling me that I'm trying to be God."

"You are, at least insofar as your own life is concerned. When you realize that you can't have everything your own way without the chance of making mistakes you freeze or worse you try and adjust life

146

to some ridiculous pre-existing idea of how everything should turn out.”

“Isn’t that what Nietzsche meant when he reduced everything to the will to power?”

The psychologist smiled, “And it drove him mad. He ended up frozen into the awareness that the instinct of compassion was still alive in him. He would never be a superman … and neither can you.”

The room was silent and the sound of the waterfall continued patiently and without ceasing.

The client spoke up at last. “Alright, so what do you recommend?”

“You mean take two aspirin and call me in the morning?”

The client smiled. “Yeah.”

“Why don’t you write a story about your experiences down there on the coast and how it relates to some of the other of your discontents that we have been discussing during your sessions with me and we’ll take a look at your composition together next time?”

“Alright; any length requirements…?”

“It isn’t an assignment; it’s a suggestion. The rest is up to you. I won’t be grading it. Next week then…”

“Right.”

The client turned again before leaving.

“Oh one more thing though…”

The psychologist looked up.

“Yes?”

“I’m still not that happy about all of this, this whole therapy process.”

“Well, take two aspirins and…”

The client interrupted smiling, “Call me in the morning.”

“No, just show up next week and give yourself a break once in awhile. Just live.”

Coastal Credo

I discovered the Oregon coastal towns early in my life. I would have discovered them earlier still had prudence not opposed my will, when I proposed to my father a plan to follow Highway One to California on my little burgundy-red one-cylinder Honda 90 Scrambler. The fact that it could reach a speed of sixty miles per hour on level ground and with a tail wind did not augur well for any sort of highway travel. My proposed adventure was met with an immediate veto as manifesting the same optimistic frame of mind and impulsive desire as when I proposed to raise a pet alligator in the shower stall that no one ever used of our home's auxiliary bathroom.

For me the impressive idea always came first and thereafter one naturally used the means at hand. I managed to preserve well into adulthood a sense that fantasy could not only infuse reality it might actually be found there just waiting to be discovered. I had little conception of the dull struggle for existence that pervades most coastal communities as logging and fishing waned leaving only tourism and retirement as bases to support the economy. For me there was only the majestic presence of the sea and a dim apprehension that a pirate galleon under full sail might at any moment round the rocky headlands to seek shelter in one of the bays that provide illusory shelter due to the presence of treacherous reefs.

I was raised in a benign and complacent era when good and evil seemed equally matched in a bi-polar, Cold War obsessed world. It was a world in which men like Simon Templar, also known as The Saint, could work their magic of detection and justified violence against villains without the more realistic limitations that beset the hard-drinking detectives of the 1930's like Sam Spade or Philip Marlowe whose exploits were honored with little more than effort, neglect, and at most an uncrowned moral victory. In those early days before the tide of fantasy had waned I wanted to write mystery stories.

In the golden age of Agatha Christie, Mary Roberts Rinehart, and Mignon Eberhart, all women writers, and of Ian Fleming, Earl Stanley Gardner, Rex Stout, and Mickey Spillane the male writers, the world was peopled by spies, smugglers, and an illustrious international set of seductresses. All of this was bound to keep the hearts of readers beating as they served to bridge the gap between childhood and the pubescent dreams of adolescent romance. But perhaps the writer I most admired was Daphne Du Maurier whose masterpiece *Rebecca* revolved around Max De Winter and his hereditary manor house, Manderley. Coincident with this was the television series called *Dark Shadows* with the great estate of Collinwood, haunted by ghosts and the remnants of ancient loves. It was these that set the parameters of my quest for the perfect coastline where I could set up shop and quietly become rich and legendary. I saw myself walking the sea cliffs in a heavy fog drawing inspiration from mysterious vessels hovering just beyond the moaning channel markers manned by a crew of indeterminate but desperate nationalities and determined to deliver a cargo of raw opium or enriched uranium to various criminal masterminded societies whose cunning operatives were waiting to arrange a rendezvous. Even into my late twenties I had not surrendered these visionary versions of my life that supplanted sensible career planning; so when I drove up from California one November day to begin graduate school in Washington and spied Whale Cove just south of Depoe Bay I thought I had found at last the site of my retreat from the boring world and the base for my future literary eminence.

As a gesture to realism and a possible academic career (just in case) I set aside my immediate impulses to embrace years of study allowing texts to speak for themselves stripped of any semblance of authorial intent or idiosyncratic readings tracing the impact of various personal signifiers when filtered through a post-Marxist sensibility. I had already seen industrial America up-close and personally and vowed that this experience was to be my only concession to necessity in a life of sustained rebelliousness. At best it might provide a resource to add a seamy texture to some future narrative that would touch in passing the squalor of rust-belt America, the legacy of the cost of our collective involvement in the endless struggles between the various European empires for relative dominance, and a warning to America to return to a comfortable isolationism.

It is hard to say when life ceases to be an adventure like the one that painted my early dreams with romance, when magic finally resolves itself into a sober and severe appreciation of the nature of life and its struggles, but my attendance in law school might have had something to do with it. The legal mind is gradually attuned to the vast amount of human preconceptions and ideas that are simply legally irrelevant. This breeds a certain cold-blooded attitude if it is not counteracted by a stern prior grounding in the humanities. It is these literary studies that explore the tension between human aspirations and the workings of what the Greeks called fate or fatality.

The world of the 21st century is an engineered age. We have come to believe that technology can answer most problems and that information and the flood of data will fill in the insuperable gap between our limits as human beings and the worlds of quantum physics and fields that provide the stage for all human actions. What cannot be coded and reduced to software is held to be immediately suspect in such a world. It is a world where the old conflict between story and fate has been superseded by mere narratives that may be further subdivided into atomistic signifiers assembled into chains.

All of the above is a mere prelude to the real subject of this ... well call it a reflection on the position of the author as he approaches his senior years. (I will not say retirement years because few authors ever retire. The flow of ink becomes a habit). My early experience of the Oregon Coast was an interwoven one: a blend of July sunlight, salt and sand, and my body still bursting with that nuclear life-force that we imagine will endure unaltered as the years progress. I felt its power when body-surfing in the chill waves, that the great Pacific and I were equally matched. Yet for all of that there was a sense that the sheer multiplicity of possibilities before me entailed their own sorrow.

Already you see I was facing the peculiar way that a thread of fatality becomes gradually interwoven with our lives until the garment it weaves takes definite shape and acquires the stiffness of form that finally leaves us with a sense that we have lived the majority of our days and nights without reaching any of the definitive resolutions that we once imagined that we alone could provide to the eternal dilemmas of existence. Of course I may be presuming too much when I say, "we." No doubt many people assume a place in life that is defined by a context of limited economic and cultural options but as a child of the sixties who believed that I was part of a generation with a new explanation, anything seemed possible to me then.

Americans have always been arrogant and optimistic while at the same time haunted by a sense that in the last analysis we are intruders bearing a burden of guilt for the atrocities committed by the previous generation of dreamers. I suppose that the real burden carried by the recent rhetoric of "Make America Great Again" is a desire to restore the lost virginity of the land so that we can rape it all over again, the search for clean coal as a modern day version of the search for the Holy Grail. My own sympathies have always been with the writers of what might be called the American Gothic sensibility, writers like Nathaniel Hawthorne, William Faulkner, and Edgar Allen Poe. Writers like Edmund White and Andrew Holleran have explored our national epic of paradise lost after the brief effulgence of 70's gay America. Perhaps that was when the tipping point occurred, before the election of Ronald Reagan condemned America to making the rich richer and to exalting a new Puritanism as the remedy for the excesses of that age of reform and revolution that still has my personal allegiance.

It was an allegiance refined by early disillusion and rebellion. In my youth I had a tendency to only grow indignant after the fact, when my first instinct towards escapism had failed me. I expected things to be easier than they were turning out to be. I was spared the trauma of personal involvement in the fighting in Viet Nam but fell into the same national trough of disillusionment post-Watergate. My early forays into a definitive career were met with disappointment. I took as a remedy that traditional anodyne of becoming an expatriate on a bargain budget. I left a job in rust-belt America and fled to Paris and beyond anticipating garrets, café culture, and discussions about the future of a post-colonial world. The decision to travel abroad seemed quite heroic even if not as unique as I supposed it to be.

When I returned from studying in Europe I was determined to become a writer so I proceeded to steep myself in our American prophetic authors, men like Walt Whitman and Henry David Thoreau, while imbibing yellow Chartreuse while I read, a decadent recipe for instant advancement into the ranks of the immortals. I hoped to make it easier for my future biographers by living my life in discrete periods each punctuated by a signature stylistic development and passionate commitment to inappropriate but promising attachments.

I discovered no unique vices, was sheltered by a providential sense of caution, and managed to skim along the ridge of the various disasters that have weeded out so many creative spirits over the course of my life. The end result is that I am still here to reflect upon the interplay between story and fate that so perplexed the Emperor Marcus Aurelius in his meditations. Perhaps his primary insight was that fate is governed by the whole as opposed to the particular so that even an emperor could not expect to be held immune from the trials of fortune that often seem so disproportionate when viewed from the point of view of suffering individuals. He considered it the height of impiety to ask that the universe adapt itself to our needs and desires rather than the other way around. The task of the man of wisdom is to adjust his expectations to results in the vast web of cause and effect that surrounds us. To do this of course works a termination or at least a severe corrective to most human meta-narratives, to all of the vast projects and projected dreams on which we repose our hopes for a fortunate set of outcomes to our actions from the major to the trivial.

American idealism of course finds such a limiting proposal to be anathema to its national creed. What are we if we cannot dictate events? This is not held to be special-pleading; it is our richly deserved destiny. But so deeply rooted is this ethos and perception that it has become the underlying theme of the present hour in its most extreme form, determining national policy and domestic economics. Many people already sense that we are hovering at the fulcrum-point between two historical eras. The magnitude of the incipient changes has forever altered the balance between story and fate among us. Our ability to dictate the text is restricted by the fields that must be filled in before the document may be forwarded to whatever central processing unit is recording the perhaps inconsequential history of the human experiment. It is precisely at such a time that the past is to be consulted it seems to me.

So by this circuitous introductory route we return to the Oregon Coast where my spirit has of old found that sustenance that makes life possible. Nothing so reminds us of the brevity of our days than the all-witnessing, all-embracing tumult of these immense waters. Sameness and succession—can any two words better express the course of our lives as individuals? Uniqueness combined with mortality—therein is the source of all tragedy. It takes a mind like that of Marcus Aurelius to take the oceanic view of insentient futurity and to make it his own—to the rest of us it is precisely the local, the particular, the things that we love that must somehow survive the welter of events, the accidents, the deep currents of the irrevocable. So when I grow weary of the sea with its play of light and shadow, its winds, fogs, and squalls I seek out the wisdom of the ages in the many bookstores that act as a sponge to absorb coastal visitors when the insouciant and constant interplay of water and atmosphere bring rain, wind, or fog to the coastal environs.

The siren call of used bookstores is universal at least among that sector of humanity that is willing to court solitude as the price of deeper colloquy with the written word and those generous minds that are willing to sacrifice a portion of irreplaceable time to communicate across an abyss of anonymity with unspecified strangers. It is no small part of community to create these spaces where fortuitous meetings are made with antiquity. The best evidence of tangential immortality is provided by the written word. I for one feel the same sense of intimacy with many long-dead authors as for people whose time I share but whose minds are more elusive despite our propinquity.

It is said that every city contains a million stories, most of them unnoticed and hence untold. All of them share the interplay between desire and outcome, expectation and result. When the law of disproportion favors us it is called good luck or fortune; when the disproportion emerges like a great sea monster to devour us and to maim us forever it is called a tragedy. Between these two there is only the dull passage of linear time, the quiet meeting of presupposition and outcome that we call ordinary life. We depend upon routine and a blanket of supportive relationships to act as twin custodians; yet we sometimes contemplate trading boredom and obscurity for exposure and renown the two biggest enemies of the private life. Limited individuality is the progenitor of story as opposed to history which traces only the great abiding current of events. This foments the illusion that storytelling is trivial precisely because it is not general or immediately replicable as science-mindedness demands that it should be to qualify as data to feed the hungry gigabyte maw of the information superhighway.

Of what use is it to meander as I do down the country lanes of coastal villages or to look back upon eras that are already being washed away by sand and surf into yellow-paged oblivion? Yet still we write. We join the silent denizens who have left only this medium behind as witness to their passing perceptions and reflections, deficient in graphics, irreducible to design and governance, demanding of attention that would otherwise be drawn into countless multi-tasking inventories that keep feeding the great totality of the theoretically accessible but inconsequent sloshing-about of the tub of raw data devoid of organizing principle and final utility to us as human beings. So in its place we alter not our narratives but ourselves as constituent parts of whatever the abiding technology demands of us.

This is the background, the setting, and even the thematic undertone that drones through our days and nights like a wailing foghorn; this is the thing that reduces us to cells and corpuscles, mere sea anemones clinging to rocks waving our fragile tentacles about for whatever might come our way to nourish our fragile selves.

As a writer I am absorbed and enmeshed in the ecosystem of fates and of personalities that surround me, the antidote to the fatal introspection of youth that because it fears that no one can ever really care fears to reveal itself fully, to transform confessional into tale. As a writer I feel a sense of story in the ebb and flow of the human tides about me, each as individual, each as hopeful as I am that it all has been worth it, that my life matters, and that wisdom differs in some essential way from the noise of the political hour. I hope for more for Americans even as the MAGA-Hat wearing throng cheers for embodied banality in the incarnation of the great hamburger-glutted attention glutton who migrates between his golf course in Florida and his television tuned to FOX News in Washington. The wreckage left behind gluts the American mind in an unprecedented way and makes books suddenly seem to be irrelevant counter-cultural artifacts. Why add to the supply of dinosaur bones of the already expressed when only such clinging store front repositories as are found scattered in abundance on the coast preserve what the publishing warehouses have already long since remaindered? Shouldn't all utterances be only momentary effusions, blogs and broadcasts, meetings over coffee and gossip?

The sea breaks and I know the answer. This impulse to select and to refine is as constant within me as these waves. Recognition will always lead the avid seeker to harbor in these labyrinths of authors describing and interfacing with other times and places finding there the still and solemn pulse-beat of the eternally human spirit that unites us all and bridges the gaps of age and sex and nation. I in turn will leave the sea of tranquility of the desiccated moonscape of this present hour of our tormented history hoping for something better, knowing that the value of ideas only emerges when thinking itself falls into shadow as in the innumerable dark ages of humanity that have come and gone before us.

Perhaps we took progress too much for granted in the days of my youth so that this present penitential era was foredoomed. Attentive observers might have remarked more on the general drift towards self-interest and materialism long before various algorithms doomed us to sordid repetitions of yesterday's atrocities: new tears for old stories, another shooting, another hate rally to stoke our fears, another evisceration of the fabric of our collective lives. Fate only becomes story when story ceases and response becomes pointless because the market has already discounted the response in all of its possible permutations before it happens. Out of this realization grows resistance opposing wind and wave by the transient but undeniable fact of our own existence. This is the remnant of the confidence that was once in my youthful arrogance presumed to be a permanent possession rather than lent to me for an indeterminate span of days and nights while all along the fabled coast of cape and estuary the great Pacific quietly whispered its name.

In precisely this way we come from the realm of past convictions and present concerns to the present minute of undigested life. A single kite flies over the beach. The morning clouds have fortuitously cleared away; an empty Tudor-Style and steep-roofed store front across the cobbled way still beckons for a tenant. A swift dust-devil just gathered its burden of dried soil in the unpaved parking lot. Couples are passing or coming in for a swift coffee or sandwich. An unclaimed guitar leans against the window. The afternoon ebbs and the light on the sea changes, grows more slate blue and silver as the emerald green of morning has waned away while I write. The swift haiku of impressions melts and improvises. Is it story or is it fate that I have endured so many times and places to write these words this day? Where is the floor of my being on which all impressions are grounded? Is my skull a shell where a little grey creature lives? What will become of me when it is ground to gravel and sand and washes away? Yet who can deny the prescience of the moment when I may decide to strike the next keystroke or indulge in the cup at my side with its coating of cream and mocha, long since a victim of my ardor and subject to my neglect?

What have become of my usual haunts and the people who once gave texture and substance to my life at home? Where is my home, this thing that I am always leaving behind and then perpetually trying to regain? The insight, the conclusion, the reduction to formula, they are as always elusive. Has my cranial balance sheet gone up or down in this particular trading session of inquiry with my own mind?

I look up to decide and suddenly I realize the full impact and color of the ocean as though I had never seen it before, realize its absolute beauty. I think of those who I did not know how to love. The crowd passes me, each retaining their secrets and the sea is as ever breaking along the coast. The lighthouse out on the end of Yaquina Point is blinking, warning the night-bound vessels to maintain their seaway and steerage room until the fog clears. The day dawns and they can then proceed safely onwards to harbor while I, guided by only a dim and flickering inner light, must seek again the open sea.

American Elegy

braham Cardozo had a problem. Since his graduation from law school four years ago everything in America had seemed to go into freefall. Everywhere there was contention and an abiding nastiness broadcast at full volume from the various absolutist discourses and narratives, each contending for supremacy. Some of these claims were religious in nature, others political, and others still simply the fracas bred of contending egos seeking attention on social media.

"I am living in the age of the *prima donna*," Abraham said to himself in the course of the inner narrative that each of us possesses as we try and make some sense of the world and fill our fleeting hours with at least some measure of stability and satisfaction. Abraham's mind was disturbed by events. Everything had become so strident, rising in pitch and volume to a sustained squeal like the sound of microphone feedback at a rock concert. Among other items of note it was the fiftieth anniversary of the Stonewall Inn Riot that by 2019 had become the LGBT equivalent of the shots that rang out between British and American troops at Concord Bridge in 1776. Rainbow Flags were expected to be flown everywhere in celebration of the event and of the full emergence of LGBT rights on the world stage from sleepy villages in Botswana to Greenwich Village in New York where it all seemed to have begun one summer night.

Meanwhile in the world of beleaguered heterosexuals various petitions were circulating to keep drag queens out of libraries where they had lately been introduced as purveyors of a so-called story hour, just one more instance of the nefarious effort to normalize the unspeakable among the young in the view of various religious groups. Disorder was everywhere. Across the vast Pacific Ocean an American and a Russian ship had barely avoided a collision in the South China Sea. The food situation in North Korea was growing more threatening each day due to poor harvests and the sanctions that remained in place even after the "lover's meetings" between Donald Trump and Kim Jung Un. In Europe Brexit looked inevitable and it seemed quite possible that noble England might be heading for a reprise of the post World War II style rationing if its economy should collapse. Below the border, Mexico had avoided tariffs for now by agreeing to act as a more efficient buffer between the fleeing hordes of refugees from Honduras and Guatemala and the safe harbor of America. At the bottom of the world in Antarctica great ice shelves were calving daily into the southern seas off Patagonia. The yearly forest fires had already started in California. In the internecine conflicts between liberals and conservatives within the Catholic Church a statement had been issued by some Bishops in Kazakhstan to remind the diminishing number of church-going Catholics, let alone the remarried and sexually rebellious, to toe the line or risk the consequences. Rain was still causing flooding in the American mid-west and south. Only Vice-President Mike Pence seemed at ease as he looked up with hound-dog-like devotion to the all-wise Commander-in-Chief (and a hell of a golfer) Donald Trump.

Things were being shaken up everywhere it seemed. Everybody was yelling at everybody and Abraham Cardozo, product of reason and tolerance, felt compelled at last to intervene. Abraham Cardozo put on his glasses to read over the text of what he hoped would be of some use in the political struggles of the present hour. A little effort on his part he felt, a little cool judicial reasoning and all could be put right. What was called for at this critical hour was an *amicus brief* to unmask the catastrophic trend of the Trump agenda of spurious populism masking corporate rule.

Abraham, as we will familiarly refer to him rather than by the august name of Cardozo (no actual blood relation to the famous jurist) like many Americans of this particular time and place was suffering from the confusion bred from the daily deluge of events. Each new day brought its own spate of revelations, assessments and counter-assessments in the endless factional currents and entrenched interests of America. Like many of his generation he had been accustomed to the concept of on demand services and the ability to remove the unpleasant and the intolerable by simply hitting the delete button on whatever device was handy. Reality might be virtual or actual depending upon one's underlying view of metaphysics, but in any case it should be subject to framing and manipulation. If Abraham had learned anything in law school it was to present the facts, whatever they might be, encased in an overall narrative that would lead a jury to adopt the client's point of view. Facts were flexible like the space-time continuum; they merely provided the field that could, if skillfully presented, lead to a favorable verdict. As in the reaction to the New Criticism by the post-modernists, it was all a matter of point of view. No text could be expected to speak for itself under changing conditions. The young attorney almost feared to read what he had just composed though because he was aware of the utter transiency of all narratives and the lack of a common point of reference for meaning and relevance.

The provisional text of his manuscript read as follows:

No narrative can hope to exist in utter isolation from a receptive community that can at once be its audience and the source of its relative value assessment among similar discourses. This is the first step along the journey towards general acceptance as truth. As discourses have increased in number and variety the communities that can receive them have similarly fragmented so that a general sense of meaning is absent.

As an example of this truth, Thomas Wolfe, the great American novelist, is famous for saying that you can't go home again. This phrase has always had for me a certain nostalgic ring because it implied that one was caught in the dilemma of desiring to return to a predictable and unified world but were doomed to rejection and misunderstanding, as though exile contained within itself a just punishment for ever having left home in the first place: abandon us and we will abandon you. As the years have passed however I have come to see things differently. Thomas Wolfe was simply making a statement of fact: the reason that we cannot go home again is that home no longer exists as it has been preserved in our memory after long absence. The accuracy of memory is such that it preserves images and structures in all of their former integrity long after those structures may have altered or ceased to exist. We assume a set of relations in space and time to endure so that although *we* may have changed *they* remain locked and frozen, just waiting for us to take them up again.

We even go so far as to apply this standard to people and to resent the temerity of their daring to grow and to change even as we have. We thought to return from a long expedition, laden down with dromedaries of wisdom, riches, experience, and in possession of triumph while they, poor things, could only stand looking outwards into the barren distance awaiting our return. After all, we Americans judge progress always in a comparative sense: there is no such thing as prosperity until it can be held up against a standard of deprivation and penury. This is why Americans are so jealous and afraid that those just below them will move marginally up the ladder of social or economic status. Meanwhile we grant *carte blanch* privileges to the upper classes to pursue their lives of indulgence without fear or even the burden of our resentment at their good fortune. We may even derive a certain degree of reflected glory from our native aristocrats so that when Donald Trump refers to other nations as "Shit-hole countries" rather than as "developing nations" his avid followers can congratulate themselves and agree, *"They shore as hell are!"*

In the year of 2019 then when everything remains suspended and the great and hoped-for deliverance of 2020 (when pray God we will see clearer and return our nation to some measure of sanity) it is becoming ever clearer that we can't go home again. Integrity is that quality that bestows identity and we have pawned it for a short pay-day loan. Imagine if you will if the various qualities and characteristics of a substance should become suddenly lacking in that adhesiveness that creates order and security. This adhesiveness goes by various names but in law it is called precedent and the stricture of tradition that precedent imposes is called *stare decisis.* It is not that the past is always wiser than the present; the rule is imposed for another purpose entirely. The conservation of precedents creates what may be called the body of the law. Theoretical structures such as contract and tort are elaborately balanced and highly evolved relationships of multiple factors just as living organisms are. Precedents are the genetic mutations that when selected and preserved over time finally evolve into the extended predicates of the law. So it is that when mere political rhetoric is willing to cast this bastion of order aside in order to secure short-term gains it is a warning that civilization is tottering and the eyes of hungry beasts in the outer darkness begin to glitter.

It is not the advent of Donald Trump that is so appalling, America has known the temporary triumph of vulgar opportunists before this; the thing that terrifies me is the readiness with which approximately one-third of our fellow citizens are prepared to surrender everything upon which democracy is based simply to get their long-deferred wish-list met. It shows that a significant number of Americans have no idea of what such cherished terms as due process and basic honesty mean. This is why each new fantastic claim or instance of personal abuse to his enemies or former enablers is becoming less shocking over time as the President proceeds in his one-of-a-kind Presidency. Each impact further dulls our sense of propriety and decency so that the public sphere now smells like the abandoned stall of a fishmonger. It is all so familiar to anyone who has ever studied the gradual consolidation of power under Adolf Hitler. I keep waiting for Nancy Pelosi to appear, tear-stained on the evening news, as she looks up at the smoking ruin of the Capitol Building. So it isn't that we cannot go home again: the problem is that our home has been disintegrating before us every day since 2016…

With the prospect of his annual visit to the Oregon coast for his vacation in the offing Abraham decided before he left Seattle to put the matter of his proposed literary intervention before his old con/law instructor for a provisional opinion. He waited for an answer while Professor Manuel Cortez, law professor and aficionado of liberation theology, sat back and considered the matter after reading the rough draft.

"Well, that's all that I have so far. What do you think of the general tone?" Abraham queried hopefully, the general sense of awe that former students have for various favorite instructors remained with him still.

"It won't make law review material, but perhaps an op-ed piece."

"I didn't think it sounded like a note for law review; too general and too contemporaneously relevant for that. A public policy review perhaps?"

Professor Cortez considered the suggestion.

"No, not even there, I don't believe. I'm not sure that such a thing exists anymore anyway, commonly rooted public policy I mean. Have you thought of an archeology journal? We may just get the Trump wall after all along our southern border out of all this. It will be a great tourist attraction one hundred years from now, a symbol of our national ethos in decline."

Abraham smiled, "You are being facetious. You think I'm too earnest in writing a piece like this."

"No, I think you are saying what most people think already, but it's too late. Can you see that? You are making a general appeal after the filing date has passed. This whole Donald Trump phenomenon was already foreseeable thirty years ago when education began to break down in this country, maybe even earlier than that. I saw it coming as early as the Bork nomination and the eventual arrival of the Rehnquist Court. Do you remember your Constitutional Law course with me when I pointed out that it all came down to an act of faith. Law is a religion. As soon as the outcome becomes more important than legal due process the whole thing becomes meaningless. It is the unwritten covenant of judicial probity in reasoning that is our only guarantee that civilization will prevail. Law school isn't a trade school; it's a novitiate in the order of a religion called jurisprudence. The students who realize this don't make the most money, but they keep the whole thing alive. You were one of the ones who I thought might keep the old faith going for one more round at least."

Abraham smiled. "I had a head start. Talmud study you know."

The Professor smiled.

"Me too, ever read Canon Law? The Roman Church finds its ultimate principle of order in God, but for the day-to-day work there is always Canon Law to keep the heretics at bay. We both have a healthy respect for the transcendent in our religious traditions but we know that in its pure form only the mystics try and deal with the transcendent dimension directly. For the rest of us there is only the comfort provided by doctrine and by law. When you break the laws you plead guilty and hope for a reduced sentence on the other side. We call it Confession."

"So you think that religion is comparable to the criminal law?" Abraham asked.

"It started there, remember the forbidden fruit? Of course that presumes a historical reading of the text of Genesis."

"Is there another way to read it?"

The Professor considered the question before explaining.

"What if you read the text like an example of the Wisdom Literature, more like the Book of Job or Proverbs? What if you look at it like a novel by Franz Kafka describing the human predicament and the dangers of premature acquaintance with moral questions that we haven't the strength to confront or to surmount? By reading the creation account in Genesis as an historical text all sorts of problems emerge that are otherwise avoidable. Christian history is awash in the consequences of what may have been an initial misreading by assigning the text to an inappropriate genre and distorting authorial intent in the process. I'm not saying I am right, mind you, but if the study of law teaches us one key skill it is to dispute established precedents."

"I thought lawyers were the bulwark of established interests," Abraham commented dryly.

"Only Republican lawyers," answered Professor Cortez archly.

Abraham Cardozo reflected.

"Then Donald Trump is not a revolutionary populist after all."

Professor Cortez sat back in his chair and placed his finger tips together as of old. He proceeded at last as he had once done in the classroom.

"Trumpism … and I speak of it as an institution rather than as the individual political program of one man (it is more like an opportunistic infection) is a strategy rather than a movement. Its guiding principle is to win power and to retain it for as long as possible. I watched in the primaries as the various Republican contenders for the Presidential nomination in 2016 fell by the wayside like so many straw men and suddenly it dawned on me that they had misunderstood both the temper of the times and what the Presidency as an institution has become for all of us. You see Abraham we don't elect Presidents on the basis of qualifications and intelligence any more but on their ability to confirm our prejudices, to flatter our dreams, and to alleviate our anxieties. Donald Trump realized long ago as a speculator that from the perspective of the buyer symbols are more important than substance. What is the whole Trump Empire but an example of leveraged illusions? It's all about branding. Donald Trump may be the first President who considers living in the

Whitehouse to be slumming. That's why he is always off to Mar-a-Lago. By the way, the name means: "sea to lake." The resort forms a bridge between the sea and the Intracoastal Waterway. In the same manner Trumpism bridges traditional conservatism with the illusion of a populist revolution from below. You get the best of both worlds. You can be a stodgy, fundamentalist, climate-change denying, rapture-awaiting, religious conservative and you can be a rich Plutocrat ready to dump the last shovel-full of earth onto the grave of the American middle-class. You can be an out and out bigot ready to scare black folk back to carefully policed ghettos. You can be a woman who thinks that ill-mannered and dominant men are a turn-on. You can in fact be anyone who wants to clock-in on a vicarious win to keep from the dawning suspicion that indebted America could collapse at any moment and follow the British Empire into the annals of past glory. You can be any of these and Donald Trump is your man. In politics rhetoric is everything; it even trumps truth."

"And the other candidates didn't realize this?" Abraham inquired.

Professor Cortez laughed.

"They thought they were competing for a job interview. They showed up with lengthy resumes and lots of earnestness and Trump made mincemeat out of them because only he realized that Presidential elections are a game-show. When the voter steps behind the curtain, he hopes that the box that he chooses will contain a new car and not a hundred cans of minced squid."

Abraham considered. "What about impeachment?"

"That might seem the best course constitutionally speaking, but only if you want another four years of Trump."

"I don't understand," Abraham looked puzzled.

"Really, what have we just been talking about? Trump is a master of leveraging. By handing him an impeachment that will not be confirmed in the Senate the House of Representatives would be giving him the one boost that he needs to come back as a winner in "season two." I am sure that Nancy Pelosi, smart lady that she is, knows this. Her task is to let the horses rear but keep them attached to the chariot. Once impeachment breaks loose Trump wins and he knows it; he even invites it. The one thing that the great egoist can't stand is sustained suspicion. It's like swamp-gas percolating up from the ground on the fairway of a golf course, not fatal but annoying, and Donald Trump is not accustomed to being annoyed. He wants a quick victory not a sustained campaign because in a sustained campaign actual results matter. What has he to show for the first years of his Presidency?"

The Professor continued, counting his points off on his fingers.

"No wall built, no new health care plan, a tax deal that has added over two trillion dollars to the national debt, a runaway stock-market just begging for a correction, a series of trade-wars that are bankrupting farmers, a love-affair with the fat-kid ruling North Korea who is running out of patience while his people starve under sanctions, and a lot of alienated allies from Japan to England. All Trump has to run on is his assumed victimhood and all the Progressive Wing of the Democratic Party wants to do is to hand that cherished status back to him on a silver platter by impeaching him when he only has one effective year to go in his ill-advised Presidency. Believe me Abraham, the calliope of the whole Trump circus is running out of steam: the rhetoric is getting threadbare, the promises are unfulfilled, and people are tired of his jejune name-calling. The whole thing is just one more mortgage loan on Debtor America. The real answer is to give the man free rein and wait it out. The one person who can defeat Donald Trump is Donald Trump. Otherwise…"

"Otherwise?" Abraham asked.

Professor Cortez shrugged his shoulders.

"Well think about moving to Denmark or New Zealand."

This was the context of the reflections that pursued Abraham Cardozo as he headed out to the Oregon coast for his annual recuperation from his fourth year of practicing law in a small eight-person Admiralty firm. He had drifted towards Admiralty Law because it allowed him to place daguerreotypes of Clipper Ships on his office wall and to practice in Federal Court rather than in the squalid state courts so often reminiscent of the world of Charles Dickens' fog-shrouded London with prisoners in orange suits being arraigned and quarreling couples fighting over their children. It was comforting to apply law to stately collisions between vessels and personal injury claims under the Jones Act. But he was tired, chronically tired as most attorneys are, and it was always a joy to slip the traces, to pass his caseload on to another lawyer, and to seek the open sea again.

There are many routes out to the Oregon Coast but Abraham preferred the slow road down from Aberdeen to the Columbia River and across the bridge to Astoria. On trips like this Abraham was accustomed to undertaking that most neglected of pastimes, introspection and retrospection; the search for what Thomas Wolfe had called "the last lane-end into heaven." The ethos of America was never explored so vividly as in the novels and short-stories of that most neglected of America's great 20th century novelists. Seventeenth century prose evidently did not play well with the staccato rhythms of mid-century America. But perhaps it was Wolfe's sense of the tragic that did not sit well among a nation always avid for the next cheap delight. Faulkner had the advantage of comparative incomprehensibility combined with the slow majesty of a funeral dirge in his prose, or perhaps it was Wolfe's youth that worked against him, dying so young at thirty-eight. His disappointments always seemed only proportionate to his hunger which was limitless. He never quite managed that most difficult of authorial tasks: to climb out of one's own skin. It is a task that is spared to the lawyer who always writes within the established texture of the law. There is nothing more intimating than using the elder tongue of language to speak new truths or to devise a new music from old chords.

Abraham observed the flow of his thoughts as he turned southwards at Aberdeen. The road unspooled before him in the late-spring light of a June day. The southwestern counties of Washington

State are comparatively undeveloped. They consist of sloughs and estuaries, of oysters and lumber, salmon and light tourism. The restricted economy creates an aura of migration and abandonment, of boarded up shops and empty pavements. The dollar is the lifeblood of communities such as these and where dollars are lacking everything dries up like a mirage in the desert.

But these were not the sole basis for Abraham's subdued mood as he threaded the narrow roads between timber cuts and outlooks across the wind-ruffled waters of Willapa Bay. It was rather the sense of passing opportunities that led him into the habitual sense that like his namesake he would always be a wandering Aramean with only the vestigial promise of his various faiths to sustain him. A habit of reflective thought can be a great disadvantage. He had long ago lost the capacity for mob-enthusiasm; his joys were personal and often difficult to explain to others.

The curves of the road were compelling and hypnotic, yet he wasn't sleepy, only mesmerized by the sense of movement and the passing foliage of the trees. Suddenly the great waters of the Columbia River were before him and then the great high span of the bridge that grants access to the further shore of Oregon. His spirits picked up as they always did when the first sector of his journey was behind him. This was the Oregon land that had inspired the pioneers to cross a continent of plains and desert; this was the goal and the vision.

He stopped for lunch in Cannon Beach and walked the familiar streets munching an apple turnover and looking in the shop windows at summer clothes and trinkets, all part of early family vacations on the coast. He remembered college parties here as well, falling asleep in strange beds with the floor littered with the sleeping bodies of college friends after a night of beer and hilarity, everything swaying like a ship in an unquiet but not stormy sea. Was he that same person still, the one who as yet had everything before him but no clear idea of what anything was really about? How strange that he did not feel at that time the vast vacuum of all that he did not yet know. But then youth brings its own fullness. There is, if nothing else, that expectancy that earth has been awaiting one's particular advent to finally reveal its long deferred promises. Was that what the first Abraham had felt, he the father of peoples?

Upon leaving Cannon Beach the road climbs steadily upwards. At the crest the view south from Neakanie Mountain over the little community of Manzanita down to Tillimook Bay was as always inviting to the wanderer, majestic and intimidating at once, as the land suddenly ends and plunges downwards into the frothing surf. He found himself envisioning the many prairie towns lying behind him and the great Rocky Mountains of Colorado, then the plains, the Mississippi River and the rich, green yet populous eastern states.

This was the America that Trump promised to make great again. Had it ever ceased to be great except in the smallness of our commercial obsessions? Abraham thought of the great Redwood forests, gone in a century, with only a few forlorn representatives remaining in groves around Eureka. The west must have been one vast cathedral then. Surely that was when America was truly great, before the great exploiters ever arrived.

The problem with the command to fill and subdue the earth was that no exact figures were provided. Did filling the earth demand that the other animals should all be in cages or shrink-wrapped in the meat department of big grocery chains? Is there no residual value to frontiers, to untouched wilderness with no exhaust smog obscuring the likes of El Capitan in Yosemite? In reality no one possesses more than a life-estate; the very idea of a fee simple absolute in the most nefarious of legal fictions. And as to future interests the only real reversion is to the bare plot of the grave. He recalled the poet Thomas Gray's *Elegy in a Country Churchyard* and thought again of the current President. Would his empire resemble more that of Shelley's *Ozymandias* "Look on my works ye mighty and despair?"

The sea gives the lie to all such presumption; year in and year out the tides wash immense chasms through volcanic outcroppings. History is dwarfed by geology. "Round the remains of that colossal

171

wreck the lone and level sands stretch far away." The meaning of history is always the creation of some later author long divorced from the original event. We bestow meaning after the fact seeking to find a pattern in random circumstance.

What is the initial impetus that has propelled human life from the beginning? Are we only the latter inheritors of a defunct line about to be transmuted by technology into inorganic hybrids? Should we each patent our particular genome to prevent infringement by some future corporation that will dig up our bones to mine genetic material for splicing into zombies, full scale replicas of ourselves with the brain left out, eyes staring into nothingness but ripe with livers and kidneys to be harvested at will by elite survivors? Will the soul be present in miniature in every fragment of our genetic legacy seeking a lost composite integrity?"

Thus did Abraham the potential father of many people query the changing scene before him and the ocean, mother of all life-forms.

As the afternoon waned Abraham Cardozo passed Tillimook with its green farms and after another half hour had passed crossed over Neskowin Head and entered Lincoln City named for the man who once saved the Union but was viewed by the Confederacy as a tyrant.

"Will there be a Trump Memorial some day in Washington or is there still a little residual room on Mount Rushmore for one more face to rule them all with the great comb-over the best place in America to take a selfie?" Abraham wondered as he headed through town to his hotel. The thought made him smile and his mood began to lighten.

He was home again in the place that was so transient by nature that it would always remain the same. Coastal towns are less aptly described as cities than they are as encampments, temporary refuges before the great waters. No doubt there were traditions and old families here, but for Abraham Cardozo one of the chief charms of the coast was its transience and anonymity. There is an advantage to be gained by being a perpetual stranger, the advantage of not entering into the squalor and narrowness of local politics, of not knowing who the movers and shakers are, who constitutes local royalty with a stranglehold on influence and social prominence.

It was good to know that each community was like a separate pearl on a linear strand reaching from Astoria to Brookings on the California border. Abraham had learned from his namesake the danger of occupied settlements with borders to defend. As a practitioner of reformed Judaism he saw that the genius of the Jewish culture lay in its combination of tradition and adaptability. When necessity demanded it tradition became sufficiently cosmopolitan to adapt to changing environments. Personally upon looking back on Jewish history Abraham preferred the Diaspora to Zionism. He left it to the millennial Christian Fundamentalists to salivate over the prospect of Armageddon. Abraham saw nothing wrong with being a 21st century incarnation of the perennial wandering Jew.

It still seemed strange to him that he had ever chosen the law as a profession, but then with a name like Cardozo, no actual relation to the great Justice Benjamin Cardozo, it had seemed the natural course to pursue rather than journalism. Now in the age of so-called fake news when journalists are scorned as "enemies of the people" he was glad he had made this choice. People still maintained a fear or at least a grudging respect for lawyers. No one was quite sure of what going to the law actually entailed but there was a sort of awe reserved for people who can sign a complaint and summon one to court, to file an answer to a lawsuit, submit to the processes of discovery and depositions, and quite possibly to force one to pay reparations or damages to the prevailing party. Lawyers understood where the landmines of liability were located amidst a general plain of mistrust and animosity between various factions in the vast mottled political tapestry of American discontents (to mix about three metaphors). Maybe that was the problem: that no overriding symbol or narrative could ever capture American reality, not even when Twittered each day from the sublime office of the Presidency by a man who claimed to know all of the best words (a boast never put to the test of actual display).

Insofar as there remained any primary residue of value in modes of communication it did not reside in words, metaphors, or even in concepts but rather in the flickering modality of images. Hearing had given way to the sense of sight – story as transposed from syntax to a mere succession of video frames. Connectivity not of meaning but of mere sequence to produce the desired response was the key to achieving the desired end, a following of likes. The sheer emergence of mass approval equaled power and power translated into money. The companies with the highest capitalization were mere agencies of communication and influence. Marketing had triumphed over the returns of finance, and finance over management. All was a big economy version of the old "rock, paper, scissors game." Bodies were big bucks. Body was metaphor. Body was economic juice. Never underestimate the commercial value of strategically placed and jiggling silicone on the penile responsiveness of the stock market. "Today is today is today! Forget yesterday! And as for tomorrow ... by then we will already have changed our position in the endless round of the cultural equivalent of day-trading."

These were thoughts of Abraham, bright young attorney and aspiring reformer, as he looked down on the beach from the hotel dining room and saw the ever hungry pelicans wheeling about in tight formations over the sapphire hued morning sea.

"I want to forget these things on my vacation," he said to himself. "I don't even want to see the coverage of Trump's visit to London. Poor Theresa May is on her way out and the shadow of Brexit is nearer every day. I wonder if I will ever get back to St. Ives in Cornwall or to Scarborough in Yorkshire. I miss the pubs, cozy places, friendly folk... Maybe I'll run up to Nye Beach today, have a pint of Guinness stout, look out to the lighthouse on Yaquina Point, settle down a bit and forget national politics..."

"But events matter surely," returned the omniscient narrator that haunts us all with the recalcitrant points of living in an era that claims to possess ultimate significance, as though the fate of all human life and of the planet itself resided with us by right of temporary possession. That narrative voice is a one without personality but only the x-ray ability to scan thoughts, to strip away mental walls, and to leave us, naked and alone, trapped in the aquarium of written narrative where we swim about like fish bumping into walls seeking escape but seeing only our own reflection in the glass.

The checking in process at his hotel was routine and an hour later Abraham was on the road again. He passed the sleepy little town of Depoe Bay and ascended to the top of Cape Foulweather, named by the redoubtable explorer, Captain Cook. Below the viewpoint stretched the clear expanse of empty space. Abraham could just glimpse the outline of what may have been Cape Perpetua on the furthest margin of his vision looking southwards while below him the kelp forests waved about beneath a frothing green sea.

"I never get tired of this," he said to himself feeling within that inner frisson of delight that can only come with a summer morning by the sea.

"Why don't I stay here always?" he asked himself in that silent dialog of impulse and intentions that are never finally resolved into a sense of complete and lasting happiness so that we push on towards lesser pleasures forgetting that just for a brief moment all desire has ceased in a transient and therefore contradictory nirvana.

Abraham thought of that poem by Wallace Stevens *The Idea of Order at Key West*. Various lines from it came back to him lingering like Proust's Madeleine pastry.

"Imagine a world not littered with mental traces of stray lines by the great poets," he thought. "How do people manage to navigate without such guide-posts for their perceptions?"

He thought again of the wasteland of what must be Donald Trump's imagination, oozing out its various diatribes of resentment and mediocrity, distilled in order to intoxicate a salacious group of his avid followers. Abraham thought of the Great Plains from Iowa to Arkansas, flooded and tornado-lashed for week after week. But then this was only 2019 and by next year the news cycle will have passed and all have been forgotten.

"But what if there is war with Iran or North Korea?"

Abraham queried the open space of the gradually warming day.

"I will look back on this day and its prospects then and wonder why I wasn't grateful for just this day when my life still lay shining before me."

Abraham pictured the various types of chaos that might break forth from just beyond the ever-receding horizon lying westward from where he now stood. He wondered if there really were dragons in the sea.

"How does this day relate to all that has been before? Will I make a decision today that will make all of my prior plans suddenly lost, superseded, and irrelevant? Some new insight perhaps … some foolish gesture of protest to capture the roving eye of the media, be granted a 15 second manifesto before being locked up for streaking at a MAGA rally?"

He smiled to himself.

"I would rate the honor of a Presidential Tweet! When did we start first start thinking in little corpuscles of expression?"

Maybe that is the problem: thought cannot exist without context. To present an argument in little machine-gun bursts is inherently and methodologically flawed. What would Montaigne have thought of this method of discourse when he wrote his great essays or the great controversialists like Defoe or Voltaire? In our era it is adequate to simply berate the other person, the triumph of the *ad hominum* argument must be supreme.

Abraham shook his head and resumed his survey of the pageant of land, earth, and sky that lay just before him, reflecting that the curvature of the earth limits our perspective from whatever height we are able to attain. The ocean is essentially ungraspable in its full magnificence. Even at sea one is limited to the compass-bound circumference set by the location of the vessel. One sails for days and weeks with no sign of progress and suddenly one has arrived at Old Cathay or the Malayan archipelago with streets crowded with rickshaws and all of the picturesque genius of native handicrafts.

Abraham smiled. The Kiplingesque image vanished only to be replaced by high-rise office buildings and polluted air over vast industrial complexes all churning out goods to be sold on credit to the bottomless appetites of American consumers.

"We simply have a head-start over them rather than keeping them as juridical colonies like the Dutch, the French, and the British," he said to himself.

"Perhaps it will go on and on. Dick Cheney says that deficits don't matter, at least if you are top-dog."

He put on a British manner, "The poor blighters have no choice old man. They don't want to go back to rice-farming. Besides, the almighty dollar is the world's reserve currency. Of course the Americans are a bloody crass race but they always know what they want and find a way to get it. No doubt one day they will decide to have a culture."

Abraham had always been an Anglophile or at least one who adored the American literary aristocracy of New England. He revered Emerson, Thoreau, Hawthorne, and Melville. These exalted the individual and aspired to no greater empire beyond the empire of the possession of one's own soul and integrity. It was hard to say where America had gone wrong, perhaps when the country pushed beyond the Appalachians or built the Erie Canal. Maybe it was the presumption of the Louisiana Purchase or the Lewis and Clark Expedition that set America on the road to Empire by slaughter and conquest.

In any case America was top-dog and determined to remain such. Still there was the phenomenon of Trumpism which betokened the fear of Americans that they just might lose status or be nudged aside by a billion Chinese or a billion workers from India who would steal their jobs in the few remaining industries that cared to build factories in America. All of that potential future anxiety was focused for now south of the border and within our own hemisphere. Meanwhile the North Koreans were building missiles that could hold the entire west coast of America hostage and China was seeking to establish complete hegemony over the South China Sea. America no longer sought as in the Bush years for a cobbled together "coalition of the willing," now we were determined to go it alone.

Abraham looked for an image that he could use later in his proposed op-ed piece. He thought of the lumbering figure of Donald Trump, the very embodiment of the William Howard Taft school of physical culture for Presidents. He thought of the aggressive yellow comb-over, the pursed lips and squinting eyes, all somehow betraying fear more than actual confidence, rather like a polar bear on a shrinking ice-floe.

He thought of Trump's chief enabler, Senator Mitch McConnell of Kentucky who always looked like he had just eaten too many prunes at breakfast and must seek a swift refuge of retreat. But maybe it wasn't a matter of image but of vision, historical vision into the causes of the fall of empires that was needed today above all else. Could America ever embrace world democracy as opposed to one tilted towards and enabling American exceptionalism?

Abraham doubted it. He wasn't even sure if Americans wanted freedom in the real political sense. If the truth be told we sort of envied the Chinese even with their hegemonic surveillance state. At least it produced impressive economic growth and everyone had a job. The real image of America, as judged by the Republican vision, was more like this: I am content to work until I drop dead of a heart attack or Jesus comes again as long as I get to keep my non-union job and my gun. When did Americans decide to settle for beads and trinkets from big-box stores rather than for real freedom?

"The first freedom must be the freedom from existential fear." As he reflected upon this realization Abraham understood that American determination to build a wall around itself was a sort of collective confession that we are terrified that the great expanse of morally vacuous and narcissistically indulgent America might better be filled by a more industrious people. The best image of the Trump Presidency was derived from the super-indulgence of his golfing vacations at Mar-a-Lago combined with his plebian taste in the preference for hamburgers.

Before returning to his hotel room in Lincoln City for the night Abraham drove up to Newport. In the quaint old neighborhood of Nye Beach he sat before a meal of corned-beef and potatoes and a pint of frothy Guinness Stout. He was starting to relax at last; it always took him awhile to adapt to the slower rhythms of the coast after the hurly-burly of Seattle. It was hard to disengage from the six-minute interval that the interior meter demands in the regime of billable hour requirements of legal practice.

After his second Guinness the interior rhythm began to flat-line and give way to the long slow pulse-beats of the ocean outside. It was a pleasure to simply look about and see people having a good time around him. The noise of the place was reassuring with its unfocused laughter and talk. This was the America that Abraham loved, one of leisure and of simple largess. He liked the blend of unconscious ethnicities that made Americans in their heart of hearts naturally hospitable. It had taken years of indoctrination by the devotees of various exclusionary Christian sects anxiously awaiting the separation of the sheep from the goats to close the door of the American mind to other people. America had begun as a secular Republic content to manage the country with the same dignified aloofness that God exercised in the Deist view in managing the universe. The laws of the nation should be as frugal and few as the law of gravity. It was hard to say when things had changed. It was hard to imagine an area of life that was no longer micro-managed by some administrative body or penetrated by some information gathering algorithm. It was a relief for Abraham to be effectively off-line for a time.

Freedom in the last analysis may be summed up as the right to disengage. Instead of seeing freedom as a prelude to action perhaps it is better conceived as the ability to do nothing, simply to listen to the great base-undertone of existence. When did Americans forget the value of silence? What were the great prairies like when they harbored only the soft sighing of the wind through the long-grasses? No wheat or soy-beans then but rather only the unbroken sod and the grazing bison. What were the Oregonian seas like when the salmon thrived and the whales had yet to be hunted for lamp-oil? Could any of this natal largess ever be restored? Each day brought new studies of species extinctions before the sheer onrush of human expansion and development.

Disengagement at one time was thought of as the equivalent of alienation, of loss of community, to risk being an outcast or to be viewed as a malcontent; but that was in the days when conformity was seen as the equivalent of virtue. Now to disengage seemed the only way to maintain one's individual sanity. Collective America appeared to be committed to a course of destruction. America had once manifested a unity of purpose around unselfish goals such as the defeat of Nazi Germany and of Imperial Japan. Who could ever dissent from such noble enterprises? The war was followed by a period of consolidation around the idea that America was the bulwark of freedom and democracy. The Alliance for Progress and the Peace Corps helped to undo any thought that victorious America would use its power to advance the old colonial rule.

There followed the domestic liberation era of the freedom riders and of the Student Non-violent Coordinating Committee to advance desegregation and the various liberation movements for women and for homosexuals. The presumption that was most prevalent as the century came to an end without a nuclear conflict was that victory had been achieved and a new era had dawned at last. It had come as a great surprise then when in the wake of the terrorist incidents of 2003 the subsequent elective wars of George W. Bush and company took over a trillion dollars out of American hands to support a new colonialism.

This in turn was followed by the Great Recession of 2008 that brought the realization that far from being delivered from the ills bred of past evils the 21st century would likely bring about unprecedented challenges to our collective planetary survival let alone question American supremacy. It was this realization that had provided the backdrop of the education of young Abraham Cardozo and he reacted to it by embracing the solutions offered by the Progressive Democrats as opposed to the equally strident call of conservative Republicans for a return to a version of America that had ceased with the publication of *The Saturday Evening Post* and *Life Magazine*. All that remained of the old journalism was represented by survivors such as: *The New Yorker, Atlantic Monthly,* and the twin publications *Time* and *Newsweek.* For more specialized audiences there was: *The Economist, Mother Jones, America, Commonweal,* or *Rolling Stone.*

But even these could not supply the unified consensus of the no longer existing mainstream American consciousness. Instead there was only the nightly vituperation of the feuds between Fox News and CNN. It was the age of contention and vituperation. He thought of the bile spewing forth from pretty faces. He thought of the almost monthly stories of shootings in schools and workplaces. Still the Republican dike held firm, the Second Amendment and the refusal of service to homosexuals must stay firm; guns God and glory were the American motto. For Abraham detachment meant to get beyond all of this in order to recover what had once been the collective peace of mind that had once enabled Americans to pursue collective goals simply as Americans.

Abraham was young. It takes confidence to make commitments to a way of life. It takes a sense that the future is at least marginally predictable in its general trends. Absent this inner sense of stability it is natural to abjure commitments and to refuse to invest the scarce and irreplaceable capital of one's youth in any sustained project. Even to have attended law school may have been ill-advised, he reflected, considering the supply of young attorneys and the shrinking availability of clients who are both able and willing to hire private outside counsel to solve their legal problems.

But where besides the law could a young reformer look to combine a sense of mission with expertise in the mindless but automated rush of events? Abraham felt doomed to the institution of the law, set aside by the same impetuous impulse and colloquy with the divine that had led to the founding of Israel. He had awoken one day to the fact that he possessed a world conscience, one that demanded that he address various ills over which he had neither influence nor control. It was an attitude that when less politically grounded and more a result of metaphysical melancholy had been called by the German term, Weltschmerz. This was the pain that accompanied our young hero each season as he set off into the desert of sand and sea on the coast to seek an answer to his ever receding question: what is the meaning of it all and where do I fit in.

The following day he awoke to a day of high clouds and wind. It was time to move southwards so he checked out of his room in Lincoln City and moved south to Yachats, a town of retired academic types and artists just north of Florence and the Oregon Dunes.

Yachats is the perfect place to seek the serenity of reminiscence while looking out from the cliffs to the never changing panorama of rock and sea. It is rather like the early Carmel of Jack London and of Robinson Jeffers, a place of retreat and individuality for people who know that nothing good can ever come out of a faculty meeting. Comfortable but unpretentious its natives divide the day into the quadrants of early morning coffee, afternoon tea, sunset, and sleep. They enjoy the lassitude of enlightened discussion without the obligation to leave serenity behind and to plunge back into the fray. Yachats is a good place to recuperate after victory over a protracted illness or to forget an unseasonable love affair. To Abraham it was only a wayside in his endless quest for beatitude.

Beatitude, that was the actual origin of the term "beat" as in "beatniks," the band of young writers in the 1950's who sought redemption and ecstasy in New York City and along America's highways. These were the true believers in that absurd and antiquated term, the American Dream. Instead, what most of American literature does with the term is to chronicle the American disappointment instead.

One need only read such works as *The Education of Henry Adams, Pierre, The Marble Faun, The Grapes of Wrath, Day of the Locust, or The Great Gatsby* to prove this point. America is all too often the story of betrayed innocence. It is the same drama that was being enacted daily on our southern border with Mexico. America combines opportunity with moral entropy in a way that is distinctively American. It was just as Arthur Miller noted in his great play, *Death of a Salesman*: the ones who are most lethally wounded are the true-believers. America lacks the comforting cynicism of the French and the long adaptation to suffering of the Russians. This makes our literature the perfect candidate for tragedy, the ruin of one who once had such great expectations.

Abraham had no desire to court disappointment by engaging, by joining in the final orgiastic feast. For this reason he had early on elected to pursue a policy of selective disillusionment to serve as an inoculation against the illness of despair. He sought the sub-text to every claim of easy redemption. He realized that the Promised Land was always just over the horizon and at least one generation distant. His abiding sense was that enough would be provided to fill his momentary needs but no more. To aspire to more was both unnecessary and foolish; therefore he detached himself from any attitude of expectation beyond that of simply awaiting the logical resolution of social forces. Yet, in spite of this conscious policy he felt driven to embrace a reformist agenda as applied to those general social trends that transcend any individual decision. The worst disasters of humankind were not matters of deliberate policy it seemed but rather spontaneous eruptions of disaster from the elusive threads of minor causality. Insofar as he possessed heroic faith it was not based upon any creed or singular proposition but rather stemmed from his refusal to accept the opposite, that this world is inherently flawed, the off-scouring of a better universe by the demiurge. While not a formal stoic he was more apt to adopt a bitter frown and a stiff upper lip than tears in the face of misfortune. If he was prone to any lasting weakness it was irritation that corrections did not produce immediate and salutary results. Life simply continued and one must make do as best one could. That was then; this was now. There was no more to be said.

He did not assume that an overarching deity micro-managed events nor could he accept a negligent deity that by shifting its attention elsewhere simply overlooked noxious or terrible agents until they had done their nefarious work upon prostrate humankind. If he had been Christian rather than Jewish he might have found comfort in the cross. Instead there was only the comfort of the Torah as the best devotional path for life to follow and the assurance that behind the many distinctions of the Talmud there was an abiding and comforting presence the nature of which could never be expressed directly but only indicated by that name that could never be uttered.

Upon arriving in Yachats Abraham left his car in the parking lot and opened the driftwood studded door where he confirmed his reservation at the front desk for the next several days while he explored Yachats and its environs. His room was on the ground floor with ready access to the winding shore path along the tidal pools. He deposited his luggage and lay down fully clothed on the bed. Outside the sound of the surf was gentle and soothing. Already the journey seemed distant and dreamlike to him as though he had always found here his restful abode and place of solace.

Was this what detachment meant? To be in a place where all that mattered was a sufficient credit or debit card balance? As he drifted off to sleep Abraham imagined an endless series of just such picturesque and remote establishments designed to enhance the comforts of their guests. Was travel the final achievement of civilization? In that case of what possible use or necessity could there be for any particular promised land? Were these concepts anything beyond a justification for various nationalisms or ethnic expansions? Was the idea of a greater Serbia anything beyond a Balkan version of the old American doctrine of Manifest Destiny? For the eternal wanderer no home is needed or even requested. A traveler is never a refugee because he seeks no other refuge than the fastest way out of town, his only goal the distant horizon. To stand still is to allow the tendrils of routine to entwine their choking grip and with long acquaintance comes insolence and contempt.

When he awoke it was time for a quick shower followed by dinner. He was near enough to walk to a restaurant that he recalled from prior years where he ordered a Pimm's Cup to drink and a salmon filet seasoned with tarragon. The high tide of evening was running into the cove and the sea had that silver sheen that betokens a clear view of the coming sunset. He felt relaxed but not lethargic and the crisp icy taste of his cocktail brought his appetite to a razor's keenness. The big world seemed very distant here. The various struggles, migrations, threats and counter-threats; what were these to this narrow band of pearl-like hamlets strung along the great green plain of ocean. Time slowed here. It seemed as though he had traversed a great expanse already since dawn, not of space but of existence and its accompanist, perception.

"Why do I ever leave here?" he thought to himself.

But there is always the need to get more money, to retain one's job or to maintain one's business and all the while our constituent cells age and the threat of incipient mutiny lies harbored within our tissues. We imagine an accounting of time that is self-replenishing so that every withdrawal will be recouped by an equal margin of interest on our investment. Each promotion brings the life of permanent vacation and retirement closer. The plums of affluence grow riper on the tree. But suddenly we realize that by harvest time we may have forgotten or lost in some obscure manner that electric excitement that once gave a point to everything. Joy cannot be summoned up at will. When we lose scarcity we lose meaning. There is a mocking law of diminishing returns at the point where we can afford the preconditions of security. For this reason we should allow nothing to escape us. Walter Pater was right in his description of the transient nature of all things and the need to pay attention to life's incipient seasons.

Suddenly his dinner was before him, piquant and redolent of the local waters. He ate with contentment, savoring each buttery morsel. The sun sank slowly lower and by the time his coffee and dessert was served the day was perceptibly cooler and the outer doors were shut. He was happy to have brought a sweater with him from his room. The wind often rose just before sunset. A sense of quiet awe sets in; the world comes alive as though protesting even this minor death although tomorrow the same pageant will be repeated as it always has been. Abraham felt though that with each sunset there should be enacted some appropriate ritual to ensure the sun's return. Even minor partings bring their weight of sadness.

He arose and paid his bill before exiting to the sea path. Great plumbs of spray arose as the breakers thundered into the narrow chasms that could not accommodate their impetuous onrush. The sun sank lower and lower and even the mists on the horizon seemed to melt and give way before it. At last the whole sea seemed to catch fire and the distant clouds to glow with yellow or orange reflections.

A silence descended upon the people walking slowly along the path with him. A sort of community of matched thoughts possessed them all and the sun began to burn its way into the sea. A short six minutes later the contracting disk was no more, its light only an upward projection from where it now reclined beneath the horizon. The wind was more intense now and a chill grew gradually on the driftwood studded sands by the river. Abraham watched as the little groups passed him with a nod or a complicit smile as though all and each were sharers in a vast conspiracy born of witnessing this universal event.

A short time later he had returned to his room. He took out the third volume of Sir Osbert Sitwell's autobiography, read for an hour, and then fell asleep to the slow pounding music of the sea.

The next day Abraham had planned on visiting the northernmost reaches of the Oregon Dunes lying just over the bridge from Florence. He decided to retain his room in Yachats to return to that night. A quick breakfast of an orange butter-horn and coffee sufficed for breakfast and he set out to see the nearby sights.

He paid the entrance fee and climbed the winding road to the top of Cape Perpetua just south of town. From its summit a vast panorama of rock and chasm is visible and the sea seems to climb until it lies within a few centimeters of one's eyes gazing outwards, a great bank of blueness that might at any moment overflow and falling inwards lap about one's feet. He sat in the long grass with his back against a stone to savor infinity. He recalled the German students he had met up here once in days gone by. They had all exchanged addresses and promised to write in order to preserve the remnants of an instant friendship but had never done so. Or was it he who had failed to respond? How many open invitations do we pass up simply through neglect?

Abraham wondered at the number of strands of parallel lives that died of just such negligence and attrition. It made him think that no one is really a stranger. If time allowed it should be possible to reach a lover's depth with all the world. He wondered if there was such a thing as an omni-sexual, not in the genital sense, but in the sense that one quivered to the passing embrace of eyes on a subway platform or a smile that might have been only courtesy but in its completeness managed to sum up a lifetime of foregone acquaintance and intimacy.

His namesake, Justice Benjamin Cardozo, had never married—for him there was only the infinite play of the great man's mind and the all sufficient power of words. While for the great patriarch of old, Father Abraham, there was his wife Sara and the servant girl Hagar. From his loins came the people Israel and the long history of suffering and exile that was the greater part of Jewish history. What could he learn from these men regarding what changes and what might just possibly abide? Would our young hero ever marry or father forth offspring to be cast adrift on the surging waters of the 21st century? This brief narrative must be all encompassing and his life trail off into that infinite regress implied in the word "maybe." He liked to consider himself a procreative optimist. In spite of the challenges the human race must soon endure it would be a false prudence to fail to procreate out of fear that human beings are not up to any challenge, even the wasting of the planet itself. There must be someone left to bear witness even to cosmic ruin and to write a final codicil to the last will and testament of humanity.

With this vow in his heart Abraham descended to the ribbon of highway below and turned south towards Neptune Beach and Strawberry Hill. From there he turned the tight corner of road at Heceta Head and climbed to the access point to the Sea Lion Caves. He pulled off the road at the top of the cliffs and got out of his car to look back on the Heceta Head Lighthouse where it lay tucked just behind the Devil's Elbow with its white encrustations of guano from the various seabirds.

The great foaming waves at the base of the cliffs revealed great colonies of brown sea lions. Flocks of hovering seagulls surfed in the sky over the abyss. It was an awesome place of land and ocean: remote, adamantine, and primeval. He remained there poised on the balance-point of wonder yet summoned again to resume his journey by the insistent tug of his outlined plans for the day. The next stop was to be Florence-by-the-Sea. Had he attended law school in Eugene rather than in Washington this town would have associations different from those that had actually prevailed. Eight law schools had accepted him, each boding a different subsequent fate. Had he chosen correctly? How could he ever know? Who can bear up under the awesome chains of contingency that life imposes? But he was here now and in that "nowness" resides our only true freedom.

Florence lies along the Siuslaw River where it meets the sea. He stopped there before proceeding across the bridge to the dunes overlook for a bowl of clam chowder, a mild violation of kosher prohibition. He would make it up later by a prayer intoned over the sand dunes, blessing all that is. He was sure that the Baal Shem Tov would understand.

Abraham's relation to his faith was hereditary and tangential rather than strictly observant. He valued the essential virtues that had emerged among his co-religionists over centuries of historic marginalization. Not least among these were the sayings of the Hasidic Rabbis. It seemed obvious to Abraham that the best way to resolve the endless religious contentions that were dividing the world would to be for God to call a general colloquy of representatives from the major monotheistic religions together, have everyone bring their favorite proof texts along in little binders, and proceed to show them in detail how historical drift and animosities had blurred the essentials in an ever-growing mound of miniscule accretions.

It seemed to be an insuperable task to sift through all the claims and counter-claims of religious discourse to discover the original bond between God and humanity. The beginnings are shrouded in the dense fog of illiteracy or else the records were simply misfiled or destroyed. It was pointless to apply the metaphysical equivalent of the Best Evidence Rule and to request an original rather than a copy. Councils, synods, schools, commentaries, speculations, original sects, revelations, prophesies, mystical visions, ecstasies: all had restated and amended that first encounter where the Celestial Presence addressed the two dripping bipeds with loins still wet due to the mindless mandate of copulation and enjoined the first codified rules of human conduct. Perhaps the most salient characteristic of the 21st century was not the threat of technology and artificial intelligence after all: the major wars would likely be over a zero-sum struggle over competing revelations and contrasting versions of metaphysics.

After a late lunch Abraham left Old Town behind and with a pocket full of salt-water taffy got back on the highway, crossed the bridge at the far end of town, and headed for the dune overlook exit. After leaving the highway a cut-off to the left beckoned and he found a parking lot where various trucks were unloading dune buggies to join the many noisy vehicles that were engaged in climbing a seventy foot mound of sand before him. The top was invisible but a path to the right through the evergreen trees beckoned and Abraham began to climb.

He found that others had been there before him and by placing his feet carefully in their footsteps he could minimize the soft subsiding avalanche as he asked the sand to support his weight. By means of this strategy he managed to climb to a fairly level surface at the crest of the great dune. From this vantage point a marvelous sight emerged. There before him lay a virtual desert as of fabled Arabia, dune after dune only interrupted by small copses of evergreen trees like sheltered isles of repose in a fawn colored sea. The great expanse of sand dunes fell off westward in steep cliffs and a mile distant the ocean appeared beyond the lower moonscape of sea grass and beach blue and infinite. Abraham climbed higher still towards where the cliffs began and sat down on a fallen and bleached out pine tree to catch his breath again after his long climb. Here he was almost beyond the roar of the dune buggies and something of the primal aspect of the scene was restored. Isolation returned and with it the luxury of thought.

He returned to his speculations upon time and history. He thought of the great disproportion between texts and actuality. If God were to write anything down then surely His text must be creation itself existing above any interpretation. It seemed strange to him therefore that the great religions seemed to emphasize the jurisprudential aspect of the Divine Intellect rather than simply to contemplate the wonder of being. The emphasis upon the will of God seemed secondary to a contemplation and appreciation of what God had already accomplished.

Abraham was neither a pantheist nor a disciple of Spinoza but he did feel that commandments had more to do with human needs than with divine mandates. Morality appeared to him to reside at the metaphysical level of parking regulations. The oscillating rhythm of sin and forgiveness, of mercy or retribution, of command and acquiescence seemed to be too infused by the human element to really matter, at least from the distant perspective of the philosopher. But on the other hand, who could quarrel with revelation provided that that revelation was authentic and not biased in some manner by the one who initially recorded it? To understand the intricacies of Divine Inspiration though was beyond the present ambit of the time and place of Abraham's speculations.

But as a bare proposition subject to correction: assuming that the reflection of God's essence lay within his creation, it showed a variety and even a quality of spontaneity that was alien to most supposedly definitive summations and interpretations by the major religions. It seemed to Abraham that closure was one of the last attributes to be implied in regard to the Godhead. All of the huffing and puffing of various imams, clerics, and avatars of the sublime to ensure that God not be offended seemed to forget the sheer silent witness of being in places like this, holding the slow accretion of eons of wind, sand, and season. Humankind lies awash in conflicting mandates and proposed punishments so that the justice and majesty of God might be vindicated at last.

Abraham thought about it all. Could God do nothing for Himself but he must rely upon various factions of our fellow men to threaten us into compliance? He thought of his proposed manuscript at home and wondered whether what so many of his conservative countrymen were calling for was a theistic version of the absurd red hats that appeared at various Trump rallies proclaiming that America could be great again; God could be great again as long as we make it happen.

Was it an accident that political fundamentalists were usually religious fundamentalists as well? What a shock it must be for those who believe that they can speak authoritatively for God himself to discover that they are powerless beyond the grim circle of their own rhetoric. How frustrating it must be to recall the days when they could call forth armies and wade through seas of blood to impose their doctrines and covenants. Now they were reduced to mere frothing diatribes and appeals for sacrifice on the part of the faithful to advance their particular crusade, jihad, or ministry. In America there was the great alliance of the born subjugators of others whose uncertainty demanded compliance as the proof that they had been right all along in the cosmic sweepstakes. All of history was a reflection of how they had used their power when they still possessed it.

Suddenly Abraham saw what was really happening in this critical hour of history. For the first time all contending absolutes were stripped down and lined up on an equal starting line on the final sprint to the finish, winner take all. There they stood with sinews lithe and straining, great chests heaving with maledictions towards the heretics and false witnesses lined up next to them in competition. Each contender pointed at the skies where ranks of serried angels awaited the outcome, fearsome and furious but determined to let some inscrutable inward certification be rewarded by victory while all others must watch as their laurels turned to chains dragging them into a pit of more than defeat, a pit of utter punishment, shame, and desolation. Victory! A blare of trumpets, the great city arises…

Abraham Cardozo awoke to the sound of the wind blowing through the trees above his head. It was late. He would obtain no more food tonight. The stars already floated in the clear sky of night, silent and remote. Restaurants close early on the Oregon coast. He might just stop for some kippers at a grocery store before heading back to his room in Yachats.

He retraced his thoughts assembled like grains of sand in the face of this great immensity. If he had possessed a papyrus roll he might have recorded his thoughts even as St. John had done in exile on the remote island of Patmos. He could slip the manuscript into a vessel or tie it with a ribbon only to have it be discovered years later like the scrolls of Nag Hammadi. Scholars would puzzle over the mysterious author and the size of the community of followers that he must have gathered about him.

Alas the city that they had envisioned had long since crumbled into sand and all that remained was this sacred testimony as witness to the vision vouchsafed so long ago. Abraham thought of the new versions of Mishnah and Gemara that might ensue from his simple act of climbing the dune alone on a summer day. He bethought him of the various schools of thought, the carefully calibrated distinctions, the condemnations and excommunications, the many dying in anguish still unsure of their salvation, lamenting their sins but secretly knowing in their heart of hearts that granted youth and time enough they might commit them again, not to offend God, but simply because they were human, overwhelmed by the passions and uncertainties spared to those who parsing sacred texts knew better, or feared more, or simply had a professional interest in being right. Perhaps they were. Who was he to say?

He took his notebook from his pocket and stood there, ballpoint pen in hand. What was his vision? Abraham looked about him at the moonlit sea, the sand, and the beacons of starlight as the darkness deepened. He listened to the wind sighing in the long seagrass. The granular presence of this little slice of eternity blew softly about his sandaled feet and he who might have been the great lawgiver and father of nations put aside his writing implements, trudged wearily back down over the sifting dunes and drove quietly away.

Confession

Allison McCarthy entered the sacred precincts of St. Peter the Fisherman parish at or about four-thirty in the afternoon of a hot July day when many Catholics were at the beach or otherwise engaged in committing new sins rather than confessing old ones. It had taken her a few moments upon entering before her eyes adjusted to the dim and peaceful interior of the Church and for the traffic noises outside to abate. She scanned the pews for those with long imposed penances and found few. There was to be no evening mass for Hispanics that night and she counted on having some uninterrupted time with Father Hanlon without some other pressing parish duty interfering with her plans.

Allison was what is known in the ranks of head-shaking Catholics as, well, let us say rumored to be, a lesbian. Her spinsterhood should have long since yielded to the importunate advances of some nice Catholic boy who had taken to heart the admonition that it is better to marry than to burn. Catholics may be the last group of Christians who take the prohibition against fornication seriously. Allison had manifested an early aversion to boys except as tennis partners. Her attitude towards her own beauty was one of benign neglect. Her short page boy style of hair worked in all seasons and she found make-up to be cloying and mask-like. She wasn't transgendered or anything as extreme as that; she could even look conventionally pretty at times if she made any effort to appear so but her attitude was such that men feared to approach her in any of the usual ways which is the same as saying that she wasn't an easy lay. This had made her unpopular in college where it was merely assumed that youth would have its way and the strictures of Catholic doctrine on artificial birth control might yield if only to prevent the greater evil of abortion.

College as she saw it was primarily ordained towards the task of getting a degree and a good job. Children were something that only the uneducated could paradoxically be expected to be able to afford to produce. Student loans rather than a love-nest in the suburbs came first in the minds of most graduates. Marriage was something to be put off for five or even ten years until a girl could have a wedding at a proper resort or a country club and a glamorous honeymoon in Hawaii.

Of course as an incipient lesbian none of this mattered to Allison. For her learning came first, politics second, and relationships... well, whenever the first two were completed to her satisfaction which wasn't yet she would deal with the issues that marriage might raise. She was not therefore technically guilty of the mortal sin of actually having slept with another girl but she had managed a few lingering thoughts in that direction from time to time and in strict Catholic doctrine this was as bad as just going ahead and executing a long rehearsed and elegant swan-dive toward the ripe and forbidden fruit. Even to touch oneself impurely was forbidden beyond a certain prudent care for hygiene.

So it was that Allison had reached the ripe old age of thirty-four with no sexual experience of any kind, no sacred vows given as a nun, no panting husband waiting for her at home ready on the slightest pretence to explore the untried wilderness of her private parts. In fact the most phallic thing that Allison possessed was the short barreled revolver nestled in her handbag, the same gun that she had brought with her to St. Peter's that night, the gun that she intended to shoot

Father Hanlon with should his answers to her long delayed questions prove to be unsatisfactory.

There was nothing particular in her choice of Father Hanlon to bear the burden of her anger and frustrations. In point of fact she barely knew him beyond the fact that he had been assigned to the parish where she had once attended school as a young girl, a parish that she had not attended since moving away, first to attend college and then to assume a job in a distant city. She had returned to the place of her youth on an impulse, to try and connect some strands of her life that had remained unattached for years, only occasionally ripping across her face in a high wind of doubt and an impulse to seek some form of reprisal for a series of nameless offenses inflicted over the course of her religious past.

Considering that most people think of religion as a source of solace it is surprising how many people are prevented from finding it by reason of being frightened early away from the very God who is described as being the very embodiment of love. But for one in Allison's position who harbored in her deepest self like a boll-weevil in cotton a desire that had been defined as an intrinsic moral evil that could in no way be approved, let alone blessed and celebrated, some degree of wounding was perhaps inevitable. Still, it seemed a little strange to her to be going about with a gun, particularly since she was not a Republican among which group gun carrying goes right along with prayer as a sacred duty.

She did not covet devices of mass destruction. In fact she had always had a certain degree of confidence that she could rely upon scorn or upon swift repartee rather than upon an extra clip of ammunition for her defense. She had never required a gun so that she could send a series of sharp or hollow nosed (she forgot which was worse) objects ripping through the flesh of a fellow human being.

So why should she even think of violence toward plump, bald Father Hanlon rather than flying off to Rome to seek out the people who are most likely to know exactly what God thinks about everything, as long as they can hang the basis on some Hebrew text or other written before you could buy bottled water at the dollar store and had to hit rocks with staffs to bring it forth in the desert? Who gets to decide these things and write texts that are like so many improvised explosive devices just waiting for someone to drive over them and be blown to hell ... literally?

Teachings on such matters were only harmless if they are ignored and this she could not manage to do. She had long sought a way out by reading Diderot and Spinoza and even Feuerbach but to no avail. The question of salvation and the ultimate sanction for failing to attain it kept creeping up on her. Lately she had been much impressed by various theories of textual criticism for relief. One of these maintained that for a text to be preserved it must mirror the ideas and the world-view of the initial audience. This seemed to undercut any claim that a text can be trans-cultural and be read as decisive authority by different cultures placed within entirely different conditions of existence. Two thousand years had passed since most of the Bible had been written and the very idea that it constituted a univocal witness to the one and same God seemed to be undercut by the various perspectives on the deity represented therein by the various religions tracing their origin back to Abraham; texts no matter how definitive sounding emerge from the context of prior beliefs and must harmonize with them to an extent or be immediately rejected. This seemed to imply something less than dead-on accuracy within Scripture. Of course the Catholic Church could always fall back on various arguments drawn from what was called natural law to back up its claims even if no textual authority was available on which to anchor moral prohibitions.

Two women can't make a baby and two men can't even provide a vehicle of gestation, lacking an accommodating uterus between them. This alone made any genital rubbing together the equivalent of friction with no flame; so if you were gay or lesbian your particular inclinations were not seconded and approved by the most obvious and indeed all inclusive purpose of the genitalia: to further the procreation of the human race. For such people their entire affective and sensual appetite was at best inapposite and at worst willfully perverse. There was no accounting for such deranged appetites but the remedy was clear, life-long continence or a return to what nature intended in the creation of man and woman. Surely this was obvious and only a stubborn rebelliousness could account for the determined resistance manifested by organized impiety in the form of gender and sexual relativism. We live in a world of convenient opposites that make the world turn round. Just look at any magnet and see what happens when you try and force two of the same poles together. So at the end of the day even the best of girlfriends must part company and go home to their respective male mates because nature has designed people to fit together just one way and no other without violating the universal call to chastity.

If this seemed a hard teaching it must be remembered that God sends hurricanes and floods to drown the innocent as well as the guilty and that everything that happens is just so because God is waiting and watching to see how we will bear up under adversity. This was all so much easier to accept in the days when it was not uncommon for one in three children to die in childhood. Better health care and nutrition had allowed people to live longer and finally to even imagine that this sort life should carry its own meaning apart from sin and repentance. Of course the Calvinists had always managed to be both good businessmen and religious simultaneously by merely assuming that they were of the elect while for Catholics the gates of hell were kept open, wide and swinging, at least until the last brain-wave flickered into a straight-line. After that the particular judgment took place and, wham, eternity begins.

The sheer brutality (so it seemed to her) of such definitions troubled Allison. She knew that she was expressing her inner doubts badly, perhaps even blasphemously. Allison hatred the way she was; she realized that nineteen out of twenty girls would be ready to zero in on the virile member like a bee to honey while giving a miss to any sprawled and waiting "delta of Venus" even if it was perfumed and gift wrapped for them. So what was wrong with her that her desires manifested such contrariety?

Allison could partially understand the condemnation of gay sex. Men were equipped with a sort of water-cannon that was likely to spin out of control like an ungovernable fire-hose in Alabama at an early civil rights protest. This was why gay bars had back rooms while lesbian bars had coy tables for two. The closest thing to lesbian group sex was an after victory group-hug after a soft-ball game. As for the transgendered crowd the closest that most of them came to sex was when they looked in the mirror and echoed Barbra Streisand in the musical *Funny Girl* by saying to themselves in glorious solitude, *"Hello beautiful."* Still Allison liked it that there were four main letters in LGBT. After that those four there was only a trailing asymptote of other letters indicating contradiction or indecision.

Yet she had skipped the fiftieth anniversary of the Stonewall Riots. It seemed a little early to celebrate with a potential four more years of a Trump Presidency in the offing. By then America's Fuehrer might just decide to stay permanently, forget term limits, or maybe just pass the crown on to his daughter Ivanka as his cute new designee. Americans have always secretly craved a royal family to give us a little class among Europeans. Just read Henry James. No doubt about it; it was still too early to prance one's way to victory as long as one-third of America thought that God wanted Sodomites to be put to death or at least deprived of a proper wedding cake of groom with groom and bride with bride.

Of course many Catholics expressed their disdain for sexual minorities in ways that were more restrained in rhetoric and philosophically rooted than was true for most Fundamentalist Protestants, but Allison knew that she was an outcast all the same and that was the problem. Allison didn't understand why God had so many grudges to bear towards his own creation. She simply didn't understand sin, at least sins of the flesh, unless they involved bringing forth children from what was meant by both consenting parties to be only a transient connection. She realized that sex can break hearts. She was not an envious libertine.

Still, the fertile earth seemed to speak a radically different language than restraint. Even the most disgusting worms and amoebas were still allowed a few plots of soil to squirm around in without being scorched to death for eternity in punishment for excessive worminess or squirminess. It just didn't seem fair or worthy of a Divine Being to share the same basic attitude and mind-set as a Fundamentalist housewife from Tennessee or Mississippi. Allison could dismiss the former because they were heretics in any case but she expected more out of Roman Catholicism, more comprehension of human frailties.

There was the whole matter of comparison. Two thousand years of uninterrupted recourse to God for forgiveness for things such as murder, nepotism, oppression of multitudes, slavery in silver mines in South America, and imposed tortures seemed to be somehow cheapened and made irrelevant when compared to two horny young people getting off in a parked automobile and then dying unrepentant on the way home. This was why as our story opens she was to be found kneeling in the front pews after the last penitent had left the Church still waiting to talk to the man she had come here to see and hopefully receive some satisfying answers... or else.

She looked at her watch; it was ten minutes to five. It was unlikely that any more penitents would arrive to interrupt her. Allison got up from the pew at the front of the Church where she had been kneeling and began a long walk to the box at the rear of the Church where the priest was waiting on his side of the screen for those who desired to retain anonymity in confession. No one was present on the other side for a face-to-face confession as indicated by the lights above the respective entrance doors. She entered and knelt down in the darkness. A few seconds later the slide opened and she was just able to see through the cloudy plastic shield the side of Father Hanlon's face where he sat with his right ear poised to hear her confession.

She still recalled the old formula.

"Bless me Father for I have sinned. It has been... ten years since my last confession."

There was a significant pause.

Allison spoke up again. "Perhaps you don't have time tonight for me Father. I could make an appointment or come another day... earlier."

The pause continued. Then quietly, the priest spoke.

"No, that will not be necessary. I cook my own meal at the rectory on Saturday nights and I have no engagements this evening. We will have time to hear your confession."

Allison hesitated. Was she really about to do this thing? Time passed and she could hear the priest breathing, slow and ponderous.

"He should exercise more," she thought to herself.

Suddenly, she didn't know where to begin. It had all seemed so easy when she had contemplated the whole thing at home, but now in this quiet church it was all so different, as though the angels were watching.

"I have to say something first," she finally managed to explain.

"Yes, what do you wish to say?"

"I'm angry."

"You wish to confess the sin of anger towards somebody?"

"No, I'm angry at the church."

There was a pause.

"I see. Why are you angry at the Church?"

"I am angry because I am tired of the church sending everybody to hell."

There was another significant pause while the priest considered this, then he said gently, "I think you may have it backwards. It isn't the mission of the church to send anybody to hell but to proclaim the good news of salvation though the passion, death, and resurrection of Our Lord Jesus Christ."

"I know that, I was raised Catholic, Father. The problem is that those phrases, beautiful as they may be to you, just don't seem to mean anything to me anymore. It's like the creed; I've said it so many times at mass that it's now just words to me."

"Do you think you've lost your faith then?" the priest asked softly.

"No, it's more like I never had any real... *faith* I mean. I simply took it for granted that what my parents told me was true and what I heard in Church was even more true. But I think real faith is much more than that. It is something rooted deep down inside that you can count on every day; you just know it."

The priest considered, "That sounds very real and quite accurate as a definition of faith as well."

"Yes, but you don't understand; I know other things just like that... bad things."

"Are those the things that you want to confess?"

"No, those are the things that make me mad at the Church."

The priest hesitated before answering. "I don't think I follow you."

"I want the Church to stop saying bad things about good people... like they are going to hell."

"Is that what you think the Church is doing? And what do you mean when you say 'the Church?'"

Allison thought for awhile before answering. "I mean... you know, the Vatican and all that, and the... like Bishops and theologians, people who are supposed to know what God thinks about everything... those people."

"I see. I wonder if it would help if I told you something about the way the Church works. You see the Church is a living body composed of various elements, each acts as a balancing influence on the others, and no part can operate in isolation. So when you say, 'the church,' there is already a problem because no generalization can capture what the Church ultimately says about something."

Allison found this statement puzzling.

"So the Church is just a confused mess; is that what you're telling me?"

The priest smiled. "No, that isn't what I mean... although 'the Church' as you use it often goes through some major trials. What I mean is that the Church is a discerning body doing its collective best to manifest the Spirit of Jesus Christ to the world and by doing so to fulfill the apostolic mission assigned to it by Our Lord before his Ascension to take his place at the right hand of Father."

"See that's just what I mean. How can God even have a right hand?"

"Well, you can't take metaphoric language like that literally."

"But people always do and they just sound dumb unless you are in a big church all saying the same thing at the same time... and that makes me mad. Why does God want us all to say such dumb things?"

"I think you would see it differently if you understood what the Church means by saying such things. Let's take this business of saying that Jesus sits at the right hand of the Father. The language is metaphoric and meant to convey the kingly sovereignty of Jesus. In biblical times to sit at someone's right hand was to occupy a privileged position, a place of honor and authority. Jesus is now in a position to act as our priestly advocate before His Father in heaven... Does that help?"

Allison thought about it, but then shook her head in the darkness.

"No, it just adds to the confusion because if Jesus is God why did He even have to go through these perambulations just to get back to where He once already was? Why does God work like that?"

The priest sighed. "You are describing it as though God were some clockwork-like mechanism. You must remember that you are using, and the Church also uses, biblical language to convey mysterious realities. These are deep and interrelated theological concepts that cannot be divorced from the entire context in which they are uttered anymore than a line of Shakespeare makes any sense unless you understand the entire purpose of the play. What would you make of, 'To be or not to be; that is the question' unless you were aware that it was uttered by Hamlet as a reflection of his ultimate sense of being overwhelmed by the conflicting duties imposed upon him by his father's premature death?"

"Well I have never been able to make much of Shakespeare in any case."

The priest smiled behind the screen.

"You see what I mean though?"

"Yes, I guess so, but I will need you to go into it deeper."

Father Hanlon said, "Alright, we have time. Let's go back to your concern about the 'right hand of God' and your sense that such terms are meaningless or at least dulled by too frequent careless repetition. You recall that I said that the Church, in its ideal structural components, acts organically even though to the outside observer it appears to be a strictly hierarchical organization from the Pope to the Cardinals to the Bishops to the Priests and finally to the laity, the chosen People of God. The truth is that we are a confessing Church, not in the specific sense of the Sacrament of Confession, which is a specialized use, but in the sense of bearing witness to a meaningful historical event. The basis of all Church teaching resides in the proclamation that 'Jesus is Lord.'"

Allison objected. "You just keep throwing phrases at me!"

The priest remonstrated, "Try and be patient with me. That proclamation states that one individual human being, Jesus, has been given all legitimate authority in heaven and upon earth and even over the realm of the eternally dead that goes by the name of hell. That authority though is an authority of salvation, to bring souls to an eternal happiness with God through the forgiveness of sins. So you see that God isn't the one that ever sends people to hell."

"But why even make hell in the first place?" Allison objected.

The priest explained, "Well strictly speaking God does not make hell; he merely permits it. During biblical times there was no sense of secondary causality in texts, everything was referred back to God as its first cause as well as its teleological or ultimate cause. God is the beginning and the goal of all things. This means that the Church is confined to talking about the upside of creation not the downside."

Allison thought about this before objecting again, "Oh yeah?

Then what about all the commandments? What about all the enumerated sins; how about all that stuff?"

The priest answered, "Well how would you give someone directions without providing some moral guideposts or warnings?"

Allison answered, "Guideposts sure... but what about threats of endless retribution. How did that come about, if the Church isn't... well... just nasty!"

Father Hanlon objected. "You keep going back to that phrase, 'the Church.' Who are you really talking about?"

Allison looked around her in the enveloping darkness of the confessional box for an answer. "Alright, I am talking about almost every official source that I have ever consulted on Catholic doctrines from the Catechism to the Catholic websites. They just make my life miserable."

Father Hanlon thought about this before venturing an answer. "You seem like an intelligent and deeply thoughtful young woman so I will try and answer you as forthrightly as I can... Most people are not capable of understanding complex relationships but they are at least capable of memorizing rules. In its chosen pedagogy the Catholic Church in its broadest sense has recognized this fact of human nature, therefore it has often taught doctrines in isolation from each other and the easiest way to do this is to adopt a rule-based catechetical formula. For most people this is all that is possible for them to understand and even then many go astray into various vain speculations about God. A simple review of history will show how even the various objective threats have not managed to alter human behavior very much. If you stick with an objective mindset it is therefore logical to conclude that many people are, as you have said, going to hell. But God does not place them there. This may help you to understand... hell is simply a logical category if you are willing to accept two prior truths: first, that God is love and second, that human beings are free to object to love and prefer to escape it by any means possible."

Allison was surprised by this unusual explanation. She spoke up at last, "But everybody wants to be loved, so who would anyone choose hell?"

The priest asked her, "May I ask how old you are?"

Allison answered, "I am thirty-four."

There was a long silence from the other side of the screen of the confessional.

At last the priest spoke wearily, "I am sixty-three and I have been a priest since I was ordained thirty-four long years ago. I have heard many confessions. The seal of confession is absolute and I can never reveal what I have heard here in specificity, but generically speaking I can tell you that I have heard stories here that show how easy it is to embrace hatred instead of love, misery instead of joy, and mourning over rejoicing. I don't know who may be in hell, only God knows that, but I *can* say that hell is possible because I hear rumors of it every day when I hear people's confessions and try to offer them God's forgiveness for their sins. Some don't want it."

Allison was silent for a long time after hearing this. It was not what she had expected to hear from a priest. For one thing it was not simple. It meant that the clarity that she had sought might not be possible to realize or achieve and if not here then where was she to find it? She had wanted to find a bad guy in the confessional, someone to blame for her doubts and fears, and she had only found a weary man doing his best to be a bridge between history and the everyday lives of people just like her. She suddenly felt sorry for him. It can't be nice hearing all of other people's dirty moral laundry. Why couldn't they just keep their sins to themselves?

"Why do you do this," Allison asked suddenly, "Doesn't it just make you sick hearing all the crap that people come up with?"

Father Hanlon answered, "I do it because I am a priest and this is one of the seven sacraments of the Catholic Church."

Allison protested, "Why don't you just send them away; let them do whatever they want. Who cares anyway?"

"How can I send people away when people are the reason that the Church exists. In its widest sense the Church is people helping people but with the indwelling grace of God to help them. So you see... may I ask your first name?

"Allison."

"You see, Allison, the Church is rather like... well, have you heard of the Heisenberg Uncertainty Principle?"

"No."

"It is a theory in physics proposed by Dr. Werner Heisenberg that states that when considering an electron it is possible to know only one but not both of two things; an observer can know only the speed of an electron or the location of an electron but not both simultaneously—I think I have that right. The Roman Catholic Church is metaphorically like that: it is possible to know in the most literal sense what the Church teaches about the means and the order of salvation, or on the other hand to know the results produced in the soul according to the providential will of God, but not both simultaneously. We are locked into time so that an eternal condition cannot be concretely imagined. The best that we can do is to attempt a rough road-map of the hazards to salvation and leave it at that. This often makes the doctrines of the Church to appear harsh or arbitrary, but they are neither; they are only evidence of the seriousness with which the entire body of the Church takes its mission: to offer a definitive solution to the perplexities and disorders of human life and to promise happiness at the end to those who are poor in spirit, for as Jesus has told us, theirs is the Kingdom of Heaven."

A great silence fell upon the little enclosure, where according to Church tradition, the soul of the penitent meets God through the ministration of another human being, not merely as a witness, but as an agent of forgiveness, not of condemnation, but of healing.

This was not what Allison had expected to find but she was unwilling to simply let go of the dread purpose that had brought her to this miniature outpost of the great and powerful Roman Catholic Church made manifest in the great St. Peter's Basilica in Rome. For Allison Rome had always been allied with remoteness and incomprehensibility, with the intricate distinctions of Canon Law, and with men in red robes and fringed sombrero-like hats. Why should they care if Allison was a lesbian or not?

She spoke up suddenly, "Father, I am a lesbian or rather I am a lesbian wannabe. I can't help it. I just don't like penises and I haven't even seen one up close. I don't want some wormy thing crawling around inside of me; is that so terrible?"

Father Hanlon wiped the sweat off his brow before continuing. "So if I understand you correctly you are virginal but prefer the idea of a woman as a mate and sexual partner rather than a man… any man. Is this what you mean?"

Allison answered, "Yes. I feel things, sexual things you know, but so far I just rub against stuff in my bed and not much of that because it frightens me. I don't know what to do with these feelings but they are my feelings and I don't think it is anybody else's business."

Father Hanlon answered, "It isn't easy learning to be at peace with our bodies."

Allison cried, "Except I have read that it is a serious sin. I want you to tell me what to do about it but…"

"Yes?"

She looked down to where the gun was secreted in her purse.

"I have to warn you that you better say the right thing to me."

Father Hanlon hesitated before replying, "So you think it is up to me?"

"Well you represent the Church don't you?"

"What do you think?"

"I think you are the nearest thing to the organization that has always frightened me because it was old and big and powerful… and intrusive."

The priest spoke softly, "But it was your decision to come here today, not mine. Why did you come?"

Allison hesitated but managed at last to choke out, "I wanted to fight back… somehow to fight back before I got sent to hell for all eternity for loving a woman."

There was a long pause

The priest said, "Right, I see now. It isn't me but it is me."

Allison protested with tears in her voice. "It isn't, you know, personal... but what else can I do? I mean I can't kill an institution can I?"

The priest was quiet. At last he said, "Why kill anything?"

Allison felt the anger rising again within her like a dark tide.

"You must know the answer to that," Allison spat out. "Why else did you study theology if it was not to bamboozle poor dumb girls like me into telling you all of our secrets, making us feel foolish and ashamed for even being here?"

Father Hanlon was quiet for so long that Allison thought that he had unaccountably gone to sleep.

At last he spoke but so quietly that she could barely hear him.

"Is that what you think it is all about for me really... my being here alone on a Saturday afternoon... that I was just hoping for some thirty-four year old like you to tell me that she wants to sleep with women? The litany of sins is what is really boring. I wish sometimes that people would come in here and tell me of a corresponding virtue for every sin that they confess. I need something to keep my own faith in humanity alive too. I need that as much as anybody. How do you think an institution like the Catholic Church has managed to endure for two thousand years in spite of persecutions and trouble if its priests are as shallow as you make us out to be? We have some bad ones of course. I know a couple of them myself, but just think of what we are asked to do? We are asked to embody the compassion of Christ, to make God present to an unbelieving world, to put our own bodies on the line for what we believe. All around the world priests are standing up against social injustice and reminding people that this life is not the end, that there is an eternal realm where they will be answerable for what they do, if only to their own consciences standing before God. I can't answer all of your questions, Allison, nobody can. No one can force you to believe what you don't already want to believe. The Church presents normative dogmas that are the fruit of its reflection on scripture, history, tradition, and from talking to people just like you. It can only do what it was commissioned to do. You think of the proclamation of the gospel as some sort of rape rather than as an invitation; even God acts more like a shy lover than He does like a seducer. You are the Church Allison as much as anyone… if you believe that is. I can't give you an answer that you have not already given yourself."

"But that isn't what I need from you. I don't care about… *normative dogmas*, whatever! I need answers for *my* life. I can't go on just alone. I need somebody to love me and I don't care about anybody's natural law. You talk as though I should be impressed by all of these councils held by bearded old men figuring everything out and tying it all down to other texts and these referring to still other texts during ages when hardly anybody could read, least of all women. You ask for my faith and then unfold this huge panorama in front of me and ask me to swallow it when I don't even know enough to nibble a little around the edges. Don't you see how overwhelming that is to me, just this one little me with my limited life experience? And that isn't enough: you dangle me over a pit of fire and threaten me with eternal punishment if I don't buy into what you are saying. How can I see that not as a threat, a personal threat to me, to my life, to my peace of mind on a daily basis so that I can't even kiss a girl and not feel dirty and worse… damned to hell because I am a woman too, for doing what everything in me pulls me toward? And what about you; don't you have a life? Aren't you even just a little bit mad that your job forces you to tell people these things? Is it so bad to just find a little happiness without being called *intrinsically disordered?*" Who talks like that? Who are they talking to if not each other? What about us, the poor disordered ordinary people who don't wear robes and walk around blessing each other all day for not fucking each other? What about us?"

Father Hanlon shook his head behind the screen before saying almost to himself, "I guess this is what the Second Vatican Council meant when it spoke of engaging in dialogue with the laity."

Allison reached into her handbag and felt her hand close comfortably around the thick and solid grip of the gun she had brought with her. She felt its brutal power to preserve life or to inflict death. Father Hanlon's life lay securely in her hands at that moment, at her mercy and discretion. She saw the headlines, "Priest Found Dead in Confessional; Police seek killer." She thought how loud the sound would be, only slightly dulled by the thin walls of the confessional box and the thicker walls of St. Peter the Fisherman parish church. Maybe no one would hear. She would be able to exit quietly, let herself out of the side door where the honeysuckle grew luxuriously and unimpeded, make her way through the rhododendron hedge to the sidewalk, and quietly walk away. She could do it; she knew she could. She saw all of her anger like a great wave washing over the dead body of the priest. She saw her trembling hand restoring the gun to its place with her hairbrush, facial tissue, and lip-gloss. She heard in her mind the tapping of her heels on the poor cheap linoleum floor that was all that the parish could afford as she would make her exit. It was all so dramatic and yet so sordid. Was this really what she was like, a killer at heart?

At last he summoned up the energy for a reply, "Are you asking for a customized approach of the whole moral law to your particular requirements Allison? Do you understand what that would mean? There are over a billion Catholics in the world today? Who gets to decide? The Church teaches moral norms as guides based upon a long collective meditation on human experience and the historical interface between God and humankind in the covenant of salvation history. That is all that it can do. Even more, it is all that I can do. I can't give you my personal assessment of everything. If I did you would be even more upset because now it would all be coming from me instead of from a two-thousand year old human institution? I can't spare you from the agony of personal freedom? For whatever reason human beings appear to have opted out of the comfort provided by strict causality. We will never be as innocent as the animals, creatures governed by blind instinct. Your very individuality is cherished and guaranteed by God but at a terrible price. You must decide what to believe and what to do. It isn't easy. God understands that. Even if you were an atheist you would still be burdened by human freedom, just read John Paul Sartre and his magnum opus *Being and Time*. People come in here seeking a remedy for guilt that they already feel, because there is a moral law written within us. The point is to seek the truth as best you can. I think you can find it here or at least some help but it is up to you. No one is attacking you."

"But they are, don't you see because people who read that we are *intrinsically disordered* won't serve us or hire us or give us places to live."

"To its credit the Church has spoken out against such things," Father Hanlon replied.

"It needs to talk louder, at least if it insists on saying things like *intrinsically disordered.*"

Father Hanlon nodded, "I think that is a fair request."

Allison suddenly felt very tired. It began to dawn on her that perhaps nothing has one localizable location of responsibility and power, that everything is interconnected. Her plan to resolve it all by one final battle with the man speaking to her from behind the plastic grille could not be conclusive. She had wanted life to have simple answers and it didn't. She realized that some generalizations were necessary if only to thwart other generalizations that might be even worse. She saw now why people like absolute answers because it spares them the burden of wandering like the Israelites in the desert for forty years just hoping that somewhere they just might find Ten Commandments so they would stop lying, cheating, and stealing from each other. It would be worth it to carry around an Arc of the Covenant and build temples and to write the Talmud and St. Augustine's *City of God* and St. Thomas Aquinas's *Summa Theologica* to get a little insight on human existence because without these things we would just do whatever we wanted and most of that wouldn't bring us to the point of love for each other.

The silence between them had lasted for quite some time.

At last the priest said, "Well Allison, if you have no sins that you would like to confess tonight perhaps I could simply give you a blessing and we could talk of these things some other time. I am fasting today but it must be past six already and I am hungry."

Allison hesitated before speaking up, "Well, I suppose that I have one sin that I could confess before we say goodbye."

"What is it?"

"Well, I might be going to shoot you."

The priest was quiet for what seemed an overly long minute.

"Are you really going to shoot me?"

"Yes."

"And with full deliberation and intent?"

"Yes."

They returned to silence. Between them they embodied the latent opposition between two equal realities, the reality of a two thousand year old institution claiming the mandate and capacity to define the purpose and ends of human life in general and the position of the individual who must wrestle with good and evil within the limits imposed by the short span of one single human life. The reality that alone can unite them is the overarching Deity that institutes and inspires the first and hovers over, nurturing and guiding, the second. Ideally there should be no opposition between the two if discernment and decision posed neither difficulty not obstacles. Surrounding both, of course, there is the encircling ambience of a secular society that cares for neither. It is a society where tolerance is born less of mercy than sheer indifference. The world didn't care if one lived or died while God, if He existed, just might care.

At last the priest broke the silence.

"Well that would be a very bad thing, Allison."

"I know it Father."

"But you haven't done it."

"No."

"So perhaps you did not give full consent of the will. Still, as venial sins go, well, it's a whopper, planning to kill someone."

"I understand."

"Strictly speaking you were not bound to confess it but I'm glad you did."

"How can I be sure that I still won't do it? And how can you in turn ever be sure that I won't be waiting on the other side of the confessional grille some Saturday when I have been having a really bad day?"

"I suppose I will have to rely on faith."

"Faith in me or in God?"

"Well, both, I guess."

"And you can live with that... uncertainty?"

"What else can I do?" the priest inquired.

Again a great silence filled the empty church.

This time Allison broke the silence

"I suppose you will have to tell everybody... about me."

"I can't, seal of the confessional remember... But I do hope that you have a firm purpose of amendment... for my sake at least. If not you might try going to confession across town at St. Andrews Parish. Father Paul beat me at golf last week and I have wondered how to get even with him."

"Are you making fun of me?" Allison asked, tightening her grip again on the revolver.

"No Allison, but I think you can see how close tragedy is to absurdity by what has happened between us today. Try and see your life in a more balanced framework as much for yourself as for the people that you will encounter."

Allison remained silent.

At last Father Hanlon said, "Now if you are truly sorry for your sins I will conclude with the words of absolution, give you your penance, and allow you to have some time to leave the Church to preserve your anonymity. Would you like that?"

Allison suppressed a sob and said, "Yes Father."

"Very well, make a good act of contrition."

Allison put the gun back into her handbag and joining her

hands together said the prayer of contrition that she had learned as a little girl: *"Oh my God I am heartily sorry for having offended thee and I detest all my sins because of thy just punishments but most of all because they offend thee my God who are all good and deserving of all my love. I firmly resolve with the help of thy grace to sin no more, to do penance, and to avoid the near occasions of sin."*

The priest said, "That was just fine. Now by virtue of your contrition and penance and your good resolutions to live a better life and by the authority vested in me I absolve you Allison from all of your sins in the name of the Father and of the Son, and of the Holy Ghost."

Allison said, "Amen."

"Now Allison I will give you your penance. It is a very special one so listen carefully. First, I ask that you will get rid of that gun, sell it, return it, or destroy it, but get rid of it. Will you do that?"

"Yes Father."

"Good, then I want you to read some of the short stories of Flannery O'Connor. I leave the choice and number of them up to you. I think you will like her. She understood the violence of the human heart as well as anyone living. She may help provide you with some of the answers that you seek."

There was a pause.

"Is that all?"

"Well some anger-management classes might be helpful as well but I will leave that up to you rather than imposing it as part of your penance. Your success in counseling is your own responsibility anyway."

"So I guess that's it huh."

"It is unless you have decided to shoot me after all."

"No, I changed my mind."

"Forgive me if I tell you that I am glad that you did change your mind. My golf game is getting a little better and I have hopes of breaking ninety before turning in my golf shoes for a harp."

Allison said, "Good luck."

"Thanks, Allison. Go in peace…"

Allison got up from the kneeler. It seemed as though she had been kneeling there for an eternity rather than the hour or so that it must have actually been. The evening shadows were lengthening and the church seemed somehow different to her, the light more golden, the silence more redolent of another presence that she did not dare to call God. She walked to the altar and said a brief prayer for Father Hanlon. Then she walked to the door, pushed it open, let it close noisily behind her to let him know that she had departed, and re-entered the outside world of sin and confusion.

LOVE AND DEATH

Of love and death much has been written; they are two of the great human universals. America in the year 2019 might have been portrayed as in the grip of both. It was a year of a triumph of the sort of pseudo-patriotism that speaks of love of country while secretly courting the policy and prospect of an early death for those young people who are too poor to build real-estate empires on credit and serial strategic bankruptcies.

In popular Republican political rhetoric past, present, and future are viewed as simultaneously existent, all of them manifest in the glorious figure for whom any mere mortal exaltation must prove inadequate, Donald Trump. History has now become the equivalent of a personal trademark. The contraction of fact to meet the demands of expediency implies that in a sense all of the diverse voices of America can find their prophetic realization at last in the daily Twitter-feed of our king and prophet.

One looks in vain for a parallel beyond the realm of American politics although physicists are beginning to play with the idea that in the space-time continuum, although subject to accretion and expansion from our particular point of view, it does in a very real sense already exist as a completed project and is perhaps only one of many similar universes. Beyond this multiplicity that beggars the imagination there exists only the singularity of unconditioned being from which all else emanates while in itself it remains at rest and beyond partition or comprehension.

America, as a unity of territories variously acquired, is now in the process, subject to its own center-point in the ponderous gravitas of its President, of claiming its unique right to command and seeking to make its existence a sort of metaphysical absolute through making itself great again. Of course the question remains unanswered as to just how America managed to ever drift from its appointed destiny. In the mind of many conservatives this drift was caused by the election of America's first black President. This unaccountable veering away from the appointed dominion of white men had almost prepared the ground for a woman to covet the exalted office and only the fortuitous circumstance of the Electoral College and its frustration of the manifest will of the electorate had prevented the popular will from having its ill-considered way.

No American Balzac has arrived yet to capture American society as it has veered away from the optimism that greeted the advent of the year 2000. None has yet emerged since the attacks on the World Trade Center, the wars of intervention that followed, and the economic contraction that brought America's new gilded-age style of speculative boom to an end. By the year 2019, the third year of the Trump Presidency, it was becoming every day more evident to many Americans that trumped-up military parades to celebrate American might were not quite apropos to our real condition because with over twenty-two trillion dollars of national debt America's next wars could be waged only with the permission and financial backing of the hard-working Chinese whose collective industry was fueling the world economy and supporting America's position as still number one.

In the absence of a Balzac the particular Human Comedy of America must rely less upon the novel than upon the short story for insight into the American ethos as it has devolved from the optimism attendant upon the new millennium into the sordid aspect of the

Trump era and the equally vacuous display put on by the Democratic party while harkening back to the New Deal, its own most glorious era. Both parties have ignored the fact that the American continent was once an integral unit long occupied by its own indigenous group of humans whose descendents are now claiming the right of migration and admission to America.

As to our particular national ethos American culture is and has always been characterized by alternative bouts of rebellion and further projection of power and conquest. Ours is a violent rather than a domesticated and pacific republic. It is for this reason surprising that the effort of conservative institutions from the Heritage Foundation to the various assorted pro-family organizations to restore an imagined golden-age harkens back to the 18th century, an age of reason rather than of demagoguery. In contrast the ever sanguine liberals imagine that the semi-literate working-class of white American males will be willing to surrender the illusion that Donald Trump would make a good drinking buddy and is out to get their auto-plant welding and coal-mining jobs back rather than cementing the economic power of the oligarchy.

Both political approaches imply that it just might be possible to engage in some miracle of restoration rather than simply admitting to ourselves that three centuries of rape and pillage have exhausted the virginal resources of the largest of earth's undiscovered places. The sad truth is that we are not in decline but still briefly at the apogee of America's long presumptuous attempt to circumvent the exigencies and limitations of the human condition. As it begins to dawn on more people that rapacious Trumpism is as native to our spirit as National Socialism was to the Teutonic spirit of industrialized Germany in the 1930's a long over-due admission of culpability is in order. Arrogant, selfish, materialistic, narcissistic, and contemptuous towards other nations and cultures—bigoted, mendacious, and self-indulgent—find any adjective and apply it to Trump and it is as apposite to America as well.

If America is ever to expiate its collective guilt we must look to the young to do so; but to date this prospect is unlikely. Anyone who has ever looked at pictures taken of children's faces whether rich or poor drawn from the 19th century must entertain the opinion that childhood as it is presently understood here is an American invention. There is little resemblance between the construction of the wooden figures and rag-dolls of that period and the sophisticated fashion-model dolls of 21st century girlhood. These figurines whether pouting and adolescent or sophisticated and elegant all betoken an early preparation for a way of life that may be vanishing in America, at least for the majority of young women.

The actual laborers engaged in manufacturing these early artifacts for the molding of the domestic dreams of American girlhood are located in foreign factories and undoubtedly do not look back on the same sparkling summer days that are fondly recalled by the grown-up daughters of those families that can afford a second home at Pinemont-in-the-Cascades (or simply Pinemont as its residents refer to it) the subject of this tale.

These fortunate daughters of the well-favored elite can look back on summers of unbridled nature-enhanced bliss in addition to their recollections of their family's main domicile whether in Washington or in Oregon. At Pinemont-in-the-Cascades the owners of companies or those playing an executive role in budding industries can spend a summer in nature at least until global warming and bark beetles decimate the great Oregon evergreen forests. At Pinemont the air is fresh and clean. The pollution from the great industrial core of China has been filtered by thousands of miles of ocean before it gets there. It arrives in America on the Pacific Coast, travels over some of the richest and greenest agricultural and grazing land in America and then climbs and spills over the volcanic peaks of the Cascades to where Pinemont rests with its golf courses, its bike trails, and its mountain lodge first built by the early timber and railroad barons and now inherited by their software and technology successors to economic dominance.

The children of Pinemont parents are granted a childhood not seen since that of children of the Victorian aristocracy. Each year brought its memories and traditions of bathing in the sea at Scarborough or Deauville. Life in England's empire days began unencumbered by student debts or the prospect of years of servitude spent in the nine-to-five rat-race, relieved only by the prospect of that coveted two-week yearly vacation. At Pinemont of course such respites were reckoned by the season rather than in weeks. After the season ended the house would be closed up again until next year, the snows would soon seal everything in white, most of the resort amenities would cease operations, the imported staff would return to their winter jobs or to school, and in Seattle and Portland more money would be made to finance this gem-like lifestyle.

In places where the American Dream has thus been realized, at least in terms of material prosperity, the year of 2019 only promised more to come. The market was booming and interest rates were low. Only in a few jaundiced authors' darkened imaginations did it appear that the present moment was more akin to the 1920's than to any other period of American history before or since, that fabled decade when F. Scott Fitzgerald found that as if by magic he could turn words into money, at least on this side of paradise. With this brief topical reflection as a prelude we will turn now to the scenery familiar to one of the protagonists of our tale.

Mercer Island is located in Lake Washington and is connected with the freeway by way of the Mercer Island Tunnel to Seattle. Boats from the salt water of Puget Sound can reach Lake Washington via a lock system to emerge at last into fresh water with the shimmering Cascades visible behind the houses that line the lakeshore. Mercer Island provides the very summit of gracious Seattle living to those who can afford it. The commute to downtown Seattle is a short one and inhabitants of Mercer Island are spared the daily ordeal of crawling up Highway 5 from Kent in the south or from Edmonds in the north into the proper core of the Emerald City. The high-rise buildings that are located there have over the decades transformed the former sleepy and quaint city with its fresh waterfront salmon drawn from local fishing fleets and its picturesque native totem poles, the city that once hosted the World's Fair in 1963, into the northern version of California's Silicon Valley and one of the busiest ports on the Pacific Rim.

Even though it was the original home of Boeing, Seattle's inhabitants realized that it is trade rather than aircraft and armaments that really make the world go round. Seattleites know this instinctively and this realization accounts for the fact that Seattle and King County always vote Democratic rather than following the archaic voting practices prevalent in what has been called "fly-over America." The Pacific Northwest can ignore the insignificant states that host soybean farms and foster the remnants of yesterday's hard-hat industries, whose citizens believe that the best way to make America great again is to keep it white and high-school educated, to keep a lid on the Black ghettos, and to bar immigration to refugees.

Since an ill-considered love affair is the primary topic of our tale (as will presently be seen) we may reflect briefly here on death. By the year of 2019 it was becoming evident that war and the implements of war were really America's primary export products. America's chief ally in the Middle-East was Saudi Arabia and in the Far-East President Trump was engaged in wooing the fat little Stalinist dictator Kim Jung Un while ignoring the fact that any missiles launched might just land on our former ally and former chief creditor Japan.

Most Americans had by and large adjusted to the idea that our blue-collar military fights and dies wherever Presidents wish them to while Congress simply votes the funds and goes off on vacation. The money presses roll and more empty dollars flood the world. There is even talk of going to Mars soon. By mid-July the east coast had ceased being flooded and tornado-racked and merely had to endure a kiln-like heat wave, but these changes were no doubt well within the normal curve of weather variability.

None of these trials were endured by the blue-voting west

coast states however. It was a lovely and smoke-free summer at Pinemont-in-the-Cascades while in Seattle the sailboats departed from local marinas regularly and headed north to the San Juan Islands. The mountains beckoned just beyond the blue waters of Puget Sound to the executives who had not yet left for their summer vacations. Seattle after all is a lovely place to be rich, but even prosperity must have its places of respite: therefore places like Pinemont exist.

Anthony Westin, a fortunate son of Pinemont, arrived in the mountains a few weeks after his classes at Pepperdine University in California had terminated. It was July now and the first blush of summer was relieved by the mountain winds behind which there was just the faintest premonitory hint of autumn. He was glad to escape California. The golden state had not lived up to his prior expectations. There was something cloying in the series of unclouded days and the boundless optimism entertained by the cell-phone wedded millennial generation who were his classmates. Over the last year he had found himself longing for just a touch of 1890's decadence to ameliorate the crystalline veneer of perfection that he found everywhere else. He was in the process of exploring a gay identity and his best models were drawn from other more closeted eras. He had skipped the 50th anniversary of the Stonewall rebellion in New York in 1969. He did not see himself donning a dress and heels and waving coyly from a Cadillac convertible. He wanted something that was at once daring and distinctive to encompass his personal rebellion. What was the use of being homosexual he felt if one was to be denied one's proper allowance of tragedy?

If he had been born in England in the 1890's he would have spent his days reading novels by Huysmans, sporting a green carnation at his club, and laughing uproariously at the latest bon mot of the divine Oscar. In the Paris of the 1920's he would have been seen drinking ice-cold absinthe and watching a black chanteuse writhe sinuously and virtually naked on stage while the smoke from opium tinged cigarettes wove their wreaths about his solitary table as he waited for someone who might never have kept their promised assignation.

In the 1970's he would have been out walking the beach at Fire Island with all of the aplomb of the Lady from Impanema. After a few years of indulgence he might have returned to school with an unknown virus in his blood and ten years later he would have died perhaps of pneumocystis pneumonia in a San Francisco Hospital surrounded by weeping friends and lovers. Now fifty years after Stonewall his sense of the tragic could only be sated if there was the chance that some fundamentalist-inclined baker would refuse to bake him a wedding cake.

He reflected that he might as well just marry one of the series of svelte and simpering debutants that his parents kept sending his way, various daughters of friends of theirs who had majored in art history at Stanford or Berkeley. The only readily available tragedy in 21st century America was to marry a girl who becomes an alcoholic and sues you for over half of your salary in alimony and child-care. It was with this un-encouraging frame of mind that Anthony had left California behind and drove his vintage collector's edition T-Bird up to Pinemont to spend a few weeks before returning to school in September.

Family tradition at Pinemont consisted of an invigorating hike in the morning, golf in the afternoon, and the ritual watching of FOX News at night to see what mischief the socialist democrats were planning for the election year of 2020. A quick look at the swimming pool during his first few days revealed nothing more than a bevy of budding female adolescents, a population that Anthony often referred to as "nymphets and crumpets." The rest of the "swimmers and soakers" were even more depressing consisting of overstressed mothers on the nether side of forty and their hirsute but pot-bellied executive husbands. It was all a long way from men in Speedos on Laguna Beach.

With a sigh Anthony had almost resolved himself to a summer

without dramatic incident until one night at the lodge when an unaccountable fate, the same that appears so often in short stories, arranged an acquaintance with a bewitching young woman who had caught his attention by her own expression of sorrow and studied desuetude as she sat at a nearby table and nursed a gin fizz.

Their eyes had met a few times without either of them exchanging smiles. They were the only two occupants of what was called colloquially at Pinemont, "the Eagles Nest." The bartender was engaged in a mild flirtation with the sole server so he paid his two customers little mind. Anthony was studying the menu when he noticed an item called, "cheese tray for two." It sounded good but perhaps too substantial for one so that he looked up again quizzically in the direction of the young woman whom he was shortly to learn was named Allison McCarthy. She had likewise been raised as a child at Pinemont.

As Anthony continued to stare at her she fixed him with an unfriendly glance and asked, "Well what?"

"I beg your pardon?" he replied.

"You keep looking over here and I was just wondering why."

Anthony considered her manner before answering, "It must be because I'm bored."

"How sad for you."

He was quiet for a few minutes before looking up again.

"Now what?" she looked up irritably.

"Are you hungry?" he asked.

"No, I'm buzzed."

"Then you should eat something," he suggested helpfully.

"What are you my mother?"

He was quiet again before asking, "Are you always nasty when you drink?"

Allison answered, "No, I'm nasty all the time."

Anthony took this in before replying, "It's nice of you to say so; I thought it was personal."

"Well it isn't … why did you ask if I was hungry?"

"Forget it."

"No why? Do I look too skinny or something?"

"Hardly?"

"Too fat!"

Anthony heaved a sigh before saying, "You are just right."

"Well thanks junior. How old are you anyway?"

"I'm nineteen."

"Well I'm thirty- four, but if you are looking for a Mrs. Robinson I'm not her."

"I just thought you might like to help me finish a cheese tray if I ordered one," Anthony said.

Allison came up short.

"Oh ... well that was nice."

Anthony returned to studying the menu but when he looked up Allison was standing by his table.

"I accept your offer. I mean thank you."

Anthony got up and pulled her chair back for her as he had been taught long ago to do. Ten minutes later they were both munching brie and camembert spread on thin toast and with a side of smoked oysters. The room was still empty. They sat by the windows and looked out at the Sisters Mountains where they shimmered in the August sunlight.

Allison asked at last, "Are you a newbie?"

"No, my family has been coming here for years. You?"

"Me too. It's funny but I don't remember seeing you here before. Where did you hang out?"

"I liked to read at home."

Allison smiled. "I noticed your glasses first thing. I play tennis."

"That explains our not meeting," Anthony said.

"You don't play tennis?" she inquired.

"Golf."

"Ugh, it's too time consuming."

"Like eating cheese with me?" Anthony smiled

"Don't be a baby."

"I'll only be nineteen once; I'm allowed to pout. It's all downhill from here."

"You can't possibly be that cynical," she said.

"I'm not cynical. I just haven't found a plan for my life yet and to tell you the truth I hope I don't."

"So how will you manage then?"

Anthony paused before answering reflectively, "I always thought that it might be nice to be an early casualty. I would like to be spoken of as one who died before his true promise could ever be realized. It is the perfect disguise for mediocrity."

"That's a chicken-shit attitude to have." Allison scoffed.

"My family expects me to do great things," Anthony stated decisively as though she should have deduced that already.

"Like what?"

"Have my own spot on Fox News after Hannity."

"You have to start first in radio." Allison smiled.

"Or I could go into investment banking."

"Do you know what investment banking is?"

"Not particularly."

"Well it's dull and stressful at the same time. Most high-paying jobs are."

"How do you know?"

"I grew up listening to my father's friends," Allison said sagely.

They each helped themselves to more food.

"What does your husband do?" Anthony asked.

"I'm not married." Allison replied.

"You will be. You're pretty."

"How would you know? You like men."

"How do you know that?" Anthony looked up alarmed.

"Please! You're such a drama queen. *I just thought I'd be an early casualty…*"

"It might be the only way that I can ever be free," Anthony

said looking down at his lap.

"Free of what?"

"Great expectations."

"Yours or your family's?"

"Both."

They were both silent again for awhile. Allison reached for another smoked oyster.

"These are good. I'm glad you asked me over."

Anthony smiled.

"You have a very fetching smile. You'll break hearts." Allison said.

"Do you really think so?"

"Yes … but not mine. I'm a lesbian."

"You surprise me."

"Why is that? Do I need a duck-tail haircut to prove myself?"

"I just meant … oh I don't know."

"You can say it. I don't expect you to know about any girls gay or straight. You probably went to an all-male prep school."

"I was quite a hit with the upperclassmen."

"I'm sure you were."

Anthony looked at Allison for awhile.

Allison began to squirm. "What?"

"E was just thinking that my family would like it if I brought a girl like you home."

"Well from what you have said so far I think they would be happy if you brought *any* girl home. Besides … I'm old enough to have been … your babysitter."

Anthony looked up candidly, "I used to have a crush on my baby-sitter. I even wanted to be her I suppose. I remember that I stole one of her lipsticks once out of her purse."

"Don't tell me that you're a drag queen too."

Anthony smiled. "Darling no, I can't afford Gucci handbags and for me it's everything or nothing."

"You could always do tacky-drag. You could shop in junior

ready-to-wear. You look like about a size 13."

"Please, not with my antecedents. I demand haute couture."

He paused before continuing ruefully, "You see how limited I am when it comes to sexual options."

They were both quiet again before Allison asked, "Why not just simply break out? Do a year of foreign study in Italy for instance. You might find some Italian nobleman who won't mind keeping you at his villa in Capri. All you will have to do is look pretty and pour drinks for rich queers that come over to visit and see his new acquisition."

"Things like that don't have good pension benefits."

"Who cares? You are planning on being a casualty anyway. Pick your moment and do a swan dive off the cliffs into the blue Mediterranean if you notice any wrinkles in the mirror some bright morning."

"I think you're making fun of me," Anthony pouted.

"Well somebody should."

"I think you know more about me than I know about you."

Allison smiled.

"I've lived a hard life. Besides, I'm a woman: I will always know more about you than you will ever know about yourself."

"So that's why you don't like men?" he asked.

"No, it's because I haven't learned to be a good liar. I could never convince a male mate that he knows more than me … at least about the things that really count."

"Is that all?"

"No. I also don't like the idea of being kept. No offense, some people are made for it. I want to know that I can always just walk away if I want to."

Anthony attempted to sound very mature. "Sounds like fear of commitment to me. Why doesn't the same thing apply if you left a woman?"

"I wouldn't leave a woman."

"Why?"

"Because I'll never find one who loves me…"

"Now who's being the casualty?"

"Don't be impertinent! I'm over ten years older than you."

They both resumed eating from the cheese selection. The brie went first and now they were getting down to the Spanish sheep cheese.

"Ugh, this stuff is too strong," Allison said.

"Don't eat it then."

"I don't want to be a cheese-wuss."

"Don't you mean cheese-whiz?"

"Don't tell me what I mean."

"Well, can I ask you something?" Anthony asked after a minute looking directly into her eyes.

"Go ahead."

"What do you want out of life?"

Allison considered. "I want to get even."

"With who?"

"With everybody."

"That sounds scary," he said spreading some more sheep cheese.

"I once held a priest at gunpoint," Allison confessed.

Anthony went on chewing.

"Did he molest you?" he asked.

"No, I just thought he represented power that was denied to me because I'm a woman."

"And that made you mad enough to kill him?"

"I didn't kill him … I even prayed for him."

"Did he ever have you traced?" Anthony asked.

"No. The seal of the confessional was inviolate he said. He let me walk away and I never saw him again."

"That was nice of him. I mean letting a dangerous lunatic escape."

Allison looked up sharply. "I'm not a lunatic; I'm just terminally pissed-off."

Anthony considered this before replying, "I'm not sure that I can appreciate the essential distinction."

"It isn't a formal distinction, Dodo-child. It means that I have a right to be angry. My anger makes me who I am."

"What do you mean, Dodo-child?" Anthony asked.

"Dodo, like the big dumb birds that are now extinct and child because … well, look at you; you look like a big baby doll."

"Charming," Anthony commented dryly. "So what does your anger ever get you?"

"I don't know," Allison said sulking.

The two were silent again. Other people were entering the room now.

Allison leaned forward and smiled and whispered conspiratorially, "Do you think that people might think that we are a couple?"

Anthony looked about before answering, "Hardly, I'm too cute for you."

Allison answered, "I knew you were a bitch."

Anthony smiled. "Before you even sat down here?"

Allison smiled too, "You cross your legs like you your maxi-pad was slipping."

Anthony said with dignity, "Ad hominum attacks are always the refuge of the intellectually inferior."

Allison grinned, "Don't toy with me tartlet I might just still be armed."

At this auspicious moment Allison's mother came up the stairs looked about and seeing her walked over to the table where they were both sitting.

"Allison, we'll be eating downstairs in the dining room in an hour. Don't you think you should go home and change?"

Then as if seeing Anthony for the first time she said, "Oh hello… Allison, who's your young friend?"

Allison blushed. "I don't know his name."

"And you are eating his food?

"I'm eating his food, Mother, not sleeping with him,"

"Allison!"

"My name is Anthony. Happy to meet you Mrs. ... "

"McCarthy, Amelia McCarthy and this is my daughter, my very ill-mannered daughter, Allison."

"Pleased to meet you Allison. Mrs. McCarthy, we have been discussing casualty insurance."

"Oh are you into insurance Mr. uh Anthony?"

"No, actually I am more into risks."

"Ah, you are an actuary."

"No, my task in life is to ... how did we decide Allison ... it is to live dangerously and by that means to court untimely disaster. It's a new field but quite promising."

"I'm not sure I understand," Allison's mother said awkwardly.

"Well it wasn't clear to us either although we were just coming to an interesting point when you arrived."

"And I interrupted you. I *am* sorry. I merely wanted to tell Allison that her father and I will be eating downstairs with the Hanover family and we would like her join us. Um you could join us as well. We are quite a diverse company."

Allison shook her head at her mother.

"Well it does no harm to ask, Allison. I mean I find you here in earnest conversation with a ... young man, so I naturally supposed..."

"I'll be back at the house in twenty minutes to change."

"Do and try and look nice Allison if only for your father's sake. Mr. Hanover is a client after all."

"I will Mother."

"Thank you. Goodbye Mr. Anthony, it has been so nice meeting you."

Allison's mother went back down the stairs.

Anthony turned to Allison and said, "And from this domestic ambiance you ended up being a dangerous lunatic?"

Allison answered, "You could give me a little Tea and Sympathy at least."

Anthony replied, "You should meet my parents."

"Tell me later; I have to go home and change."

And from this disjointed beginning a summer relationship of sorts began between them.

The following day Anthony encountered Allison again where she sat gazing out at the lake from the gazebo. He came up behind her quietly before saying loudly and clearly.

"Don't shoot; I come unarmed."

Allison turned around and smiled. "Dodo-child! Come and sit with me. I am looking for an intelligent confidant and since none is available it might as well be you."

As Anthony settled down comfortably in a deck-chair beside her she said, "By the way, I thought that you handled my mother rather well yesterday. You aren't as brainless as you look."

Anthony drew himself up, "I will have you know that I am on a full scholarship at Pepperdine in English Literature."

"Surfboards and sonnets, eh?" Allison answered.

"My parents think I am studying finance and mathematics though, a joint major."

"What will they do when they find out?"

"By then I will be off to Capri like you said yesterday."

"Well I am not a qualified career counselor. Just ask my mother."

"Well you must have learned something in your twenties."

"I learned how many false starts a person can make and still retain sufficient credibility to keep getting financing for the next one."

"I don't think I could I could keep that going," Anthony said ruefully.

"You may have to if you are anything like me. But then you are a man and for a man something may always turn up for you ... even if you are queer," Allison commented.

"I've always hated that term," Anthony said.

"Well it's very in right now: LGBTQI, just pick a letter,

something will fit you."

"I prefer invert or homophile."

Allison laughed. "You are so antiquated, so very Henry James, all the Nancy-boys of that era were running about Europe or going off to Morocco and calling each other my dear boy. England had a fairy on every square foot of English soil and yet no one ever apparently got laid."

"Lytton Strachey certainly did," Anthony said in defense.

"Nobody reads Lytton Strachey anymore."

"I'm surprised you have heard of him," Anthony said with a sneer.

Allison answered haughtily, "I will have you know that I am well grounded in the humanities, philosophy specifically, which means that I am consequently virtually unemployable. I will always see all of the logical flaws in any company policy."

"I thought people in human resources would value culture," Anthony objected.

"Hardly," Allison answered drily. "Only basic grammar is required. Cultural depth can even be a handicap as they try and find a slot for you to fill. Meanwhile people like you and me study in an effort to overcome our sexual alienation; when our contemporary world provides no valid interior role models we turn to the idealized past for sustenance and support."

"Well I hope to make it as a charming ingénue, so why am I studying anything?"

"Well I hope you are not studying in hopes of earning money. People like you and me study to form ourselves into something besides an empty gullet with an impressive expense account. It allows us to feel superior to those upon whose good-will our survival depends."

"But we still fancy an elegant cheese-tray from time to time don't we?" Anthony smiled. "It is the old problem of elegant tastes coupled with an empty wallet."

"People like us need sponsors to enable our gracious living or we might if we are lucky attain the security of a good marriage to rescue us from genteel poverty."

Anthony sighed. "Well there will always be Capri for those of the inverted demimonde."

"For you maybe, but the number of rich lesbians is … well, you have to be another rich lesbian to find one."

"How do you know?" Anthony inquired. "I thought you were above being just trade."

"Trust me, I know." Allison replied mysteriously and Anthony already knew enough about her to leave it at that.

Their next casual meeting was along one of the hiking trails that threaded Pinemont; he was walking, she jogging. Allison ran up alongside of Anthony and yelled, "On your left." He started and moved aside quickly and Allison burst into laughter, "Lesbian coming through."

"You startled me," Anthony remarked as she jogged in place beside him.

"Well you're up early. I pictured you lounging about in a Victorian dressing-gown to the consternation of your parents and reading decadent poems by Ernest Dowson or Arthur Symons. You had best be careful venturing forth from your yellow wallpapered chamber or you will lose your fashionable pallor."

"Down, you presumptuous strumpet, do you dare to imagine that you understand me?" Anthony replied laughing.

"Well I expect that you have reduced superficiality to an art-form. You practically admitted as much to me at our first meeting," Allison chided him playfully.

"And from that fortuitous encounter you presume to have insight into my real character?"

"What character? The best that you can manage is an orientation. You are so quintessentially gay. Quite honestly I was surprised that you asked me to share your cheese sampler. Aren't you afraid of getting female cooties?"

"My dear girl I am proof to any and all effusions and distillations emanating from the female sex."

"You always talk as if you had just stepped out of a book."

Anthony smiled, "Why whatever do you mean Allison dear?"

"There you see!"

"Perhaps you are unaccustomed to good breeding."

"There is a difference between breeding and affectation. A little less Jane Austin and more of Jack London would do you good if you are determined to be gay, Anthony. Effete isn't in right now."

"I stand corrected," Anthony bowed.

They walked on side by side in the morning shade. The sun had not as yet climbed above the towering Ponderosa Pines nor had the usual heat of the day descended. The air was dry and bracing and scented with the trees and with the sweet scent of the meadow grass of the horse paddock toward which they were walking side by side.

"I don't suppose you ever ride do you?" Allison asked.

"Not without a proper hunt and the sound of hounds in my ears."

Allison stopped short. "You don't expect me to believe that you have actually hunted foxes."

"On my last trip to Bedfordshire…"

"Stop, you mean that you actually pursued a helpless little fox and…"

"No, I must confess that we only followed a drag. Bloodsports have been outlawed even in the home counties."

"How disappointing for you that must have been. You might have been awarded the brush."

"You speak scornfully. Evidently you don't understand the pageantry of the whole thing. There was a reason after all that the English came to dominate the world. The desire for conquest is part of human nature. As an English public school trained young man the English elite was taught to endure pain and if necessary to inflict it."

"I knew it! You probably like wearing harnesses and spiked chains too."

"I believe that we were talking about the refinement born of manly endurance and the ability to read the classics in their original languages."

Allison remained adamant. "Men in academic robes beating little boys with canes; it's disgusting."

"History is the record of pain and brutality."

"That's why I don't read history," Allison stated firmly. "When women have more power and can influence events then maybe…"

"Oh yes, here is where we hear about the golden era that will come when women rule," Anthony interrupted.

"Don't be so condescending. It is coming you know. We are almost at parity in the professions and many world leaders…"

"How many times did Theresa May try to get a Brexit deal through parliament and she left in tears. Do you think Churchill would have gone out like that?"

Allison looked down, "She was treated abominably."

"Excuses!"

"Besides, Brexit only happened because your precious English are afraid that the whole country will be soon overrun with Syrian women and children. Women will always fight for their children."

"Then they should stay where they are and fight. It isn't economics at stake really it is a question of cultural integrity; that at least must not be diluted by an Islamic effusion."

Allison walked on beside him but Anthony could feel her sudden coldness.

At last she said, "Borders are unnatural things anyway. Survival takes precedence over mere legalities. Forget Europe, how do you think America got settled in the first place? Do you think the Indians invited them?"

"You prove my point; it all comes down to the will to conquest of under-settled and undefended lands. Take Pinemont for instance: do you think that just anyone can come in here? It costs a pretty penny and those who have the pennies work for them in the city so that their kids can retain a privileged status to ride horses about and play tennis in nature's wonderland without being bullied by some Compton kid in a drug gang in sunny California."

"What do you know about it Mr. Pepperdine? They wouldn't be in a drug gang if they had a chance of a good education and a decent job."

"Over fifty years of affirmative action and all that it has produced is rap music from the hood. At least the Black Panthers knew how to dress well, radical chic."

"With you life's big issues always come down to a fashion-statement don't they?"

Anthony was quiet and they walked on in silence. At last he spoke up.

"Well if you want to know I don't really care about politics and sociology. I just think that it is nice that some people can afford gracious living and I think that most of them have worked for that privilege. Would you want to entrust some kid of yours to the tender mercies of the ghettos in L.A.?"

"I don't have any kids, but if I did I would want them to have a social conscience and not become some nasty little Republican prick whose best idea of rebellion against being an investment banker is just to become a spoiled effete snob!"

"Who said I was a Republican and who said you get to call me a snob?"

"If the shoe fits wear it."

Anthony walked on in silence before saying despondently, "We don't know each other well enough for you to fight with me like this."

"Well I was in a good mood when I jogged up."

"Well who asked you to stop anyway?"

"It was just that you looked so pathetic walking here by yourself with your head down. What happened did your family ask you not to embarrass them by hitting on the waiters here or something?"

"As a matter of fact they did."

Allison stopped walking, "Oh."

"Well in effect they did. I keep being asked the usual questions about who I might be dating at school. I think that they might even be relieved if I could demonstrate a little inconsequent promiscuity as long as it did not compromise my future by drawing into our orbit some girl who as my father puts it might act as a drain on the estate. A wife is an accessory not a partner in life. Well I said some catty things back to them and we had our annual fight last night."

"That's too bad. So what were you doing before I came up to you all inappropriately chipper?"

"I was wondering how long it would take to drown in a mountain lake from hypothermia or if I might just be able to locate a mother grizzly bear and her cubs and grab one of them up by its little furry feet."

"Don't you think that is a rather extreme solution?"

"I'm very emotional and reactive."

"I guess you are. Remind me not to fight with you; you're fragile."

"I'd certainly appreciate it."

The two young people emerged from the sheltering forest and the meadows lay before them with the great mountains in the background. Clouds backed up behind the ridge and spilled slowly into the valleys below. The path wound along the open meadow and descended into a grove of aspens beyond. They walked side by side again and Allison looked up at Anthony's face and saw him brush away a tear impatiently.

Allison said quietly, "I hate fighting with family."

"With us it's a tradition," Anthony said with a catch in his voice.

"Is it a religious thing?"

"No, we aren't religious at all; to them being gay is simply a social impediment, but so is any entanglement with another person. Investment bankers are allowed a family as long as it doesn't interfere with business. But, to have a proper relationship means that one is socially respectable. In the world of investment bankers a homosexual is bound to be viewed as a socialist and of course every socialist is bound *mutatis mutandis* to be a homosexual. I hope you haven't planned on being a professional yourself; straight people will only be sure that you are a reincarnation of Emma Goldman."

"Darling, nobody remembers Emma Goldman."

"Then they'll think you are like the squad, another Alexandria Ocassio-Cortez."

"I am what is familiarly known as a professional student. My parents think that if I remain in school long enough I am bound to find some up and coming guy and marry well someday. It always comes down to a choice between tuition and therapy and they figured a degree is worth more than just being told by some shrink that I'm not crazy anymore."

"Are you really crazy?" Anthony asked in alarm.

Allison pondered his question before replying, "Who can tell? What do you think?"

"I just think you're abrasive and mouthy," Anthony said loyally.

"Thank you. I like you too Dodo-child."

"I probably know more than you do," Anthony said.

"Perhaps I just hide my education better than you do," Allison replied.

As the summer days passed Anthony and Allison found as if by accident that rather than spend their time in moody and solitary introspection while in a lovely mountain setting or the even worse company of their respective parents they would rather be with each other. Yet the days passed by without significant incident or issue. Although they appeared to be on alternate routes regarding sexuality both of them had been born to privilege and to all visible appearances should have been capable of attracting a mate of the opposite sex thus ensuring the perpetuation of the human race and the fulfillment of nature's design in creating sets of perfectly matched genitalia. By this cunning ruse intelligent design had so sculpted the human bodies of each that what one possessed in abundance the other was correspondingly denied. To frustrate this design implied that each was manifesting an attitude of evident contempt for the efforts expended on their behalf by being determined to seek love from one who was a mere replica of themselves. Worse still in its political and cultural impact this penchant or disposition was not an individual idiosyncrasy but was one evidently shared by a sufficient number of other human beings that it was not inconceivable that given sufficient time and opportunity one or the other might possibly encounter another person so inclined and perhaps even see the initial prompting of their misguided appetites ripen into the simulacrum of a romance. This was not a case in other words of a dearth in population of one or the other sex so that from strict necessity and lacking all other viable options friendship might unaccountably tip into the forbidden confines of sexual exchange between persons of the same sex. Rather their joint propensity was due to the lack any goal other than the sheer pleasure of the concupiscent act and as such socially unacceptable and reprehensible. Each had declared to the other a determination to follow a barren path into an inextricable jungle of sterile passions without social support or sanction let alone the security that nature's intent would be fulfilled. This was clearly a case of wayward and recalcitrant genitalia. Yet so it was that these two young animals were daily in each other's unsupervised company without any danger that lulled by the gentle summer breezes and seduced by the softly shaded potential bed provided by fallen pine needles on the forest floor they might disrobe and spreading their garments to protect their flesh from any untoward abrasion in their frenzy so commune with each other that the folly of their former proclivities might be made at last manifest.

Instead their walks through the forest along the spring-fed river were confined to the prosaic topics better reserved for people of twice their age. They discussed pedagogy, careers, politics, and even touched upon matters of metaphysics and epistemology. They discovered that they shared many of the same views, had many memories of the same things, and saw their lives terminating at some future date with the same summation as to life's ultimate meaning. In this they were already somewhat estranged from their peers who were too busy living to speculate about life's end. Both confessed to times when the possibility of extinction beckoned as the premature end of unwarranted pain rather than the termination of all prospect of fulfillment and contentment by finding love at last.

Of course it is easy to hold time as cheap when one is burdened by a surfeit of days. Age would no doubt have taught them otherwise. It is trite to say that youth is wasted on the young, but it is only older people who mutter such nonsense, imagining that if they could as if by magic be restored to that era of taut skin and radiant form, of lushness of limb, and charged with an energy that can only be revived at a later date by hormone supplements that they would do better this time, that they would be grateful for each hour rather than callously lavish with that one irretrievable commodity, time.

Bathed in unmerited riches however these two found nothing odd in the thought that their stories might end in a self-determined manner. Enamored of tragedy from reading various books they did not really know the true cost of anything. Happiness seemed something owed to them so that the only real question was whether any particular happiness would prove adequate to their imagined desserts. They thought it strange that their parents were so obsessed with externals and appearances when they each enjoyed finding ways to give the world the metaphorical finger on the slightest pretext. Everything seemed slightly ridiculous to them. Surely life must be easier than their elders made it out to be.

"I don't know why I can't find anyone to love," Allison confessed to Anthony one day after one of their comfortable silences when walking together along the spring-fed river that wound through the woods near Pinemont.

"Don't be ridiculous," Anthony said, "The only problem is finding someone who is sufficiently hung."

"Don't be crude," Allison remarked.

"Well if you can't stand honesty…"

"Are gay men really that shallow?"

"No, just gay men in their twenties; by forty they would rather gossip about things like opera or *haute cuisine*."

"I think you may have read too many books by Edmund White."

"And what is a lesbian doing reading Edmund White?"

"He functions as a reset button after reading *The Well of Loneliness*."

Anthony reflected. "You should read *Dancer from the Dance* by Andrew Holleran. The period that he deals with is gone forever of course, it is more remote and idealized in its way than *The Great Gatsby*, but it gives one the same feeling of inevitable and pervading doom and loss."

"If you like doom and loss…"

Anthony shrugged, "What else is there really?"

"And I thought I was the morbid one."

"What makes *you* so morbid?"

"Well for one thing I'm in love with the music of Lana Del Rey," Allison confessed.

Anthony considered, "Well I guess that qualifies, at least until you turn eighteen."

Allison bridled. "You're so supercilious, what makes you an expert on everything?"

"Extensive reading."

"Oh really! What have you read?"

"In English or in the original languages."

"Come on."

"I mean it; test me."

"Okay - Lautreamont."

"The Song of Maldoror, a bit affected but graphic. I think he was going for shock value just like *Justine*, horribly boring really, both of them.”

“You mean Lawrence Durrell.”

“Please! De Sade of course.”

“Henry Miller.”

“Wishful autobiography, sordid heterosexuality.”

“Anais Nin.”

“Most of it never happened.”

“Who says?”

“Gore Vidal.”

Allison objected. “And you think *he* never told any lies?”

“Who cares when he’s so witty?”

“And cruel, you must admit that he could be cruel, to poor Truman for instance.”

“Capote deserved it; besides truth is always cruel.”

Allison reflected. “Who have you read in the 21st century?”

“Nothing. I only read classics. I am a man born after my time.”

Allison mimicked a fit of nausea and said, “You make me so sick.”

“Then why do you keep hanging out with me?”

“Deluded Dodo-child, it is you who are hanging out with me I thought you knew.”

They both laughed.

Finally Allison said, “You won’t ever become an investment banker you know.”

“And you won’t have any kids,” Anthony countered.

“Stop it.”

“Oh? I didn’t think you wanted any kids.”

“Why should you think that?”

“Well don’t look at me as a prospect; go and find a doctor with a Petri dish or whatever they use.”

“I wouldn’t want any sperm from you. It’s probably tainted with virus.”

“What virus?”

"You have probably found a new one: California Streptococcus Herpes 5."

"I'll have you know that I always play hard to get. I am only an icon for admiration and unfulfilled longing."

"Until your third drink maybe."

"Nasty bitch."

"Easy trollope."

"Don't make me cry."

They both laughed.

Anthony shrugged. "Alright so I won't be an investment banker so what?"

"Well how will you get money to live?"

"I'll repair to my garage and invent something with popular appeal that will save people money or something."

"Like what for instance?"

"A re-usable condom."

"You just can't be serious can you?"

"Not with you."

"What makes me so special?"

"I don't know. I have been trying to figure that out. If you want to know I find it a little disconcerting."

"Do I remind you of a man?"

"No."

"Then what?"

"I told you. I don't know."

They walked on in silence for a bit.

At last Allison asked, "Are we friends?"

Anthony replied. "I don't like friends; they always make demands … especially women."

"What do you mean by that?"

"I mean there are only so many hours in the day and I am not interested in spending one or two of them hearing the details about some incident that even the woman in question will have forgotten by the next day."

"You better stay gay then."

"I plan to."

Allison was quiet again before asking, "I am trying to figure you out. What if you are worse than just an unpleasant little twit? What if you are evil?"

"Then go back to the lodge and find another sucker with a cheese tray on whom to exercise your frustrated motherly instincts."

"Remember I have a gun."

Anthony pulled-up short. "I thought you told me that the priest told you to get rid of it."

"I might have bought a new one since."

"Oh."

"I can help you realize your ambition for a tragic and premature end."

"Psycho."

"I can see the headlines now 'Blond Youth Murdered at Cushy Resort\Deranged Lesbian Held in Custody.' Then the copy, 'The distraught mother was quoted as saying "We did everything we could for the poor girl. She was the most beautiful debutante in her season.'"

"Were you?"

"My dad says I was."

"He would have to."

"You *are* evil."

"Artists are dedicated to the truth."

They walked along side by side.

"Your problem Allison is that you are a cliché."

"Me! Well so are you. I bet you've never done anything outside the Castro Street playbook in your life."

"Alright, let's be daring, I'll ask you out on a date, how would that be?"

"Come on."

"No I mean it, a real date. Call it mutual revenge on our parents."

"You might have to kiss me to make it appear authentic," Allison warned him.

Anthony made a wry face. "Very well, I'll think of England and jump, parachute or no parachute."

"You might get to like it."

"Only if you start calling me Foxy Dude instead of Dodo-child."

"But you are a dodo-child the proof is that you don't know that you are."

"You're such a girl."

"Well I suppose at thirty-five that's a compliment."

"Take it any way you want."

So it was then that Anthony and Allison started dating. Their parents were at first skeptical and then cautiously thrilled. It would save so much in expensive conversion therapy and in making lame excuses to friends of the family for their unmarried state. Days passed and the pair became one of the seasonal collective memories at Pinemont that summer. They made a beautiful couple, especially when Anthony kissed her hand or they toasted each other with Shirley Temple's designed to look like pink champagne. Each had an element of untapped theatricality and had watched sufficient movies to recreate classic love scenes in pantomime. Sometimes they didn't even talk but simply engaged in a series of passionate expressions made and exchanged between them to the delight of the surrounding tables. Each tried to top the other in simulating restrained passion so that even older couples seeing them together began to smile with nostalgia and a few reached out and joined hands shyly.

It was all a grand lark but as the days passed Allison would occasionally have to excuse herself. She would go into the ladies room and cry for no reason that she could comprehend. She would splash water in her face and reapply her make-up before returning and going on just as before. Anthony in turn would pose as one who was growing impatient for his beloved's return and light up in simulated delight when she walked up again in her full-length dress to resume her place at the table by his side.

So did the summer days pass and September imperceptibly neared. The wind shook the aspen trees outside the windows of the lodge. Autumn seemed at once infinitely far away and close at hand and the faux-romance became a fixture in both of their lives. Allison thought back to her time with a cousin and her family from some years ago and of how hard it had been for her to bid them goodbye at last and return to her own solitary life again, a life spent without context or meaning.

Perhaps it was natural that she was more preoccupied than Anthony by existential questions; after all she had majored in philosophy. He on the other hand was obsessed with the expressive possibilities of literature rather than whether any particular proposition was true or not. In addition there was always their difference in age, not a particularly large one of course, but a significant one to a woman whose available window for child-bearing is rather narrow. Love and death as ultimate realities are more the concern of the sex that gestates life and thus comprehends its inherent value.

One day Allison asked him. "What's your objection to women anyway Dodo-child?"

Anthony walked on in silence before answering at last. "I suppose the problem is that I see them as competition for what I really want. They have all the advantages, a sort of direct line to most men's libido, breasts and all that. Other than that everything on a woman seems designed with babies in mind. It is all just too physical. I crave sterile refinement punctuated by short bouts of focal passion with no encumbrances attached."

"Selfish through and through," Allison said in disgust.

"Oh I don't know. After all someone must preserve the culture. The Greeks knew that. Children are the death of superfluous leisure and it is leisure alone that creates monuments of culture. Besides, I don't think women like men all that much. Just listen to them when they are meeting in one of their various cabalistic discussions. The primary topic is usually men's shortcomings. Women immediately set about dismantling a man's interests after the marriage ceremony is concluded. Out go the toys, gone are the old drinking buddies, and what is left to him but yards to mow and garage doors to fix. The highpoint is the occasional weekend barbecue with "mutual friends" which means the wife's BGF and her desiccated mate brought along from the mummy case to help carry plates out from the kitchen while she and her hostess sit laughing by the pool asking over their iced-teas if the burgers are ready yet."

"Evidently you've never visualized a relationship of gender-equality between men and women."

"That's the last thing that most women would ever want! Women maintain an icon of the ideal man, a sort of combination of their idealized fathers and some lobotomized stud with an Austrian accent."

"And you men want some endlessly nubile young blond thing to worship you combined with a twenty-four/seven cleaning machine and secretary."

"Thus the whole LGBT movement: everyone is freed to seek their own kind."

Both were silent until Allison asked, "Then why aren't we happy?"

Anthony looked surprised. "I thought it was me who wasn't happy and you were acting the part of the wise older sister and confidant."

"I'm not that old," Allison said defensively.

"Everyone's old after thirty; it's all in the LGBT guidebook and bylaws."

"There isn't any such thing."

"Well then it's an unwritten rule and those are the most binding of all."

Allison was quiet for a time before muttering to herself, "I hate rules."

They walked on in silence. At last Allison stated, "Your problem is that you don't understand love."

"Me?"

"Yes you. You are leading an entirely derivative existence as though everything can be expressed in a book. Henry James! How disgusting!"

"What's disgusting about Henry James?"

"It took him until he wrote *The Ambassadors* to realize that you have to grab life or it escapes you. Besides, it always takes him a whole page to describe the most trivial actions, description run amuck. He dug so deeply into his characters that they became ciphers and not people anymore. It might have worked for that wacky governess at Bly with the two possessed kids but most people just aren't that neurotic."

"So you *have* read Henry James."

"Nobody *reads* Henry James. They labor though him like a particularly painful delivery. He isn't an avocation, he's a punitive sentence imposed on those who want to sound extra sophisticated. I'd rather read Faulkner with all that dust and old Civil War monuments to a vanished age of glory, all the decadent and incestuous families too proud of their heritage to let anyone else in."

"Well I think incest is tacky," Anthony said fastidiously.

"You think everything is tacky unless it happens in a men's room at a bus station."

"And I think you are too into stereotypes, a poor excuse for your poor skills in argument. You better go back and read some more philosophy."

Allison smiled before saying triumphantly, "So! Did I finally get under your skin a little bit? I knew poking critical remarks at Henry James would do it. Maybe now you can understand why I said that you don't understand love."

"I do too."

"You don't. I bet you never even saw *Picnic* with Kim Novak and William Holden."

"Well I haven't, so what."

"So there's something wrong with you if you never saw *Picnic.*"

Anthony objected, "How can you make blanket statements like that? Who makes you the almighty film guru?"

Allison turned away. "Well maybe I just want you to know something about love that's all. Love is worth any price you have to pay for it."

"Well *Picnic* as a title sounds pretty trivial."

"It's by William Inge, a gay man who ended up dying by suicide … interested yet?"

Allison walked ahead of Anthony and ignored him. After several minutes Anthony conceded, "Fine, tell me about your *Picnic.*"

"It isn't *my picnic* Dodo-child. In fact love isn't a picnic. Did you ever think that people die over love or better still they realize the full value of living by being in love? You have to take risks to love. Sometimes you even have to endure endless betrayal and cruelty from the one you love. And sometimes for no good reason at all opportunity introduces you to someone who is completely wrong for you and you still love them anyway."

"Tell me about *Picnic,*" Anthony said.

Allison looked around for a fallen log by the hiking path. "Alright sit down with me and I'll tell you."

The two walked over to a fallen log covered with a light dusting of dried moss and sat down there side by side.

Allison said, "Okay. *Picnic* is the story of a few short days in little town where everybody is stripped of their illusions."

"Well that sounds fairly typical to any drama."

"Do you want to hear this or not?"

"Yes, I do."

"Then be quiet. The main character, Hal, is an ex athlete, a real jock."

"I think I might like this after all."

"Will you shut up!"

"Okay."

"Anyway, he comes to town to look up an old buddy of his because he's out of work and riding the rails. His buddy comes from a rich family in the grain business. His old buddy is at first really glad at first to see Hal because he can show off his foxy fiancée Madge, the prettiest girl in town."

"So the buddy isn't gay."

"No. Try and pay attention will you."

"Alright."

"So anyway by coming to town Hal ends up stirring up all these hidden feelings among all the other characters and Madge falls for him like a ton of bricks. It all happens at a picnic where the town elects the Queen of Neewollah."

"The what?

"Neewollah, Dodo-child, Halloween spelled backwards, a sort of harvest queen. Madge gets elected of course and through a series of circumstances Madge ends up dancing with Hal and oh my God this music called *Moonglow* starts to play and they dance too and ... oh I guess you have to see it, but it is so beyond sexy ... and then this stupid middle-aged lady school teacher tries to muscle in and dance with Hal too and she ends up tearing his shirt almost off and the buddy thinks that Hal tried to seduce Madge and he claims that Hal stole his car and suddenly Hal is on the run again because he doesn't want to spend a night in jail because his Mom once had him thrown into juvenile detention and he hates jail even if it is just until everything can get straightened out."

"Slow down."

Allison paused to catch her breath. "Anyway Hal is basically suddenly a fugitive with no job, just lost his good buddy, and all he can figure is that he has to get enough cash to split town. But before that he runs into Madge sort of in the woods and he tells her to just leave him alone but Madge starts to tell him how great a dancer he was and what it meant to her when he held her in his arms. And then…"

"What? Did they do it or something?"

"No, disgusting twerp, they didn't *do it*; they didn't have to. She tells him how tired she is of being just told that she's pretty and then she kisses him. I mean she *really* kisses him and, oh my God, there's something there that's … well it's iconic, it's *love.*"

Allison stopped talking and it was quiet in the woods and the dry heat of the day was only softened by the breeze in the high tree-tops.

Anthony said nothing.

Finally Allison continued, "Well Hal can't believe that this beautiful girl loves him but events are moving fast now and he goes to the boyfriend of the dopey teacher lady that ended up tearing his shirt almost off at the picnic to borrow enough money to leave town because the ex-good-buddy said that Hal stole his car and he has to get away. Anyway, the father of the ex-good-buddy doesn't want his precious son to marry Madge anyway because she doesn't come from their social strata."

Anthony interrupted her story, "Is that it then? Does Hal get away?"

"Be quiet. Madge and her sister are talking in their bedroom and Millie, that's the little sort of butch sister, she tells Madge she should go off with Hal, do something smart for once. Madge's mother doesn't want Madge to go. She knows about men, how fickle they can be, how shallow they are, even if they say that they love you. *But Madge doesn't care…*"

She paused.

"Why?" Anthony asked.

"Dodo-child! It's because *she loves Hal.* She'd go anywhere with him now, but even then he has to ask her to go away with him and he does."

"What does he say?"

"He pulls her away from her mother and he tells her that she belongs to him but even more than that he makes her feel like no other woman has ever done before. She makes him feel…"

She paused again.

Anthony showed some interest at last. "What does she make him feel?"

"She makes him feel … *patient.*"

Anthony hesitated and then he blurted out, "What the hell does that mean, she makes him feel patient?"

"Well you wouldn't know Dodo-child. And I thought you were a literature major! Think about it. Hal's problem has always been that he just moves along from flower to flower like a bee and here is this girl who has *brought him down!* Do you see? Now his life has meaning at last. He'll do anything now to keep her; she belongs to him."

Allison stopped talking.

"So how does it end?" Anthony asked at last.

"Hal runs away and hops a train yelling back at Madge to remind her that she loves him. The mother tries everything to keep Madge from going and the old neighbor lady tells her Mom that Madge has to go out and discover life for herself for better or for worse and then the camera pans back and it shows the train crossing the dry grass plains and Madge is riding on a bus past the high school leaving her little going-nowhere-town to meet up with him and start her new life."

The two of them walked on together in silence.

Finally Allison spoke up, "So what do you think?"

Anthony thought about it before answering, "I think that girl could use some counseling."

Allison said, "You're just lucky that at this moment I am unarmed."

But later Anthony thought about it and resolved to see the movie at his first opportunity.

"So what are you reading today," Allison asked Anthony a few days later when she came up to him at the least used pool at Pinemont.

Anthony looked at his faded book-cover. "Oh it's an old biography of John Galsworthy, you know, the author of *The Forsyte*

Saga."

"There must be something in the gay genes that can only imagine true fulfillment as season tickets to the opera and an upper-middle class existence," Allison commented.

Anthony ignored the remark. "I am masochistically drawn to family sagas. I guess I always imagined myself the scion of a wealthy family with an elegant family townhouse in London and a great manor house in the country for weekends. The closest I can come to the image of a tolerable old age would be this: me clad in old tweeds grown curmudgeonly with the years and a wife rather like Vita Sackville-West keeping the gardens at the old place in trim, bringing in asters and zinnias from the garden to place in vases hither and yon, and her listening to me complain about the state of the empire. The vicar and his wife would call later and we would discuss the latest poems by Tennyson over tea. Does that sound good to you?"

"Is that an indirect proposal?"

Anthony cringed, "Heavens no, but I thought the image of me in a straight guise for once might please you."

"Well I have my own cherished images," Allison said turning away.

"Would you care to share them with me?"

"No."

"Too personal?"

"Yes … and painful."

"You aren't as tough as I first thought you were," Anthony remarked.

Allison made no comment.

"I think people are buying it," Allison said quietly as they sat in a corner table in the lodge looking out on the lake shore and the mountains beyond.

"And why shouldn't they," Anthony answered. "Aren't we both accomplished performers? Isn't that what we have both been doing all our lives."

"Not I," Allison returned, "I consider myself to be an entirely frank person. It goes with being a philosopher."

"Hah, you are a basket of emotions and secrets," Anthony scoffed.

"I am not."

"You ooze feminine mystique and estrogen from every pore."

"Shush, people might be listening."

"Of course they are listening; we are the hit of the season."

Allison slammed her fork down.

"Is that all that this means to you? You thrive on inauthentic gestures and pretence; you would make Sartre nauseous."

Her outburst of passion disturbed him at first but Anthony tried to pass it off, "Very cute, a play on words. I think I am doing you lots of good. You have moved from being a lunatic spinster to being almost a match for my foil."

"Conceited twit, I let you emerge at times into the footlights because I know that your ego just thrives on any escape from being one of life's little unnamed extra players."

"I caution you not to bandy words with a gay boy; my talons could shred you on the instant."

"Smile Darling, people are watching. You might take my hand you know; you haven't touched me all evening."

"I am a model of strategic restraint. The audience must imagine that I will pounce on you in the backseat the moment we cross the parking lot and reach the comparative solitude of my T-bird."

"Who drives a T-bird? You are so retro."

"You're the one who thrives on a movie made in 1956."

Allison ignored his jibes. "The people can tell that you are all tied up in your Oedipus conflicts and I in turn am terminally frustrated by your male frigidity."

Both of them lapsed into silence to regroup for another assault. Finally Allison said, "We aren't laughing like we did a few weeks ago."

Anthony said tight-lipped, "I'm smiling. It's you that are betraying the game; get with the program."

Allison whispered, "I don't have to follow your orders you little martinet. I'm older than you are."

"It's never out of my mind."

Tears blinded Allison, "That was unnecessarily cruel."

"Love is an anthology of unkind actions."

"Only in your twisted conception of it!" Allison began to dab at her eyes with her napkin.

Anthony protested, "You would hurt me too if you could."

"Stop reading Edward Albee; he's too grown-up for you."

Allison was about to excuse herself and go to the ladies room but Anthony grasped her wrist and said in a voice tinged with desperation, "Why isn't it working for us tonight?"

Allison answered, "You know why. I brought love to close to you and you can't stand it. Human warmth causes you to curl up like the little snail you are. Back into your shell you little escargot!"

She scored with that one.

"Time of the month?" Anthony inquired.

"Trite!"

They both fell silent.

The older couples shook their heads and went back to eating. "Just lover's quarrel," they thought complacently. "Nothing perfect lasts."

Time passed and things returned to normal between them.

One late-August day the two conspirators sat looking out to where little cat's paws played about on the lake. Several small sailboats skimmed over the waves appearing to be destined to collide and then turning away at the last moment. It reminded each of them of when they had been children at Pinemont in days gone by, each entertaining dreams of finding their proper place in a society that has only been preserved in the literature that they both read when they should have been learning the intricate art of mixing, meeting, networking, and of course concealing. Romantic success is the fruit of conformity and duplicity with just a spark of charm or beauty thrown into the mix.

It was strange that being raised at and around Pinemont had somehow passed over them like a summer wind leaving them tossing about in agitation but still rooted in their native illusions. Each had evolved an armored persona to shield them from an uncomprehending majority to whom same-sex loves will always be disordered and anathema.

Another season in the mountains was ending and already the night temperatures were showing the disturbing alteration that betokened the chill to come when snows would close the passes and the summer houses would groan unheeded through the long winter nights.

Anthony was ineffectively throwing stones into the lake when Allison spoke up.

"You know you can't drive me away," Allison said.

Anthony wearily sighed, "I'm not trying to drive you away; I'm trying to keep you grounded in reality."

"Reality is always a matter of contention," she answered.

"Time resolves all conflicts," Anthony said to console her.

It didn't work.

"You only talk like that because you can't hear it," Allison said.

"Hear what?"

"Time's winged chariot."

"I know: Andrew Marvel, a 17th century poet."

"Someday soon we won't be young anymore," Allison said disconsolately. "We'll be like the people who have watched us all summer."

"I know. It worries me considerably," Anthony answered. "People like us are creatures of a season not tethered to home or family, at least..."

"Yes?"

"Nothing."

"No, what were you going to say?"

Anthony shrugged, "I was going to clarify a point of gay taxonomy, at least in our pure form. I mean all the Castro gays in jeans and with shaved heads trying to look like the kind of guys they hope will be interested in them, these know all about time's chariot."

"Are you one of them?"

"Hardly! I am literary gay through and through; we never get down to actually doing anything. Can you picture me in leathers?"

Allison laughed. "No. it wouldn't work for you. You are pure tenderized chicken through and through. You better find yourself a Gustav Achenbach somewhere out there in Venice Dodo-child. You were born to be admired from afar."

"You promised not to call me that, Dodo-child; I'm not a child."

"I did not promise you that."

"Well you did … and what about you? Where will you look for identity and permanence? You're as lost as me."

Allison tried to sound blasé. "Oh I suppose I'll eventually get to look like Alice B. Toklas and find my own Gertrude Stein."

"Now who's being the drama queen?"

They both fell into silence.

"Actually, I think I will end up permanently single," Allison finally remarked.

"Well with your attitude…" Anthony smiled.

"I like my attitude," Allison said with something of her old anger.

"I remember; it's who you are right?"

"That's right," Allison said quietly.

The wind came up again and shook the leaves on the aspens over their heads turning them into silver hearts.

"I love it here," Allison said softly. "I know that it costs a lot to live here and when my parents die I will have to give it up but it is the same land that the Indians once wandered over, never thinking that anyone would ever land here from Europe and take it all away from them.”

“Rich people take what they want,” Anthony agreed.

“I was speaking about the original settlers,” Allison looked up.

“So was I,” Anthony answered. “What is a better example of an invasive species but a settler, a so-called pioneer? What was present is pushed slowly away until there is no place for it anymore. The survival of the fittest is not as violent as it is usually supposed to be, it moves incorrigibly and insidiously into new lands treaty by treaty and suddenly my father is ensconced on Mercer Island and the Suquamish dead are buried on a little reservation next to Agate Pass just west of Seattle.”

“Is that where you are from, Mercer Island? You never said.”

“Yes.”

“I’m from Lake Oswego.”

“Right… lots of nice homes there.”

“Yes.”

The two of them were silent.

The wind continued to blow and the clouds began to drift over the Cascade Range and to fall down the other side like an airy avalanche. The air began gradually to cool and there was a promise of thunderstorms before evening. Behind them the activities of Pinemont continued unabated impervious to the changes in the atmosphere. Love affairs were concluded or broken, deaths occurred, summer residences were sold, new staff was hired, new expansions were planned, yet Pinemont remained Pinemont and the children of Pinemont played on the golf courses and the tennis courts or swam safely in the pools surrounded by parents who knew each other from prior summers.

At last Allison spoke up. “If you weren’t gay you could ask me to marry you and if I wasn’t lesbian I might accept and our parents would be happy and we would get married down there by the lake and all of our friends from past years would gather to wish us well. We might have to move away for awhile until you found your wings and your business began to grow. I would get pregnant of course in due time and we would come here for summers as our parent's guests and our kids would be able to return to school and tell their friends about how exciting their summer had been in the mountains of Oregon; their friends who had spent their own summers running through sprinklers on the back lawn to cool off, they would envy them. Some of our children's little friends would have packed a tent and a cooler full of soft drinks and stayed in a state park with barking dogs only a few yards away. Others would be trapped in the city and hear only the rap music from next door all summer long. Some of the girls would come back to school pregnant because they let themselves be fucked because their boyfriends got tired of blow jobs…"

"You paint a pretty picture of heterosexuality," Anthony said. "Maybe you should be a publicist for the family-values groups."

"Do you think they would have me?"

"I was speaking ironically."

"You seldom speak in any other way."

The pair was silent again.

"The worst part about heterosexuality is that I wish I could have just a little bit of it just to feel really connected to something…"

The wind in the trees rose again to a wail and the water on the lake shivered.

At last Allison said, "I will miss you when you go Anthony."

Anthony looked up, "I thought you didn't like men."

"Sometimes I don't know what I like."

They were both silent again.

Anthony spoke up suddenly like one who wishes to end a long debate. "Well nobody will stop you now. It's all up to you what you become."

Allison hesitated before blurting out. "So I'm in charge of my life?"

"Yes."

Allison shook her head and said quietly, almost to herself, "If that was true then I would ask you to marry me."

Anthony started as though he had been stabbed with a pin.

"You are a dangerous lady to share a cheese tray with." And then immediately, "You know it wouldn't work."

Allison protested. "It works for other people, why not us."

Anthony turned and gripped Allison by the shoulders before crying out, "I think this is just a game you are playing with me because I am just a dodo-child like you said."

Allison closed her eyes and shook her head violently.

"Tell me it's a game!" he insisted.

"No."

"Tell me."

"No it isn't a game; it would solve all of my problems don't you see? God, my parents, everybody ... they would just rejoice. I could dig up the last of my old college classmates and ask them up to Pinemont for the wedding. We could choose any music that you like and you could look just all spiffed up and your father would be able to see you as a proper investment banker at last or at least gainfully employed. There would be a great wedding feast and I would be there all in white, sacramental but sexy, and I could have babies before it's too late for me and you wouldn't have to go off and become some little gay Euro-slut just to pay for room and board in Capri and years later emerge sick and jaded when your beauty fades and die on the streets in Milan or Naples. Don't you see, Anthony?"

Anthony shook her by the shoulders, "Stop it. That isn't the way it is with us."

"What does it take to reach you? Tell me what I have to do!" Allison cried.

Anthony spoke slowly. "It isn't you. Maybe it isn't even me. Maybe we received poor modeling in our youth so that love and sex got separated somehow and death became the uneasy tag-along to both. I don't think either of us expects to be happy or even loved. I'd settle for just a lustful glance from the right guy and you ... Allison you deserve someone who will be for you..."

"What?"

Anthony searched for the right word.

"Allison, you need somebody who will be patient."

Allison was silent as the beautiful vision of sexual complementarity between them faded away. She saw herself, an object of pity and disdain, not all that much different from when pictures of lesbian love appeared on lurid paperback book covers sold in drug stores across America. She did not know how she had come to feel something for the blond youth before her but she felt his fear, not just of her, but of everything that went along with upper-class suburbia where decade was linked to decade as the hard-won promotions succeeded each other in the inevitable march to the possession of a coveted corner office. Had she betrayed their little conspiracy and ruined whatever was between them by popping the question that he had dreaded most to hear because even if it was offered to him by a man it would have meant the surrender of his only real possession: his pretense to the possession of inextinguishable youth?

She felt him fading away from her like the sun that was declining to rest upon the mountains west of them. An unwonted chill was rising from the grass around the lake and she clasped her bare shoulders to ward off the cold. She could feel the full impact of the metaphor of night.

When she spoke again it was with the voice that he had first heard from her earlier that summer. She looked away from him into infinite distance.

"You are right of course. But you can see where and how I might just get thoughts like this from time to time. My mother is thinking again of having me sent into treatment. It's what they do with dangerous maniacs like me who carry guns and threaten priests and propose marriage to little dumb gay boys. The ones like you who had already made up their minds about love and death before we even met."

"It may help that I have not made my mind up about anything. I think you will haunt me Allison for a very long time."

"Well that's something at least."

"It is ... and it isn't flattery."

"I wish it was. Flattery my dear Anthony will get you anything, even me."

Alternative Ending...

And that might have ended the story for each of them and they would have parted each to pursue a separate tragic fate according to their original conceptions but Anthony suddenly said, "Unless..."

Allison looked up at him, "Unless what."

"Oh I don't know. I just felt suddenly uncomfortable that's all."

"Why?

"Well, I didn't like that image of you in a lunatic asylum. Do they still have places like that?"

"They do if you can afford them. Otherwise you have to get an old grocery cart and push it around town filled with ugly tops, knit stretch pants, and old yellow bras."

"Disgusting! I'd never allow it."

"Well don't worry about me. My family will find me a nice place with a name like Oakhurst Rehabilitation Center or something."

Anthony thought about it.

"I still don't like it. After all, you are a friend and you sounded so tragic."

"It was just a crazy dream. I mean me, the Lunatic and you, the Dodo-child."

Anthony thought more about it. "Well you sprung it all on me kind of quickly. I mean a girl likes to be prepared."

"I thought you wanted to be a fetching boy chased about Europe by aging noblemen."

"You always made that plan sound so sordid."

"Well it just seems to me that if you want to end up a trollop that you could do better as a girl. I don't think you would have said those awful things about women if you weren't a little bit envious of us."

"Well it does seem a bit much that you can make big money flashing a little leg on camera. If I looked good enough I could be a reporter on Fox News or one of the real housewives of … someplace. I mean literature doesn't get you very far these days. Nobody can read above a sixth-grade level. I might end up writing nauseating love stories like Nicholas Sparks just to make ends meet."

Allison thought about it. "No, the real money is in televangelism. You can be a complete drag queen as long as you are pushing the prosperity gospel on Christian broadcasting. They love it if you bleed mascara when you cry. How are you at crying on cue?"

"All I have to do is picture myself as an investment banker tied to a desk in some suffocating office building."

Anthony tried to picture himself as a lady televangelist rather than a European Trollope.

"If I'm going to be a televangelist I'll need a partner, couples do better at that kind of work, bleeding the faithful."

"We'd have to be married," Allison said.

"I think it would be the orthodox thing to do," Anthony admitted.

Allison considered the idea, "I'm not that butch."

"Sideburns and some fake facial hair would do the trick," Anthony suggested. "But won't you have trouble promoting generic Christianity as a Catholic, I mean with the Council of Trent and all?"

Allison considered this objection and then her face lit up as though with celestial illumination.

"We'll do a Jonathan Swift on them. Did you ever read Swift's *A Modest Proposal* or Defoe's *The Shortest Way with Dissenters?* No? Well that's your next assignment. Here's how it will work. We'll start our own religion. We'll call it umm, Cosmetology! We'll emphasize the virtues of studied triviality. You'll be the perfect spokesperson Dodo-child; you're half way there already and sculpted eyebrows and a little lip-gloss will do the rest. Our religion will have affirmations instead of commandments. We'll just tell people to do what they are doing already; it's so much easier, the exercise of stoic virtues and discipline are passé."

Anthony considered the idea, "Well you know I'm not as dumb as you are always saying I am."

Allison put her arm around him, "That's alright Sweetie you can be smart, just don't let anyone know that you are; it will spoil the illusion."

Anthony smiled happily before asking, "Alright but what would some of our affirmations be? What is a religion without doctrines?"

Allison though about it and finally replied, "Okay, how about these for starters: 1. be nasty it's the new nice."

"Super!"

"Of course in our religion we'll change and substitute doctrines depending on how well they play with the faithful."

"So it's sort of religion on demand," Anthony said.

"Right," Allison said.

"It might just catch on."

Allison explained, "Well if you've been paying attention everything is moving in that direction anyway from business to education: degrees on demand, studying optional, Presidency on demand knowledge of government optional, faces on demand see your plastic surgeon, nothing just is what it is so why should religion be what it is. Look at the Indian casinos, the Indians finally figured the settlers out: we all want something for nothing."

"It still sounds a little risky."

"Well let's face it Dodo-child does any of your other options sound any better?"

Anthony thought about the summer, its swiftly fading days and the vague and impressionistic sense that he had of his own future. Already prep school seemed a distant memory and he had failed to adjust to the complexities of California's ersatz culture of plastic glamour and dried mesquite hills.

He desired a world of convenience and an ever-ready supply of cash to meet his occasional passions for silver trinkets. He was not extravagant; he preferred zircon, topaz, and amethyst to the sterile glare of diamonds that were said to be a girl's best friend. So far his life had been characterized by a dull sort of resistance to whatever carefully designed and pre-bottled essence his life was to assume.

Allison on the contrary appeared in her daring to possess what he lacked, passion and decision. Surely then any conception that might come from her was at least as likely to lead him to the small measure of freedom that he required, to open a fissure in life's unyielding granite face. He felt words of consent trembling on his pale lips but one last matter troubled him still.

"Alright, suppose we end up being a big success, what about our home life afterward?" Anthony asked. "I could learn to cook but I have to warn you that I might flirt with various tradesmen when I go shopping."

"If you do I'll paddle you," Allison assured him.

"Promise?"

"Yes."

"Will you be quite severe with me?" Anthony asked coyly.

"Yes."

"You'll probably be quite demanding sexually I suppose?"

"I'd consider it my duty" Allison said quietly.

"Very well then," Anthony offered her his hand, "I accept your proposal."

Colloquy

The new millennium about which had gathered so many hopes and visions of a new and brighter world, enabled by technology, enlightened by reflection on the errors of history, and devoted to the spread of the benefits conferred by an interconnected and collective web of thought has yet to justify those hopes and visions and instead appears to reward precisely those trivial occupations and vain pursuits that least deserve our esteem. As the year 2019 relinquished the fullness of its summer days a reflective observer looked in vain for a unifying concept whether in politics, culture, or religion to arrest the nation's decline into commercial mediocrity and the stale and re-heated rhetoric of American supremacy. It was not a time when transcendent principles could contend with slogans and mendacity. Old alliances were failing even as despots promised efficiency exacted at the price of freedom. Demagogues were catapulted into office by disgruntled electorates. Once securely installed in office these did not scruple to claim auspicious and exalted titles for themselves. Honors were bestowed where least deserved while in America at least minority voices were stilled as unpatriotic because they dared to question the status quo.

This ought to have been a time for prayer and prophesy if these activities had not fallen into obsolescence. The seriousness of these former pursuits was now reserved for the utterances of the

Federal Reserve Board and its decisions made regarding the optimum prime lending rate so that the economy could pursue its headlong growth to the detriment of the biosphere. Prayer may be a lost art today less from neglect than from the general realization that the divine has long since been trivialized by over-familiarity. If we could comprehend the full measure of contradiction entailed in the act of prayer, no one would dare to pray. It is ironic but it is religion that diminishes the inherent daring of the act of prayer by making presumption commonplace through memorization and routine. It seems that some sort of prelude then would be in order before we kneel, clear our throats, compose our minds, begin a preliminary search for proper words, elevate our eyes (under the assumption that God can be assigned coordinates in space), and begin to pray.

Against this background as regards prophesy an arduous search discloses as our story opens the solitary figure of Jonah (as he was originally named at birth when all things are assigned according to initial appearances). As the years passed after the birth of this prophet various contradictions first manifested themselves and then grew. Jonah had cherished for many years a negative attitude to the transcendent realm since it displayed a variance with his particular experience and identity. It appeared that denial would be the price exacted to reach a satisfaction and accord with God in order to discharge a primeval debt that had only grown larger through the years. Finally Jonah admitted that he had a substantial bone to pick with God and began to ask how to address Him directly.

The problem was to find a proper node or network where he might feel assured that his message had some chance of being transmitted intact without any superfluous editing or alteration before reaching the intended recipient. He did not want some vast filtering apparatus or set of ministers, ordained or otherwise, to soften various individual phrases, translate them into Latin or Greek, add various bits of archaic diction, or make any extra cross-references to an existing sacred text. These particular requirements had for many years delayed the transmission of, what for want of a better term, we will call "Jonah's Prophesy." He was aware that there was already another book in the Bible by one with the same name, but he considered his own work to be of the same tone and tenor. It might therefore serve as a worthy addition or sequel to the original.

With this plan in mind Jonah began to read and reflect on the salient characteristics of the present time, as any prophet should do before daring to compose a prophetic text. Ours is not an age that delights in doctrine or in deductive reasoning from infallible premises grounded in ancient texts. Indeed so natural has it become for the daily data streams to be called into question that any affirmative categorical assertion, let alone a definitive Kantian categorical imperative is thought to be an instance of overreaching and arrogance even if traceable to venerable and long-established institutions. Of course this means that the aspiring believer occupies the lonely post of standing in the theological equivalent of John Rawl's "original position."

The universe begins somewhere beyond the thin envelope of our atmosphere and stretches backwards and outwards in space-time to either a big bang or to some leaky wormhole from an adjoining universe. The idea of a universal regress however in space-time is as daunting to us as it was to St. Thomas Aquinas when he considered the problem. Sooner or later one comes up against the metaphysical question of why there is something rather than nothing.   This fundamental question of metaphysics is complicated by the apparent fact that when matter and anti-matter collide, they evidently vanish and are transformed into energy. Is the former matter something or nothing? Of course existence is not confined to matter and energy but to fields and dimensions as well. In the last analysis the inquiring mind is confronted by various cosmological instances of behavior: things simply work out a certain way and mathematics can describe those ways by reducing them to stable equations and constants; but why these particular relationships prevail we cannot say, we only know that they act as they do. At any given moment of human understanding then, the world of existence simply emerges before us and demands our assent. Even if we are not satisfied in all respects by possessing an encompassing view of reality we can at least manage our daily lives and map out horizons for future research. Meanwhile we have men like Descartes and Husserl to help us to see the limitations of human knowledge and reason and to open the door to the transcendent.

To most religions of course philosophy is an afterthought. Philosophy may help to clarify religious concepts, but those concepts are often rooted in direct human experience rather than intellectual apprehension. When Abraham encountered God the meeting was exalted but simultaneously as informal as any other meeting leading to a dialog. Clearly any God, if He is to be considered from the viewpoint of His being a metaphysical absolute, must then have engaged in a vast act of condescension to engage with Abraham and others so directly and verbally.

Both Judaism and Christianity derive from similar intimate encounters. This intimacy with the Deity as recorded in the Bible had always troubled Jonah. He would have preferred a few more special effects just to prove that God was really God. He preferred that God act on a broad screen that if not quite "Cinerama" was at least equal to the broad screen treatment of "VistaVision." Jonah loved it whenever God smote (or smited) people or places and reduced them to ruins, pillars of salt, or at the very least caused them to tumble over dead at the precise moment that their sin was brought home to them. Jonah did not want comfortable metaphors to be used to diminish whatever ultimate reality was out there. If God spoke to various bearded prophets who smelled like sheep and goats and wandered around the Hejaz, Jonah could not understand why God couldn't speak to him with equal candor and directness. Jonah considered that faith was a binding contract and he deplored the way that it was presented by various evangelists as some sort of unilateral agreement with all of the equities on God's part and none on the part of the other contracting party. After, all a covenant should bind both parties to fair and open dealing and the form of those promises should emerge from adequate negotiation so that all viewpoints might be aired.

Instead Jonah found that he was already in a one-down position with God simply through his status as a human being. His source of knowledge was limited and dearly acquired. He was not subject to vast intuitions let alone universal agency; God needed only to will a thing to have it done. Only God could do that. Worst of all Jonah wasn't particularly holy. He wasn't overly wicked either, but he would be the first to admit that he could be a real S.O.B. on occasion. He wasn't particularly lustful, but he had as they used to say, taken certain liberties when occasion offered. He felt no particular need to engage in truly rebellious tendencies against God: there was no Friedrich Nietzsche or Alistair Crowley lurking within him. Nor did he desire some spurious New Age substitute for revealed religion. He was not impressed by Frazier's The Golden Bough either. Antiquity did not equal relevance. The idea of going about sky-clad or meeting in a circle around a naked woman in a grove of oak trees while wearing robes and chanting in Anglo-Saxon about some hypothetical Great Goddess seemed to Jonah to be carrying rabid feminism too far.

All that he really asked for was a religion that would meet any critiques imposed by British logical-positivism but without vaulting into existentialism with its practice of long Germanic word-coining and the circumlocutions of Karl Jaspers and Martin Heidegger. Most of his other objections to religion were confined to the practical order: why did bad things happen to the innocent while truly maleficent figures often lived long and luxurious lives and went unpunished, at least in this world. Even if they went about un-smitten, God could at least give them jock-itch or a really bad case of hemorrhoids. Jonah had brooded on these wrongs for many years but at last he had decided that he needed to as it were to finally have it out with God.

Technically as the challenging party Jonah realized that he should leave to God the time, place, and choice of weapons for their proposed duel. Normally these options would be handled through a party agreeing to act as second and conveyed to the responding party. Jonah finally concluded that in the absence of a designated second, formally and uniquely qualified to represent God, that he would have to proceed to God's likely local domicile and call him out to engage in direct battle.

So it was at long last that Jonah slipped one night into the Cathedral of St. Philip Neri in the Archdiocese of --------- when the Cathedral was to be kept open until midnight for anyone desiring to engage in private prayer. As he entered the cathedral the solemn majesty of his surroundings modulated to a degree whatever initial casualness and confidence he had brought with him as he marched through the streets of the city composing in his mind his initial diatribe. He realized of course the disproportion of his enterprise. Two thousand years of Catholicism had, in addition to numerous doctrinal formulations, created a legacy of art, music, and literature, one not only impressive but the foundation of Western Civilization. Kings have left their crowns aside to bear homage to Popes. Great wars have been fought over sticky points of theological interpretation. Inquisitions have probed under torture for deeply held if inadequately expressed divergences from residual Paganism and later on in its turn from any variations from orthodox belief. One does not approach prayer then or challenge theological certainties with a casual frame of mind.

Yet Jonah was simultaneously aware that the literature of the Old Testament honors those who wrestle with angels and protest manifest injustices, even before the throne of the Almighty. Truth may appear to be a gift but it is in fact an achievement and the outcome of contention between opposing views. God may have more respect for the honest heretic than for the complacent believer who is never troubled by doubts because religion plays only a marginal role in his life, rather like an insurance policy the premiums of which are automatically deducted every month. It was this reflection that enabled Jonah to proceed once he had entered the church. He walked therefore up to one of the front pews before the high altar and the suffering figure of the crucifix and began without preamble to talk to God.

Jonah came quickly to the point, "I don't know how best to address you but I think you should consider a radical review of the whole literature that has been written about you. I mean don't you think it's time?"

He suddenly realized that he had spoken out loud. Jonah looked behind him but the few lingering church-goers, evidently caught up in their own devotions, had decided to ignore his brief outburst. Jonah decided that if it was really God to whom he was speaking then mind-reading would be a fairly elementary skill for Him so the rest of his monologue was conducted in the form of silent thought.

Jonah continued, "I mean I don't want to be disrespectful to you or, what do you call it, um blasphemous, but I think it's time for a complete textual revision of your collected works in the light of recent discoveries. There isn't much about string-theory in Genesis and, I don't know if this particularly embarrasses you, but that bit about a dome of water over the earth is poetic but pretty poor astronomy. It doesn't seem much of a leap to extrapolate from things like that to a few other premature conclusions or cultural encrustations in the written accounts about you. Did you mean for everything that you ever said to be given equal weight? You seem to me to get angry about some pretty trivial things while letting other more serious stuff slide and I just need to know why you do that!"

Jonah paused before continuing.

"And what have you got against Hittites, Amorites, and all those other ancient tribes who just happened to be settled in Canaan before the Hebrews showed up? Why couldn't just one of your commandments have been, 'Live and let live?' It would have saved a lot of superfluous slaughter. I mean why not give people a break? And you should have known that Adam and Eve would mess up one day or didn't you figure that two people who were dumb enough to run around naked all day, without even knowing they were naked, might also be too dumb to even think of disobeying you. At the very least you could have given them a fair shake, turned a mongoose lose in the garden to eat the snake. Have you ever heard of a do-over? Maybe Adam and Eve would have taken a break to reconsider their choice and the next day everything might have been back to normal. Adam would stretch when he woke up and say to Eve, 'I just had the craziest dream last night. I dreamt that you were naked!' And Eve could shake out her long blond tresses and stretch and say, 'So what's naked?'

Instead look what happens: they get kicked out of the garden, they have two kids, and one of them kills the other. It's the first generation and we've already got a dysfunctional family! And it just gets worse from there on: angels come down and start sleeping around with hot Jewish chicks and make giants … or were Adam and Eve even Jewish? The Noah thing bugs me because I keep thinking of all the species that might have been lost forever because they got stepped on in the ark by the elephants or the hippos. I used to lie awake as a kid and think of things like that. How for instance did the animals from Australia get to wherever the ark was loading up?

But I don't want to get off topic here. The point is I think you might consider commissioning a re-write or at least a consolidation. I'm talking about the big texts of course like the Bible and the Koran but that's only the beginning. Whole institutions have grown up as authoritative interpreters of these sacred texts, finding ways to graft their values and world-views onto new problems raised by new eras and to make them normative for other cultures. I don't want to be pedantic here, but exegesis and hermeneutics are really elucidating the full complexity of scripture. This more or less weakens the naïve single author approach of fundamentalist literalism.

I have to ask you if you think that conservative Christians are paying any real attention to your main message anymore or whether they just use selected quotes to beat up on certain groups of people or to justify various atrocities. I think we are entering into an age and a set of problems that requires something beyond what the old texts can provide. I'm not sure that people are really appreciating some of the more symbolic aspects and metaphors. The decline of an agrarian culture for instance definitely undercuts the efficacy of sheep metaphors. I think many people live their whole lives and never even see an actual sheep. If you are talking to an urban audience you might consider using a more familiar animal. Ritual purity and styles of women's fashion by the standards of older cultures seem a little antiquated today.

Suggestiveness is all in the mind anyway. In Victorian times even a well-turned ankle was provocative. Of course the really big problems are in social justice and ecology. Slavery still exists but today it's called wage disparity, predatory credit practices, and the student debt crisis. If things go on as they are a tiny minority of billionaires will monopolize most of the equity and purchasing power of the world. I think that you had a more communitarian vision originally in mind didn't you? You always said that you felt a special empathy for the poor and the forgotten. I also think that you must like animals; you made so many of them.

I think this might be the time to be specific. Let's take Brazil as an example. Of what use was it to the indigenous tribes of the Amazon River Basin who had cultures that were perfectly adapted to the conditions of their environment to suddenly learn about some Semitic King named David, the conditions that prevailed in Jerusalem two thousand years ago, and the rejection and death of a young reformer and that his death and resurrection was the basis of their own salvation. Their minds had never been troubled by these concepts, let alone their alien solution. Why not just leave them alone and you deal with them directly after they die? Were they any worse than the people who did get the word? Instead, what happens is this: missionaries arrive and behind them come various conquistadors and silver miners and before long the Indians are being worked to death for the profit of fat-cats in Portugal.

It hasn't gotten any better either. Now it's 2019 and some idiot right-wing, family-values, creep named Jair Bolsonaro has just been elected as President of Brazil and what is he trying to do but favor business over indigenous people's rights and the rainforests where they live are burning. Bolsonaro says that the fires were started by the NGO's which is just like Hitler when he said that it was the communists that burned town the Reichstag instead of his own people thereby removing the one threat to Hitler's assumption of absolute power.

Don't you think it's funny that every right-wing group, no matter what the country may be, is always conservative theologically as well? I think that the LGBT folks are like canaries in the coal mine, if they don't like us or worse want to kill us then I can tell what stance they will take on most of the other really important issues. Do you think that it is just a coincidence that one in three people in Brazil is now an evangelical Christian? In other words they are the same people who just can't wait for Armageddon to happen so that you will have to send Jesus back here to earth to start his thousand year millennial reign. What do they care if the rainforest burns in Brazil? All you will have to do is snap your fingers and just fix the whole thing, right?

Besides, they figure that they will all be floating up in the air watching the fires down below burn up any unconverted Indians and of course the residual Catholics who share the concerns of Pope Francis in his encyclical urging environmental responsibility as a moral issue. My only problem with Pope Francis is that he's just too nice to people.   Couldn't you tell him to excommunicate some people starting with that creep, Bolsonaro? After all Bolsonaro has been married three times and he says that if he had a gay son he would prefer that he died in an accident. Is that disgusting or what? He also believes in beating young gay children to change their minds about being gay. How do you put up with people like that? And these modern day Pharisees claim that they are really tight with you! Are you surprised that people like me are alienated by religion?"

Jonah paused. He looked up and saw that the Church had emptied around and behind him. The solitude gave him renewed confidence and he continued.

"Of course the little stuff doesn't trouble me now but I'm not a scripture scholar. In any case I didn't come here to talk about you. I mean, what do I have to tell you about you that you don't already know? I'm not even sure why I came here tonight except that I'd like you to understand me a little better, let you get inside me a little. Would that be okay? Isn't that what you always seem to desire? I mean otherwise why mess with people like me at all? Why put up with our sins? You could just squash us like bugs or do like that kid in the old Twilight Zone episode and wish us out into the cornfield. You could time-transport a few T-Rexes and watch them gobble people like me up. So I'm talking to you like I can just, you know what I mean, just talk to you and I hope you don't mind because you scare me a little ... okay, a lot. But I don't think you really want people to just tremble before you, do you? I think that would be pretty shallow. I guess I think that you're above that sort of thing. So I'm like taking a chance here, talking to you... "

Jonah knelt tentatively for a moment just to see how it felt. It wasn't really all that bad. He kept the position for a few minutes and then placed his butt back comfortably into the firm embrace of the carved wood of the pew. "I guess this is sort of what your priests refer to as confession."

"Well, to begin with I always tend to fall in love with the wrong people, desperate people, even if I don't know them personally. I guess that I first fell in love with the model Gia Carangi during the two years when she was all over the covers of Cosmopolitan and I was still in junior high. After a couple of years she descended into a really bad heroin addiction and died at twenty-six of AIDS that she had probably contracted in the shooting galleries of New York City.

What is it that people look for in each other? Is it an ideal image that in line or shadow paints our dreams of a perfect union, or do we love what we cannot find to honor in ourselves? Is it a twin we seek or a contrasting vision? Perhaps it is a correspondence with variations like a musical score. Is it pleasure that we desire or a carefully attuned agent of pain, one poised just far enough out of our reach so that we cannot grasp and keep it?

When I say that I fell in love with Gia I don't mean that I wanted to sleep with her or anything like that. I wanted more than that. I wanted to be her or maybe not her exactly but beautiful like her as though we belonged to the same species because I just felt so inadequate all the time, so that even talking to you now, with no barriers between us like I'm doing, I still feel the same wrongness inside, even though I had my chance earlier than most transgender people to pursue my dreams. More about that later, even though you must already know a lot about me, because I am sure that you have been watching me for just a long old time! You probably know how everything got started inside me, things that even I don't know. How could I? I just found them present there from the beginning. I mean I am glad that I was born healthy and all that, but how could I enjoy it when everybody insisted that I act differently and feel different than I really felt? I had to dig down really deep and erect a bunker to keep the incoming mortar fire at bay.

But I don't want to talk about my childhood as a transsexual kid. Let's begin much later when the shell began to crack and I came out blinking to look at the world. Those were the years when Studio 54 was raging and disco and recreational sex turned the world upside down. I know all about how carefully you clock sexual sins, so I hope that talk like this isn't too uncomfortable for you, but I know that I'm not telling you anything that you don't already know ... about people liking to get off and all that. Well in those disco days people thought that everything came cheap and without any price attached, but sooner or later the bill always comes due. Don't get me wrong. People want love too and if you can manage to find both love and sex in the same person at the same time it's fantastic! But sometimes love is really hard to find and sometimes you love people that don't particularly turn you on. For instance there are lots of really bitchy women who everybody would like to have sex with but they're so nasty that nobody loves them, least of all themselves. And there are guys who are just walking crotches with handsome faces, buff virus carriers, the ones that haunted the gay bathhouses until they died. That's the power that sex can have. I don't think most of them wanted to spread the virus, but by then the infection was everywhere. I guess the reason I'm still here is that for me sex is an aesthetic thing more than it is a matter of fluid exchange. I hate that term, bodily fluids; it sounds so gross and sticky.

Anyway Gia Carangi was so on the top of her game in the modeling world in those days of my youth. You only had to say "Gia" and everybody knew who you meant, sort of like AOC is today but in politics. In those days though modeling was the top of all games for a woman. She made big money and as you know money is what makes our world go round, money, not truth. I don't think that truth carries much weight anymore. I know that guys who know all about you talk a lot about the efficacy of Divine Grace, but it's sort of like radioactivity isn't it, it's real but you can't tell that it's around except by its effects. Meanwhile there are other faiths that don't get all caught up in sin and redemption and just deal with what people can see and feel. They see you more in what you have made than in whatever exists outside our perception. Still, it is nice to assign a face to all this wonder and have somebody that you can thank by name or at least point to and call the Supreme Being. Don't you get a little tired though by just having people going around all the time calling you great? I mean it's like when a really hot girl keeps getting told that she's so hot; it gets really boring after awhile for her. I guess that isn't the best parallel, but you see what I mean. She already knows she's pretty. She would rather hear something about you unless she's really into herself and that's a real turn-off no matter how beautiful she is.

So anyway I just had this whole sort of Gia thing going and her sad eyes and her dark edgy look. She could summon up though a sort of freshness at times that was so sweet and innocent that it made me ashamed to look at her picture. I thought to myself that I had no business trying to be a girl when I could never be like her. I'm transgender. My name is spelled Joana now not Jonah. You probably thought I was like the prophet Jonah, the swallowed by the fish guy. (By the way, that whole fish story is pretty hokey). I mean how could he breathe in there? I think you should have a word with your editorial staff and make sure that they specify when they want you to be taken literally because there are people who think that everything in the Bible means exactly what it says. They're a real drag for the rest of us. For instance they're completely hung-up on Sodom and Gomorrah. I mean people are starving and shooting each other in this world; why not deal with those things first?

Oh and people are really messing up your creation. We withdrew from that international agreement to help preserve the planet because President Trump doesn't believe in climate change. Does he ever bother you when he is holding one of his little Nurnberg rallies? He drives me crazy! And what about that little gnome that he appointed as his Attorney General? Doesn't he look like he ought to live under a bridge or something with the other trolls? All of the Trump people ought to be in a carnival. Just you watch Mike Pence sometime. He looks like he's having an orgasm every time he can take Melania's place and stand next to Trump. They've got this little "me and my shadow" game going on. He's so pathetic. I bet you don't like him either because he used to be Catholic but he flipped over into being some sort of Protestant, one of the really flakey sort. You know, the kind that gets all teary-eyed every time you say America and just can't wait to condemn Islamic moderates while they snuggle up to Saudi Arabia. Go figure! I mean you probably don't even have to figure; you just know things. I bet people tell you that you are very intuitive.

That sounds so stupid. Nobody can tell you how you think. Besides … here's a real brain-teaser. If we know things it is because we have to learn them, a state of affairs exists outside of us and by some process we attune our mind to some outer reality. But with you there is no outer reality until you make it happen. You can have everything anyway you want. Who's going to stop you? So I guess for you, as God, you know things by simply willing them to be that way and they are. So does that mean that you can never know yourself as God completely because you might just change your mind about something and then everything would just be reversed? What if you, metaphorically speaking, got out of bed (pretty big bed) and were just sort of pissed-off about everything and just turned the lights out on everything BAM! Everything would just disappear and you'd be left floating around in a big empty whatever. I hope you never do it. I know that a lot of people use your name in vain and pretend you aren't around and act all atheistic and such but I expect that they must know at some level that they don't have all the answers either. I think they are just afraid that you are watching them. I think that they would rather that they be the only beings that can think. It makes them feel closer to what people call closure. Life sucks and then you die, so just face up to it … I think that shows a really bad attitude!"

Joana stopped to re-gather her thoughts for verbal formulation in her mind. She began to think/talk to God again.

"But I was talking about Gia wasn't I? Anyway, she was just one of the models that I would have loved to be in those days. I'm even talking to you now the way that I talked then, not like my real age. I was like most of the other teen-aged girls then looking for the perfect role model. My mom loved magazine subscriptions and we had everything: Vogue, Life, Look, Mademoiselle, Modern Screen, Cosmopolitan, and Ladies Home Journal. That's a lot of pretty girls and I wanted to be most of them. You see I got a double-whammy: a girl's mind and a dose of high-octane testosterone. Man … I mean God, that's a pretty deadly sexual cocktail combination!

Anyway I used to go in the bathroom and put on my Mom's lipstick and then just scrub it right off again. I used to be so disappointed at my own sad eyes looking back at me from the mirror. It wasn't until much later that I learned how to really transform myself, until I could look pretty good … but never as good as the models that I had worshiped … I mean really admired a lot. I'm a great deal smarter than I sound when I'm talking to you but part of me is still like a teenager inside because I don't think that I ever really grew up. I'm still sort of locked into becoming a girl rather than just being one. I know that sounds very existential.

So anyway, I went away to college and I majored in psychology so that maybe I could figure myself out and discover why I was so different. I got really into it. I read all the big names in psychology: Carl Jung, Eric Fromm, Karen Horney, Harry Stack Sullivan, Otto Rank, Fritz Perls, Wilhelm Reich... Did you know that Reich thought you could store up sexual energy in little "orgone boxes?" I mean talk about the perfect gift, the gift that just keeps on giving, whoa!

Anyway, none of those great psychologists dealt specifically with my problem. Finally I heard about Havelock Ellis who wrote in 1903 about a thing called Sexo-aesthetic Inversion and BAM that sounded just like me. Anyway his book didn't catch on too well except with Magnus Hirshfeld in Germany and the Nazi's soon shut him down so that by my era all that was left in the media that seemed to pertain to me was Andy Warhol's little coterie of drag superstars: Jackie Curtis, Candy Darling, and Holly Woodlawn. Otherwise there was only my abnormal psychology text and that wasn't too comforting. I was apparently just suffering from a persistent delusion. So I just tried to shut the whole girl-thing down. I gave away my bra and stockings, tossed my mascara and lipstick in the trash, and burned my wig. I was a boy again … but I was miserable."

Joana was quiet for awhile in the vast empty space and a tear trickled down her cheek. Somehow since starting to talk to God she had loosened up. She wasn't as angry anymore. It was sort of like talking to a friend, someone who might just sympathize and understand. She had never thought of God in that light particularly. He had always seemed somehow inaccessible if not rejecting to her. After she had composed herself she began again.

"That's was really stupid, me crying like that, and all. It was all a long time ago and anyway I kept coming back to being a girl so I figured what was the use of trying to reform? I started trying to find a way to just live as a girl. I grew my hair long, started to buy girl-jeans and tight little-tops that made me look like a flat girl who refused to wear a padded-bra. At least a nipple-show was worth something. Guys would check me out once in a while but I didn't take too many chances. I didn't want to be just another dead-tranny statistic. Finally, I heard about the few seedy bars in town that catered to a gay clientele and about the drag court system, you know, queens competing for titles. It sounded cool and I started filtering into the shadow world of the 1970's bar and club scene. But I wasn't into drugs and I could already see that some of the queens weren't living a very healthy lifestyle. Besides, I had a college degree and I didn't want to give that up for work that I could have done right out of high school.

So I sort of stalled out in my life; I couldn't move forward or backward. I sure couldn't afford sex change surgery. All I could manage was to get hormones and maybe get my breasts done, thinking that would give me just enough credibility to pass full-time. But you see there is always something that might still give you away as having been a boy. I might get clocked in a grocery line and want to take my top off right there and yell, 'Hey stupid what are these? Do you see? I'm a girl!' But I never did. I'd just go home and cry…

So I lived like that for a few years and suddenly people around me just started dying. I mean they were young and suddenly they just started dying. It was called the gay cancer at first and then GRID, 'gay-related immune deficiency syndrome.' It was only called AIDS later. Well, that sort of wrecked me for thinking about sleeping around. I didn't want to die. I had just been very lucky that I had been scared back into the closet so often."

Joana was silent for awhile … remembering.

"Would you like to hear what AIDS was like in those days? It was a closet illness just like our whole life was closeted then. We were all like moths that only come out at night and circle about a light-bulb until they fly too close, singe their wings, and fall to earth dead. Only we died slowly, or not me I guess, because I'm still here. Only my friends are dead, only they weren't my friends really because

I never slept with anybody. I just watched them from a sort of sexual remoteness, from the shadows on late autumn nights when the rain was falling. I wonder where all those autumn leaves are now. They used to float down the gutters to the corners and clog the drains. I used to drive home, west to the good end of town where I could live my little immune life overlooking Puget Sound. I felt sheltered then by time and guaranteed of my own eternal youth. When I arrived home I would wipe off my lipstick in the mirror and look again for the boy that I had tried so hard to erase. I couldn't afford a pussy so I just wore tight panties and jeans to get the right look. It isn't easy to be an ingénue five to ten years late but I pulled it off anyway. I used to stop traffic on Broadway and Pike in those days up on Capitol Hill in Seattle. I walked in my own little spotlight of imagined glamour, only they were really only the headlights from the passing cars.

A little money came my way and I bought my silicone tits. Finally I was right. They should have been mine at fourteen, but if they had been I would have been sent to some institution or enrolled in a circus I guess. Now they were my passport to what the queens called realness. I liked being envied in the bars. If I was any more real I would have caused a lot of trouble. It was my little revenge to offer what I could never bestow. I would come home later and take a long bath and go to bed on the couch in my sleeping bag and say my usual mantra, 'No one can touch me, nothing can hurt me.'

I could distill drama out of nothing during those years. I could get off on songs as though they were written just about me. I could absorb a character out of a movie and walk around for hours afterwards as though I was them. Maybe that's dissociation; I don't know. What do you think? I guess I was just a poor deluded creature of vanity. That's why I envied the ones who dared to do what I only dreamed about.

The death of so many beautiful young people was an accusation pointed like a dagger at the frozen heart of America. It was as though each life had sprung into bloom overnight in all of its strength and ardor only to falter and fail. The decade of the eighties throbbed to a pulse where everything seemed simultaneously possible and infinitely remote. AIDS arrived unannounced as though on little cat's paws. It sunk its talons deeply and rode about for years while talents were fostered and dreams were achieved. Then suddenly it leapt forth in swollen glands, a persistent cough, an inexplicable weight-loss, anything really that implied that the well-tuned bodies of youth were coming unstrung. In Africa the disease was called, 'slim.' Fevers followed on fevers. Eyes floated in a sea of unshed tears while every bone grew in definition and the skin once so vibrant grew pale and slack. Ailments arrived like unwelcome relatives on an endless train. I felt the presence of AIDS when I walked through the old neighborhoods that now never seemed to escape mourning.

Joana paused...

"I don't think there is anything lonelier than downtown streets with the rain falling. I shiver to think of all the places I have been in my life. I have walked to the very edge of so many abysses and turned away just in time. To be honest I miss the days when we were not as accepted as we are now. Incomprehension made us sort of scary, like vampires. People thought they could become infected by simply being near us. They didn't know that I was as squeaky clean as a nun. I never even kissed anybody! I lived in my head I guess, but isn't that where everything ends up anyway? It's all just a lot of electrical impulses...

I know you haven't felt this but with sex you feel it gathering like storm-clouds and then everything starts condensing and bearing down and Wham! And you're just lying there in the after-wash and he gets up and goes to the restroom to pee. You can still smell his sweat in the empty bed ... And the funny thing is [whispering] I never did it ... that's how good I am at imagining things. I can look at an apartment from street level and tell you everything that has ever happened there. It means that I need a pretty severe filter to keep experiences at bay. A little thing upsets me. People seep into me and all of a sudden I am them and I don't know who I am anymore just as me. So nobody gets inside me. I guess that it's good that I wasn't born with what I wanted … yes and dreaded to possess just as much. I can't figure it out.

I pull my identities out of a box like costumes in a harlequinade. I dance on the ends of my strings and no one sees behind the curtain where I hide. They just toss silver pieces at me and I gather them up when the carnival closes for the night. The moon rises and I walk with bare feet along the sands and feel the tide tugging time away from beneath me. Words materialize out of nothing and I write them down before they can vanish … And all the time I know that if it was tomorrow I would have written something different... Am I wandering? You should have interrupted me. I'm simply connecting the dots of discordant memories looking for a theme.

Anyway my roommate at the time saved up newspapers to recycle, but he never did get around to dropping them off at the recycling center so when he moved away I was left with two years of newspapers. There were so many newspapers that I made logs out of them and burned them. The sheets would peel up and catch flame one at a time as though a demon was reading them slowly and finding nothing there to his liking reduced them ash. I guess I thought sex was like that: a quick burst of flame and then the cold creeping back into my soul. I liked to read poems by Ernest Dowson. 'I have been faithful to thee, Cynara, in my fashion.' Was I Cynara? That would have been such a great name to have chosen for myself. It sounds like the name of a snake or like some poison. Is it a dreadful thing to want to be admired to distraction? I wanted to haunt the city streets at three o'clock in the morning and hear the ferryboats out on the sound, somewhere out there in the fog. I wanted to hide my face in a cloak with just my lips visible, scarlet and trembling."

Joana paused again to savor the image she had created.

At last she smiled and said, "I think I'm just saying these things to impress you or just to see if you are paying attention. You shouldn't listen to people who mistake poetry for prose. It was easy to mistake passion for reality in those days and then just watch while people faded away like mist and vanished forever. I would sit on the floor in my living room at night and reach across town by phone to talk to the drag-queens about the various dramas that they once had to tune into Dynasty to find. It was clean and safe for me. I would drink bourbon whiskey straight-up in little sips because it was sour and harsh. I guess if I was a real fem I should have been drinking pink daiquiris in a bikini somewhere in the Bahamas instead of talking on a rainy night to gay boys living communally in the old apartments across town that comprised the gay ghetto. I guess it was enough for me that I was living in the clean and sparkling suburban end overlooking the water and the mountains whenever the rains cleared away. If I had been in Manhattan I might have been in a spendy up-town condo or out on Fire Island or the Cape in the summers. I would then have been at the center of the unfolding AIDS disaster instead of living on the outer northern periphery of the plague's reach clear up in salmon country."

Joana returned again to that realm of reflection where our lost lives remain unchanged and unredeemed in that inscrutable domain of memory preserved there in all of the blindness and inconsequence of our immaturity and flawed choices.

She began again, "I remember that I called Madeline to see how her roommate was doing the night that Cayenne-Pepper died. She had been the first to show any symptoms of her collapsing immune system. Madeline was my first friend in the community. When she heard that Cayenne was sick she had quit her job in the Tri-cities and come home to nurse her to the end. The funny thing was that they weren't even lovers. What straight person would do that, make that sacrifice, and take that risk for just a friend? Even families were exiling their children then. Nobody knew what caused AIDS in those early days. Doctors and nurses were coming into the rooms of AIDS patients like they were going into a nuclear reactor. Good Christian families left their children out to die on the streets while they piously listened to televangelists proclaim that AIDS wasn't a disease it was a cure! It was all part of the wrath of God, imposed, they said, for committing the unspeakable sin of loving across the impassible chasm of the gender divide. I'm always amazed at the various Christian family values organizations even today. I don't think I can ever forget how their representatives appeared on the various popular talk shows explaining why God hated us, overlooking the vast numbers of gay and lesbian youth abandoned by 'family values' to the tender mercies of the streets.

It was shortly after Cayenne Pepper's death when I started fighting for civil rights for us. I was about as startling in my own appearance at the time that you could get.   This was when transgender people seldom appeared in daylight. I was feeling my oats as they say. I thought I could be just like Evita and command my hometown from my imaginary balcony at the Casa Rosada and it would all just happen. But it was harder than that, harder because I think that people enjoyed shaming us and treating us like we were nothing, that we deserved to die because we were rebelling against the natural order, the one that said if you couldn't seem to manage in your assigned sex ... well that was just too bad. We should just suck it up and be what God or fate had made us. Even today it isn't much different.   Transgender people are beaten up and murdered and proper health care is denied us because any alterations that we require are deemed 'cosmetic' rather than a passport to avoid ridicule and violence in daily life.

That was my acting-out era big time with big Tina Turner hair and tight sweaters and jeans. I spent every night listening to Andrew Lloyd Webber soundtracks and later on it was Enigma or Depeche Mode. Dark moods are cheap if the bad news applies to people other than you; depression embraced as an art-form. I fell in love with women and kept men at bay. Men seemed to have all the physical demands but no real ardor. They lost all interest after one brief tornado of passion while women could communicate by the slightest touch for hours. Their expressive faces and sense for nuance made of love a symphony rather than just a song. I know that all this has little to do with procreation, but did you really make us so sensual and communicative if all you wanted was just a quick ejaculation as long as it hits the right target spot on? Can you understand why women might prefer to love women? Do you ever listen to the way that men talk about women? Are the theologians really any better? It's all a matter of getting the penis securely in place at the critical moment before blast off; otherwise the duty to fill and subdue the earth becomes a sin. I've always been startled by that choice of words, 'subdue." Doesn't it imply that the earth might be putting up at least some token resistance, the earth seen as just one big vagina just waiting to filled? Would it make a difference if we referred to the planet as Father Earth?

This disparity of respect is the natural consequence when men are taught to view women as nothing more than occasions of sin or as easy prey. Does it take someone like me to bridge the gap of indignation by being both a man and a woman inside? As long as woman is viewed as somehow alien and only partially human this stuff will go on. I don't think that femininity is ever seen by men except as a threat. I think that's why gay boys get beaten up. It's because they are a sort of fifth column behind military lines implying that men can also be penetrated and used just like women. I think that is what you meant when you said that sexual sins could be serious, because when people are raped, simultaneously their hearts are broken, their will crushed. To be used and abandoned; I think abandonment is the greatest sin. I think we all want connection and respect."

Joana's memories were flowing in now like a flood and her past began to yield its deepest secrets.

"You may ask how I know and feel these things so deeply. I lived with a man once. He was an alcoholic and I never even knew it. Can you believe it? I let him move in as a roommate upstairs and we seldom ever talked. His room became like a little abstract island cut off from the rest of the house. I think they call it denial. When he moved in he promised to be my protector as a sort of side-benefit. He said that I was lucky because nobody would ever hurt me again as long as he was around and I was so anxious to be real that I believed him. I should have told him that I didn't need a protector, but the sad part is that I did.

Later on I asked him once if he loved me and he started to cry, but he never answered my question. One day he came down the stairs and asked me to drive him to the hospital to dry out because he couldn't drive himself there. I hadn't seen him for days but I would hear him upstairs so I thought he was okay and just didn't want to go to work. I thought that he knew his own business. Maybe he was sick; I didn't know what to do. So I just waited to see what he would do. It seems so strange to be now but that's what I did. I guess that unconsciously I didn't want to know how bad he really was. I was so alienated at the time from everything that I guess some amount of indifference was to be expected ... or maybe I was afraid of him. I don't know. When he got out of treatment in the hospital two weeks later he told me that he would be moving away. He called me 'baby-doll' and took my picture by the couch that last day.

Later on I heard that he had settled in with a woman and her child. I guess he was finally happy because he had a family of his own at last, even if an inherited one. I guess he always wanted to be a Dad and I couldn't give him that. After that we lost contact until one day I heard that he had died. Maybe she left him. Maybe he started to drink again. Who knows? People come in and out of your life and you still never really know them. But the funny thing was that I was downstairs all that time when he had lived with me and he could have talked to me anytime if his soul was broken, but he never did. Anyway, now he's dead and I guess you're in charge of him now. Maybe you know how to heal the wounds that life never could."

Joana was very quiet now. The setting sun slanted through the tall gothic windows of the church and made splotches of gold on the polished and worn walnut wood of the pews. Generations of believing Catholics had come to pray here, to be forgiven for their sins, and to celebrate Mass. The altar light burned red up by the tabernacle as visible evidence that the Blessed Sacrament was always present. "God is here," it proclaimed: the miraculous is honored by the genius of artifice but not dependent upon it.

At last Joana stirred and addressed God again. "Well I guess you've got the idea. I wasted a lot of my youth on living out a self-produced drama. I'm sorry for that now. I know the value of time a lot better, but in those days I internalized societal rejection like a sponge. It sort of took me down as you can imagine, but it just made me even more radical and determined than before. If the world doesn't make room for your existence you have to create your own space. I decided at last to selectively withdraw from the place that had been my home. I moved to a little town that had never had a transgender person before and just said, 'Here I am.' They didn't know what to do with me at first, but year by year they adjusted to me because they could see that I hadn't any other defenses, only my own honesty. Everything else had been stripped away, all my dreams and pretenses, even my anger."

Joana was silent for a time hoping that God was considering her story and might respond in some way so she said, "And there you have it, my life in a nutshell. Why does this gender thing happen to people? How do so many of us just shut down? It is only now that I am waking up again as though after a long sleep to ask myself the old questions once again. So I just thought that I'd come in here today and ask you this question: are you satisfied with the way things are going with me and well, with the whole world for that matter? I mean it's your planet, right? It's your universe even. Why don't you do a little smiting down here again like you used to do in Biblical days? This would be a great time for it; only leave the LGBT folks alone okay? We get smited enough every day! America is completely awash in real assholes and most of them think that they speak for you. Sorry about my choice of words but what would you call them?

I remember that the prophet Jonah was really upset with you once because you were a little too sparing of people that he thought you should go after. Well I'm a little like him I guess but my name is spelled Joana (two-syllables by the way not three) just like Jonah, the name my parents still call me. I don't want to argue about what stuff you might have done in the past or how messed up your followers have become but I'm getting really worried about the future here. I don't have any kids as you know but I do care about our earth and about the course that human history is taking. I think we all have a stake in those things and it's a real shame if all we do is fight each other about what we think that you want us to do. Why don't you just do another Mount Sinai thing like you did with Moses and say something like, 'Thou shalt stop fucking up my planet, like right now!'

I'd advise you to use really harsh language even if it doesn't seem particularly holy because otherwise some evangelical creep will just ignore it and say that what we should really be doing is going after the transsexuals and the immigrants and making their lives miserable. I think we should restore a sense of proportion in the moral realm especially in America, don't you?"

Joana paused to consider whether God would like some more specific suggestions. She reflected that the whole problem might be that God was getting poor advice from his advisors or staff or whatever passed for such in the celestial court. Joana had never really aspired to be a prophet, but then if she remembered rightly most of the prophets had tended to shun their vocations. Maybe if you wanted to be a prophet in the olden days you just had to start talking and later on if God liked what you were saying he made sure that it got into the Bible so it would get wider play. This was, after all, before the Internet and Facebook. Maybe God was like a DJ with good taste who sort of intuits the best songs to play and before long everybody is just dancing to it...

There was no light visible outside now except for the dimly reflected streetlights of the city. With the darkness the building had seemed to cool as if craving human warmth. She thought back to her childhood training. She had been taught that the Church was not a building but the Living Mystical Body of Christ made up of all the baptized faithful. She thought of how many people had left the Church to join one of the fragmented sects that claimed to represent a reformation of the two-thousand year old mother-church founded on the twelve apostles, the first bishops. She had never been tempted to embrace Protestantism with its sterile buildings, its lack of veneration for the saints, and its lack of full appreciation for the Virgin Mary. For Joana it was either Catholic or nothing. She thought of all the Catholic women and children seeking admission to America just as Mary and Joseph had sought shelter for the new-born Baby Jesus. She thought of all the ministers hailing Trump for keeping them stuck on the border or worse having their children ripped from their arms and put in cages. She thought of the contempt that conservatives had for Alexandria Ocasio-Cortez for pointing out how inconsistent it was to be pro-life but to always vote down pre-natal care and a living wage. She didn't see why God would ever be merciful to people like that. Worse still she didn't want God to be merciful to them. Joana made a decision.

"Okay, Lord, I'm going to just start talking and you can do a playback later and have it transcribed, if you want to, just in case you want to issue a new book or testament or whatever. You could call it, The Really New Testament or something. Not that the first two were bad but there's nothing wrong with a sequel when you've got a good thing going, I always figure, just to slam the message home. So here goes...

The Book of Joana

[Taken in down in the year 2019 by the angel, Amanuensis]

In the year 2019 the word came into the mind of Joana while she sat in the Cathedral of St. Philip Neri and she spake forth forthrightly unto the benefit of all who could hear her... [Editorial note from Joana to God: It's coming out with a sort of Mormon flavor. I'll skip the archaic diction from here on in. You can put the fancy language back into the text later if you think that it will help us to sell the message. I'm talking like I'm you remember...]

I, the Lord, have after much reflection decided that I have been silent too long in addressing my children with an extended prophetic utterance. Readers of the collection of disparate texts that is familiarly called the Bible will note that it was once my habit to inspire various prophets to speak in my name or to narrate various frightening and improbable visions in an apocalyptic manner. Interspersed with these were histories, poems, and collections of wise sayings as well as accounts of various pious persons such as my faithful servant Job. After the death of the last apostle of my Dearly Beloved and Anointed Son Jesus I meant to give no further public revelations until the Second Coming. I figured that I had left all of you with adequate means to procure the salvation of your souls. Imagine my surprise then when various and assorted later seers, who will remain unnamed here, came up with texts claiming to be amendments or additions to the Jewish and Christian traditions. Not that I abhor any source of wisdom; after all, I had long since made allowances for various epic eastern works of a speculative nature as to the complex being that is mine in the Upanishads and the writings of Lao Tsu and Confucius. I even looked the other way when the Buddha, Siddhartha Gautama began his program of dealing with suffering by detaching from the things of earth and coveting a form of philosophical non-being that he called nirvana. I imagined that you would all arrive at some sort of peaceful accommodation of divergent views.

Finally, after two thousand years my head angel came in to see me one day with a report. After reading the results of a surprise audit conducted by one of my accounting angels I was appalled to discover that the earth was, well, a complete mess. So it is that I have determined to have a little fire-side chat with all of you through the lips of my servant Joana. I want to warn all of you as once I warned the wicked city of Nineveh that you had better straighten up your collective act or I won't be responsible for the consequences.

Quite frankly Joana is of the mind that I should not delay retribution but rather to strike at once a few members of the Republican Party just to let you all know that I am serious. To calm her down in her feminine ire I have caused a plant to grow over her head to provide shelter for her in the heat of the day. There a dissociated part of her sits brooding even as I compose this brief admonitory missive, bitter and threatening to jump into the sea so that she can be eaten by a big fish if I don't do just as she says to preserve her dignity and status as a prophet. Personally, I think that she has been taking a few extra hormones in her seemingly endless pursuit of transition, but I am unwilling to risk another tirade by telling her so. So while she broods I will speak and she can look over the text hereafter and amend it to meet her own aesthetic preferences. Of course the final decision regarding publication as scripture remains with me. Here is what I have noticed taking place on the earth, a place that is nearer to paradise then you might think.

I could let the text be confined to what you call bullet points but these might mess up the division of this book later into chapters and verses for memorization in Sunday school classes so I will stick to simple narrative. It surprises me that you often choose some of the very worst people to lead you, people who will never advance your desire for justice, equity, and well-being but who will instead do everything possible to enrich themselves and their friends and meanwhile decimate the earth. I think you know who I mean if you read Mother Jones. It surprises me that it has never dawned on you that I am a socialist and so were the early Christians. You need only read The Acts of the Apostles to discover this. But apparently Christian conservatives think that I am really just a big investment banker in the sky.

I'm also really into non-violence. In fact Gandhi, Martin Luther King, and I were discussing this just the other day and we all agreed that I should instruct Congress to rescind the latest tax reform bill. Most Americans only saved enough for a few extra trips to Walmart. We also agreed that Congress should sponsor an amendment to drop the disgusting Second Amendment to the U.S. Constitution or to pass some statutory program of strict liability for annual gun-induced injuries upon any lobbying group that desires to retain it. I would also like to make it clear that LGBT children and adults are not to be bullied on playgrounds or denied jobs and housing later on in life when they grow up. Oh and I'm a real fan of Taylor Swift's music. Try and just be nicer to each other: feed the hungry, clothe the naked, and get rid of those ridiculous MAGA hats, please. Oh, and you might tell the current President of Brazil that I will hold him personally responsible if he burns up my rainforest in the Amazon. Try and eat less beef, stop smoking, and try and get a little exercise every day. You'll live longer and most of you could use a little extra time to repent. I really hate judging people, but it's in the job description. As for the over-population problem, tell the people in China and India to take more cold showers. I like keeping my commandments short and sweet because every new commandment only increases your chance of offending me. Try and think up a few of your own and just seek to be better people. As your all-seeing and benevolent father it is natural that I have a great concern for each and every one of my children. I hope that you understand though that in a universe as large as this one, abounding beyond your imaginations in galaxies, let alone solar systems and planets, I have many concerns. To speak quite candidly and truthfully (and how else would you expect me to speak) I was of the opinion that if I gave you the rudiments of religious insight, particularly in the case of Christianity, you could manage affairs without further interference from me; but just to be certain I am in the habit of dispensing bounteous amounts of divine grace to guide and fortify you. It helps if you recognize seven sacraments instead of only one.

But to return to the surprise audit, imagine my surprise after two thousand years (a mere eye-blink in celestial time-keeping) to discover that (not to be too harsh) you have all made rather a hash of things. I had hoped that an inspired text or two might give you a few points of guidance to keep you from each other's throats, but apparently that assumption was ill-advised. I think with a few thousand years more of evolution the orangutans might have been a better choice as the dominant species on earth. They have a little problem with melancholia but that may be because you are depriving them of their timber habitat in Indonesia. I hate to think that I simply made a bad choice by making you in my image, but historically speaking it looks like I might have given the decision a little more thought. (No one ever said that I am not impulsive at times, just look at the big bang!) Anyway this certainly looks to me like one of those problems that can't be successfully delegated. I have hosts of angels of course but as one of your famous politicians once said, "The buck stops here."

So here is what I have decided to do: I clearly can't simply allow the consequences of your actions to fall upon you, even though that course is the most natural pedagogy to follow. You would then have no one to blame but yourselves if you manage to destroy the earth. As for other alternatives this leaves either supernatural intervention or a major liquidation of assets; in other words to just tell you all to go to the devil. But as you can imagine I am not the sort to accept defeat gracefully so the latter course is off the table. This leaves divine intervention as my best option.

So here is my warning to you: I think that Ten Commandments were overly optimistic due to their brevity. They may have worked in a simple agrarian society, but they are wholly inadequate to cover every contingency in a post-industrial age. It will take more specific guidance to turn the tide of destruction. I would hate to go all the way back to the era when plagues and afflictions were the only way that I could get your attention. I know it sounds trite, but that would hurt me more than it would hurt you. I really like erring on the side of mercy, but well, I would hardly be able to look myself in the mirror if I was incapable of managing my own creation. I think it might help if you looked into your hearts and attempted to find that lingering spark of divinity that I planted there so many years ago. Is it too much to ask, that you adhere to what might be called a basic decency? Once you get that down we'll talk about more refined concepts of morality.

Yours truly,
God

After her mental recitation which she felt captured in its spontaneity and basic friendliness how she could imagine God addressing his poor beleaguered creatures, Joana withdrew her mind from that special state of utterance and vision that is termed prophetic. The vocation of prophet is a rare one. Even at that though, at any given time, many false prophets will be going about peddling their wares. Their spurious concoctions lessen the respect due to the real thing in the eyes of the general public. It is sad to say this but success in the prophetic line is usually inversely proportional to its inherent value and credibility.

Not that being a prophet is easy. It is always a strain for a mere mortal creature to presume to penetrate the inscrutable mind of the deity; always something is lost in translation to the printed page. This discrepancy is always presumed to be covered by the guarantee provided by faith that whatever inaccuracies or approximations may be present, whatever variances from the purity of divine truth, they will not lead the believer substantially astray. God sees that his word is properly preserved although the fate of the unwelcome prophet, speaking to a recalcitrant community, is not one to be envied. The order of grace is above all pragmatic. The word of God is not uttered in vain. This is not to say that prophets are never impatient with God even in the throes of inspiration when one might imagine them to be caught up in some manner of ecstasy. Many a prophet has been tempted to decline the honor of being chosen to convey messages from on high to the humid valleys below where human passions reign and divine missives are not greeted with alacrity.

Then there is the whole matter of gaining general acceptance. This troubled Joana no less than it has troubled all of her brother and sister prophets in their turn. No doubt later scholars, if her particular prophesies are ever accepted by some designated faith community, will parse each phrase to see if the human element has in any way disordered or confused the primary intent of the ultimate author who is God. Those scripture scholars who presume to submit prophesy to critical study rather than simply blind acceptance seek to discover whether the writings are inspired as opposed to being simply dictated by God verbatim. The resulting text requires a competent and discerning community to allow its true meaning to blossom forth. There persist certain grounds for interpretation that require a guiding spirit, often embodied in an ordained hierarchy, to weed out spurious or fanciful interpretations. Certain factors, personal or cultural, may render the text less than the photographic copy of the mind of God that we might desire.

Joana, having finished her recitation saw at once that, as prophetic utterances go, it was far too mild. Where was the great and fearful Day of Judgment? Where the wailing and gnashing of teeth? It definitely needed some more volcanic imagery to season the boiling broth of admonitions. It was almost as if God was pleading with his people to believe in him like a recruitment poster that shows military service as one big party in well-tailored uniforms instead of watching while your buddies catch shrapnel or are shot to pieces in front of your eyes in Afghanistan after fifteen years of fruitless engagement.

It seemed to Joana that real prophesy needed a little more pizzazz if it was to gain general acceptance. She should have brought a written draft with her instead of trusting to the inspiration of the moment. Narration has its own tricks. One of the best devices was to pick a natural and inevitable disaster and to read into it a deliberative intent like the destruction of Sodom and Gomorrah for being a little too imaginative in sexual expression instead of blaming the city fathers for building the cities in an undesirable location. After all, what about Pompeii?

To spice up her own work Joana thought of an idea. As Hurricane Dorian approached Florida Joana thought of an ideal location for it to make landfall. It might be an amusing sight for people to throw paper towels at the President for a change and trivialize his losses with absurd symbols. Now that she thought of it, any number of things made her crazy and roused her ire and a desire for some sort of payback. She had long kept these things close to her heart. Now they could be focused on the appropriate targets. This would include various types of conservative evangelicals: phony faith-healers, televangelists living in multi-million dollar homes and with their own private jets, and conservative news commentators who saw nothing contrary in the proclamation that the real King of Israel is Donald Trump as opposed to reserving that appellation for the humble Jesus of Nazareth.

Who was the best living example of the prosperity gospel in action if not Mister Prosperity himself who can fire anyone no matter what their exalted position in his cabinet at a whim, made public on Twitter? Real power after all is lies in the ability to act arbitrarily without consequences. Who could best judge the proffered word of God if not the man whose vast education has revealed to him the very best words, like "You're fired?"

And what about the cheering throngs at his rallies? Could any right-thinking person imagine that these good folk were misled when they proclaimed His Trumpiness to be God's choice to run America? Where would white prosperity be in America if we allowed it to be diluted by extending charity to the homeless women and children refugees driven from their countries by the dug-lords financed by America's addictions? We already have enough dependants of our own. Didn't the Lord's ministers know just who God perceived as the sheep and who God perceived as the goats?

This was America in 2019 as the majority of Americans, those who had not voted for the Donald Trump, watched in horror every day as America devolved into an anti-intellectual morass. It was definitely time for a new prophet but Joana? Why would God ever pick a transgender person (as if such a thing was even possible, a man is a man and a woman is a woman) to tell her those who know that they are saved how God felt about the direction the world was taking at this late date of 2019? Wasn't the millennium at the very gate now that Israel was restored? With a little careful handling Armageddon might break out any minute. Donald Trump was just the guy needed, at the right time and place to light the fuse of global conflagration and bring on the rapture for the elect. When seen in this light, Joana, not less than the four women referred to as "The Squad," was a clear and present danger to America, little better than Hilary Clinton. Surely Republican led providence would intervene in time. Was it any mere coincidence then that the lights in the cathedral were suddenly extinguished at the precise moment when Joana had just completed her oration of her pretended book of prophesies? Such darkness! It was as though the entire sacred space became the metaphorical equivalent of the belly of a great fish and in that belly Joana now reposed.

After her initial surprise and natural trepidation at being thus deprived of light, Joana allowed her thoughts to turn inward to seek the reason why she had been deprived of that one most essential aspect of life, the light of God. She wasn't sure what to expect now. Had she been guilty of the worst form of overreaching in daring to pray in this direct fashion? How would God manifest his discontent if not by withdrawing his grace and guidance? Where had her wayward thoughts come from in the first place? Is it ever possible for a sinner to channel God's word? Who was she to think that she could hold herself out as a prophet?

When she had entered the cathedral it was primarily to seek personal understanding and affirmation, to discover if there is an ultimate witness and guarantor of our uniqueness and value in the face of constant alteration and change. If there was no God then, Joana thought, we are all thrown back into a mere cacophony of assertion and counter-assertion. What was history but one long set of oppositions without any final resolution? How could there be any resolution without a point of absolute stasis to exercise its majestic sense of moral gravitation and awesome peace? Wasn't this what was meant by the long slow utterance of the majestic syllable Om? Why should we expect God as the great universal to manifest himself to us in particularity? Yet wasn't that precisely what Christianity had claimed to be the essence of its faith, that Jesus was Lord, simultaneously both God and Man? This was its great and unique innovation: that being human mattered, that we are not a cosmic disgrace. Is it possible that God likes us?

If so then why, Joana thought, had she been plunged into darkness? Was this darkness any different from the shame and exile that had for so long beset her? Joana had always felt that she was living a parallel life from the one that she should have had rather like someone who has taken a wrong exit from the freeway and ended up on one of America's endless but futile back highways, the ones sketched like blue veins on the road atlases. How did some people manage to connect to one of the great ski-lifts that exalt them from obscurity to fame and fortune? Not that fame and fortune are everything; but why shouldn't she have her own combination mascara and lip-gloss and make millions from her Internet followers, JOANA COSMETICS.

Instead here she was trying to break into the old prophesy game with only God to listen to her. God was having his own branding problems. It was getting so churches were sort of like brick and mortar retail outlets, closing every day. The only way to make religion pay was to go digital or to operate a media empire, hire a few fat guys in powder-blue suits telling America that women's restrooms were being besieged by millions of men in cheap thrift-shop dresses and thirty dollar wigs who were claiming to be transgender for the day just so they could sneak a peek. There's trouble in River City for you! She thought about how hard it was to be transgender; the statistics didn't lie. No doubt about it, America was committed to gender bi-polarity; no mix-and-match allowed. After you left the coastal blue states you took your chances as a trans-person. Naturally this state of affairs had left Joana a little bitter and that bitterness translated itself into a desire to rain curses and imprecations on the self-complacent purveyors of "Gospel values." It seemed to her that fundamentalism had missed the fact the religion is mystery rather than knowledge. The comfortable and crude Gnosticism that denied anything not found in some individual verse of the authoritative bible while missing the message of the whole made her furious. Even from a more sophisticated and universal point of view, one open to discovery, the seeker was brought up short by the fact that so much of dogmatic theology is the proclamation that two contraries can both be affirmed simultaneously. Theological questions are not so much resolved by such answers as frozen into place in a matrix of belief by the very act of presentation. How does the individual interface with two thousand years of theological conflict? Was there a more direct path through and around so many contentious offerings? Is it even possible to locate the source of our discontent in the comfortable way that Sigmund Freud had in his book, The Future of an Illusion? Religion did not seem illusory to Joana; it affected world politics on a daily basis. Its various contentions might just result in the next world war. Of course economics always plays its part as well. What would the ubiquitous Christian broadcasting networks be without well-healed sponsors? Conservative Christianity wasn't so much about relieving anxiety anymore, Freud's "the opium of the masses." Most of the audience already knew that they were saved. The whole point of evangelical Christianity had shifted away from individual salvation to the proclamation of who was not going to be saved. This inversion seemed to her so contrary to the evident intent of Jesus that she could not believe that so many Christians seemed oblivious to it. If the whole point of salvation history was to vindicate the offended dignity of God, then who was God anyway? If God cherished offenses, then who could hope to stand before God? How could they believe that God was so petty and cheap, so insecure that he needed to vindicate his dignity by squashing the very people who were most pitiful because of their sins? Surely this was to take the name of the Lord in vain if anything was.

This explained hateful religious rhetoric and the central importance in American life of always having someone to feel superior to: racial minorities, the homeless, or best of all the whole lavender crowd in all of its various manifestations. This also explained the disconnect between the conservative Christians' supposed reverence for life while it reposed in the womb and their utter contempt for poor children who might get a free and nutritious lunch at public expense or any publicly funded pre-natal care so that the baby might be born healthy. Was it any wonder that most of the Republican base was drawn from people beset by envy and convinced that only insults and petty meanness could deliver them from some democrat out to pick their pocket? It had always seemed strange to Joana that oil depletion allowances for corporations aren't socialism but public education and Medicare are.

"The real problem rests with us," she thought. "In our blindness we are seeking an answer when it is already around us reaching into every crevasse of our being just as air seeks to fill every vacuum. We are loved!" In an instant her anger at God vanished and she felt how sad it was that she had not long since affirmed as Henry David Thoreau once did when he was asked during his final illness if he had made his peace with God. Thoreau's answer was, "I was not aware that we had ever quarreled." If this was so then Joana realized that her indignation was pointless if it was directed at God. Any answer that God might give her had preceded the asking of her question. It was pointless to pray for acceptance if one was already accepted, to ask for love if one was already loved, to seek immortality if one's soul was already immortal.

She did not turn to see if she was still alone in the cathedral. Was her lament any different from that of others who might have left the busy streets that night one at a time to seek God's presence in this special place set aside for divine worship? The shadows of mistrust began to lift.

"I have wasted so much time!" she cried out and her voice of lamentation echoed from the dim recesses of the gothic vault upwards to the empty choir loft.

"Where has my life gone? I was always so unprepared for everything and now it's too late for me!"

Joana saw her days and nights cascading downwards and adhering to her in their sheer irrevocability, frozen like a glacier into immobility. Could anything ever deliver her from the brittle etching into slate of every thought she had ever entertained, every action she had taken, each decision she had made however trivial and indubitable it had once seemed? All certainties seemed to vanish before her like water in the desert. She was left alone as only prophets are ever left alone, to trust in darkness the witness that they give to others of what has been revealed to them alone. To enter the desert is the most risky thing that a human being can ever undertake.

"No one takes this upon themselves unless they are called to it," Joana reflected. "Was my calling always inherent in my confusion? If I had known who I was and if love simply blossomed from within me with the usual certainty that comes from an automatic congruity of sex would I ever have become the person that I turned out to be? Was my life the exercise of freedom or the living out of some pre-ordained plan the nature of which is only now being revealed within me from behind the veil of circumstance?"

Her thoughts hovered over the same abyss as that described by Dante in the first Canto of The Divine Comedy where he says that he came to himself in a dark wood where the true way was lost. Sooner or later everyone finds his or her way there. Despair beckons and the adversary is very near at hand. Human life for all of our differences is a universal—our interface with the absolute.

Only a single phrase came back to comfort her now in her darkness. She could not think where she had first heard it.

"Behold, I make all things new."

And with that recollection whatever glitch in the electrical circuitry of the cathedral had caused the blackout was evidently repaired by someone because inexplicably, or maybe providentially, the lights suddenly came back on and Joana, the transsexual and would-be prophetess, was restored to her fellow human beings in the land of the living.

Triptych

In October the month of harvest and completion nature puts out her finest show of color and variety so that even in dying there is the promise of fullness and rebirth. It is the month of gaudy display culminating in a grand masquerade where everything can both assume its disguise and simultaneously reveal what has been latent within it all along.

As the year 2019 began to ebb away into the great dust-bin of history Americans were beginning to wake up to the costs imposed by a streamlined approach to attain heady results that would ignore law, prudence, and the fact that the days when America needed only to will a thing to have it done were passing away. It turned out that there were other nations in play after all. Still there was time for one last blow-out of self-indulgence. Americans would not relinquish power easily.

So it was that in retreat they had decided to elect a man who could embody in his very person the lumbering imposingness of American self-indulgence with the piggy-eyed suspicions and paranoia of American supremacy. Who could foretell the events of 2020 when as its name implied vision must triumph over masquerade? Story telling is not prophesy; the accoutrements of even tomorrow are beyond our grasp. Still, it does not seem too great an exercise of imagination to presume that it will be a contentious year on all fronts. But from the vantage point of harvest-time when nature shakes out its frills and furbelows for one last gay extravaganza we might imagine a story such as the one that follows…

Scheherazade was a drag queen; she had never claimed to be anything else. She was neither particularly pretty (real in drag parlance) nor was she less attractive than the majority of biological women who had reached, as it is coyly expressed, a certain age. She had never procreated because even with the greatest act of determination she had never been able to even imagine herself as a man, let alone adequately perform the male role in an actual act of coitus. That role always reminded her too much of what her avid Irish setter had repeatedly tried to do to her leg when given the slightest opportunity. The net result of all of this was that Scheherazade had remained as it were genitally arrested at that stage of growth when she merely wished to imitate the women of the household where she had been raised in a semi-fatherless environment as a child.

Scheherazade resided at the time of this story in one of the states between the Rockies and the Appalachians referred to as the Great Basin or more colloquially as "fly-over America." The states in this region are basically interchangeable with each other as to their acceptance of sexual non-conformity … NOT ACCEPTING. So we will avoid being more specific as to the specific town or county of her domicile, less for fear of outing anybody there than because our story is so generally applicable to many individual biographies that many poor souls would be in distress as to how a remote author might have divined their most private dreams and histories while making only a few alterations in the name of fiction.

As we have mentioned above, our heroine, for such she is, had no children of her own. The years had slipped by in that way that they have of slipping by unnoticed in a series of acts balanced between pleasure and pain to simply keep the whole process of an individual life going on from day to empty day. Gradually her women relatives and early role models had grown old and died so that finally Scheherazade had come to the realization that she was quite alone in her life. She had never made it out to New York City or to San Francisco where she might have performed in a drag review while still in the first blush of youth performing to the whistles of an appreciative audience of straight people who would afterwards chuckle at the very idea of a man in a dress.

The lights has faded early on her aspiration to declare herself as one of the disciples of what is now referred to as "gender ideology" that in the first quarter of the 21st century poses such a threat to American security that various religious groups have brought the issue up constantly as a sure-fire fundraiser for various evangelical political crusades. This has always puzzled Scheherazade. As far as she knew no drag queen had ever commandeered an aircraft to fly into buildings or shot-up an outdoor concert in Las Vegas; but still to the conservative mindset if a guy is going to wear mascara and lipstick there was no telling what else he might do.

All in all Scheherazade considered herself to be a relative non-entity. She worked at the local grocery store outlet as a grocery checker by day as a man so as to keep her job and she still lived in the same home where she had grown up as a child. She had a few friends left over from high school who she still met on occasion for a lovely walk or a night of cards; mostly though she watched lots of movies on cable television, old classic films in black and white. She ate a little too much and as a result had developed in middle-age the breasts she had wished for in adolescence, but she had never qualified for female hormones let alone considered the big operation that would have confirmed her deepest sense of herself.

So it was that this particular Midwest daughter of the great American soil sat one day before her antique mirror looking at herself in a girdle and an old-lady bra as she applied acres of pan-stick before applying contour, blush, and loose powder and asked herself what the sum total of her life added up to. If she had been a character in a book by Albert Camus or by Andre Gide her existential problem could be summarized as a state of alienation and anomie, but in the Midwest she was just another depressed queen wondering if she should drive out to the highway rest-stop on the chance of finding somebody there to love. The nearest gay bar was sixty miles away and on the few occasions when she had visited there her dance card had, let us say, not been filled.

She thought back often, recalling the name she had chosen in youth while watching re-runs of *"I Dream of Jeanie"* on television while eating Hostess Twinkies on the couch after school and before substantial dinners of roast beef and potatoes. In her mind she always saw herself though as Barbara Eden and it was all she could do to avoid using her magic powers to nod and blink and make the bullies at school just disappear or turn into the little toads that they really were. She used her fertile imagination to visualize herself as a favored courtesan in a harem, the one drawn from the other silken-veiled concubines and made love to by the hour, leaving the muezzin unheeded, by a sloe-eyed and turbaned Prince or Caliph in some garden hidden in the remote recesses of far-off Baghdad or Arabia. She would tell him tales by starlight and bathe his weary brow in scented waters drawn from a carafe of gold while he nestled in her lap. She would nurse all manner of young princes and princesses appearing regularly from her fertile loins and tell them to go play in the sand because mama was resting after a busy night with their father, the Caliph.

But this vision was soon replaced by the sordid demands of the hour and her reflection in the mirror before retiring was always the same ginger-haired boy with the requisite and functional crew-cut that only made her appear more odd with her broad hips that made running difficult during the required physical education classes that serve more to isolate and ridicule gay kids than to instruct. It was all part of America's winner-take-all culture that cannot be acquired too early in life. In this world the function of woman was to admire and praise and to learn that her future could best be assured by securing a good male partner and then to keep him from straying by constant attention. Still Scheherazade envied the women she saw about her and felt her isolation more keenly when denied their company because of what for her was an irrelevant appendage. The net result for Scheherazade was isolation all-round and the creation of her own inner world where her inner reality could be confirmed and validated.

So had the years passed by when one day, while perusing the unending cellular feed of news that a non-judgmental algorithm had selected for her based on her customary usage, she heard of a program that allowed drag-queens to perform at libraries by reading stories and singing songs. Scheherazade thought instantly of how much such a program might have meant to her in her youth and the solace it might have brought to her and decided to apply. What had she to lose, except maybe forty pounds? She broke the pencil twice in her excitement in filling out a letter of expressed interest to the organization involved. She enclosed one or two selfies taken in dim light and crossed her arms over her bosom and blinked three times to carry the missive upon the flying carpet of magic to its intended destination.

Imagine her surprise and delight then when she was invited to an audition held at a local church where members of the LGBT community were not anathema. She had inherited a vast collection of vintage dresses from a deceased aunt and in one of her favorites she gave a brief recitation in a loud and clear voice and a week later heard that she was in. There was no formal induction ceremony. There were several branches of the local library system in various bibliophile prairie pit-stops of education across the lands where the buffalo used to roam. She was assigned a date at one of these and expected to show-up in a timely fashion, keep her act age-appropriate, and do the community proud.

All looked well for our heroine therefore until, in that mysterious way that fate has of playing a role in our lives that is disproportionate to our deserts, a determined force of opposition arose to prevent Scheherazade from performing and sowing confusion among the youth while promoting the insidious agenda of gender ideology thought up by people who had already bid fair to causing chaos among the hitherto secure realm of English pronouns. The gig was not only suspended but cancelled until further notice.

Our story might have ended right there but for the fact that it is always the function of the determined protagonist to never take no for an answer. Opposition is the name of the game, as a quick reading of Northrop Frye's *Anatomy of Criticism* will make perfectly clear. So it was that Scheherazade was not only unwilling to consent to having her name and picture, which she had seen in all of the glory of the lights of Broadway, taken down from the library bulletin board where it had been stuck up with thumb-tacks the week before, but she determined to take her two-week vacation and travel to Washington D.C. to make a statement and to express her outrage at the lobbying headquarters of the *Society to Keep Perversion Out of Family Life.*

In that same year of 2020 at a casino on the west coast it was Disco Mania Extravaganza Night and Deco la Tage was to be as usual the mistress of ceremonies for the evening. Her usual haunt, venue, and pied-a-terre was the Frisky Frisco, a gay bar done up in 1890's elegance reminiscent of an up-scale, turn of the century, cat-house in the fabled city by the bay, San Francisco. Deco had come to the FF as it was familiarly known as a young street queen with little to her name but big eyes, a pouty mouth, and an elaborate notion of her own worth as a potential lay. After having most of her attitude beaten out of her by a drag mother who announced after their first meeting that she didn't put up with *no I'm-all-that bullshit* from her daughters, Deco had emerged with a certain amount of style and a soupcon of wisdom and had succeeded in due order to her present post of prima donna at the FF by sheer grit, time, and tenacity.

Deco was what was once called a glitter-queen. She never felt that her body was complete unless it shown like a night sky in Montana with various tiny metallic sparkles from her peacock blue-green eyelids to her scarlet mouth. She preferred to perform under black light in silver or deep purple gowns with three inch nails that glowed green and with the deep silicone-enhanced bosom that a generous sugar-daddy had once allowed her to purchase so as to live up to her stage name. Deco watched her figure and avoided the excesses that made so many queens flame-out like a fighter-jet diving into a hillside in Afghanistan and as a result passed sufficiently as a woman so that, even deprived if her nightly finery, she turned heads and got whistles on the street. Better still, she saved her money rather than drinking it up in her room above the FF after hours or wasting it bailing no account lovers out of jail or defunct business schemes.

Deco had always lived as part of what was once called "the life" and was still HIV negative (which was saying something). Her big turn-on was to be looked at but not touched, playing her lover's fantasies in the light and shadow game of suggestion and nuance. In a part of her inner life there still resided hope for a grand romance and in her vague idle hours she imagined herself inhabiting a villa overlooking the Mediterranean Sea in the south of France where she could entertain guests lavishly while drinking Pernod and sampling delights from the local patisserie. By then of course she would have silver hair and a face where every bone revealed the underlying structure of her former beauty. She would have many tales to tell to her adoring chamber maids who would never stop giggling and saying, "Ooh la Madame!"

However in banal reality as the year 2020 arrived she often sat in the bar after closing hours and took stock of her life with all of its faux glamour and illusions and she didn't like what she saw. She thought of her dressing room, strewn with collages of seasons gone by and the signed autographs from real celebrities that had visited the Frisky Frisco over the years. She saw the panorama of her past glories fading into a uniform visage beneath increasing layers of pan-cake make-up and paint. It seemed necessary now to have nightly conferences with Pedro the light-man about how best to illuminate her on stage.

In recent years her stage patter hadn't evolved much since the glorious years when she had begun as a drag performer and she could foretell that she was rapidly becoming that most horrid thing for an artiste, a flesh and blood anachronism. Deco felt that she needed new skies and new material or she would be gently nudged aside (or rather pushed into the gutter) by some up and coming young thing. There were no stock options or golden parachutes for aging drag queens.

So it was that while the Frisky Frisco was closed for two months for a much needed roof repair and renovation, Deco decided that it was time for her Sapphire Extravaganza Tour. She packed up her old van with wigs and costumes and three cases of various cosmetics and set off on her road tour of the east coast and the southern drag circuit to assess the state of the art. As a grand finale he decided to include in her travels a stop in Washington D.C.

Meanwhile at her home base, when not appearing in cyberspace, there lived one of the princesses of social media. Sherry Dallas was five feet six inches tall and lived in Wilsonville, Oregon, an attractive suburb just south of the expanding freeway traffic jams of the greater Portland area. Sherry was a full-on transsexual and the final product of several skillful plastic surgeons. So successful was she in fact that she had joined the bevy of constructed beauties that had ridden the wave of social media to viral stardom. She had a respectable following for her make-up tutorials and her personal web-site showed her assuming various wistful attitudes as she went about her suburban day from early juicing at breakfast, yoga at mid-morning, petting her angora cat on a white couch in the living room while leaning against a luxurious fringed pillow with her bare legs stretched out in the afternoon, and ending by getting ready for an unnamed (and unrevealed) gentleman caller by night. Sherry was well-paid for simply living out other people's fantasies of the good life. Her business was to appear to be having fun while subtly suggesting to each of her followers that they enjoyed a special, behind-the-scenes, relationship with her beautiful self.

Sherry had reviewed all of the options before as it were choosing a face for herself. She divined that in the last analysis feminine beauty might be reduced to a set of formulaic computations based upon various sizes and symmetries. Once achieved these proportions were immediately translatable into various currencies from the dollar to the franc to the yen, because beauty is the gold-standard of humanity. This was made clear to her every day. What for instance could be more charming then a privileged blond news anchoress on conservative television stations frowning prettily as she announced the latest plans of the socialist Dems to destroy America and open our borders to various baby-toting Latinas? (Everyone knows that they all get fat at forty! Besides they're all Catholic and not respectably and non-denominationally evangelical).

Sherry Dallas of course didn't care one way or the other about politics. She hadn't gone through all that she had just to fall back into heartache or be encased again in tranny ghetto life through fruitless advocacy. She had realized early on that she was locked into a body-modality that could make her a sitting duck for abuse, a blank screen for other people's projections and agendas. She had finally reached a level now where she could mock them opening and get away with it. Sherry had recently even gone to a major annual conservative Christian conference and received a proposal of matrimony from a co-attendee over wine in the evening after listening to various lectures all day on the infestation of gender ideology in our schools.

Another attendee, the corporate founder of *Puritan Pierogi*, a national fast-food chain that threatened to edge into the burger market with the Ukrainian version of ravioli, offered her a modeling contract to push pierogies. Her figure was hardly typical though of the average patron of his drive-through business with its high caloric count and the whopping load of cholesterol it carried due to the bacon and potato filling and generous topping of sour cream. This was put into perspective however by the advertising slogan, "Hey

Babushka! Live a little!"

Sherry had politely declined both of these offers, preferring to make her money quietly at home by simply existing before a camera and going about her day. She was not about to be the Maria Ouspenskaya of greasy little Slavic pastries or to rush into marriage with a man who would no doubt hate her if he knew what she was, or rather, had once been. Sherry's life-path was designed as a quest for legitimacy which in this world demands a combination of visibility and simultaneous inscrutability. The key quality she had always aspired to possess was moral and emotional self-sufficiency. She realized early on that there were primarily two main types of men: the ones that seek out insecurities in women so that through flattery they may possess them sexually, and men whose own insecurity needs require a woman to validate and admire them. Both see women as a resource to be used until depleted before moving on to more promising fields. Now and again true devotion may appear, but as is usual with anything of true value, whether earth, sky, sunlight, or water, these are taken as just another of life's constants to which neither gratefulness nor conservation are required.

At first at the week-long conference, Sherry Dallas had been concerned that her internet notoriety might have preceded her there, but after days of earnest exhortations followed by socializing over rare cheeses and vintage wines with nightly prayers after steak and salmon dinners, she realized that any inquisitorial instincts were directed beyond the attendees towards those who dwelt beyond the circle of light in the outer rings of darkness: socialist Democrats, Guatemalan border-crossers, unionists, gender ideologists, and assorted liberals.

As the days at the conference passed Sherry felt a sense of conditional acceptance and belonging that was worth every bit of the hefty fee she had paid for attendance and accommodations. If she had any doubts at all she needed only to reflect that she was spending the money so that sin could be made more clearly manifest and so that rational Christianity could prevail over emotion-based and misguided toleration for vice. She knew that she would return like a charged-dynamo radiant with virtuous umbrage at the follies of the age and determined to resist any innovations set afoot with cloven hoofs by for instance the misguided papacy of the Catholic Pope Francis. If she weakened all that she needed to do was to look again at the workbook provided to every conference participant that pointed out on page one that "God is a capitalist" and to review the handy proof text that, *to those who have much, more will be provided, while those who have little will be deprived of even the little that they have.* In the last analysis heaven might be looked at as a perfect candidate for merger and acquisition by a determined corporate raider. She had especially enjoyed the session entitled, *"Why should you be only an ordinary Christian when you can be a CEO for the Lord?"* By the last day of the conference the cumulative effect of the inspired rhetoric had raised a fire in her heart and made her aspire to greater things. The attendees were given their final marching orders until next year's event prospectively denominated: *"Don't Keep Your Dogma in A plastic Bag."*

On impulse she had put her name up to be one of the delegates to march in the nation's capitol in support of the Republican slate of candidates in 2020. The inroads of liberalism and immigration simply had to be stopped. South America was the breeding ground to Amazonian Paganism even if it wore a mask of Christianity. Unexpectedly she was chosen and stood there blushing to the sounds of applause and halleluiahs. Who would believe that this little T-girl had final climbed the slippery ladder to the ultimate heights of invisibility, to be sent as a delegate by the very people who despised everything that she was (if they only knew)?

She had heard all week about how as a minion of Satan the transgender-mafia was taking over "our schools, our libraries, our rest rooms, in fact our whole American way of life." The sanctimonious umbrage had elicited gasps and raised goose-bumps on the flesh of the attendees. Never had Sherry been more grateful that she had wisely invested in obtaining for herself the vaginal equivalent of a shiny new Cadillac. She personally had nothing to fear from the restroom inquisition. Her size eight shoes would never give her away. The days of her bitter high school gauntlet experiences in the boys' locker room were like memories drawn from a nightmare of a previous life. In other words she had finally arrived. As the cheers continued she found that she simply could not find it in herself to decline their commission and their trust. She would go to Washington, D.C.

Washington D.C. in the year 2020 was less a stronghold of democracy than an armed camp awaiting the outcome of the election in November. Not since the 1960's had the culture wars more resembled a conflagration. Marches and demonstrations were a daily event and the police presence was supplemented by troops drawn from the National Guard in adjoining states just to keep order. This was the fulminating atmosphere that prevailed in the nation's capitol when our three aforementioned gender non-conformists hit town.

They were not alone. Also demonstrating were the contingent from *Leviticus is Forever,* a group that advocated physically stoning adulteresses and sodomites and the *Dead Cold-Fingers Coalition* that made it clear that they would die before surrendering their guns to the Democrats. These made common cause with other groups listed in the top ten of America's Taliban. The other members of the big ten included *Christians against Catamites* and various groups claiming to do research on *sexual anomalies and perversions* in order to preserve family values, particularly the right of parents to dump their gay kids on the street for disobedience and for promiscuous behaviors. Meanwhile representing the ever-present liberal fringe were *Wiccans for a Free Lunch, the Conspirators for Astral-Projection,* and of course the *Drag Queen Bibliophile Association.*

Keeping these groups apart, while still allowing then to harangue bewildered middle-America on the nightly news broadcasts was no easy task. Even the ardently fought Presidential contest was dwarfed by the outpouring of the unleashed political passions of fractured America. The fissures ran long and deep from sea to shining sea. The carry-over sometimes bordered on the ridiculous, such as the case of the Christian Delicatessen owner who refused to serve people requesting kosher dill pickles or anything using curry powder because even such condiments promoted non-Christian values. It was no surprise that even various Christian sects had rediscovered old grievances against each other. Various hospitals refused admission to dissenting denominations without the presentation of a certificate of proper and sect-congruent baptism. With no reliable and common bond as Americans every possible source of fission was being exploited and a general attitude of mistrust was the order of the day. Rather than lamenting this condition, Americans had learned over the past four years to embrace a radical sense of mine and yours as the national ethos and the phrase: *Community is just another name for communist* was as popular as the charge of purveying fake news.

All in all it wasn't the best place or time for Sherry, Deco, and Scheherazade to hit the shining city on the hill, each wishing to make some sort of personal statement before returning to the little zone of safety and acceptance from which they had come. Each of our lady-emissaries wished to escape lives that were summed up in conventionality and irrelevance. Each imagined that they had been commissioned to pursue a higher cause and each found herself wandering through the taper-lit streets to the sounds of vile imprecations thrown back and forth across the various barriers that had been erected to keep the contesting parties from actual assault and mayhem on each other.

Of course the media of the world took notice of these events occurring in the land that had once been a source of hope and inspiration to a struggling world. Now emulation had given way to either pity or ridicule as America pursued its seemingly endless culture wars and the currently reigning masters of discontent smiled in satisfaction. Any street corner would do as a place for any one of our heroines to announce her presence and make her proclamation but each, now that she had arrived, found that the arena was already thronged with roaring beasts.

So it was that as if drawn by a familiar and common inspiration to seek out a place where she could nurse a pink daiquiri and assemble a melded message and visage to draw the gaze and attention of the crowds assembled to hear her, each of our heroines converged at D.C.'s most famous gay bar, *The Monument,* at the same day and hour. The art of storytelling depends on just such synchronicities and fortuitous events. Can it therefore surprise us further to hear that these three that we now regard with some measure of curiosity and affection were to be seated at a single table? Yet such it was to be…

Scheherazade, as was appropriate to the old adage of age before beauty arrived there first. She had spent the late hours of the afternoon adorning herself in her best Midwestern idea of eleganza. She was readily admitted and chose one of the smaller rooms off the central core where the music was less loud to seek solace and to set up court. She could see through a glass partition into the main area of the bar located at a lower level. It was as though she was in one of the boxes in one of the old classical movie theaters she had attended and admired while growing up. She only wished that she had brought along opera glasses or a fan to add to the effect. The table she had chosen combined spaciousness with intimacy and comfort and she hoped that she might make some friends in the course of the evening.

The architecture of assignation in gay bars had changed since the days of *Studio 54* and *The Mineshaft.* Being gay was no longer about blatant sexual display or back-room indulgence let alone the more imaginative fantasias of pain and pleasure. The elaborate significations and coded communications of desire, battened on repression when suddenly unleashed into mindless indulgence, now seemed quaint reminders of a bygone era. With respectability, and above all legality, came order and responsibility. In spite of the outrage that same-sex marriage had provoked among conservative heterosexuals, legitimacy had exerted a civilizing influence in the former steamy jungles of desire. The interlaced communities of LGBTQIA had come into possession of sophisticated nomenclatures and codified manners so that the choice of partners appeared no longer to indicate or entail a promiscuous lifestyle.

Of course this cut little ice among those who could never imagine two people of the same sex forming a domestic unit let alone having that unit encouraged, celebrated, and blessed. Drag of course had always been subversive of gender norms even as it celebrated the radical divisions between the sexes. Drag queens did not embrace androgyny but instead thrived on high style and excess. As such they were mistrusted and sometimes ridiculed from both ends of the gay-straight spectrum. The full unleashing of raw female sexual power was always threatening no matter if done by transgendered or by a cis-gendered individual. Gender is largely a geographical demarcation and woe must follow the trespasser and border-crosser. Of course looking at Scheherazade, who even in her flowered print dress was more reminiscent of a church bazaar in Kansas than of an Arabic harem, no threat could be imagined. She seemed the ideal storyteller whether to children or to adults. How different was our next entrant on the scene!

Deco la Tage believed in the big entrance no matter where it might be.: even when grocery shopping it was customary for her to stand before the various displays and to lovingly caress each item with her long-nailed hands before arranging it thoughtfully in the grocery cart and pushing it further down the aisle while allowing her hips to slide first to one side and then the other displaying her well-padded derriere. Now and again she would look coyly over her shoulder to assess interest from the patrons with one eye hidden beneath her blond tresses like Veronica Lake before proceeding in search of further delicacies.

Of course Washington D.C. had its own style of high camp so that now, as she entered *The Monument* the various denizens of the establishment spared her only a perfunctory look-see before returning to their drinks and conversations. It must be said that she bore up well under the unaccustomed indignity, but diva that she was Deco knew when to make a strategic exit from the stage and as a result entered the private room where Scheherazade semi-reclined at table and joined her, greeting her as she deposited herself delicately on a chair with an aura of familiarity assumed for the occasion to hide her embarrassment.

"There you are! I hope I haven't kept you waiting long. Perhaps you don't remember me; I'm Deco la Tage but you can call me Deco, everyone does. I see you've already ordered a drink. My that looks delicious but I will need more than a drink. I'm simply famished. You have no idea how many barricades I had to traverse simply to get here!"

Caught off guard Scheherazade could think of nothing better than to simply offer her a hand while smiling and giving Deco her name in return.

"Scheherazade! How perfectly oriental! Shouldn't you be wearing a veil or a burka or something? You've done marvels of adaptation; you look positively American, very Betty Crocker."

Deco took time to look around her and assess damages; no one was paying any attention to her so she relaxed.

She whispered, "I'm sorry. Please don't think me rude but I'm from out of town and quite honestly I'm used to coming into a place like this with an entourage."

"Quite alright," said Scheherazade smiling. "I'm from out of town myself and it is a bit overwhelming. Do you think riots will break out?"

"Who can say? If anything happens I brought along some pepper-spray. Just look, see; it is guaranteed to stop a biker, a grizzly bear, or even a Bible wielding church-lady. You stick with me Honey and you'll be okay."

Scheherazade felt a sense of sudden sisterly warmth for the brash newcomer. She was even willing to overlook that Betty Crocker comment. It was a novelty for her to have a brash ally.

"Where are from?" Deco asked as she signaled to a cute

waiter in shorts for a drink and a menu.

Scheherazade hesitated, not wishing to seem too provincial. She suddenly wanted desperately to live up to her exotic name.

"Well, I live in the Midwest now but I was born in Lemon."

Deco froze and then began to giggle, "Don't you mean Yemen?"

Scheherazade blushed, "I still keep the local dialect of course, the Y sounds like an L … it's a habit."

"Oh. So when did you come to America?"

"My father was in the service and we were stationed all over the world. I always had to learn to adjust to new places."

"That must have been very difficult, I mean when you're gay and all. Don't gay people have real trouble in Arabic countries?"

Scheherazade said demurely, "I didn't make it a point to tell people."

Deco assessed her new friend from head to toe before commenting, "Honey that must have been like hiding the Sphinx in the Egyptian desert. I mean just look at you! You're just a woman. I bet you even carry tampons around in your purse."

Scheherazade took it as a complement. She looked enviously at Deco's trim figure and evident confidence. This was always what she had wished to possess.

"Well what about you? I mean, you're beautiful."

Deco gave her a radiant smile before her face collapsed and she brushed away a sudden tear. She confided, "Thanks honey but the clock is ticking for me. It won't be long until I will be doing a Gloria Swanson and telling Mr. de Mille that I am ready for my close up."

Scheherazade smiled and asked enthusiastically, "Do you like old movies?"

"I love them," Deco answered.

"I mean really old."

"RKO and Universal."

"Who played Dr. Frankenstein's wife in *The Bride of Frankenstein?*"

"The bride of the monster was Elsa Lanchester and the doctor's wife was Valerie Hobson," Deco answered promptly.

"What other great monster movie was Valerie Hobson in?"

"She played Wilfred Glendon's wife in *The Werewolf of London* in 1935."

"Right! You know your stuff," Scheherazade said on admiration.

"And she played the grown-up Estella in David Lean's version of *Great Expectations.*"

"Stop, I believe you!" Scheherazade laughed.

"Of course I don't spend my time these days watching old films, plenty of time for that later."

"Later?"

"When I'm old of course."

"Oh, I see. Well, since I'm old already, not elderly of course but old, I find movies comforting. They give me a sense of stability and permanence in a time when that was why people went to see movies, to find a little glamour or to get a respite from the world around them."

"Isn't that still true?" Deco asked.

"No, I think people go to movies now to be stimulated or alternatively to have the world reflected back at them. I only want peace and maybe, oh, a refuge."

"Are you hiding from something?"

"Aren't we all?

Deco shivered for an instant. "It's cold in here, too much air-conditioning."

She paused before continuing, "I don't like to think about growing older. I'm an entertainer you see. I do drag shows for a living. I've made a career out of shocking people by degrees in a pretty tame venue. They walk out thinking that they have taken a little walk on the wild side. Actually my life is pretty boring. Making being gay respectable is killing the industry. Now you can see us on cable-TV whereas you used to have to go slumming. It takes away all the adventure. It's like religion that way: take away the candles and the incense and what have you got?"

"You're Catholic?"

"Yes. I mean I was."

"Yeah, me too."

"I miss it sometimes."

"How are you with your family?"

Deco took a long drink from her daiquiri before replying airily, "I haven't seen them in years."

"Really?"

"Nope. They disowned me; didn't want a faggot for a son."

Scheherazade paused before replying, "I think that's terrible!"

Deco shrugged, "Yeah but what are you gonna do? I made my choices and paid the price."

Again Scheherazade paused before asking, "Have you been happy?"

Deco smiled, "They pay me and I don't have to do tricks for it. What more can a tranny ask?"

"Are you a tranny?"

"Well as good as one but I still get read once in awhile. I might as well just be a woman the only difference is that when I'm on stage I dress better."

"What brings you to Washington?" Scheherazade asked.

"I just thought I'd check it out. I'm touring drag shows down south here looking for new ideas. You?"

"I came to protest," said Scheherazade proudly.

"What are you rebelling against?"

Scheherazade did a Brando impersonation and asked, "What have you got?"

Deco laughed. "I mean really."

"Well I wanted to read in libraries, as a drag queen. I like books; I read all the time."

"Reading to kids? I've heard of that … a tough gig."

"Reading to anybody is. I wanted to do as me though just to

let them know we are here."

Deco tossed her head. "I think they know. We're the boogey man."

"Doesn't it get tiring though pretending we will just go away somewhere?"

"You mean over the rainbow? We serve an essential purpose, didn't you know that?"

"What purpose?"

"We serve to remind men of the awful fate awaiting them if they allow themselves to feel anything that women pretend they want them to feel. Women pretend that they want their men to be sensitive and vulnerable while denying that they are attracted to precisely the fact that men are not."

"Can you speak for women?" Scheherazade inquired.

Deco paused before replying, "Probably not, but I can observe. For instance, take that chick over there."

"Where?"

"The one in the black dress like she's just come from church, over there, the real pretty one, the one that just came in like she's never been in a gay bar before."

"Oh, her."

"Yeah. I wish we could talk to her."

"Why?"

"Dummy, don't you know she's one of us."

Scheherazade looked again and said with bated breath, "No she isn't."

"Yes. Fishy as hell but she's one of us," Deco assured her.

"How do you know?"

"Baby, I've seen them all. Besides, I watch her show on the Internet. She does her own reality spot. What's she doing here?"

Sherry Dallas had wandered around Washington all day after leaving her hotel room. She had chosen her clothes carefully with an image of a first lady in mind. Her red hair had been given a body-wave before she left home and now it cascaded down her back and curled over her pale shoulders. Her aim was to achieve a soft but imperious glow, respectable as befitted her mission as a conservative woman, or at least one commissioned by a conservative organization, but still suggestive that the first prerequisite of all family values is that a family should exist. Her aim was to convey simmering fertility but as demurely as possible.

Sherry's former life as a male now seemed as distant as another lifetime and it was only with great effort that she was able to conceive ... wrong word, imagine that she was without a uterus and hence unable to bear children. Behind her vagina was only the usual viscera shared by both the male and female sexes. Her beckoning labia led only to a cul-de-sac rather than a womb. She had not thought to freeze any sperm prior to her surgery so in her the long line of genetic succession had reached its terminus. Generations had made sacrifices, suffered, migrated, and perished merely to create this perfect image in a glass crafted of flesh and silicone into the simulacrum of perfect femininity. Was perfection always a matter of construction wedded to imagination while the real world is always patterned and plotted on a dark grid of imprecision and disappointment?

Sherry tried not to think of these things. She kept always before her the image of unfilled decades of sunlight and display when she could awaken male desire without price or consequence. Essentially she saw the sex act as a male convenience. They went away swiftly after satisfaction at precisely the moment when the body of a woman curls about the spring of life within her. There were good men of course, willing to exchange variety for security of supply and of these there were some of heroic honesty and devotion but they were swimming against the tide of nature that merely mandated fecundity. Besides, as a partial product of artifice Sherry considered herself to be as much a product of her surgeons as of nature—Sherry was an idea come into form. It is not easy to exist as an image.

But recurring to her mission to carry to Washington the ideals and transcendent principles of conservative Christianity as discussed at the caviar, wine, and cheese discussion groups she tried to recall now what she had heard there. She thought of the threat posed by Democratic socialism if embraced by the masses, of the emphasis placed on keeping America safe from the marauding tide of brown-skinned and hybrid refugees from Latin America, and she thought of how essential it was to banish the LGBT acronym forever and to restore the people it designated to invisibility.

She thought of what a shame it had been that Pope Benedict the XVI has resigned and left the church to be run by the reckless man who had succeeded him as Pope, a man who evidently refused to rule with stern declarations in all that really mattered while wasting his time in a neo-pagan dedication to preserving this passing world. Of what significance is a planet that will soon be supplanted by a great wedding feast held in celestial realms far beyond this mundane sphere? Were we not in the end times? Any concentration upon or obsession with matters that distracted one from efficacious ritual were a mere waste of time when the real work is always a matter of prevailing grace. The poor would always be with us and liberation theology had been rightly unmasked in the end as nothing but creeping socialism by another name. Now was the time to gird our loins and level the mountains and fill the valleys for the eruption of glory. So great was this new advent that its prosperity was already evident. Jerusalem had been restored as the capital city of Israel. The Persians had been reminded that America still had the power to order the affairs of the pseudo-nations of the Middle East as Britain's successor to empire. Wealth was power and could be wielded as a mighty sword to advance the will of the true deity, a jealous deity who could only hold in distain the presumption of a bunch of ignorant Indians who worshipped the rhythms of the rainforest when it should be cleared and transformed into good grazing land for cattle to fill the woks of the hungry Chinese.

She tried to remember all that she had heard and must now convey to the liberal secularists who were massing on Washington this year demanding change and equality. For Sherry this was the long-awaited chance to finally feel good about herself as a woman by breaking once and for all from her past. It humiliated her to think that she might be included by some people under the LGBTQIA acronym. She would never know if she was really free of course until she could split forever from the very people that had made it to the top three of the issues to be condemned at the conference in the minds of many of the attendees there. Sherry decided therefore to go and observe the disgusting behaviors exhibited by the very people whose lives served to remind her daily of her own origins before her fortunate deliverance and readmission to the ranks of well, everybody else.

Sherry Dallas entered *The Monument* with fear and trepidation. It was unusual for her to enter any place where people were massed together without being a focal nexus of eyes and attention. The atmosphere would bristle and change as though an electrical current had run through it. In this case however she was disappointed. Gazes were polite but transient and she found herself looking for refuge under a sudden attack of what amounted to the gendered version of agoraphobia. It had been years since she had entered a gay bar where the value allotted to femininity was far below its par value in most exchanges where people gather. The only sustained attention she was receiving appeared to come from a pair of what looked like straight women seated at a table in a private room looking down on the general activity below. They at least had made sustained eye contact with her. She was drawn in their direction by a common feminine bond. She walked through the open partition and over to the pair and introductions were immediately exchanged. Sherry sat down and within minutes a spirited conversation ensued.

Deco said, "So let me get this into my head. You are here representing a conservative group that advocates the rejection and condemnation of people like me and like Scheherazade here. They use their money and privilege to tell others what to do and claim to speak for God while they condemn minimum wage laws and fight unions so that the rich can live better and there is supposed to be *nothing obscene in that.* Did I understand you correctly?"

Sherry looked down and said, "Well there's more to it than that. You see these people believe that it is the wealthy that represent the real talent pool that makes the world run and that as a result the rewards that flow to them are only just and in accord with natural law. Where would the jobs come from if they were not there as innovators to create and provide them? Competition is the essence of the natural order of things."

"Then where does charity come in?" asked Scheherazade.

"Well many of these people make charitable contributions of a substantial order," Sherry replied.

"And they're still no doubt filthy rich even after you spoon off the gravy," Deco commented with a scornful toss of her head.

"The people that I represent believe that charity must be an individual choice but the right of private property is more important still. Sharing is an act of virtue; it cannot be compelled."

"Sounds more like Nietzsche or Ayn Rand than Jesus," Deco commented.

"Who is … what you said?"Sherry asked.

"Oh he was just the philosopher who said that power is everything, and she was the guru of selfishness … right Scheherazade? My friend here reads lots of books. She even identifies as a practicing bibliophile! I thought it was something kinky when she first told me what she was until she explained what a bibliophile was: a person who likes books. This was before you joined us here. I thought it was people who like to have sex in obscure corners of libraries."

Sherry looked embarrassed but decided the best answer to Deco was to ignore her and just continue with her explanation of her mission. "So I came to Washington D.C. as a sort of combination observer and advocate. It's really quite an honor."

"What do you normally do?" Scheherazade asked.

"I'm a sort of Internet model. Maybe you've seen my show,

Crème Sherry. I travel around with a camera crew and go to exciting places and lie on beaches and do my make-up and talk to people like they are my best friends. I have quite a following. Oh, and I endorse things by saying that I like them."

Deco stared at her wide-eyed, "And they pay you money, just for liking stuff? They should come to me; I like loads of stuff that I can't afford to buy."

Sherry looked at her with great earnestness, "Yes they do; but mostly they do it because, well, I'm pretty and I have lots of clothes. I get my clothes for free by liking them."

Deco pouted "Honey I like all kinds of stuff but nobody gives me anything. There are lots of pretty girls out there so how do you rate such special treatment?"

"It just grew; I can't explain it. I suppose I'm somewhere in the top twenty of reality stars."

Deco said, "It used to require you to sing or dance or act to be a star. Scheherazade and I were just talking about old movies before you sat down. You must do something more than just like things."

"Well I do I … well I sort of react to things. I look worried or sad or delighted and things happen to me and I meet handsome guys and I say no a lot and people like that because I look like I ought to get lots of, you know, action but I let people know that I have other plans then just spreading them."

"Like what plans?" Deco asked.

"Like another season of traveling around, and saying no, and liking things."

Deco shook her head and said, "Well like my mama used to say: if that don't beat all!"

Sherry suggested, "You could try it. You're very good looking."

Deco said, "No forty year old drag queen gets paid for just liking things."

"Then how do you survive?"

"I challenge people and trade insults and make people laugh

at the Frisky Frisco."

"The Crispy Crisco?"

"No, sweet thing, the Frisky Frisco as in San Francisco; it's a drag bar."

"So you're already in entertainment. I do the same thing only at another level and with the help of the world wide web." Sherry turned to her other companions and asked, "And what about you, Scheherazade? What do you do for a living?""

Scheherazade looked down and blushed beneath her layers of foundation. "I work as a checker in a grocery store."

"Well that feeds people at least. I think you should be proud of your work. If you want to know, the real reason that I'm here is that I wanted a change from feeling like a phony everyday in my life. The people who sent me here liked me, me instead of things! They trusted me to carry the torch and keep the demonic Democrats (that's what they called them) from ruining America by destroying the work ethic and just giving people things. Without pain and fear people have no motivation. They would want more than they could ever afford to buy and they might turn to violence to get it like those French people with the guillotine."

"As opposed to affording things that no one could ever want or realistically use or consume because they are billionaires," Scheherazade mumbled quietly.

Deco heard her though and started to laugh, "You say it Mama!"

Sherry disagreed, "I don't think you understand. It's a matter of principle. People need it that some people do better than they do. People like stars because it gives them something to look up to."

"Oh please! I'm a diva if anybody is but I don't think people envy me and I've always been suspicious of principals since one tried to do me when I was twelve when I got sent in for skipping school. Honey I know all about power and I have learned over time how to survive people trying to use it on me."

Sherry answered, "It wasn't always easy for me either. For

instance ... I wasn't always the woman you see here today."

Deco laughed, "And we don't know that? Who you think you're talking to girl?"

"Well, I can't always clock people so I couldn't be sure you knew. I just assume that they are as they present themselves," Sherry replied. "I give them the same respect that they show me. Is it so awful to want to be just normal?"

Deco shook her head, "But you aren't like everybody else and even if you were don't you know that everybody is pushing everybody else around just for breathing space. I feel it and I don't ask for much, just a stage and some good lighting and a chance to be myself in a space that I can control. As for love I don't know who finds it but it sure ain't found me. I'm smarter than I sound you know, but my drag mom was black and I'm Latina and she told me how it was and saved me a lot of heartache as result. I'm not into protesting because it only makes you a target. I don't need the Supreme Court to grant me any rights because I know that nobody will enforce them anyway. It's enough that I know what to do and who to avoid while I'm doing it and that gets me by. Sherry, if you want to represent people who don't really know you well go ahead and do it but you are only betraying yourself and your sisters if you do. Scheherazade would have made a great mama but she has daughters out there if she looks for them. We're all children really feeling around in the dark."

Scheherazade had grown strangely quiet and in a pause in the conversation of the other two said, "It's hard for me to hear you two comparing your lives. I have missed out on almost everything and when I tried to tap into what I had missed and tell my stories at a library they cancelled the program. That's why I'm here. I want to tell what it is like to be a storyteller who has lived her whole life in silence."

The other two stopped talking but at last Deco said sympathetically, "You could tell us; I think we of all people would be most likely to understand."

"Thank you. I have been looking for you both for a very long time," Scheherazade said with tears in her voice. She smiled before looking at them both appealingly and saying, "I feel like a dinosaur. It isn't just that I recall a world that will soon be forgotten, one that demanded greater proximity and human touch; it is that behind that world there were three thousand years of civilization based on the written word. The sheer multiplicity of digital memory bits now overwhelms us. Worse, it confuses information with inspiration so that words become as identical as grains of wheat in a storage silo at home where I live. We have gone beyond abstraction; we now model ourselves out of images as recorded on silicon chips. We are not in an age of storytelling now but of images; the word has never been more neglected and stories are made of words laid out in succession. Words are grounded in sense experience which lends them concrete references. Where is truth if it has no locus and set-point? Against the noise and the mere chaos of graphic appeals to vision only in silence are words still able to form at the deepest level of our being. It is there that storytellers take residence now in their solitude."

The other two sat still trying to take all this in even as below them a ceaseless party atmosphere reigned and in the streets outside groups of opposed zealots shouted insults at each other over the policed barricades of the American capital city. There were even speculations about civil war or secession ever since Congress had been paralyzed for the past year. Calls from the White House had proceeded from accusations of treason to stern demands to the Justice Department for the immediate arrest of various members of the opposing forces for interfering with the power granted by the people solely to the President to make of the nation an entity that would forever wear his image as its final summation and realization. In the last year speeches had been given to the effect that the Constitution should now be suspended or better still abrogated since it had finally achieved its God-ordained purpose by bringing to power an administration that would rule America according to the dictates of the Bible and to smite those who opposed that rule. The definitive war over the fate of Israel was now tantalizingly close to the institution of the thousand years of millennial rule after which those who has opposed America would be cast into the lake of fire.

The Europeans had watched all of this in horror while it was reported that Vladimir Putin was considering rewarding various experts in computer hacking with dachas on the Black Sea to express the esteem of a grateful nation. The Americans had fallen on their own swords at last. The southern Russian border was secure. After mopping up the Kurds the Turks were eyeball to eyeball with the Persians and the Saudi regime, all in competition over Muslim supremacy and the whole world teetered on the edge of a new global war. The Republicans blamed the fake news media and the breakdown of traditional values due to secular libertine culture as promoted in the schools and therefore suggested that there be an end to public education and its replacement by charter schools. Public education was a failure anyway and some foolish liberals even proposed a student loan amnesty by assuming the loan burden under a new collective bankruptcy bill so that the students could escape debt slavery and get on with their lives.

The recent plunge in the stock market and general uncertainty had caused a flight of capital from America to various offshore tax havens and malls around the country were likely to dim out one by one as retail sales continued to decline. The country was in short reeling about like a drunken man. The old stories had failed, including the epics, and even the privileged literature of the Jewish people that had sustained western civilization for the past two thousand years seemed inadequate to deal with the general meltdown in world affairs. To expect too much from Scheherazade therefore was more than even her broad drag queen shoulders could bear, but she gallantly tried anyway. She went on speaking to her new friends.

"I think our problem is that the world is escaping us just when we thought that we understood it and could control it. We seemed to be making such progress that we could afford the luxury of triviality and excess. It is sort of like the Savings and Loan crisis if you can remember that. Everybody thought that the government would stand behind poor investments in commercial property so there was a wave of speculative building followed by a collapse that was passed on to the taxpayers by a subservient government. Similarly we all thought that we could burn up fossil fuels in a few hundred years that had taken millions of years to be produced out of decaying and compacted vegetation. Now the world is divided between those who think it is too late to come to our senses so we may as well enjoy whatever marginal advantage our nation may possess for the last hundred or so years before a great extinction of all life occurs on this planet and those who think there may still be a margin of hope if we act swiftly and comprehensively to amend our ways. It is also at precisely this hour that various apocalyptic narratives promise relief much as the government did in the Savings and Loan Crisis. God will come to our aid and simply wind the whole show up and restore in a twinkling what we have ruined of a paradise of evolution that took millions of years rather than six days to create."

She continued, "Like all stories this one has a beginning, middle, and an end. We live encased in this story though and our actions can affect its course. It is the greatest story of our time. Rather than concentrate on it there has been a cacophony of other stories to distract us. We are like children running after toys and candy when a piñata is broken at a children's party: the toys are our pet ideas and the candy is our preferred mode of gratification. Meanwhile the oceans are warming, the glaciers are melting, the forests are burning, the poorest are suffering, and the wealthy are celebrating the success of the present economic order. The world is running at full speed just to buy another twenty-four hours of survival and the dream of endless prosperity. It will be nature that suddenly fails us and we will look about at the ruin that we have wrought and wring our hands in sorrow but it will be too late."

Scheherazade paused and reached out for the right words, "If I told a story like this every day for one thousand and one nights it would take 2.74246 years. There are now 8.97 billion mobile phones on the planet and 7.71 billion people to use them. The word is out there in other words. We are in the story. It is occurring in real-time. The disk scans and it is not re-writable. What you see in the streets of Washington today is only the beginning of what is too come. Ideas are no longer a common possession of reason and consensual reality but of mere assertion and the power to command assent. You will see more of this. If prophecy is the ultimate end of storytelling while history is at the other end of the temporal continuum, then I exist in between them, merely recording events through perception and the ability to record what I see. I thought of writing about these things but does the world really need another blog and books are what we use to fill-in extra shelf space. So I thought I would come to Washington and read aloud what I will not be given a venue to read at home. There is still something appealing in the human voice, crying in the wilderness. The first storytellers were the bards and ballad singers. Maybe drag queens are what the shamans and oracles once were. We always somehow manage to draw a crowd, don't we, so maybe we may be of some use after all."

Scheherazade fell silent and so were the others.

Finally Deco said, "Whoa girl! You sure are one dangerous bitch once you put your storyteller hat on. Where do you get that stuff anyway?"

Scheherazade smiled and looked over to the third member of their little triptych. Sherry Dallas just sat silently, her political mission seeming now fragmentary and biased. She felt again that old gnawing uncertainty that could only be overcome by feeling around her the admiration and desire that her youthful beauty and image provoked. How could Scheherazade manage knowing as she must that for her generation transition was only a lonely journey into the oncoming waves of certain rejection, isolation, and the prejudice inflicted non-being that came with the surrender of one gender with no ability to establish a new identity on the other side. She had simply been forced to make-do with what she had in a time and place that demanded silence and obscurity from its gender-variant members. These left no stories behind them of their silent suffering. Where had their strength come from, these early gender pioneers rejected by family, condemned by their religion, deprived of partners of either sex, and even now seeking protection under the facile umbrella of the laws?

Even now were things much better for the people she could now view as sisters? Each year added to the number of dead transgender women, mostly sex workers, found beaten-up or killed only to be blamed for their own demise by those who imagined that they could always just have buckled down and accepted the fate of blind biology as the sovereign will of God. As she reflected on these things Sherry no longer wished to be part of America's shouting dialectic of accusations and counter-accusations. There must be something higher if she could only find it, a place where the multiple absolutist solutions applied to intractable human problems posed by other eras could be put on hold until the earth itself stabilized sufficiently to support and permit a return to the luxury of fixed ideas.

Until then all weapons and talk of warfare, economic or otherwise, was futile and force still an exercise in mutual annihilation. Sherry wondered if she could use her immense following to simply say, "I like the earth and all the diverse people in it!" It wouldn't get her many endorsements and the vast coalition of the conservative minded, who paradoxically seldom ever really conserve anything, would no doubt call her a tree-hugger or worse, but so what? After all she could afford to lose a few accounts. She wondered if she dared go further still to establish a nexus with her presumed community. Maybe some of her on-line followers would forgive her possessing a Y-chromosome shouting out from every cell in her body that the missing genetic information that another X-chromosome might have provided was inconsequential after all. She thought of the pain exacted of women over a lifetime in betrayal and in loss. It was only accident that nature had made the female sex the default pattern for human beings while in every other respect men were granted immunity. It had taken divine revelation though to clarify God's original intent to create man first, directly and without the aid of a woman. Even her late advent was a mere concession to the fact that the man needed a partner that both shared his nature while remaining in so many ways superfluous at the same time. The sole original act of woman was to crave knowledge and by that inopportune appetite to doom all of humanity to undergo its various ills. Was this the beginning and the typology of the shame that had never really left her since she had been discovered at age four wearing her mother's lipstick and earrings and gazing at once in rapture and dismay at the little boy looking back at her from the mirror? Haunted by an image of what he did not possess, for to all appearances at the time he was only another of the scruffy little things that later blossom into manhood, Sherry first entertained the hope of being a beauty like the ones she admired and wished to emulate.

If transition had been difficult, would remaining as she was ever have been a real possibility for her? Sherry felt in the innermost recesses of her being how fortunate her own gender transformative journey had been as she looked over at Scheherazade and she determined then and there to stand by her new friend's side when she gave her readings and told her tales about the fractured loyalties and severed consciousness of America. Immune from condemnation in her presentation of femininity Sherry would traverse again the long journey that had ended with a video camera as the ultimate wall between her and the rest of the human race.

Meanwhile, Deco had regrouped and ordered a new round of drinks for them all and a big plate of nachos that they could all share. She didn't know what her place was in the big scheme of things. It had been enough for her to keep one-step ahead of the smart young things ready to take her place on stage. She had watched the years unfold like a desk-calendar in the wind. The days had rushed by and then the years just as fast. The place where she used to go bi-weekly to skim off the best bargain shoes was out of business. The friends she had known who spent weekly evenings hand-beading gowns were mostly dead. She was afraid that when she went home that both the bar and the venue would have changed to accommodate a younger clientele. There was even talk of changing the name of the Frisky Frisco. Drag was irrelevant in a world where sexualities were melding into one glowing amorphous mass. She could sympathize with anyone who was watching what they had known and relied upon disappear.

Advancing age, the course that every performer fears most, was winding about her ankles like a snake. Suddenly she jumped up and asked to be excused and a few minutes later Scheherazade and Sherry saw her dancing on the floor below them with one of that endless supply of vain young men who had once in years gone by, shortly after the Stonewall riot in 1969, traded ten years of ecstasy for a lifetime of fidelity and restraint. Sherry and Scheherazade, the young and the old, saw the sweat glistening on the sleeveless and well-defined musculature that clasped Deco and explored her abundant but dancing-toned derrière even as they whirled about the floor to the pulsing music and flashing lights, both of them the nexus of eyes. It was the same sorry pageant of bodies relating while souls remained remote, each drawing from the other further evidence that the illusion of perpetual youth and unlimited desire could somehow be fulfilled.

Neither Scheherazade, prophet of the old order, nor Sherry, the carefully constructed image-queen that surfed just ahead of the waves of change in the new digital world, had lived what Deco represented. She was the very symbol of the defiance of the age that had produced her: late enough to have escaped the plague of AIDS, but too early to have her youth coincide with what was at least a grudging and provisional acceptance of her kind. Deco only knew what she had always known and could only be what she had always been. If the world fell in about her she would still be part of that radiant but temporary reflection of what has already occurred, recorded in a beam of light that speeds outward from the earth to lose itself finally in the expanding darkness of space-time as the great constellations flee ever further away from each other, further and further, until even the light from the brightest of the remaining stars can no longer bridge the immense gaps existing between them and the universe, at least in the realm of communication, embraces a common darkness to accompany the already existing silence of the spheres.

Ligela

In the culture of Mexico, November begins with what at first must seem a most inauspicious feast, the Day of the Dead. Rather than an orgy of darkness however it is a time of embroidery of skulls and a sharing of the color and festiveness of life. I think that the Latin people, the very ones that to so many stolid Americans represent the ultimate threat to our materialistic way of life and an unwelcome reminder that most of the area of western America was stolen from Mexico as the fruit of greed and conquest, are merely reclaiming the common legacy of earth through their migrations. They remind me that the drama of egotism manifests all that is darkest in the human soul and that the human race is a collective project towards a better life for all. I had not thought to resume again my own efforts to define myself, by adding a chapter to that most unprofitable of human endeavors, the writing of memoirs, but, as happens so often a chance event occurring in the present may lead to the stirring again of thoughts long since forgotten and open again the catacombs of regret.

I was looking in that mausoleum of mostly unread books in my library for a biography of Mary Shelley, the second wife of Percy Bysshe Shelley, the great poet of the Romantic Period in England, and herself the authoress at seventeen years of age of *Frankenstein.* I was looking for a reading selection sufficiently autumnal to mirror my mood. Mary Shelley's life was an endless pursuit of the early love denied her in childhood after the death of her mother, Mary Wollstonecraft Godwin, an early feminist rebel. I sat down with it and before long my attention had drifted away from current issues. I saw again in my mind's ever duller eye an image of the young Mary sitting in a graveyard by her mother's tomb seeking to extract some manner of warmth from the cold monument of stone at her side. Years later Mary, after meeting the reform-minded poet and running away with him to the continent, she thought that she had found in his idealism and poetic gifts the source of the undying love she craved only to be bereft again by his untimely death. Percy Shelley drowned in the silver-blue waters off the coast of Italy and was cremated by his friends after his body had been retrieved from the clutches of the sea. When the ashes were later stirred it was found that only his heart had resisted the flames. It is not impossible that my own heart will share that unique endurance.

As I say these stray thoughts set in motion a train of reflections that after many twists and perambulations led to one who is only a memory for me now. I came to reflections on her by degrees. My first thought was of the vanity of hoping for literary immortality. I remembered how I had come as if by accident upon one of Herman Hesse's novels while away at college in New England. It was an old edition from that period when paperback additions of Hesse were pushing him as an early version of the '60's flower-child movement, just another of those throwbacks to prior ages of romantic yearning for justice and equality that seem always to elude the masses to the delight of their rulers. I found Hesse fascinating and went on to read his novels dealing with various simple wanderers in search of wisdom and of peace. His German sensibility made a lasting impression upon me.

Rather than having the good sense to return to my studies towards a degree in finance or management and starting that long, laborious, but finally fruitful climb to material success I allowed myself to study the social sciences instead in pursuit of a newer and better world. It seems strange to me now that I had such little respect for history as to assume that human moral progress is ever really possible, but at that time of life my days stretched out before me endlessly and I thought that surely I would have time for anything that my vain heart desired. I would discover the magic key that would make redemption superfluous because enlightened humanity would provide all that could ever be imagined or esteemed.

From these reflections upon youth's fatuous confidence my mind turned to my present position, one still no less rebellious but now consumed by doubts that even what I had professionally achieved was now in danger of being overtaken by a world-wide turning to right-wing solutions and simplistic rhetoric. I asked myself, how these trends could be resisted? If I had been helpless in the full-flower of youth to resist the tyrants of the age what greater effect could I hope to have against such well-financed mental mediocrity as that which was daily displayed in America? Perhaps I had always been destined to write in the elegiac key rather than to sketch out the path to effective resistance by a mere economic redistribution. Is happiness and justice so easily obtained by mere material ends? I thought of Mary Shelley reclining on the greensward by her mother's grave while the leaves blew about her and suddenly found again within me a desire to write of Ligeia. I therefore took my pen in hand and began thus to reflect upon my life as though it were a miniature cameo that when opened revealed her dark visage, the face that haunts me still.

It is November again, the month that Catholic tradition sets aside for remembrance of the dead. If October is one festive display of color and of harvest as life fades away, November is the month when trees as the poet says weep their burden to the ground. Death becomes less picturesque as the likelihood of its personal and immanent claim upon one grows. One might think that I look forward to my own demise as a gateway to reunion with the one who, I hesitate to admit it, I once called beloved. In that supposition however there resides a dreadful error for the fact is I would not bring her back even if I could, or worse still share a final resting place at her side, our sodden ashes mingling in a dull repetition of long extinguished desire. No, it is far better that she rest in that graveyard that she once cherished as she deposited night-violets upon the memorials of the unremembered and the lost.

She always found death comforting as though in its insensibility she found solace for her incessant and unrelieved pain in life. Maybe it was because the dead could not reject the violent and insistent nature of her love; I cannot say. I only know that she loved graveyards and I, because I loved her, finally equated them with her presence so that even now in my travels I cannot pass one without remembering her ivory hands resting languidly upon the moss and stone. I will call her Ligeia, though she went by another name when I knew her many long years ago, years that seem like yesterday as my ability to lay down new memories diminishes.

I take the name Ligeia of course from a story that she loved by the esteemed author Edgar Allen Poe. Our periods of youth did not coincide but that was a mere accident of birth and had no effect upon the communion of spirits that can at times unite disparate souls. I think I must have anticipated her advent in those far off collegiate days in New England when I would read the novels of Herman Hesse or the poetry of Shelley while the leaves of the yellow elms and maples fell down about me from the trees that like burning tapers surrounded the old apple orchards near the college. Ligeia was one with the melancholy figures that haunt the gothic imagination in her willingness to bear and to inflict pain. She required some morose Byronic figure to languish over or to despise in order to complete some long and elaborate tale whose origin fades in the mists of some long forgotten sin in her ancestral line. It is still a mystery why she gravitated towards me. Something in me made for good casting in the role of a minion or witness of her self-immolation. Like the case in most set scripts there are any number of actors who could conceivably have taken on the role; the fact that I was chosen had more to do with my willingness to keep returning for casting calls and rehearsals than any innate ability I may have had to play the role of a tragic hero in her play.

As the years passed we took our show upon the road through the sordidness of the provinces using the few props that were at hand and the shallow stagecraft that was all that either of us could then afford. I doubt that either of us was up to the pretention of our roles. Yet perhaps I do myself an injustice here: by some magic trick of the imagination I had learned in childhood to traverse time so that my relation to certain authors was so intimate that I could consider myself to be one of their select company. It seems so foolish now but as a measure of my loneliness and as an anodyne to an empty world this illusion served its purpose. The result of course was that I could hardly be said to exist apart from the authors whose stilled voices were still preserved in these immortal texts. My reading of biographies since has convinced me that this dialog with the lost shades of vanished minds was less particular to me than I might have imagined. Perhaps literature is nothing more than a long conversation continued across time by people who have never met each other. No statesman or financier can compete with the poets, the novelists, and the dramatists because their creations are as alive now as when they were first penned. It is only the audience that ages, changes, and sometimes forgets. Perhaps Ligeia had that same gift of seeing her life course portrayed in the very course of its daily evolution to a wider audience than her own solitary self.

The mind of the artist after all is not confined to a single medium. Ligeia had the genius of seeing things in juxtaposition. She made of life a collage of varied inner moods and associations. Her métier was confined to an audience of one while I, like some phantom observer from the wings of her dress rehearsal for life, was able to witness what I could never hope to share completely. So it was that our solitudes intermeshed so that on occasion we reached each other across the vast spaces that divided us only to be lost again in the various fogs of mutual incomprehension and misunderstanding. There were long breaks when I lost all contact with her. It is these gaps that preserve sensitive souls intact when any real intimacy threatens to break through the enveloping mists of solitude and alienation.

After her death I set forth on my journeying hoping to lose in space what I had already forfeited in time. I wouldn't be speaking of her now if it was not that I have returned to Austria in the course of my travels to walk again the streets and lanes of the old city where I did my graduate work. I go to mass daily at the old pilgrimage church on the hill with its steps worn by the knees of penitents seeking to undo the follies of youth and to escape the countless separate vanities that age reveals. I am now of that number that returns to God late in life because little else remains for me. The portals of eternity are widening by the hour. My dreams now inhabit a perpetual autumn.

I have taken a small flat in the city near the flower market and I walk by the lake daily to feed the swans. There is one bench here where I hold court before occasional passers-by who wonder at my American accent and are kind enough to engage me in conversation. I suppose that I appear genial to them, well-balanced, and even gregarious, whereas if they knew me better they would see that I am still haunted by innumerable regrets. The rhythm of my days is as predictable as a metronome. I have rolls and coffee for breakfast, noodle soup or dumpling broth for lunch, and for dinner the little spiced sausages that reflect a Balkan influence in the local cuisine. I have a modest two beers each day and a glass of slivovitz after dinner to warm me as I walk home. I still enjoy cider with cloves and cinnamon and the bread smeared with bacon grease that I am too weak to abjure as injurious to my health. I have stopped running for a time from my memories. I feel that I am leasing a posthumous existence in any case. My life is united only by the endless flow of words, mine or another's. Yet I wonder what motivates me to even pen these words unless it is that I hardly know my own thoughts until I record them. It is a hazard of the writer's trade. Yes, I am becoming at long last a writer.

I may even become somewhat well-known in my time and become honored with a leather-bound set of my collected works and awarded one of those slightly absurd honorary doctorates in exchange for boring students, professors, and other interested parties at a dinner in my honor with a few scattered reflections on the decline of the humanities and of culture in general in our digitally enhanced age. Those doctoral robes make good blankets in chilly the chilly rooms of a Gasthaus or a pensione.

I don't mean to sound ungrateful but I am not so foolish as to imagine that academia is really a serious pursuit devoid of vanity and ordered to the advancement of learning. I know the predictable stages of a career in literature from present honors to final irrelevance. The playwrights have it best, it seems to me; they at least can observe their audiences reacting to their words. The rest of us exist behind a veil of silence except at those tiresome readings and book signings for the few fans that imagine that they really know an author from his works. Writers have been replaced in the popular imagination. Such celebrity as we possess can hardly match the glamour of actors or politicians. I think most people go away thinking, "Maybe if the poor fellow could learn to juggle balls or tell jokes…" We are a dying breed in a superseded medium appealing to a diminishing audience with a shortened attention span. I'm not even sure the human brain even works as it once did. But then I am drifting aren't I … from my main topic I mean. What did I call her just now? Oh yes, I called her Ligeia, a fascinating name.

Poe was quite mad of course, nerves raw and wracked by ceaseless drinking. The Europeans understood him while the Americans never really did: America never quite lives up to its creative spirits, not even towards Dreiser or Howells let alone Hawthorne, Poe, or Henry James. American roots are simply too shallow to sustain great art from the whistle-stop platforms of the little prairie towns that sprung up all over the great plains once the Indians were pushed aside, Sinclair Lewis and Willa Cather notwithstanding. It takes long seasoning to produce the likes of a Thomas Mann. Therefore it makes sense for an American author to be an expatriate. You have to leave America to really understand it ... just as I had to leave Ligeia finally before I could accept what I was dealing with ... but I don't want to talk about Ligeia here, even fictionally, to put her in some crumbling mansion and have her always threatening to rise from her grave while I or some pale alter ego remembers her beauty and the way her black hair fell in Medusa-like ringlets about that waxen brow to hide her cat-like eyes. No, I would not think of her even in writing about her here. Perhaps she never really existed apart from those endless things that she drew about her, collected, annotated, and arranged. She existed in them and they existed in her. What she was in herself perhaps no one knew, least of all Ligeia. What price admission to the great museum of her unlived life? It was all such waste yet I once considered myself privileged to share it. Perhaps I was mad. Maybe I still am mad. That would surely explain my Melmoth-like wanderings over the face of the earth. I recall seeing a sign once that said that not all who wander are lost. I suppose that this implies some sort of hidden tracery of purpose in travel or perhaps the stimulus of adventure; I know only that I must keep moving from place to place to keep regret at bay.

Let us speak for a time of other things. Ours is an age of decaying institutions or at least the old ways of doing things if real renewal is to be accomplished. Even the Roman Catholic Church appears at times to be at the end of its tether. I read this year about some sort of Amazonian Synod of the bishops of South America. They brought along some sort of statues of a maternal image, a naked pregnant woman in the last stages before birth. I recall smiling when I read of this, finding in the figurines some late stage recognition of the endless cycles of procreation and perhaps of reverence for the sex that must sustain life on this poor planet, withering under industrial ill-usage. The Pope even blessed the figures and was promptly accused of idolatry by the same conservative Catholic media that has made of Donald Trump some sort of lawless icon of their long deferred to-do list. A few days later I heard that some vandals had broken into the church where they were being displayed, had stolen them, and dumped them into the Tiber River. I was astonished to read that these men and their actions were acclaimed in the following days in conservative media as some sort of folk heroes like the book-burning Nazis and the Buddha-defacing Islamic vandals of some years ago. How easy it is to think that competing symbols can be destroyed by violence. The world's ideas and conceptions now lie in uneasy juxtaposition; shall we destroy them all in one great orgy to see who was always right after all?

As actual life is nudged aside all that remains to us are our representations. This is why I hesitate to write anything at all, to add to the great edifice of the neglected and forgotten. Who would care for Ligeia now though if I did not remember her? Where are the monasteries where in the long hour of the night the monks awaken to chant the Divine Office: matins, lauds, prime, tierce, sext, none, vespers, and compline just as I wake and think of her? Ligeia's long defiles of former devotees are now as dispersed as the worshipers in spirit and in truth. I was neither the first nor the last to love her, only the most faithful. So it is that I am in sympathy with those who deplore lost liturgical customs even as I deplore their narrowness of sympathy and conception. Surely our conceptions of God, unequal to our dogmatic convictions, are even less adequate to portray God as God really is. I feel words and concepts alike failing to bear the weight that is placed upon them. For me now everything is a great retrospection.

As I said I spend a great deal of my days, and nights as well now, in the old pilgrimage Church whose steps I first traversed at the age of twenty-five. The tapers burn as of old on the high altar above the cold stone floor and the graves in the snow outside bear only the mutest witness to the lost passions of yesterday and the poor flesh that housed then. Now all that remains are bones and wood, or perhaps the dead remnants of flowers still blooming when they were lovingly placed in the cold hands of the beloved, never to be removed.

I do not flatter myself that I shall be so honored in my death. Everyone I once knew is in a distant land or they have already preceded me to the grave. Why you may ask do I continue then with my posthumous existence? Surely the answer is not hard to deduce. After all I am hardly a mysterious character: I am the logical descendent of the character depicted in Dostoyevsky's *Notes from the Underground.* You have never read it? Dear me, that is a pity. You can hardly hope to understand me without a bit of research into my romantic forebears. Self-pity as an art form does not arise *sua sponte.* Perhaps you have read Goethe, *The Sorrows of Young Werther;* something perhaps by Georg Trakl, an Austrian nature poet? Now there's a man who understood how depression leads to despair. You can hardly be expected to comprehend my great loss without first tilling the soil of disappointed love now, can you?

Oh well we must proceed as if you as well have discovered the dark joys of lachrymose affection. Ligeia understood, ah too well, and it led her to reject everything that I held out to her with outstretched hands. We met only in the interstitial regions of her spiral into darkness. Perhaps there was something too wholesome in me. After all I do enjoy life at times and for her that was always anathema. Her specialty was to find happiness within her grasp and then to fling it to the ground like a lantern just to see the wick of the candle within expire. Perhaps it was vanity, who knows? Maybe she thought that love was an ever renewable spring. Maybe she thought everyone unworthy of her divine obsession with herself. In any case she left behind her the maimed corpses of vanished loves. I don't expect that she is a rarity; after all deadly nightshade grows almost anywhere they say.

But I sound bitter don't I? Surely I was responsible for my own actions in always returning to the same barren ground expecting roses and not thorns. My hands are still scarred as a result of encountering her rejections and ever renewed solicitations. You see she never gave up on me, or for that matter I also did not give up on her. There was always that tiny hope that I could walk across that narrow plank across the chasm to her perpetual esteem. Foolish, I admit it, but I can hardly correct my error now, can I? I mean the years have vanished, never to return. Life is unforgiving even if God is. The moving finger writes … you know the rest.

So what should we speak of now? Having seduced you with a tale of Ligeia you are now at my mercy. Shall we speak of things past, present, and to come? Perhaps we should maintain a reverential silence in memory of her. She would like that. She always wished for a bigger stage on which to manifest her epic decline. She deserved some sort of apotheosis or at least celebration for her efforts in that regard even from a poor poet like me who is derivative at best. There! I have demeaned myself in tribute to her memory. She would have enjoyed that. She was always best when she could turn away in scorn for imagined offenses. The last word was always hers to give, to leave one standing there dismayed and helpless while she walked away. She was a grand mistress of the strategic exit. One always thought that there would be a pause while the stage-lights gradually dimmed to darkness before the applause would burst forth … but there was never anyone there in the empty theater but me.

So we went on from year to vanishing year until through long acquaintance I had forgotten what human dignity even looked like. I expect it is a common enough story and thus my example may serve some purpose after all. But my purpose is neither to praise Ligeia nor to defend her: perhaps she was only a product of her times. She was born as a child of promise and expectation and denied fulfillment except in the crass terms of luxury and the search for a perfect love that forever eluded her. I met her during that era of her life when she was a student at one of the colleges for debutants, one of the last strongholds of American aristocracy where she was enrolled in one of the Ivy League bastions of privilege and power. I was pursuing an under-graduate degree at a matriculation date eight years beyond the usual age at Boston College after serving in one of America's wars pursued in the national interest in other people's lands. I came home by way of Austria where I was able to explore and to appreciate the scenes of so many battles waged along that central fault line that divided the Germanic and the Slavic nations. I imbibed deeply from the same streams of skepticism and pietism that led to the philosophy of Immanuel Kant and later to that destructive philosophy of Nietzsche and his philosophy with a hammer.

I had not yet decided upon a course of studies. I still had all of the resentment that remains the only lasting legacy of combat, resentment towards the fortunate ones who had sent us out to preserve their material interests. I hesitated to take up a business career for fear of sharing their mentality. I met Ligeia in Paris. She was there on an American version of the Grand Tour after graduating from her prep school. We met at a symposium after one of the more stimulating lectures on the decline of Vitalism in Philosophy since Bergson. She asked me if I had read Huysmans or the poet Dowson and was surprised to hear me answer in the affirmative. The conversation continued as we walked across the city through the falling leaves and to warm ourselves we adjourned to one of the quiet student retreats where we could continue our discussion in quiet but congenial surroundings.

She was less of a hermit then, less inclined to wander those dark corridors of speculation as to other's motives that latterly obsessed her. I thought she was wonderful. I thought that here at last was the remedy for all of the premature death that I had witnessed in Afghanistan. Surely it was so that American youth of which she was so representative might thrive and fulfill their dreams. I asked her at last what she hoped to achieve, where her interests might lie, and it was then that she gave me the first hint of her lugubrious imaginations—a totality of fulfillment wedded to pain. It made no sense to me at the time I remember. I had just come from a place where the difference between life and death was as strict and final as a stray bullet or an explosive device on a hillside trail. To court death seemed to me an unpardonable luxury but in justification just looking at her I would have pardoned her everything. She had spotted at once my fatal need to believe that perfect happiness is possible in this Vail of Tears, that all could be made right by simply enduring until the inevitable tidal change took place that would bring her to me once again. Having faced so many more difficult challenges I thought that determination and longevity could not fail to bring success at last. She used that flaw to keep me present to her until the end, long after everyone else had finally left her. I never understood until the end that cruelty and derision would have won her, that being rejected was the key to her heart. Nothing so repelled her as light and happiness. They blinded her in the same way that the absence of light blinds others.

None of this was fully visible at first. When we both returned from Europe I visited her periodically. I remember the exhilaration that I felt driving down to see her. As I walked across campus to her dorm I remember thinking that none of the girls that I passed on the way could hold a candle to her beauty and the intensity that radiated from her. How swiftly though the day would change! I could feel a sort of cloud made up of depression and inertia began to surround me before I even called up to her room. Sometimes the phone would ring unanswered and only on the third attempt would she finally answer it. Her explanations were always laconic and indifferent no matter how definite our plans had been. It was sufficient to her feeding habits that I had been put to the effort of driving down and by so doing paid my little stipend of tribute to her insatiable need for power and control. It pains me to think of that first year after our meeting in which there was already, if I had possessed the good sense to read the signs, the prophesy of all that was to follow over so many years of gradual submersion into her darkness so I will ask the indulgent reader to bear with me if I digress again for a moment to other things.

I have said that I have returned to Europe recently where I now reside due to the good fortune of an unexpected legacy. Only now can I act the role of a well-lettered exile filled with political conceptions: a D'Annunzio without country or portfolio. I can imagine and hold forth on the dreams of 1848 when through sheer energy, equality and liberty might be procured and sustained. Every age knows its era of similar idealism. But lately it appears that the most unworthy are being awarded public approbation and acclaim. I find that people are turning to plutocrats for their populism, reaching out with the hands of beggars for the crumbs that fall from the table. Where is the fervor in that? Where is the life force? You see I am still more of a vitalist than I am a Christian. To listen to the conservatives, those of the Catholic persuasion at least, our life is a constant struggle for inner conversion and resistance to sin, whereas to the vitalist what matters is to resist dissolution by living, even if one is doomed to defeat in the end. There! Now you can see why I hate and fear death so: because I cannot be sure that the universe or whatever is out there cares about our moral dispositions.

But what else have we? The motives of statecraft are so interlaced with venality and self-interest that virtue and vice wear the same face and all that really matters is results. I am impatient alike with good intentions and with fanatical adherence to an ideal. I know what hunger and pain look like and all I seek is a remedy. Yet, and I hesitate to confess this, I am not a stranger to a desire for comforts and unearned profit. I alternate between a hunger for impersonality and simplicity and a desire to plumb the same depths of sensation that Ligeia once made her home. She was one who could refuse herself nothing and hence she could not understand why everyone was not ready to lay themselves down and surrender everything to serve her.

Still, my impatience with dull moral strictures makes me hesitate to condemn her. After all, she had no real ability to extort such sacrifices that I and others made on her behalf. It was part of her genius to make such surrender seem inevitable and refusal unthinkable. The passing years had allowed me to witness the parade of suitors who used her and departed ... or was it she who exhausted their own patience and resources? As one always loyal to her versions of events I could never make up my mind where the truth lay. Instead I preferred to simply circle about her like some dim outer planet about its sun, satisfied with the frigid light that filters down to it rather than to embrace again the empty comfort of light from distant galaxies. It is not too much to say that I shared her illness through my own irresolution mistaking desolation and hope for fidelity. I took what was perhaps a pardonable pride in vowing that I at least would never abandon her.

So did the years drift by unnoticed until her fate settled down upon her, until I in a strange reversal rather like Mary Shelley who spent her life tending the flowers of her husband's posthumous reputation, wondered how I might properly enshrine the memory of Ligeia. But now the love that I had once entertained for her was encased in pain and an awareness of the countless instances of cruelty that should long since have brought me to my senses. How does one explain such a singular lack of judgment in this one particular instance? It was as if I had contracted one of those slow and chronic diseases that waste the victim without killing him. As the years passed I dated them by the entries of her infidelities and disappointments. Her promises of reform and reformation began to diminish immediately after issue like a currency with runaway inflation. Her demands for unconditional affirmation and availability were like one of those black holes in space that suck everything into itself, downward and downward until even time itself slows down and stops. She dwelled always in a sort of sub-basement of the soul.

I cannot say when I awoke at last and regained what was left of my senses, but I recall that it was as if I had been spellbound for years. I thought then of the poem by John Keats:

> *I saw pale kings and princes too,*
> *Pale warriors, death pale were they all;*
> *They cried - "La Belle Dame sans merci hath thee in thrall!"*
> *I saw their starved lips in the gloom,*

But that was after many autumns had fled with riotous leaves away from me. I have been no less a victim of other's narratives, just as the world is. We are born into stories whose beginnings preceded us and in which we are only links in an unending chain. The great religions exist as they do because of an *ex parte* meeting between various prophets and the deity. We were not present to raise our own questions at the critical hour. The rest of us must measure our lives by standards arrived at hundreds of years before our births. I often wonder if the world could simply begin again. What if we issued a general pardon for all prior offenses, melted down the medals and citations, re-distributed the lands and benefices, cancelled all the anointings and ordinations: could the blank slate be worse than the endless conflict we have now? What if like people in a lifeboat we were forced to do a simple inventory of sea biscuits and casks of water and had to calculate the number of days left before we were to die? What if we were forced to acknowledge the desperate straits of the 7.8 billion people on this planet that only differs from an insensate universe because of the life existing upon it? We have three thousand or so years of recorded history and before that only the assurance that our wandering forbears bequeathed to us a balanced and intact world. Can we do better now than simply to preserve it; surrender hope of eternity to the demands of the hour? What if we aren't going anywhere? What if this is it, no rescue at hand for our follies but what we alone can devise? Does God adjust the time of the final judgment to fit our contingent circumstances or was it already fixed before the oceans ever rolled? Is providential intervention adjustable or are the settings already clearly established and set at the moment of creation? If life is the material result of a genetic blueprint what will it be when we move from designing software to designing species and beyond? What will be the first silicon-based life-form? Even transcendence is being made immanent. Where is the prophet who can descend from Mount Sinai with a new set of instructions or commandments adequate for the age we live in?

Yes, I am a Catholic of the ancient Roman Rite. It is too late for me to un-think the habits of a lifetime. I haunt the cathedral here daily like a ghost and walk back to my sterile rooms afterwards to seek my repose in unquiet slumbers. It is then that in memory I walk at the side again of Ligeia or knock for admission to a presence that was always such a disappointment to my hopes. Time with her as I have said was always preceded by elation and followed by anguish and regret. I was like a bird following a trail of crumbs, scattered with sufficient abundance as to be adequate to ensure compliance but never sufficient to allay hunger and to finally allow the bird to sing. Year after year I remained faithful to a vision that was proven illusory before we ever left Paris.

She was already firmly set on the course that her life was to follow. My experience of life has taught me almost to accept the idea that our life course is set out for us before we are born. We struggle to free ourselves but ever and again the same coils enmesh us drawing ever tighter and tighter until we cannot breathe. We need a foretaste of heaven now and again to sustain us. It is vain to nourish faith on desired conviction alone; no doubt this is why the Catholic Church insists upon sacramental observance. We are after all beings of flesh as well as soul. Calvin and Luther thought that God was best found in words; only the Catholics understood the role of the body in salvation. I suppose that is why I remain Catholic. I am more of a believer now than ever before, because of my doubts I am more devoted, because of my disquiet with dogma I am more desirous of love, because it is so readily filtered by those whose province it is to guard access to the temple I seek admission to the sanctuary.

Yet I feel myself torn asunder every day. Where did all of the former certainties go? I used to feel as though culture could provide a refuge if religion failed, but culture itself is eroding around us. It is becoming impossible to locate a moral equivalent for Greenwich Mean Time. The result is that everything is in suspension from day to day as the various sources of biased and conflicting information wage their daily wars to capture the fleeting hours of leisure time that is left over after a day of work, to occupy ourselves with wider concerns rather than seeking refuge in some more mindless pursuit towards respite if not oblivion. Politics has infiltrated everywhere these days to the extent that no one can escape the clash of contending forces. To weed out the noise is becoming impossible unless one turns to the last remaining sources of silence: the churches and the graveyards. Fewer people each day care to visit either of these and be reminded that the time allotted to each generation is short. Already we are passing into history.

I am glad at least to no longer reside in America. It is still tainted for me by dreams of Ligeia. I hunger for even the cold comfort of that cemetery in England where Mary Shelley lies buried still dreaming of the smoldering and unextinguished heart of her beloved poet husband, but even that solace is denied me. Homeless now I wander over Europe in search of, I know not what.

Where is a life of sophistication and grace to be found? It is the part of the artists among us to make of life something more than just consumption and display. Even Ligeia shared that belief in her fashion and for years it was a bond between us. It only failed when all else was encased in the mistrust that made her wall herself off from any contact with her former acquaintances and lovers, even me. She read in them the betrayal that was the product of her own cruelties. She has kept me on to the last, year after year, as her chosen witness to monitor each stage toward her final decline and dissolution.

"Watch me," she seemed to be saying, as I throw it all away.

Can you bear it while drop by drop I bleed to death before your very eyes? Why don't you do something?"

So I remained. Fixed by her basilisk stare I did watch, knowing all along that by no force of will or act of abduction could I stop the process much less restore what either of us had been before we met. Even now when I should have begun to heal like a scorched forest as the tiny tendrils of new saplings rise towards the clear blue skies I wake in the night and think of her. She is the embodiment of disappointed hopes and desolation as the world pitches about from side to side and from course to course on its disparate headings. So it is that I have sought sanctuary here in one fragment of the long since dismantled Holy Roman Empire, or Austria-Hungary as it was known just before the Great War of 1914-1918 when it was finally defeated and dismembered.

I took a train journey one day into Vienna to visit the Hapsburg palaces there. Where had all of that pride and confidence led but to ruin and defeat? As I walked the gravel walks behind the Belvedere Palace I wondered whether the new Church of the people being brought to birth by Pope Francis would be able to amass the mythic grandeur that it took to embody faith. Could faith survive without the baroque grandeur of the old cathedrals with their gold-encrusted domes opening to visions of seraphs surrounding Christ or the Virgin Mary? Does it take great art and music as well as grace to save souls?

But can any human conception ever really capture divinity? Perhaps love is a quiet thing, something built up over vast stretches of time like the beleaguered Amazon rainforest with its great canopied roof filled with colorful birds. Was it an accident that a conclave chose a Pope from Latin America at the same time that this great Gothic Cathedral of nature's fashioning was being burned by purpose and design and as the rulers of the ever-hungry oil companies were bent over maps calculating profits once the last indigenous inhabitants could be brought off, pushed aside, or killed?

The forces of death are all about us now. A moral prism is emerging that will divide humanity into those who nurture life in this all too material world and those who in pursuit of some all-embracing idea forget our complete dependency upon the living systems and interconnections that sustain us. I am looking for my place in all of this, hoping to align myself on the side of life, menaced as it is by mere abstractions. As a first gesture towards a resumed life course I have sat at a table these past days looking out onto the courtyard where a gentle rain is falling through the denuded trees. I have dared to see my life as a whole searching for that first fatal turning.

I see in reading over what I have just written here with all of the spontaneity of one who travels again around a pillar of flame that our tale, Ligeia's and mine, was not a linear one. Ligeia seemed from the first to have been always with me as though a place had been reserved for her long before we met, and retained long after I had bid her a final farewell. Final, how strange that word sounds to one who wears her forever like a dagger in the heart. Was Ligeia a demon in human flesh? I must say that I have speculated along these lines from time to time. How else am I to account for her power exercised over me for so many years? Like all demons they delight in specificity, each selects its victim with infinite care. So it is that after I met her I imagined that she had always existed by my side as my portion and my cup whereas that phrase is always reserved for God alone. It is a mistake to dream of final completion from mere human love.

Yet even in saying this I know that if she rose again I might follow her pale wraithlike being as it wandered about by night, feeding upon what it could not share. Eventually she became a shadowed version of her former self as though she was being consumed by an inner fire that scorched her very soul. Redemption like happiness was for her always just out of reach.

The ashes of Ligeia have no mortal resting place. Neither mourned nor memorialized she died as she had lived surrounded by her aura of bitterness and recrimination towards a world that had finally proved itself unworthy of her. It should have realized that a goddess walked upon it and bestowed upon her due obeisance.

The story, if that is what it is, ends here and I doubt whether it requires further elaboration. To catch the essence of the thing is the key. Perhaps it is enough to sound the cautionary note and to move on. My Ligeia like Poe's is in the last analysis a vampire tale and like all such tales the hope is that the undead may be stilled at last to prevent their return. Only the haunted know the price that this exorcism entails. It must be embraced voluntarily if at all by the one who is to be delivered at last. It is said that when the victim of a vampire awakens to his state in life and assesses his own proximity to death he must use as an exorcism such words as these from Edgar Allen Poe. May they be the epitaph of all who walk in the way of Ligeia and of those as well who like me have become pilgrims towards an empty horizon. Until then I am merely filling the days and nights until perhaps I will see her once again…

The lady sleeps,
Oh may her sleep,
Which, is enduring,
So be deep!
Heaven have her,
In its sacred keep!
This chamber changed for one more holy,
This bed for one more melancholy.
I pray to God that she may ever lie,
Forever with unopened eye,
While the dim sheeted ghosts go by.

Apocalypse Yesterday: A Collage

The quest for reality and for truth statements about reality is an elusive one, so elusive in fact that the great philosopher Immanuel Kant finally surrendered and admitted that what things are in themselves is unknowable. What emerge instead are various assessments of the phenomena of existence and these in turn are further modified by the limitations of the language by which we communicate those assessments. Beyond even these we have the various arts that attempt to illumine reality by a mimetic translation of reality into various mediums that highlight and emphasize various latent aspects of the whole.

This would be difficult enough but in addition the would-be knower must deal with the phenomenon of change; things do not remain static but transmute into other things; as every physicist knows the arrow of time points only in one direction. The general law of entropy yields increasing overall disorder in a system. Yet despite all of this metaphysical humility history speaks confidently of progress attained through a fundamental and gradually acquired knowledge of the past. The historian is not a mere archivist; he assumes that patterns can be discerned in history and that eventually history can become a proscriptive science.

This was what George Santayana meant about learning from history. Of course what he forgot to explain is why we *never* have collectively learned from history. Perhaps this is because historical problems always emerge in new guises just as viruses mutate season by season. The temptation to exceptional exclusion from general laws is insistent and overwhelming. Historians like to think of themselves as scientists, although historical writing is more akin to the arts. If history is storytelling, then does the plot come after the events in question or is the form imposed upon the raw data of events even as they occur? The question is a significant one because it bears upon any judgment that the discipline of literary criticism imposes after the fact upon the amorphous mass of writings that claim to be literature.

The literary arts have never existed in such low general esteem. They appear to be so steeped in subjectivism that they appear to be inapplicable when plotted along a pragmatic continuum. If this applies to the novel it is even more likely to be the assessment of the short story. The short story is remarkable among literary forms for its brevity, its impact, and its ability to allow character to manifest itself under the stress of a dramatic situation. Judging by these criteria the present story, one that will dispense from the ordinary convention of characters, must be content to proclaim its universal applicability for what "apocalypse" can live up to its name if it is not universal. We expect a certain extravagance and grandeur from our apocalyptic candidates.

However, there has grown to be a marked tendency to see such candidates as shrouded in the misty confines of the future and for this reason the title of this submission to the reader's discerning judgment must consider that an apocalypse coyly situated in the past as in yesterday may be viewed with suspicion or at least with curiosity. Have events so far eroded the normal cause and effect relationships upon which tranquility rests that, unbeknownst and as it were stealthily, apocalypse crept in among us unremarked and did its mischief while our eyes and senses were distracted and engaged elsewhere? If things are out of order at precisely the moment when progress appears poised to shift into overdrive how did this situation come about and why was it not more attentively examined when its nefarious influence began? Perhaps our collective immune system has been sleeping. If so, and having concluded this much, our weary narrative voice, one still echoing with the sonorous periods of the prose of one of the founding fathers of American literature, Nathaniel Hawthorne, we will proceed not deterred by disillusion to do what art always does: to express the reflected shadows of reality as persuasively as possible.

The three unities being long since discarded, the storyteller, balanced along the edge of irony and deconstructed discourse, must assemble a narrative out of fragments. The borders between the arts are dissolving so that rather than assembling a chain of incidents into a moral narrative of cause and effect leading to a moment of revelation and insight beset with questions of setting, dramatic motivation, and point of view the author may look instead to music and the plasticity of art here for inspiration. At once many problems of narration vanish to be replaced by effects of assembly, rhythm, juxtaposition, and contrast. The narrator need no longer be identified or to explain how she knows what she inexplicably knows about the personages or inner mindsets of her characters. Artistry in any case consists in tonality and the ability to suggest, to tickle the outstretched antennae of perception not all of which are within the parameters of the conscious mind. With this inspiration and stimulated by a Freudian spirit of free association and accompanied by a silent drum roll the camera slides backwards to reveal what follows…

Out of a soft haze emerges the head of the last male of the northern sub-species of white rhinoceros hunted into extinction by poachers to feed an Asian market that covets its horns to stimulate fertility and sexual potency in the human male. Is it imagination or does the dead eye of this ancient creature manifest a sorrow and pain beyond its mere animal mentality? "How," it silently asks, "Did we come to this?

What fate has condemned me to perish with my seed still intact so that the entire species and the long history of my kind must die with me? Where is the Sophocles to tell my story?"

Across an ocean and by the sluggish flow of the great Amazon River comes an answer from trees rooted in soil long adapted to nurture the canopy where bright birds flash in the sun from limb to limb. The Amazon Rainforest is a sculpture, a system of perfect efficiency and exchange between sun and soil, wind and cloud, plant and animal. Presiding over it is a force that exceeding all lesser forces embodies origin and process that contains it all and yet stands separate from it. Such is the imagination of symbol-making humans that the indigenous tribes called it woman and made it visible. They called it Pachamama. It was as real to them as to industrial man are the names of the great oil companies, the corporate entities that in American law are defined as 'persons' with full rights under the law. There are no statuettes to symbolize these entities but they are held to be real none the less and they are worshiped and served by countless acolytes.

Across the ocean we pass again to where a Pope, a man drawn from the Pampas, has tried to awaken his ancient church to the challenge of the times. In the course of the recent Amazonian Synod and as a gesture of cultural respect he allowed into the sacred precincts of the church the bowed maternal head and figure of a Pachamama statuette that was later stolen and thrown into the Tiber River. This is the preferred tactic of those who are unable to distinguish degrees of symbolism and the artificiality of ritual when it attempts to grasp transcendent reality. Under the belief that the Pope was sponsoring and promoting idolatry conservative Catholics have demanded his public penance. It is characteristic of the formalist and essentialist mind that it cannot see behind prohibitions to distinguish the policy or purposes behind those prohibitions, therefore anything that comes within the gravitational pull of a concept is included within its presumed domain. The worst part of this type of reasoning is that it is non-relational and fragmented so that the deity is encapsulated and eclipsed by utterances that are viewed in themselves as absolutes. This leads inevitably to fundamentalism and eventually to attempts to justify religious terrorism.

Meanwhile back across the ocean the Brazilian President, anxious to clear away the rubble of the rainforest to stimulate cattle ranching and oil drilling sees these same indigenous people as obstacles to the growth of national prosperity. Forest fires are the chosen means to manage cheap brush clearing. The great businesses are served by this but of course this service is not ritualistic idolatry and no voices of opposition or demands for penance are raised to oppose it. To the conservative religious mentality ritual always trumps reality. A list of prelates and concerned conservative lay Catholics have demanded that the Pope must do public penance for the sin of idolatry over the Pachamama incident or suffer the pain of eternal damnation. Many members of the same group, of course, see no problem in promoting the Trump brand on every occasion, discerning no idolatry in the various Trump-rallies with their chanting and vulgarity.

But stop; these linear contrasts already have drawn us into the balanced dialectic of opposing forces that like a ticking clock advance us towards some great conflagration while as the title indicates the planet is already living out a disease process long since begun somewhere along the corridors of yesterday. Besides, what we pursue is not linear but rather emergent as when a system undergoes a phase change to a new order or as is the case where an energized atom steps down from one valance orbital to another emitting a photon of light.

We move the camera once again along a circular track and focus on the fact that the past, already frozen into unalterable lineaments, hangs about us like a shroud. The generations spring up constantly so that any dividing line that we choose to impose to define epochs must be deemed somewhat arbitrary. The sheer density of events appears to give a degree of absoluteness to the happenings that occur in real time. We at least expect the cast members to stick around for the conclusion of the play. We do not expect the stage hands to whirl away the setting while the dialog is still being exchanged and while the audience, remaining in their tiered seats, is still engaged with the action on the stage.

All very well but what if one play merges into another imperceptibly so that a question remains whether one is watching scene five of act four or on the other hand scene one of act one of an entirely new play. The surge of events allows no time for an intermission. Would pausing and taking advantage of such untimely timeliness not be ... well, somewhat apocalyptic? So that even before receiving an answer to the above question we rush onwards in our devising of new forms to contain old events and to constrain the ever evolving permissibility of innovation (and we are not even dealing yet with artificial intelligence but only with the creative mind run amuck). These new forms that beckon to the backs of the patrons of the literary circus as they make for the exit (disappointed that there are no trained elephants or bears to perform but only dusty grim old T.S. Eliot or an artist drawing his designs on the sidewalks soon to be effaced by the December rains). No concert hall is to be found here filled with well-dressed men and silken ladies gracefully taking their seats as the lights dim about them. No, there is only the dark undercurrent of the withdrawing tide past the old sea-weary barnacles and mussels that cling to a long abandoned boat-hull or pier.

We gaze about us. It is closing time at the pub and the patrons walk out one by one into the solitude of a night in Belltown or in Pioneer Square. The old signs of a bathhouse beckon to no takers, the denizens being long dead victims of one of the scourges of history. So we wander about Seattle with an old Modern Library copy of Joyce's *Ulysses* or maybe one of Kerouac's *Visions of Cody*. We pass an old plate glass window in a vacant building and see our reflection distorted back to us, perhaps on the edge of tears ... Okay Boomer, no time for self-indulgence, it is time to move along now; pack up your troubles. We were unable to update your app because of insufficient memory. For technical assistance please call the 800-number provided to India or the Philippines where our call center will be happy to serve you.

We walk up to Boren Street. There is the old brick building where a student rented a room once on the first floor (wonder what rents are like now)? Remember the old movies at the Harvard Exit and years later climbing the stairs on Pike to sit on the old couch or a straight-backed chair in a circle with boys who wished they were girls. Afterwards we could dance until after midnight at one of the gay bars on the hill or eat fancy food in one of the new gentrified eateries if some rich John picked us up and paid. Gone now or did it ever happen? No one recalls a past not worth recording. From here we can look back down Denny or Pike to where the downtown skyscrapers pierce the mists coming up off of Puget Sound. The fog has made Bainbridge Island invisible tonight. The ferries work the docks like an old streetwalker crying unremarked by the passers-by.

But we are falling into the old trap of locality that leads eventually into naturalism; better to stick this side of surrealism. Genre traps exist everywhere for the unwary. Suddenly words emerge out of the darkness and arrange themselves on paper to be fed on later by the ghouls of interpretation. Who can separate the sign from the signifier? Who can distill significance from an inconclusory epic? William Blake and all the mythmakers before and after him groping for universal applicability must finally yield to the ever onrushing flood of the circumstantial. We turn in vain to the old sources of interpretation; data multiplies beyond our ability to find categories for it. First there comes redundancy and then inapplicability. Finally a red-line is reached and the system collapses.

(Pause here to change the reel)

And again we begin: perhaps the poets have the answer after all, poets the ultimate custodians of language. Perhaps life's experience should be divided into cantos; Ezra Pound thought so. Or perhaps it is sufficient to leave a case-hardened image as Amy Lowell sought to do. The poet is unperplexed by questions of before and after; there is only the now of suspended apprehension. Is all of poetry one long lamentation? One need only read the poets of the Tang Dynasty to know the answer. The poet pleads for understanding and sympathy.

Life is like this (he cries): times were once better and now I am old and I don't seem to understand things as once I did. It is estrangement the finally engulfs us. I thought to return home only to find that it had dissolved away in my absence.

(Ah at last we have a narrator, you heard him. He said "I.")

Too late he has disappeared once again and we are plunged into the rush of images and oratory. A student once set herself the task of reading and understanding *Finnegans Wake*. No apostrophe in the title to indicate possessiveness because Finnegan is universal. Even the genders merge and waver and the family is merged into one amorous and amorphous whole. After nightfall all boundaries waver and dissolve. The elm and stone discourse together by the river filled with all the soil and refuse of Dublin. Images emerge out of memory and then vanish before the recording angel can note them down, all to be recapitulated on the Day of Judgment.

(We dare not make literary use here of the Koran and suffer the fate of condemnation exercised towards Salman Rushdie. Let us rather remain within our familiar zones of late stage religious freedom in America).

"We do not serve sinners here, so tell me have you done anything wrong lately? If your sins are different than my sins I reserve the right to refuse you service as a testimony to my own righteousness."

Korea... "Our patience is not unlimited. Our dear leader will not delay to bring retribution upon America beyond its worst fears if this warning is not heeded."

"The Democrats are planning a coup attempt in collaboration

with the deep state to deprive the people of their right to choose a President. We need a true authoritarian to get thing done. There is too much talk in a democracy. We are better armed than they are and the liberal Dems better remember that we'll fight to keep Trump in office. God has chosen our President, just listen to Rick Perry, if you don't believe me."

Whose were those voices interrupting our narrative?

(Flap flap flap … time to change the reel again? No just a break in the continuity as we sit in the private theater showing this day's rushes. No editing yet; that comes later when we choose between multiple takes. 'You were looking down again dear. Try and remember your character. Alright company let's try it again. Lights, camera, action!')

"No everything is fine so where were we? Oh yes we were discussing the treatment that was submitted to our Culver City Offices, or well somewhere in L.A., about an apocalypse that just went unnoticed until its effects began to show up … hmm interesting concept but film is about showing and all you've brought me is an idea. Besides, religion is a touchy subject right now; we don't want to alienate key sectors of our potential audience. Don't forget the Red States; they buy popcorn too. Maybe we could just suggest the idea by a creative musical score for the picture, borrow a little from Strauss or Stravinsky. Look what they did with the music in *2001: A Space Odyssey*. Nobody even knew what was happening in that film but it sure made money. Man that's entertainment. A rose is a rose is a, hell whatever that old lesbian in Paris said: you get my drift anyway. People don't need an explanation; they need experiences. Okay that's it. Look I'll talk to our people in production and see if it flies, alright? Hey, stay in touch."

Thoreau went to the woods to live deliberately within the ambit of a particular time and place and in the custody of his own conscience. Emerson, another great individualist, tried to imagine an oversoul that is distributed among all persons. Whitman believed in a natural adhesiveness that draws all people together in sympathy and finally evolves a unified democracy as the best form of government. Compare these great prophets of the American ethos to the pseudo-populism of dictators whether actual or aspirational who seek to draw an equation between their own particular personhood and the unified will of the people. This is a false symbolism and in the end this alone may bring forth the apocalypse.

"Fractional distillation allows us to separate a fluid into its separate viscosities. When applied to the newsfeed our task is to confirm our readers in the opinions they already hold. Please try and remember staff that America no longer has a univocal point of view grouped about a mean. We are a country without a centrist group to moderate between the extremes so we simply have to choose: who are we trying to reach?"

The death rate of young adults is rising in the United States due primarily to obesity, addiction, and suicide. This trend has an inverse ratio to years of education. This is what allows the schools to use tuition to leverage a generation into debt and so to control them throughout their years of rebellion and vigor making them a subservient mass. By the time you hit forty and are debt free it's a little late to take to the barricades.

It is projected that most people who reach their full retirement age will live for another twenty years and most of these will not continue to work. Thank God for the kids! When they finish paying off their own debts they can support us.

"Hey that was one great putt! You have the honors on this hole. It's a four-par dogleg left."

Russia claims to have a new guided nuclear deterrent that can elude our defensive missiles. Maybe he whispered something to Trump at the last summit. "Got you sucker!"

A collage is made of many different materials or pictures affixed to a backing instead of encased in a frame. The different textures add contrast and color to exemplify a theme or idea without explicitly stating it. What looks like chaos may have an underlying strange attractor present and paradoxically be more orderly than a deliberately ordered but mendacious creation. The art of framing involves selection; the subject is confined by the scope of the lens. It should always be kept in mind however that behind the camera another world exists that is not observed. This means that there is no real escape from the laws of perspective. The mere fact of selection introduces an artificial barrier.

"You know I could just listen to you all night honey. Where do you come up with all this crazy stuff?"

(Now who was that speaking?)

"Hey did you read about the Catholics and those Pachamama things? Well its getting a lot of air-play. They're these naked mother things out of the Amazon." "

"Is that so?"

"Sure is. So the real die- hard conservatives are really upset about these things; claim they are idols and the Pope is a big sinner because he allowed them in Rome. Yeah, they think the Pope isn't even Catholic. Besides they can't stand his lifestyle; he's too much like Jesus: cares about the poor, doesn't start every sentence with an accusation, you could see how that would piss them off."

"I've known lots of people like that for instance…"

"Hey don't break my train of thought. Anyway, here's my idea: we trademark these Pachamamas and sell them. Yeah, it could go viral! Auto supply houses could sell them; hang them from your rear-view mirror. Toy stores, novelty shops, you name it. Yeah, and hey if it gets more controversial great; we hit the religious freedom angle. Hey who's going to knock motherhood right; besides these things are topless, you know always a winning point. Yeah well I'm looking into it, first kid on the block, get the early sales in the big box stores. Okay so we'll spell it funny like Pa Cha Mama; don't settle for any imitators; we're the original. Right, okay, I'll make the pitch and see if it flies with the finance people but hey keep this under your hat okay? Great, see ya."

A latent infection is one where the alien organism has been introduced but has not yet manifested itself as overt illness; the body's defenses have managed to hold its onslaught to an equilibrium, a *modus Vivendi,* a presence without any harm instilled beyond that sense of apprehension elicited by any foreign agent when inserted into the calm and oceanic integrity of the organism. Similarly, what we have called a premature apocalypse or apocalypse yesterday describes a catastrophe that has become so normalized and habituated that its signs, even when they become overt, will be overlooked by the usual guardians of sanity and health in a society. In fact the first signs that something is very much amiss will appear disconnected to their ultimate cause. The swirling currents of cause and effect may hide a larger even if latent force that is everywhere operative among us.

Thus the magician, loath to be coy, might explain in no uncertain terms the inspiration that lies behind all sleight of hand for the success of illusion always depends on distraction. In multitudinous juxtaposition there is a great weariness. We depend upon the magic of art to synthesize our intuitions for us into one great insight. The tension that exists between the real and the imaginary is resolved by a sort of crystalline process into clarity and resolution.

We will even forgive the artist his little unresolved discrepancies for the artist is only human after all. We will allow him or her a few editorial comments drawn from the insistent wellspring of an everyday life. One need only think of the constant wear and concatenation of molecules bombarding the delicate circuits of the brain year after weary year. Who can blame the artist, musician, or writer for including something of these in the very public arena of his discourse? What power has the artist to command attention or regard let alone respect?

Out of the solitary workshop of the creative mind things multiply and distill themselves into one medium or another and then the creator stands back to judge or to forgive and this before even its exhibition or publication: already it is distant from the hand that crafted it. Even the artist knows not whence has come what stands before him just as God for all of his advance warnings of the deleterious fruit of knowing the difference between good and evil could preserve the innocence of the first couple in Eden. If the artist feels that somewhere a great and fundamental disharmony has set in he would be well-advised to keep his suspicions to himself.

The only people who enjoy apocalypses are those who are let into the secret in advance so that they know when to build an arc and hoist sail for Mount Ararat. But if the apocalypse is so latent that it has already occurred, why then everyone is in the same relative position to each other and no one will be spared. Crisis will follow crisis and each will appear to have been resolved in a timely fashion, while hidden in the darkness below the infestation will multiply and spread its toxic effluvia. Tiny fissures will appear in even the most sacred and unquestioned of our certainties until at last, its force, long gathered, breaks suddenly forth in storm and destruction. Dismay will yield to a forlorn isolation and a blackened sea vessel beset by hideous and multi-legged worms that will seek shelter again in the mass of mussels and anemones that clinging together retard all progress.

Even thus do metaphors multiply so that even a possible good ending is wasted and to no avail. An apocalypse does not always imply closure; it may just as well merely mean that things become so fragmented that integrity, whether structural or merely in the form of a literary discourse becomes impossible. This process was attempted to be contained through deontology and the method of the deliberative deconstruction of all texts. It was always assumed however that the text could be re-integrated and re-inspired so that the corpse would breathe again and rise up from our dissection table and go about its business as if nothing untoward had ever occurred. This is what lies behind our ultimate fear of insight: that we might inadvertently discover that our nature is inadequate to support the full extent of our knowledge let alone our suppositions and our dreams.

Story depends upon the preexistence of a set of uniform expectations in a discerning audience for the interchange of meaning to occur. If this uniformity is lacking the exchange of contrasting and of sympathetic viewpoints does not occur. The problem that the author faces at the present hour is finding a target audience in the face of societal drift and fragmentation. The only authorial hope remaining therefore is either to adopt an overly simplistic narrative or to appeal to the subconscious mind by reducing logical narrative to a mere collection of symbols or stimuli and to push the interpretive task onto the reader, to allow his unique subjectivity to make of the literary object whatever he or she pleases.

The trend is towards the ultimate in objectivity and abstraction wherein the narrator as narrator disappears and all that remains is a suggestive artifact that escapes clear definition. It is in this spirit that reflexively speaking "Apocalypse Yesterday" is written. If this seems an abdication of the authorial role it is an abdication that is forced upon the author by the sheer number of empty seats in the theater of the mind. The basic contractual agreement between writer and reader has been severed by technology and by social drift into various polities that approach the world and the act of interpretation with widely divergent tastes and presumptions. This phenomenon forces the author inwards to confront his or her own inner experience and perceptions in all of their primal and decompensated nature.

Out of the ur-text and raw data of the ever suggestive mind arise thoughts and images out of the vast whirlpool of language that form wholes through sheer proximity and the bonding tendency of association. Literature like science advances by degrees as new forms are created to convey content. To speak of the form in the very act of evolving that form is less an act of transgression than a frank confession of what the author is about even as he does whatever authors do. The problem of the unreliable narrator disappears as soon as the author peaks from behind the curtain and unveils the machinery behind his own creation. Like the Eiffel Tower the difference between structural elements and ornament disappear when they become one and the same.

The ultimate question for the conscious mind is whether it exists in isolation. We depend upon communication to form linkages—we seek communities of interpretation. Even then the question remains: how do we ground our ethical and epistemological insights in some sort of ultimate guarantor of verification. An unprofitable enterprise entirely is literature unless it is termed to be revelation at one end at least, at that spectral zone where color fades into blackness. History has yet to escape the impact of its sacred texts because to do so would cause us to collapse into ourselves like a collapsing star forming a black hole leading to some inexpressible singularity. Humans cannot exist alone floating in endless space/time without direction or orientation without experiencing overwhelming anxiety. Deprived of beginning and end, lost in a sea of indeterminacy, brought into conscious agency and then as abruptly plunged into insensibility without hope of one last review and summation we are forced to adopt a position towards ourselves and to all questions whether asked or still forming themselves somewhere in the floating ether of the mind. We balance our absolutes each day with our morning coffee.

What if Moses or centuries later St. John of Patmos had suffered writers block? But then if words are being forced into your mouth like a set of oversized dentures I guess you just write what you're told to write by God. Anyway there's still time for correction (isn't there) just in case you misunderstood something or placed the wrong emphasis on something that was merely a parenthetical illustration of a more important but unstated point. In any case one apocalypse is enough. I mean a general ending for humanity includes everybody so that we don't need to worry about getting the daily rushes edited for our hypothetical film or who got the best distribution deal because it just won't matter anymore will it after the final waves of the metaphysical tsunami advance and then retreat?

Anyway I'm pretty tired as you can perhaps tell and I'm

running short on paste and materials for the collage and hell you can overdo anything if you stick with it too long. I'd like to enshrine all the things that upset me, what the French call my *bête noire* but who'd listen even having come so far intrigued and yet bewildered. They'd figure they had the drift of the whole apocalypse thing anyway before we even started. Apocalypses are about endings…

A Valediction Forbidding Mourning
An American Story for the Year 2021

John Donne wrote his poem, *A Valediction Forbidding Mourning* to one that he loved. He explains that love forbids morning because of its constancy. No journey is a final severance because its circle is confined by one point of a compass that remains forever fixed. Location of thoughts and desires demand a focus. In times of involuntary change a focus keeps us rooted in a sense of identity and attachment to places and to people. In the year 2020 I was exiled to the very place I had once longed to call my home, condemned to the very fate that I had long cherished as a dream of happiness. I first saw it coming home to Washington from California, a coastline so reminiscent of Stevenson's *Treasure Island* that I half expected to come upon the old Admiral Benbow Inn and see the old mariner Billy Bones who styled himself a Captain with his spyglass on the headland. I vowed then and there to return someday to walk the sands and explore the coves.

In subsequent years I visited this stretch of the central Oregon Coast often but my home, my ports and vessels were located on Liberty Bay in the Puget Sound country of Western Washington. After years of living aboard I decided in 2019 that the time had come to enjoy the sea from the landward side instead of falling asleep each night to the roll of the inland waters with seals, otters, and gulls as my nearest neighbors. So it was that I broke up a chill and even snowy period of interlude and headed south where I remain even as I write these words.

Circumstances have made solitude a necessity. I was forced into what has amounted to a long retreat this year of 2020. I thought that we would have the virus under control by now but as I listened to the news tonight I discovered that yesterday America lost more Americans to the pandemic in than were lost in the 911 attacks. Who would have thought we would be in this position, certainly not the seafarer, now landlubber, who left Washington in late February. With each month I thought that America would get the virus under control and that I could return home to visit the life I had left behind. Instead the gap widened week by week so that now I find myself entertaining choices that I left behind in my twenties as equally possible to returning to a life in my sixties that in many ways has ceased to exist for me.

But I forbid mourning for it. Whatever the coming decade brings for all of us it will not be a return to the past. We know better now. We know now that the secure ground on which we once stood can be shaken by more than earthquakes. People can become overnight little more than vectors for disease. We know that a President can hang onto office like a South American dictator and that half of America would still follow him even into death by refusing to exercise basic health precautions. Those of us who are transgender know that another four years of Trumpism would only further deny our right to exist.

To find a form in formless experience is the lesson of a year spent here by the open sea. Sky, plunging foam, and sand alter with each day and the footprints along the shore are never the same. People form tableaux of friends and family while I have remained in solitude through the accidental confluence of time and place with a global pandemic. Only ones long schooled in solitude can endure such long separations. Yet my very experience as transgender has made me well acquainted with exile and emotional self-reliance. I draw my strength from sea and sky like the plants that find root somehow in the shifting sands and bear tiny purple flowers. These are my daily companions as I sit in the sand reading or lie in semi-slumber bathed in the sound of the breaking waves.

To the student of beginnings any story begins in *media res* or to take a more usual metaphor we merge with the traffic of history. But tonight such thoughts are far from me. A fog bank has moved in on the coast, a warm one and the winds are still after a two-day blow. I have become used to the moods out here on the edge of America where I walk each day virtually oblivious of the upheavals occurring across the nation. The air is moist tonight and still as though taking a break from all the recent tumult. Only the waves breaking further out than I have ever seen them before shows that big waves riding the summit of the high tides forecast two days ago have finally arrived in full force. They have been breaking all day at the foot of the cliffs where the big houses are planted, where the lights are just coming up now like little sentinels. Looking down on me from high-ceilinged living rooms the inhabitants must wonder who that lone figure might be, the one that always walks back along the beach each night carrying books.

I wear my winter shoes now. I gave up the ones with the

holes in the soles finally just as I was getting used to the gravel burn on my feet from the road down to the beach, before the soft sand makes it feel as though my feet are nestled in the shoes that have been magically restored as they were when I bought them down in Newport three years ago. I could spend my days then in coffee bistros writing or maybe run up to the casino for the dinner buffet: smoked tri-tip roast, crepes, and all the Indian fry-bread I could eat. I am known there and they treat me like the transsexual princess that I still imagine myself to be. But then those activities and destinations are from memory. This year I only managed to catch the tail end of normal life in February and early March never imagining that I would still be here in December. I came down for just a short early visit to brush pine needles from the roof and be sure that the mice had not gotten in over the winter. Then suddenly the pandemic arrived, suddenly, brutally, remorselessly, not like this fog tonight, gentle and soothing but more like the great blade out of the *Pit and the Pendulum* swinging like a scythe of death over my head.

Everyone has a key bodily weakness and for me it is my lungs. I knew from the beginning that I could not afford to catch this virus. I thought back to when I once suffered from tuberculosis. It was 1980 then and I had gone down to California to live out my little version of the lives of Jack London or Robinson Jeffers. That summer I used to drive my Honda 360 over the coast range to Pescadero from the quiet little peninsula towns of Los Altos and Mountain View and head down to Carmel for the day. I recall that I had some of my poems printed up like bookmarks to be sold in the bookstores there.

One day in August I drove my motorbike back from Berkeley where I had gone to visit the campus and the next day I had a strange cough that just wouldn't go away. I had left my job and was house-sitting in San Francisco. I was flattered at first when I discovered weeks later that I had the same illness that had killed Katherine

Mansfield and D.H. Lawrence. I guessed that I must be destined to be like them a writer after all. Soon after my diagnosis I said goodbye to California. I came home to Washington and was cured at the county's expense. I would line up for testing and medications with the recently arrived Cambodian refugees, fresh from the killing fields of Pol Pot. I was still fresh from the romantic literary dreams nourished during my previous years in Michigan working in an industrial setting before I escaped to California. I dreamed then of the life of men like Jack Kerouac, Henry Miller, or the early John Steinbeck, a life spent around Big Sur or wandering about America and soaking up atmosphere for the big book that every author dreams about writing after the first years of struggle and neglect.

My recovery from tuberculosis gave me time to ponder my future and to travel. I drove 8000 miles the summer of 1981 crisscrossing the western states: mountains, valleys, and deserts before starting grad school at the University of Washington that fall. Everything was so intense then. Each decision was so pregnant with destiny and yet uncertain. I could have returned to Europe as I had planned to do in 1978 when I stood on a train platform in Luxembourg and said goodbye after six months spent studying abroad. Looking back now I realize how much I was living according to a prearranged drama bred of too much reading and an innate sense of the dramatic. It seemed natural in those days to think of my life through the long perceptive of dreams. Time seemed infinite then and there was always the possibility to correct course and start all over again. I forgot that American life can be brutal for those who miss early opportunities.

America tends to neglect its artists so that they often end up in places like Key West or Provincetown, somewhere on the edges of the continent that they are always trying to leave behind. The lucky ones make some money but then fortune shows its teeth and they often start that long slow road of self-destruction that their poverty had once kept at bay. Successful writers may end up like movie stars always hoping for one more big success to get them back on the bestseller lists.

Some seek to exploit their onetime celebrity status. They appear on the midnight talk-show circuit and try to say amusing things without a typewriter or computer screen in front of them. People look to writers as oracles to explain experience and capture in print the zeitgeist of the age. They don't see the lonely hours that writers spend alone with their thoughts and unsolved dilemmas that by a strange quirk of fate are not theirs alone. Writers write as long as they can. Many write the same book over and over again always looking for that magic formula of perfection that will ensure recognition and esteem. Others are one-book wonders who die young or go off into hiding to protect their sensibility from intrusion.

Some like me end up on a foggy night along the Oregon coast during a national pandemic. I climb the stairs up from the beach now and walk up through the trees along the path that I now know so well. It is enough that I will be warm tonight and that good food awaits me. When I sleep I will have the comfort of knowing that I am not stranded out there somewhere on the road or listening to the boom of tarps tied down to my deck to keep the rain at bay. Adventures are no longer sweet to me. I prefer warmth and comfort, to wake secure, and to hope that the virus will soon be the stuff of histories and the dimming memories of those who were fortunate enough to live through these days.

Where was I? Oh yes, I was speaking about the fog lying up along the coast tonight like a blanket in a chilly room. I walked up along the path not meeting anyone tonight. The beach was all mine, except for a few silent groups, separate and anonymous the way groups are now when social distancing is a must. I knew that dinner would be easy tonight, leek and potato soup with sausage and my favorite Greek seasoning. Maybe I will write a little before bedtime, maybe catch the evening news and hear the death count of the day.

Funny isn't it how the news of a thousand or more dead Americans has now become just routine, sort of like a 747 plane crash every day of the week. Now, nine months into the plague the gross death figure is like the Dow or the NASDAQ stock indexes, just one more figure to gage America a nation that lives by its indexes. How did all of this become so normal? The world that was lost in 2020 through the advent of the coronavirus and the resulting pandemic has been less a sudden inexplicable scourge and more of a revelation of what has been wrought by human expansion and invasion of the lands where indigenous peoples have lived for centuries yet survived the presence of these strange microbial agents. It is how we live in nature not nature itself that is the problem. We come to conquer subdue and decimate so should we surprised that nature reacts in kind? For every action there is a reaction. Our own seeming omnipotence has brought this disease forth as a great corrective to our pride. Was it always sleeping among us somewhere like a time-bomb ready to spring forth and decimate us whenever we brought together in a critical mass diverse species, in this case the bat and the scaly anteater so that a fortuitous interchange or chance mutation allowed the species barriers to fall? Perhaps the mechanism has a different trigger such as mass deforestation, single crop agriculture, or even too much carbon in the air. Maybe some inner memory was triggered and nature concluded that the dinosaurs had unaccountably returned or maybe we are just careless in the way that we stack crates filled with beasts in cages. In any case from some inauspicious beginning all else has followed. Now the economies of the earth tremble beneath a scourge as contagious and omni-present as its distant relative the common cold. All of the flaws of our interlaced civilizations are now made manifest like sea-wrack visible high on the shore tonight before a withdrawing tide.

All our debts to nature are becoming revealed now. They stand forth as evidence that we must perforce shut down or muffle the great engines of carbon-based commerce. All of our poor and homeless are now revealed as working families face eviction and the hobo-camps of yesterday no longer find their domain beyond the railroad tracks but rather in our city centers. We who live always in advance of ourselves are now brought up sharply like a runaway horse. The stern bit in our teeth causes us to arch our backs in rebellion at being constrained when we would love to run on ahead to our own destruction off of an ecological cliff.

All was going so well too. Who needs responsible government anyway? The reign of King Trump began with a tax-giveaway, not by raiding the piggy bank but by saddling the next generations with a trillion dollars of unnecessary debt. We pocketed our tax savings, spurned old alliances, and thought we were entitled to brag about our selfishness, the key American virtue. "Stop us if you can," we had shouted in our renewed greatness! And then suddenly a tiny globule with spiked proteins like an old World War II mine around a harbor drifted in among us ready to bump into our cells through our vagrant exhalations. The worst is that no one had heard of it before, this virus new to our species working at most a passing inconvenience to its former hosts but to us a plague never encountered before and to which we had no immunity as a species.

Coronavirus alone would have been sufficient to make the year of 2020 stressful but it coincided with the greatest social revolution since 1968. In order to remember that fateful pivot year in any detail it would be necessary to be born at the latest by 1960. A person born in 1960 would be sixty years old in 2020. People younger than sixty would then have no direct experience to draw from in order to process a period of national upheaval of the magnitude of 2020 when the confluence of pandemic, anti-racism protests, and a critical national election all happened to coincide. Coping mechanisms require some degree of prior exposure or they must be in a sense invented from scratch. This has been the real characteristic that will forever mark the year 2020 as historical in the same way that 1789, the year of the French Revolution marked its era. To young people it has been a shock that will be felt years later as their education process has been either altered in significant ways or at least deferred. The gap of a year in critical socialization skills alone may show up years later in one more addition to the Diagnostic and Statistical Manual of Mental Disorders.

Historical distortions create social tremors that reach to the furthest filaments of the social fabric just as a tsunami leaves the point where an earthquake occurs and radiates around the oceans of the world. These perambulations and perturbations are worse if they coincide with structural flaws. America, when the virus first struck, had been for four years engaged in a great social experiment of deregulation, corporate stimulus packages, and anti-environmental measures undertaken to boost profits in the fossil-fuel industry. Global warming was proclaimed to be a leftist Democratic hoax supported by a group of newly elected women in Congress known as the squad and ultimately backed by the deep state, meaning the professionals that ultimately make our complex government run. Putting a man in the White House whose idea of literature is a Twitter storm, one who conceived of the duties and responsibilities of his high office with the same enthusiasm and lack of comprehension as a kid in a candy shop maybe wasn't such a good idea after all.

The year 2016 brought on the equivalent of a leveraged buyout of America, a sell-off of key components for a quick profit, and the reorganization for resale to a smaller and more focused ownership group. In order to make this palatable Americans were promised that history could be reversed in order to "Make America Great Again." The whole transformation relied on old symbols while ignoring whatever real meaning they once had. Old emblems were dusted off, flags were waved, military air shows recalled World War II, and even tarnished Civil War memorials to long dead generals of the Confederacy erected during the period of reconstruction when virtual slavery was imposed once again by a defeated South that refused to acknowledge its defeat were suddenly emblems to be cherished.

Rhetoric from the KKK and from various Neo-Nazi fringe groups was suddenly respectable once again. Chanting at political rallies recalled the pageants once staged at Nurnberg when ecstatic Germans had wept to see the Fuhrer drive past in his Duisenberg with his palm raised to stir the people onwards to some imagined glory. Now of course "the master race" was inferred by simply being a white American and the great task was to build a fabled wall to proclaim forever that brown-skinned migrants had better stay south of the Rio Grande. The west that we had stolen from Mexico in 1848 was ours now and so it would remain forever!

Where did this new American sense of collective enthusiasm and hysteria come from? Was it merely an ad hoc Republican invention or the dream of a reality television mogul whose grasp of history was derived from the westerns that he may have watched as a kid on television? It may help to do a brief retrospective here to answer these questions.

In the 18th century a group of merchants, diplomats, and gentlemen planters motivated primarily by economic considerations and secondarily by certain romantic notions inspired by Locke, Montesquieu, Rousseau, and Paine decided on undertaking to form a new sort of government for the colonies in which they found themselves. The problem was to clothe what was a manifest act of rebellion with an aura of virtue and inevitability. Few innovators in political science or the actual governments of the earth presume to grasp power or to retain it without invoking God, historical necessity, or some other overriding principle to justify their rule. It is the part of the majority of the human race to then submit to these readings, explanations, or constructs and to avoid violence to their persons in the form of imprisonment or execution and the confiscation of their property through open disagreement or non-compliance with the promulgated laws of the particular jurisdiction. Governments begin in idealism and end in inequality and subjugation.

This group of associated gentlemen having decided to break with England first constituted the new government as a confederation of independent states but since these individually could not hope to long resist reacquisition by the jealous powers of Europe they decided for the good of themselves and their posterity "to form a more perfect union." In the smithy of a great Constitutional Convention they forged a Constitution inspired in part by the democratic structures of ancient Rome, a practice that was natural since a classical education of the times demanded a close scrutiny of the writings of the Greeks and the Romans. This Constitution has survived to the present day due to two factors: a handful of amendments occasionally supplemented as new needs arise and the imagination and sagacity of the judges who have managed to find various rights and principles within the bare structures of that very Constitution through applied legal reasoning. The end result has been the creation of the most armed and commercially successful empire that the world has known to date.

This brief prequel is meant to sum up in a few words a great amount of history and the lives of the many persons who have made this progress possible. The nation that exists today is a product of various interactions in war and in peace between that nascent nation and the other nations of the world. It takes enterprise and determination to migrate to a new country. American genius is not innate but borrowed from a citizenry made up of voluntary exiles. Immigration is not a threat but the very life blood of the nation.

The rest of our good fortune is due to possessing a moderate climate, many navigable ports on two oceans, and continental dominance in the Americas. However to the mind of many Americans ours is a story pregnant with inevitability and as such America is the favored child of fortune, the beloved of our Creator, and the natural legislator in world affairs. For these Americans long schooled in the catechism of their own greatness flattery is only our just due and it should be paid in both respect and in revenue by all of the other nations of the world.

So it was that when a man in 2016 managed by what many saw at the time as a refreshing honesty and bluntness to capture the Republican Party and its nomination to the Presidency their collective hearts rejoiced that the new President-to-be would not be a politician or even a creature of the laws but rather a magical embodiment of everything that they did not know about America but felt in their hearts with that intuitive sense of pride and entitlement that Americans of both major parties hold dear.

It had not escaped the notice of many average Americans that the promises held out to them in childhood were not being kept. Their houses were smaller than their parent's houses had been. They took shorter vacations, had a higher debt load, and were dependent upon a dwindling source to obtain the goods that made their consumption-oriented lives possible. The great producers of their clothes and in fact most of the items from pharmaceutical needs to automobiles were located elsewhere. The economy of the nation was seventy percent consumer driven which meant that most citizens simply recycle the same thin slice of all of the outstanding dollar supply among themselves at restaurants, hair salons, and gyms while the bulk of dollars goes to workers overseas or funnels upwards as profits to the one percent of high wage earners and corporate stockholders. The American pantry was in fact almost bare and Mother Hubbard was living in a shoe that was manufactured in China or India. All was looking lost until a serial playboy, one who was famous for being famous as well as a propensity for lavish real estate projects that often failed, presented himself as a disinterested Robin Hood figure who would rescue forgotten America.

Donald Trump didn't reach far for his model, perhaps recalling how far another raucous orator had managed to get by using the repeated word Deutschland and histrionic rhetoric to extinguish democracy in Germany; so why re-invent the wheel. His crudeness became forthrightness and ingenuousness and besides the bad-boy mystique is so charming to people who dare not speak out in their ordinary lives. Arbitrary rule is the hallmark of the paternalistic Christian family. Commanded obedience was a matter of recent memory or current experience for many blue-collar Americans. Even supposedly liberated women evidently found it charming to imagine that here was a man who confessed openly to wide-ranging heterosexual explorations as merely one more version of the ancient *droit de seigneur* of the lord of the manor.

So it was that in 2016 that staid body of electors defied the popular will and appointed to office a man who saw the Presidency as the place where he could see his fantasies of ultimate power not only fulfilled but fomented by supposedly conservative politicians. The essence of romanticism of course is not conservation but change, the pursuit of a vanished golden age. Imagine a Camelot Presidency without any pretence at intellectual depth; this is to grasp the essence of the "Make America Great Again" ethos. The dusty closet of a vanished patriotism yielded its old and tarnished memorials now appropriated as just part of the brand and logo of the new Commander in Chief. Every neural circuit from elementary school received a new burst of electricity and suddenly everyone was in the back seat of the old family Ford or Chevy and it was 1958 again!

Only it wasn't 1958 because time moves in only one direction. America had already passed its accidental zenith which was a by-product of our involvement in two world wars. The collapse of the European colonial empires and the terrible decimation of the Soviet Union by Nazi Germany had allowed America a free hand to exploit the early developments and the technical advancements that emerged from the war after 1945. Japan and South Korea were then virtual American colonies and China was still stuck in the 19th century with an agricultural economy and a surplus population. The tax structure of America in the 1950's and 1960's favored a vibrant middle-class and the babyboom generation grew up on toys and cartoons dreaming of endless opportunities. So secure were they in their superior position that Americans of that time developed a sort of evangelical capitalism in the form of The Peace Corps and the Alliance for Progress. The whole world might now aspire to be American!

Then suddenly the sixties decade was over. The costs of the war in Viet Nam and the expenditures of "the Great Society" resulted in inflation. Young people struggled to find their footing in an expanding world economy. The flower children became yuppies, the tide of universal liberation went the way of disco, and Ronald Reagan was elected President. The 1980's was a struggle between libertines and conservatives, the seeds of today's culture wars found their first rooting places and forged valuable alliances in government. The first Gulf War began over the fate of Kuwait and suddenly America began the long hemorrhage and transformation into the sole remaining superpower ready for a thirty year experiment at creating a new world order that was in reality only the same old order of rebellion and reaction that has always characterized human history.

Every year after the dawn of the new millennium has seemed alien to me, without a central theme. Time seems to have sped up and there is no guiding vision. Events simply happen in a random and unconnected way. As the dreams of my young adulthood have waned and the long twilight period has begun I hunger for the same security that from an entirely different mindset Republican voters thought that Donald Trump could give them. I on the other hand hope for no messianic figure. I take comfort in virtues when I find them. Maybe I never realized that I had been born into an age in decline; that the high point of culture was reached long before I was born. I find myself answering the questions first posed in my grandfather's generation. I have always been playing a catch-up game with history.

Life all seems so inevitable now, resistant to any plan or order. This great loss of direction at the macro level is replicated on the micro level, so that as I walk the beach each day reviewing my own minor place in these great events I wonder what remains to anchor my values and my perceptions. I wish I could begin all over again, although I realize that I cannot do so. My own flesh is part of that turning of cycles, those wheels within wheels. Can I be getting old after all? Is there a reason why the movie stars whose names and films I knew don't show up at each year's Academy Awards anymore? I am startled when the yearly collective obituary runs to see how many familiar names appear, knowing that film alone preserves them as they once were? As a member of a media-obsessed generation film stars were my pantheon of idols. I thought of them as intimate companions and role models, imagining that some of their glamour might become mine so that by stepping into the film I could leave behind the constraints that held me bound to a sex that didn't seem to really be mine.

My daily sense of self sifted through imaginary ideals. I found that I could slide through various characters like an FM radio dial always looking for a clear signal with no static interference, always looking for a confirmation of illustrious ideals that might have only existed in my mind. Now here I am marooned by coronavirus and forced to engage in solitude with what I have become and to look over the depository of my days and nights to see what endures and what might be dissolving away now day by day erased by the interminable waves of time.

I came down to the coast then before winter was over and by the end of March the state of Oregon was in lockdown. It came as such a surprise. I should have remembered 1982-1983 and the way that another virus was suddenly seemingly everywhere. The difference is that coronavirus is less focused on a particular community and it takes people from health to gasping for breath to death quickly whereas AIDS in the beginning might take two years from the first night sweats to the final skeletal end of its victims.

In those early days I knew drag queen friends in their twenties who turned from being delicate sylph-like creatures into the semblance of old ladies as their flesh melted away. I didn't think I would ever live through anything like that again. Doing the covid-19 numbers in real time was shocking at first but as the year has worn on the faces have disappeared and their stories with them. Maybe someday an encyclopedia will be assembled to remind us of just who these people were and how they were plucked out of life to make the bitter vintage of tears that is a pandemic. It is only now that we are seeing what exponential growth rates mean when translated into mobile morgues in city after city.

I decided early on in the pandemic that I would do whatever it took to stay healthy and not be a part of history. If nothing else I would hang on until the blessed day when I could watch Donald Trump be voted out of office. Every day I check out the conservative websites, some religious and some mainstream news. I told people in January that 2020 would be a stressful year. It would be a political confrontation of maxed-out dimensions, but never did I foresee what was about to descend upon us. I had first heard about the coronavirus on the news blaring over my head from a big-screen television while I shoveled down yummy food at my favorite Chinese restaurant. Part of being a regular customer is possessing right of first possession. I guarded my usual table like a pit bull, me with my model-length red hair and fierce blood-red nails to give emphasis to my summary dismissal of anyone who tried to turn the channel over to Fox News from MSNBC. My first impression of what was soon to be known as covid-19 was that here was just another of those predictable flair-ups of weird viruses in China that blaze up like brushfires and are soon extinguished. If a few cruise ships were infected they would go into quarantine along some dock in California and the whole thing would soon be another false alarm.

I was wrong. By the time I got down to the coast there was already a case in some school in Oregon and two weeks later coronavirus was a real issue. Suddenly my comfy routine in Washington had become an inaccessible memory. Platters of food fresh from the kitchen, big serving spoons, and nothing but mounds of shrimp and General Chou Chicken were now light years away. Days spent among crowded tables with everyone talking and eating were like a time from some former life spent in gastronomic paradise.

Yet even now, even this late into the pandemic, covid-19 denial is everywhere and mask-wearing is interpreted as the ultimate abdication of our right as Americans to demonstrate that we can muscle our way through this thing by holding it in contempt. The virus is spreading most readily in precisely those rural Republican-voting states where it was at first slow to arrive. Things can only get worse in the next three months. It isn't easy to keep screen-doors and windows open for ventilation in the midst of a Dakota winter. I find myself getting mad at the people who have deliberately avoided precautions out of supposed loyalty to Donald Trump. Next to the National Anthem and the Pledge of Allegiance nothing demonstrates rabid patriotism like ripping a mask from your face, just like the boys in 1917 when commanded to go over the top into steady machine gun fire, according to this invincible fantasy of pointless risk.

Now as December arrives I realize how I have kept putting off my return to Washington day by day and now month by month waiting for things to improve. I don't know what I will be returning to and as long as I stay here I can pretend that I have a life there that I can take up again just where I left it. The rhythm of a day is like an orchestral score but now whole pages are missing and the conductor's baton is broken.

When I walked down to the beach today I saw how the king tides have erased old landmarks and deposited new driftwood logs along the now familiar shore. Even the beach has been sculpted by the waves raised up by two successive gales with winds gusting to 60 MPH overnight. The beach is no longer flat but is broken by low hillocks of sand, littered by tangles of kelp uprooted by the great waves and flung onto the shore. Everything changes but then I have changed also in my months spent here, bereft as I have been from the mirroring influences of my usual home and community. Instead there is only this great gap between the routines of a life that I had established over twenty years and whatever remains of my life.

How shall I spend it? Is it too late to create something entirely new? Wandering makes no sense without the possibility of return to display our discoveries. All maps today terminate in a starting point and I begin to suspect that there is no land of promise to which I might escape the baying hounds of memory that pursue me. Why did I ever allow so many indignities to be meted out? But then did I really have a choice at the time? I did whatever the day demanded in order to survive and I took comfort in the little details of daily living. Isn't it that way for everybody?

The surf rises and suddenly I find myself pinned up against the sea cliffs. The friendly ocean appears menacing and the need for escape suddenly imperative. I respect everything more now, all of the blind forces of creation. I am beginning to suspect that I play no permanent part in the panorama of events and that my observations are for this day only. The waves will soon cover my footprints and a day will come when it will be as if I had never been.

How long can my heart beat so that the world can explode with each day into sight and sound before me? The sunlight today works harder to warm the air. I have decided once again to remain where I have been safe, well-fed, and granted the freedom to read and to write but even more to meditate on what my life has been, the choices that I was forced to consider and to make because they ensured survival when anything more was too much to hope for. I looked for love in the wrong places and held on too long to relationships that would have never been started if I had comprehended the many options that I could never manage to believe were my due as a human being. Transgender persons often take on the coloration of the abuse that surrounds us. It is how we end up dying too soon and living in deprivation because we take the first hands stretched out to us for fear that otherwise we will remain alone, unprotected, and bereft of all human sympathy. We are thrilled by events that most people take for granted, pathetically savoring each morsel of recognition and acceptance, and who can blame us for that?

The shame is not ours. Those of us who recall the early days when we were not only obscure but virtually invisible need to remind the present generation that as bad as it can be now it was once far worse for us. The rainbow now reaches from horizon to horizon whereas it was once confined to a single prism of glass held up against the sun through a solitary windowpane to catch the light. We were in a state of stealth even from ourselves.

I came out early and paid the price for it but not as much as many others. I owe them some sort of elegy in everything I write because I am here and they are not. The early imperatives of gender become less insistent with age as various diva possibilities fade. Humanity ceases to be two separate oceans of appearance and perception. Each sex begins to resemble the other. The spark between opposing poles is less as the two electrodes come closer together. But for all of this our souls remain grounded even when fractured by a life of multiple gender representations.

The easy binary assumptions of the first writings on transsexual identity are less mandated now. We have less to fear from doctors who once held our fate in their hands. These were the people who spoke for us because we were denied a voice. In those days it paid to be selectively crazy because that was what we were expected to be. We can take our time now and reflect before making choices under pressure from immediate circumstances. We can be honest about our doubts and fears. We can tolerate ambiguities even in our most closely held convictions. We can claim the full spectrum of our humanity without being dictated to by words and symbols. To claim our full humanity means being something besides sexual fetish objects for those who would claim an automatic right to explore and to exploit us. Above all else we don't need to compete with each other for transgender door prizes along scales of "realness" and "passing." Our bodies are not ends in themselves but gateways to being able to fully experience this world that surrounds us. Life is not an audition, not even a performance, but the thing itself.

Every day now the numbers of the dead go up in an ever increasing spiral. In the beginning I prayed for them one at time, then in tens and twenties, and now in hundreds but still under the same basic phrases, "For those who will die this day and their afflicted loved ones and their patient and long-suffering caretakers, may their souls and all the souls of the faithful departed through the mercy of God rest in peace, Amen."

Now even those days of more focuses prayers are left behind as the daily death count crosses two thousand. I have finally lived long enough to live through one of history's great watersheds. Lives that just a short year ago were immune and filled with expectations have been cut off sharply and cleanly by an organism that no matter how long it had slumbered in an alien species had done us no harm. Along the wing-like membrane of a bat's widespread fingers it lived in the blood or traversed the lungs while below we could walk oblivious of what soared aloft over our heads. In any case a vast ocean separated us from its source and so whatever swift transfer made human infection possible would surely flare briefly before being extinguished. The rich variety of our individual pursuits would go on and we would live to fulfill our destinies. But now a great interruption had taken place and tears appeared in the fabric of our lives. People who could not be replaced left unaccountable holes where we had been accustomed to seeing them each day and had every expectation that they would be there tomorrow and again tomorrow.

I thought of all matters often as the sea days arced swiftly over my head and the waves beat their incessant rhythm to mark my solitude.

I would wait it out no matter how long it took. From the hour of my awakening and the first news of the day on Democracy Now to the last hour when I would read until my concentration waned before drifting off to sleep I would hope for deliverance from the chaos of the country and the ravages of the virus. It would be hard to take up the strands of life again when the period of contagion has passed. Never before had it seemed so evident that we are flames from a common fire, sparks blown upward red and glowing against a clear sky on a summer night while the shore wind blows in from the sea to disperse them.

Ego ties us to our particular history so that we don't see that another's eyes are really identical with our own. Their pain or loneliness is identical to ours and ours to theirs. Individuation ignores how we are joined at the stem and at the root, nourished by a common force that some call the Holy Spirit. We are walled up behind our own eyes, imprisoned in a skull of bone while somewhere a ligature joins us to all other lives. A common pulse beats inside of us, a beat mirrored by the unceasing sea. We carry the same salt ocean in our blood and even our bodies are vehicles of metabolic transport so that hearts may replace hearts and lungs replace lungs. Those who receive organ donations do not say, "This part of me is not me." Are our brains any different? Can we transfuse identities? Is language only a brief signal like a lighthouse flashing outward to vessels that approach our shores? Did I come to the coast this year to find myself or to lose myself, to tear myself away from the comforting routine of the last twenty years, to return to a time of hopes that had not known disappointment, to regain an era of infinite belief? I wanted to find the freshness again, the icy thrill of new experience when everything was new. Perhaps I had thought too much, found sources of opposition everywhere. Maybe now I could grant a general amnesty to life and start over and do it right this time.

But death was close in 2020, closer than it had ever been before. People younger than me were dying and I was in a group that did not bear up well after a positive diagnosis. This thought plunged me back into separation. "I must survive because my life is not yet complete!" Others had done so much more in half the time. Their charity was a down-payment on eternity while I only leased my life in thirty day increments, always waiting for something definitive to emerge. Would another's virtues need to cover me as well? Could their surplus cancel out my debt that having lived so long I was just approaching ... what? Was it a definitive formulation? Something culled from a thousand books sifted and set out once again in my own words? Is that enough for a life?

But then the sea is profligate and human life is profligate. The beach is a littered burial-ground of preliminary efforts, crabs half-grown, bundles of kelp, empty clam shells. I walk over them to my adopted place each day when the weather permits, set my books down and begin underlining and annotating. "Ah here is a passage worth a double star!" Life is a vast allegory, the poem copies nature, no rather enhances and transports it to another level of apprehension. Very good! "Look out there, a squall line has come up over the horizon moving towards me." Unsuspected it springs upon me, the first drops falling. "Close the book before the ink begins to run! I had better start back now the wind is already beginning to blow and the squall is closer now. Look where the rain shadows like a grey curtain make the south bay invisible."

So having read passages from Longinus or Horace or Plotinus I set out for home across the sands. I have read them as though we were engaged in some long debate and I could meet them later over a beer to thrash out a disputed point, but they are long dead these two thousand years and my comments, even made with such advantages, ones born of the resources of later commentaries, cannot eclipse the brilliance of the initial formulations. For Classical writers the Trojan War was yesterday but is it less so for me when set against the slow accretion of geological time that has worn rocks into sand?

There was another autumnal gale last night, so for today warnings went out for high surf and the possibility of sneaker waves that can wash ashore and pull the unsuspecting beachcomber out to sea. Sneaker waves are like miniature tsunamis. The water simply keeps on coming as though from an irresistible source of reserves. It is a function of the preceding waves interacting with the slope of the beach which might have been eroded in such a way that hills and valleys that were absent only yesterday provide new channels of flow and retreat today. This sea phenomenon might be taken as an analogy for our present political and cultural situation as the chaotic year of 2020 slips beneath the waters of history. The certainties of yesterday are caught up in the tidal flow of events such that entire industries are being transformed before our eyes. Job categories are not merely migrating; they are ceasing to exist. Old loyalties are being broken and new and perhaps equally transient alliances are forming. Perhaps only people like those of us who have managed to surf the waves of identity and the expressive modes that support identity can find within us the skills to adapt when the ground shifts beneath our feet. Only people who have embraced instant exile as the price of personal authenticity can know what losses of this magnitude entail for a culture.

Early transgender people were solitary gender samurai. Now we senior members are people who blossomed before the dawn and are now wilting away. Our testimony is almost embarrassing because our lives were once so restricted. Our early transitions or lack of them are reminders that surgical and hormonal resources were then in short supply and not readily available at that. I am surprised at the seeming fluidity of gender-change today and the widespread acceptance of a category of experience that was formerly confined to psychiatric journals and scummy talk-show formats. Opposition now requires at least a few sidelong glances before being verbalized. We are still victims of violence and even murder but gone are the days when such events were not even newsworthy because we were deemed expendable and deserved what we got. We have made progress and no doubt President Biden will reverse some of the last gasp persecutions of our people under the recent Trump regime.

I am tired though; weary of being a cultural icon to be exploited by conservative media as a sign of cultural malaise or even decadence. Once we are unmoored from our assigned gender we are too often reduced to being piquant manikins for sexual exploitation because of our very difference. We get swept into debates not of our choosing because most of us simply want to live. Some of us are able to make careers out of leveraging our life-experience, but to do so is a subset of the entertainment industry and yesterday's star is likely to be today's tabloid tragedy.

I avoided celebrity in my youth by seeking shelter in the bosom of a small town on a peninsula during the years when I might have found a wider channel for expression in New York or Los Angeles. People like me were rarities then and like anything rare, exploitable. I opted for quiet and convenience because these gave me a semblance of what life might have had in store for me had I not been transgender. Urban enclaves in contrast invited more extreme fates of fortune or of disaster. Suburban life in contrast leaves us in a state of suspended animation between true acceptance and mere toleration. I chose the latter because it had the advantage of any pastel existence, quiet harmony with the other furnishings. I was just colorful enough to draw notice but not sufficiently aggressive to pose a threat.

After the election most Americans heaved a sigh of relief but I was still uneasy. I keep thinking of Neville Chamberlain getting off of the plane from Germany proclaiming that "peace in our time" had been achieved. I took daily comfort as case after case raised by the Trump campaign was being thrown out of court for lack of evidence. The midnight talk show hosts were able to laugh at these feeble efforts to reverse an election but always I heard the echo of jackboots in the streets and recalled how unlikely that Nazi takeover had once appeared, the dull-witted street thugs who supported Hitler, the inchoate enthusiasm of the nameless masses bewitched by his passionate rhetoric. The very fact that Trump was making these outlandish claims with impunity should have been enough to awaken people to a clear and present danger. If nothing else this man was seeding the ground for four years of domestic terrorist acts committed by those supporters who took him literally. Almost half the country had voted for him even while the hospitals bulged at the seams with the desperately ill and the dying. Would all of this disappear on Inauguration Day in the midst of an economic recession that would require further stimulus to recover even after the vaccination program?

Meanwhile I had my own personal damage control with which to contend. I had lived in virtual solitude for ten months. My former life now seemed as distant as my earliest memories. Looking at the tumultuous seas with their rip tides and brutal undertows and over-falls I wondered if I had extracted all that I might have done from the pageant of living. I was raised in a faith that proclaims certainties. Was it time now to begin the long process of repentance and reparation for a life that had been ill-spent or to rally round my convictions and even my doubts? I would like to have accomplished more in my past, but in which direction do I bend my future efforts?

Maybe I would have done more harm than good had circumstances not kept me on a short leash. To exert force in any direction after all is to set other things in motion just as the gale last night has produced today's huge waves on the shore. To see all things in motion seems to me to be a more accurate description of what exists than fixed and enumerated categories. The universe appears to have its own spontaneity. The balance of forces is harmonious without being static. Even language loses meaning when the same sacred phrases are repeated again and again. The function of literature is to constantly renew our language with new metaphors.

Thought grows a hard carapace when it is not constantly deconstructed and reassembled. But there is a corresponding danger in this. The breeding ground of every heresy always begins with the phrase, "Yes, but what if…" But a static orthodoxy finally loses contact with its original referents. Formulaic phrases become meaningless, but prior to that they become hard granules that only circle back on themselves in endless replication. This is why rebellion ultimately has a constructive and preservative role. It forces a new articulation of what has always been believed so that it becomes fresh and new again.

Rebels are always a threat though. I would have done better in life to memorize the rules and figure out who was in charge. Instead I completed the assignments while secretly questioning the purpose of the whole thing. I like to think that every equation has a remainder so that there is always something more to do. When the virus passes who will I be and where will I go? The erosion wrought by the coronavirus, as unique and catastrophic as it has been, is a subset of the greater changes that are occurring all around us in the environment and even in our inner sense of ourselves. The dense weave of the decades creates a common culture around us. It tells us who we are and what resources are available to fill our needs and where we can expect to find them.

I carry within me an inner road map of the stores at the local mall where I customarily shop when I need anything beyond my basic needs. I expect to see the same sales persons when I go to the mall and the same grocery check-out staff when I return to doing my own grocery shopping. When we all come out of our burrows blinking in the sunlight of recovery and renewal it is probable that we will return to a changed world without our favorite restaurants or watering holes. I usually notice changes even after a short vacation so what about a year of absence? What will it entail?

The worst part is that I will probably not return as the same person that I was because changes are part of me as well. I no longer have the same expectations that I had. I see my life now with an unaccustomed objectivity as though I had left the stage and gone down into the audience seats. What had once been routine for me seems now a strand of tissue neatly clipped off and floating about at random in the aqueous gel of my vision. I am connected by only memory to my former pursuits like a familiar VHS movie stored away in a box and now without the mechanism to play it. I will need to transcribe everything to the self that is over a year older. The perpetual illusion of my own youthful relevance is denied daily in the mirror by my physical body so that a re-calibration, let alone a re-invention from scratch, seems impossible. Reflecting on this makes me feel that it would be just as well if I simply started over again somewhere else at chapter one although I can no longer echo the first chapter of David Copperfield entitled, "I am born." Instead, I echo the sentiments in the poem by Alfred Lord Tennyson entitled, *Tithonus,* that begins, "The woods decay, the woods decay and fall, the vapors weep their burthen to the ground."

The nation itself has grown unaccountably old in its semblance of democracy. It will have to struggle to its feet after the

Trump attempt to impose authoritarian rule. The racial divide that exists has never been more urgent because its reality has been made more visible by the Black Lives Matter Movement. Conditions of long standing will need to be ameliorated during the Biden Presidency. Those who will have been rendered homeless or jobless will have to draw their lives about them and assess the damage.

The dead of course will not return. For them history will have ended with Donald Trump and his rallies where the disease was simply dismissed as a democratic meme. These will not rise with the dissemination of a vaccine. For them there will only be the panic as the sedative took hold and the intubation device invaded their body in order vainly to keep them alive when the efforts to draw an independent breath became too difficult. The sun of their memories will have set on a world dominated by the constant noise that Donald Trump's noxious presence visited on America with the intensity of a laser beam for five long years.

If I survive then I must count myself lucky. I will at least have a prospect of renewal and for that reason I forbid mourning. We dare not tarry long over all that we have lost as a nation. We must take our disgust and loathing and put it aside, although never forgetting that the forces that brought Donald Trump to power still exist among us, all the envy, the desperate desire for vicarious celebrity, the esteem relished on his discourtesy, and the contempt for science, for learning, and for culture. The greedy will find some new avatar and the poor having been betrayed will seek another savior as the raucous chants of the Trump rallies fade away.

The America that will emerge with a national debt approaching 25 trillion dollars will need to realize that we depend on the rest of the world for constant cash infusions to keep our national debt from collapsing in on itself like a building set for demolition. But still we must forbid mourning lest our tears never dry. It is at times like these that it helps in some ways to have been transgender, to be accustomed to disappointed hopes, and to the dissolution of dreams. Transgender exile breeds its own independence. Transgender people know what it is to leave a ballroom rented for the night, to go out under the streetlights of a winter rain, to climb the weary stairs to a shared apartment or a solitary studio, to set aside a rhinestone crown if there is one, to see the tired face in the bathroom mirror, and to see all the colors of make-up on a washrag or swirling down the drain of the sink. After that we simply go on as we have always done. We gather the spare elements of style or glamour from the rags of fortune. It is an old trick for us.

Our newly acquired status and recognition raises grounds for hope. It is a capital mistake however to use the exceptions to ignore what is true for the majority of us. Many struggles are still in front of us as a community. The current comparative visibility of transgender lives is as deceptive as our invisibility once was. When we were invisible we were presumed not to exist and now that we are more visible and receiving unprecedented attention and sympathetic understanding in some quarters it is assumed that everything is finally turning out alright for us. Instead what is often occurring is that the same cultural anxieties that once marginalized us is now leading to an assumption that we are more powerful than we are.

The myth of "gender ideology" proclaims that we are engaged in and able to accomplish the breakdown of the identities of straight people so that what is exceptional will become a new imperative; the fear that transgender identities will become the new norm for human sexuality. The same oppression in other words that was once visited on transgender persons will now, it is presumed, be turned against heterosexual and cis-gender people so that they can no longer live as they choose.

Whether this paranoid supposition is due to a bad conscience within the society that has often treated transgender people so badly or not, its effect is the same, to make of the victim the victimizer. Then, to add spice to this deadly political concoction, religion is stirred into the brew. It is now proclaimed that the very essence of religion lies in the right to discriminate by selective designation of the ungodly and then making their lives untenable through refusal of service, lack of employment or housing, and by refusing to afford to us the social amenities that usually accompany our gender.

This backlash is justified by linking us in with other marginalized groups. The present national hysteria of faux-patriotism that depends more on symbols than upon substance makes us into strangers and aliens. The Trump administration made this process all too clear by denying transgender individuals the right to serve in the armed forces and by reversing protections that had enabled transgender students to claim the right to full participation in their childhood and adolescent years, those crucial formative years when we mature in our gender expression and are launched upon adult life.

The latent fascism of the Trump Presidency and the pandemic that it did so much to promote through its own policy failures has left havoc in its wake. The recently acquired place at the table for transgender people is a tenuous one. For all Americans the reconstruction of our economy on a more equitable basis will take years. It will take even longer to disassemble the acceptableness of systemic mendacity that has made Trumpism not only possible but has rendered his noxious conglomeration of assorted bigotries acceptable for roughly half of the American population.

Conservative religion has forged an iron-clad alliance with political intolerance and a monolithic image of American life that denies the racial and cultural diversity that have always been the source of American vitality. This has been combined with an apocalyptic view of history centered on the belief that a war in the Middle East by pressuring Iran will usher in a period of Christian millennial rule. This belief system that overrides sensible statecraft and diplomacy is based on an unquestioned belief that America has been chosen by providence to insure the end of the world through an alliance with Israel that will lead deterministically to a final confrontation. The withdrawal of American participation in multiple international treaties, from environmental preservation and from arms control agreements and the constant abuse of NATO and the United Nations while exalting an American go-it-alone strategy, all are hallmarks and confirmations of this fanatically religious, dangerous, and isolationist mentality. The fortunate victory of the Democratic Candidate Joe Biden in the recent Presidential campaign gives us four years at least to return some measure of sanity to our republic.

The active engagement of formerly isolated groups demanding justice will be required. They will enter the fray against formidable obstacles raised by entrenched interests bolstered by appeals to tradition, patriotism, and an assumed favor from God, the same sentiments that have inspired every Crusade, made possible every case of genocide, and accompanied most of the wars of humankind. The deaths caused by the pandemic should have united us around a common cause of survival. Instead these deaths have left America fractured with one half of the nation convinced that to fail to wear a mask in public and even to die as a result is a sign of proud refusal to accept facts. This folly is the supreme expression of the brand of American exceptionalism that Donald Trump and the party that has enabled him has made mainstream. Together they have managed to marshal a deadly mixture of pride and insolence into a collective force of paranoid suspicions and latent violence. It will not be easy to absorb the fluid bred of this toxic abscess back into our democracy, but we must do so if we are to survive as a nation willing to cooperate with the other nations of the world to face problems of a global nature and to surpass these immediate threats to our survival without pretending that even greater challenges do not remain.

As December 2020 arrives the virus count climbs ever higher with its attendant deaths. In my place of refuge I seek daily solace by the sea. We denizens of the coast have left last week's storms behind us now; the sun has returned. I see daily groups of children wading in the ocean surf and the usual dog-walkers are out on their usual promenade. Last night the full moon rose up just behind the trees huge and round as it always is when it is close to the horizon. I was listening on my phone to a podcast promoting a new book lamenting the current crisis in the Roman Catholic Church and the remissness of the majority of the Bishops of the United States willing to reduce or curtail the usual church services in obedience to the civil authorities. To me this sense of responsibility is only to be expected from mature people in light of the present crisis. To the extreme Trump-worshiping right wing Catholic conservative movement however failure to court a readily available prospect of unnecessary death is to miss a great chance for martyrdom.

There has been much talk of late in conservative Catholic circles that we don't talk enough about hell these days. The unstated presumptions are always that conservative theology can readily ascertain the sign posts of salvation, that where God is concerned correct ritual is more important than the saving of human lives, and that God's wrath requires constant appeasement. Listeners to conservative Catholic media are reminded daily that hell is the default destination of human beings, a reminder particularly apropos when uncertain death in the form of the virus might now strike at any time and that the pandemic is a direct visitation of God to punish us for our sins. All of this of course is reminiscent of the religious hysteria that greeted the Black Death of the 14th century.

All the while as I listened to this broadcast on my phone I could hear around me the waves breaking and watch the moon rising on the placid human groups wandering about on the sand and see the rose-gold light of the sun shimmering in the tide pools after sunset. These spoke of a larger conception of creation, one that made the grim pestilence seem very far away. Death amidst such splendor was unthinkable let alone one that would only serve to inaugurate us into greater suffering still.

I believe of course that there is a wide path that leads to destruction but it begins at a Trump rally and it leads ineluctably to Wall Street. I also know about the narrow path that leads to life. It is found in the hospital wards where nurses and doctors spend each day gallantly trying to save the lives of people, many of whom entertain the idea that the virus is a Democratic hoax and that if we would only stop testing so much as President Trump insists why then the virus would simply go away.

Last night after I came home from the beach beneath the moonlit trees I turned on my computer and went up on the Gutenberg Project site to look at the books of the great philosopher and historian Thomas Carlyle. I was not aware that he had also assembled a book of the writings of the great religions of the world. I picked a few passages at random to read and was startled anew by the way that every culture and nation has found a way to embody in a sacred text the poetry of our sense of wonder at all that is and to assign some sense of order to a creator. Surely the artist is greater than the canvas of this present world and surely life as it greets us each day wondrous and immense gives the lie to death.

The phenomenal display that greets us by the ocean may be the mere test sheet of some great moral exam but if contemplated in its own vastness and incomprehensibility it augurs something more. Adjuration has its place but to make of moral disputes and ritual observances the essence of religion and of worship seems to me at least to diminish whatever eternal realm exists. I think that we know smallness and constrictive conceptions when we see them. The great religions do not exist to close us up like an oyster on a few sternly grasped truths but to open us outward to a fuller conception of what with a little generosity and compassion we could become.

I am daily astonished at the sheer wonder of my fellow creatures. I am astonished to find how love can awaken traumatized shelter animals to renewed trust and to play. Even wild beasts are turned from lions into lambs by love and if Catholicism means anything at all, and I think it does, it means to love. I rejoice at the broader sense of God's actions and designs celebrated by Pope Francis in his new Encyclical, *Fratelli Tutti.* It speaks of a brotherhood of the human race that exists even prior to evangelization, not to diminish evangelization, but rather to honor what is already present in the longings and aspirations of a created order, one yearning and manifesting a divine order that is already present in all things.

This affirmation awakens confidence that the wide path to destruction is not what many Christians think it is. The wide path to destruction is to entertain a narrow and parochial ideology that sees the other as alien and as a stranger. It is a frozen mindset that builds walls simply to keep others out. It is the paltry selfishness that refuses truth whenever truth threatens to diminish personal power. It is the lie that when repeated often enough gains in credibility, at least for the gullible. It is all that has reduced America in four short years to our collective pride and isolation. It has all been a great seduction that has finally condemned us to be its minions under the short unhappy reign of Donald J. Trump leading us to deserve the pity of the rest of the civilized nations and to become in this disastrous year of 2020 the undisputed coronavirus capital of the world.

What are we to make of the multitude of narratives that make claims upon us? A totalizing narrative reduces everything to itself. Art by its very nature enhances or transforms initial impressions into meaningful communication by various means. This involves a process of discovery mingled with active response by the artist and the final transference by this medium to another human being who in a sense co-creates the now independent artistic object by willingly subjecting herself to its influence.

Music and drama actually add an additional intermediary in the form of played instruments or an orchestra and in the case of drama by stagecraft and acting. The two essential elements however in any artistic work if it is to fulfill its ultimate destiny are creation and communication. The creation may be spontaneous and perishable like a chalk drawing on pavement or an improvised theater piece. Permanence and the ability to replicate its influence or to recover its existence at will are all irrelevant. The manuscript to a great novel may even languish in a drawer or be burned and thus never fulfill its destiny. Franz Kafka instructed his friend Max Brod to destroy the manuscript of Kafka's unpublished work, *The Castle.*

In contrast to the partial articulations that are art we have in the realm of science the pursuit of a Unified Field Theory that will reconcile all forces and in religion we have various authoritative revelations that are understood to set universal norms for conduct and authorized ritual observances. We would like to believe that human experience would make it possible to make an authoritative yet still personal choice among the various contenders for universal explanations and meanings. The idea of cultural variance implies an unacceptable degree of relativity among totalizing narratives. The certainty of the prospect of death provides the universal solvent, the one experience that every human being must share, although the meanings attributed to it vary considerably.

Something deep within us though allows us to vibrate to the chord of another person's emotions. We all know hunger, loneliness, and fear. Our joys may vary with their specific objects but tragedy is the great welding universal that awakens sympathy within our deepest selves. Pestilence! How inappropriate is such a word to our sophisticated post-industrial world. Surely that is a word that only fits the middle ages. Who would imagine that so many could die today of an affliction that a year ago did not even exist among us? Where shall we seek a source to sustain us as we reconstruct a world so recently eclipsed?

My time runs short to absorb and adjust to the claims made upon me by my past and the challenge of an ill-informed future. The sun has returned though and once again I marvel that I have been allowed to spend my year of solitude here where each day the prospect of the great ocean makes small our conceptions. I have no telescope to scan distant galaxies. For me there is only the velvet drapery of the sky filled with stars and beneath their placid gaze the midnight blackness of the sea at night reaching outward infinitely but confined by the laws of perspective to a single line along the horizon. This is wonder enough for me. I impose few limits on eternity; not because it is my allotted task to decide which gates are narrow and which are wide, but because the sea itself spurns any effort at confinement. I imagine God as equally unconfined, willing to break in among us if given half a chance.

I believe that my entire life has been spent seeking to get at the basis of things. Religion begins with fundamental narratives of origin and purpose. In this sense every religion is linear and related to how we live in time. They involve aspiration and choice. Nirvana is conceived as a way to step out of time, to prevent the endless cycle of rebirth. Dharma is the continual stepping stone path to an ultimate cessation of personal existence and a merger into the ultimate reality. Even the goal of Christianity is that in the end God will be all in all. This sense of the totality unites religions while their mode of expression may be singular and unique in their doctrines and demands.

The great Western Religions with their Judaic base take eternity as a given so that we cannot having once been born manage to step out of existence because immortality is itself our doom. Death is simply that gateway to a final judgment, a great binary that will forever separate the human species into one of two alternative fates. In heaven there are said to be many mansions while in hell there is only one shared confinement of solitude deprived of love yet condemned to occupy a single crowded cell. Even the concept of forever as endless time vanishes into a present where the ideas of before and after become meaningless. I like to imagine that something of the innocence of creation is a parallel source showing metaphors of the nature of God somewhat comparable to the written texts that ground most religions. No religion may be judged from outside the perceptual categories that each religion terms essential. Religious thought creates its own fundamental categories of apprehension that guide all further thought and talk about them. This is why religious debates are seldom fruitful. Conversion is an organic and holistic process. In Christianity, properly understood, the gateway is love, a paradoxical and reciprocal relation where each cause is at the same time its own effect. The point of entry is such that after entry the door vanishes and one exists in a different way just as once one is at sea the land disappears and on every side there is only a single embracing horizon.

Winter! The sun scans now in a lower arc across the southern stretch of beach. Only the ambient temperature separates this sunny day from what I experienced over the past months of spring and summer. My ideas also follow a lower arc. I usually begin each year with definite goals and the unfounded certainty that my faculties will expand proportionately to achieve them. Ordinarily when autumn comes I gather the holidays about me like a comfort blanket. This year of course all subsequent life and plans are contingent to a successful vaccine. I seem to have been orbiting about this year awaiting a re-entry vehicle to carry me back to the earth I once knew. Everything I valued is now filtered by this year and the books I have read and the lines that I have written. My sense of solitude is now baked into me like a hard glaze over the mobile clay that has received it.

I came down to Oregon hoping for a reassessment of my life and a clearly charted final quadrant, the last twenty years of my human life. There is no longer room for partial gestures. Every narrative matters now, particularly if it flows from my pen. I received again today pictures, samples of an endless string of cameos each to be encased and laid aside in the box of memories of one who cannot be named. People and places move like a tinsel mobile over my head now; all are echoes in Plato's vast cave of appearances.

Yesterday a cousin asked me not to forward any more political articles because they threatened family unity. A news item on the same day said that one out of four doctors knew a colleague who had contemplated suicide because of what they have witnessed this year in treating patients for covid-19. When the new year of 2021 begins there will be no time for mourning; the exigencies of stamping out the last burning embers of the virus will demand all of our efforts as will the task of putting our lives back together again.

The ocean has provided me this year will all the metaphors for such a transformation. Each day as I walk through the graveyard of whatever the sea has thrown up with the last high tide I see how interlaced are life and death so that the two bleed into each other. I sit each day with my back against the rocks and my morning selection of reading material spread out before me. I like to read in the shadow of a beach house that casts its long morning shadow out over the beach. No one interrupts me there although I can watch the walkers, single or in small groups, walking dogs or playing in the surf. One day it might be a young woman doing cartwheels for her boyfriend and then running up to him for a hug of approval that she can still do what she did so well as a girl. On another day it might be two elderly women with notebooks who were measuring and recording the dead birds lying in the sand, more this year, no one knows why. Perhaps the fish are fewer or harder to catch.

Once a college group gathered for a group hug and no one was wearing masks. There are two or three surfers who tackle the waves each day expending fifteen minutes of effort and energy for a ten second ride in, but they think it is worth it. They disappear at times beneath the waves and I am anxious for a moment waiting for them to surface again. The sand that is smooth each morning is chopped up by successive feet in the course of the day. I like to watch the horizon for brief storm squalls that can move over the edge of my vision with surprising speed. Sometimes a fog bank moves in so thick that even the expensive homes along the shore disappear and people emerge like ghosts out of the misty distance.

I have a driftwood pile where in the spring of the year I would rest my head and doze in that semi-consciousness of wind and wave that is always hypnotic. The weeks and months have drifted by with the casual inconsequence of a place that always changes yet is always somehow the same. There was no place better to return to while the virus raged so I simply stayed where I was and now it is winter and I do not know how to return. A year separates me now from everything I knew at home and I am also somehow different. Perhaps it is because this very transiency is part of me now; perhaps because I have witnessed sunset after sunset this year, each unique and distinct, and each bearing that sense that it relinquishes its grip with reluctance on the brief hours of daylight where it had once reigned supreme.

Sometimes the sun vanishes in a distant fogbank so that the final diminution cannot be witnessed. But there are days when the sun sits on a knife-edge of horizon and sinks like a lemon bit by tiny bit. At the end there is only a ever diminishing disk that grows smaller and smaller until only a fractional spot remains forming a dome of light … going, going, and then there is only a solitary line although the sky is still as bright, as if the sun now set had never left to begin its long journey to the other side of the earth.

The night wind comes up then and I gage the distance for my long walk home before twilight should engulf all that I see and leave me in darkness with only the white line of the breakers to my left as a guide. If the light permits I may read for a little while longer or engage in those quiet thoughts that we save for life's twilight hours: regrets for past mistakes, wishes that we had made better choices, or mere reflections that life is infinitely precious because it can unveil sights like the sunset that I have just witnessed.

I get up at last, not yet creaky-boned, but still with an effort, and begin the slow walk back. The beach is empty now and the long promenade of my fellow hermits of the sea is over for the day. I marvel that such an expanse of space can be my sole possession without traffic-light or buildings to hem me in. I can think now beyond the horizon and imagine destinies that I have neither time nor energy to fulfill, although at one time I felt that the earth lay golden at my feet with infinite possibilities. Time once stretched out before me rich decade after decade simply waiting to be segmented and cached into neat files of memory so that in the end I could review it all and say that I had lived a perfect life, one filled with adventure, variety, and romance and only seasoned lightly by mistakes or foolish choices.

There were few thoughts then that things are as vulnerable as they are or that the great institutions that sustain us are like cobwebs in a gale. I felt the world then like a spinning top balanced along the edge of a precipice: would it spin forever or plunge over an abyss beyond repair? I recalled then the need to never stop affirming alluring possibilities so that a time would come when I would write a valediction forbidding mourning. Until then I could always sustain a sense of hope as I do now anticipating the coming day.

An Interview with Sheila Mengert

When did you start writing and why?

The best answer to this question is less a referral back to one's first attempts at recording thoughts in a formal and artistic manner, which is what writers do, than to ask oneself first why one continues to write year after year, producing book after book? Part of the answer to this is that writing is motivated by a desire to embody fleeting thoughts and impressions that would otherwise be forgotten before bearing the fruit attendant upon further reflection. Sometimes it is to explore a single theme in depth or to surprise oneself by a felicitous creation that even exceeds the initial experience or conception that has later matured into full form and symmetry. Perhaps writing is an extension of the personality of the writer, an attempt to survive oblivion, or at least to grasp the fleeting moment by recording it before it vanishes forever. There is also a certain celebrity attending writers who dare to express what others have felt so as to recall to them those common elements that make us human.

The importance of the writer's social role has long been recognized. The power of the written word and the power of oratory were recognized by the early Greek and Roman philosophers. The law itself is embodied in written judicial opinions and these in turn to the processes of litigation where lawyers as skilled advocates pursue the goal of justice. To debase oratory with lies and demagoguery is therefore an offense not only against the body politic but to those ideals that make civilization even possible.

As a writer I have watched in dismay as these high humanist traditions have been recently debased so that the very thought processes of a nation have been compromised and diminished. Repeated terms of abuse derived ultimately from the techniques of absolutist rhetoric similar to those of the Stalin era in Russia led inevitably to the infamous Russian show trials of 1938. These same techniques have now been adapted to an American sensibility fanned into racist and xenophobic intensity by a single-minded President who would portray any critic of his policies as "enemies of the people" who should be beaten up or even tried for "treason."

The equation of a sitting President's personal interests with our most hallowed traditions is an example of the most brazen political effrontery that our country has ever seen. There are many subjects to which I would have rather devoted my attention than assessing the conditions that have surrounded all of us since 2016 but none have been more timely or urgent. There is a great tradition in literature for what might be called a literature of engagement. Early examples of this genre in America are *The Jungle* by Upton Sinclair, *The Octopus* by Frank Norris, *The Grapes of Wrath* by John Steinbeck, and *Darkness at Noon* by Arthur Koestler. In Europe this genre is represented by Jean-Paul Sartre's *The Roads to Freedom Trilogy* and Boris Pasternak's epic on Stalinist Russia, *Doctor Zhivago.*

These authors have been my inspiration during the years since

2016 as I looked on in horror while the unaccountable forces of American selfishness, racism, environmental exploitation, and centralized corporate rule found in the personality of Donald J. Trump their perfect spokesman and avatar. The anti-intellectualism, the repetition of verbal memes designed to seduce great masses of gullible or self-serving Americans, and the general breakdown of all civilized discourse was reminiscent of the processes that took hold in Germany in 1933. The following years led to the burning of books and the wholesale repudiation of arts and literature under Nazi rule.

My collection of short stories is entitled, *Auguries of Desolation.* The thought that led me to this title was that no better descriptive phrase could be found for America in the year of 2020. At the start of the final month of this fateful year we are approaching 300,000 dead Americans from covid-19. Many businesses have closed their doors permanently and the unemployment figures and the sheer numbers of food-challenged Americans show a fundamental class and ownership gap that is unprecedented in the past seventy years.

When I settled upon this title there was also the danger that Donald J. Trump might possibly be re-elected for another four years to complete his destruction of our democratic Republic and the final liquidation of effective opposition to his goals and ambitions. As the weeks since the election have shown, this President clearly anticipated that his base alliance of racists, fanatical religionists, and well-armed malcontents would bestow upon him the twin benefits of a shelter against charges of criminal behavior and four more years to leverage his office for the benefit of his business interests. He has even spoken in terms hinting at setting up some sort of family dynasty that would undermine American democratic mechanisms and ideals that have traditionally deplored any semblance of monarchical rule.

The result of all of the above has been a virtual fissure that now divides our nation into two mutually opposed camps. It is difficult to imagine the extent of the paranoia extant in this country as we approach the year 2021 and a new Presidency to restore order and sanity. The destruction reaches far beyond the traditional opposition found in politics. Various religious broadcasting networks have often become mere political arms for right-wing conspiracy theories not the least of which has been that when masses of American voters turned out to evict from the White House our only Presidential advocate of absolutist rule that this was a case of "stealing the election" rather than a fair and healthy just-in-time withdrawal from a descent into a would-be dictatorship.

The stories that I wrote in 2019 seem to me now in retrospect to have been prophetic of the climate of belief and the erosion of character that will hopefully be confined to the present brief era of American autocratic experimentation that began in 2016. Each of the stories that I wrote last year is prophetic in character and hence an augury. These are stories of fragmented identities, haunting resentments, and aspirations for some vanished land of promise and sanguine expectations.

On a more general note, short stories, in my opinion, are at their best when they hit the reader like a freight train so that the memory of the reader recalls them when similar situations occur in her own life. Two examples of stories like this are *The Lottery* by Shirley Jackson and *The Swimmer* by John Cheever. The short story format is a meeting of character and situation resulting in an abrupt confrontation with reality or a change in position of a significant character. There is little time for a series of incidents such as the novel format affords to the writer. Instead, life comes down upon one swiftly and remorselessly creating an insight into the deeper nature of things as in *Araby*, the first story in James Joyce's book of intimate portraits entitled simply, *Dubliners*.

Prior then to answering this first question of what led me to write I would like to explain what I have been writing in this year of the great pestilence, the year 2020. The term twenty-twenty vision will ever after this year have a special meaning. It will be the year when the world was brought up short by a world-spanning emergency that suddenly made death something that could not be outsourced to underdeveloped countries. Death from the coronavirus, while still revealing great fissures of inequality in our nation and the world, was just as likely to affect those who denied its very existence as for those who could not dodge its cruel scourge because they were essential workers on the front lines fulfilling our necessities.

When it is all over a final study of the victim categories needs to be made. The usual indicators of disaster have proven to be inadequate. The fact that the stock market and certain remote service marketers have actually increased in value and market share while so many people have died and so many small businesses have gone under has clearly revealed whose bread gets buttered in America and who must go hungry even while they may have sacrificed the most in this time of need for the general welfare. Ethical vacuums have emerged in surprising places. Many Christian denominations for instance have raised Donald J. Trump to a virtually idolatrous degree of adoration and accolades even as the country has spiraled downwards into division, chaos, and death.

Of course Americans have died in great numbers before in theaters of war but no President since Woodrow Wilson has presided over such extensive civilian deaths and casualties. It is the single greatest signature event of his spendthrift, corporate give-away Presidency and one that will always mark his tenure in office as among the darkest in our collective history. The relish with which various Christians have embraced his postures and his rambling cliché-ridden rhetoric has revealed a singular gap in both spiritual insight and basic decency so that the words "religious freedom" are in this year of 2020 virtually synonymous with a claimed right to infect others by refusing to wear masks, as if they were some sort of facial condom.

So it is that my writing this year has been largely confined to non-fictional critiques of various social structures and systems. The isolation mandated by the virus has made me aware that writers are always somewhat removed from positions to directly intervene in emergencies. Instead we serve the role of assimilation so that when the emergency has passed we can find some meaning in what has occurred and some hints about how better to respond next time. Thanks to the favorable outcome of the election of 2020 we may now look forward to something other than the shallow dictatorship that for a time appeared to be a real possibility.

I am influenced in my writing by a classical consciousness in conflict with a romantic temperament, by a Catholic faith in conflict with a free-thinking philosophy grounded in vitalism, the *élan vital* of the philosopher Henri Bergson. I hope for heaven while being one fully committed to the earth. I have been influenced and indeed have embodied those drives and feelings that are labeled transgender while refusing to entirely assimilate any fixed identity so as to keep an escape route handy should its use be necessary. Much of my writing in recent years but above all in this year of my enforced exile has been to dredge out the anger within me so that healing might be possible when the world again opens its doors to freedom of motion and human intercourse. Vitalism has tended to be denigrated as a mystical sense that life is an immaterial force that guides the mechanism of living matter but which in itself is unknowable except through its material manifestation in chemical processes. Science only recognizes what can be quantified.

The problem with vitalism is that it is both focused and universal but cannot be measured or even defined in itself. Vitalism recognizes a principle of organic unity and coordination that appears to transcend the constituent elements of an organism. It manifests consent of the parts without debate or legislation for the good of the whole. Lacking this coordination the organism or the community perishes. Cooperation is far more the underlying rule of nature than competition is. This surrender of discretion is not coerced as though it was ever possible for the organ or tissue to exist independently. The proper subordination of function is the very essence of each layer of inquiry as the living embodiment of the order existing just below it.

A cell requires the existence of mitochondria and mitochondria require the mechanism of intra-cellular transport and oxidation reactions. These in turn require the chemical composition of complex carbon-based molecules. Each of these levels of existence is embodied by characteristics that are encoded in behavior but the plan itself operates as a guidance system. It may appear to emerge coincidentally with the character of its subordinate elements so that any teleological extension might appear to be merely a metaphoric description applied to the final product but it must always be recalled until the final state is arrived at over time. The finality and goal was not clearly ascertainable but only predictable from within a range of possibilities. An eye lens without a pupil and a retina for instance would be useless. We look in vain for fossil evidence of the great refuse-heap of failed organ systems. Each existing being is perfected to a specified if limited formula.

This vital guiding force is to my way of thinking a source of theological insight parallel to any revealed sacred text and I honor it as such because the very existence of that force shows the fructifying nature of God. Similarly, to act disparagingly towards creation and to our own complex totality is to reduce God's own vitality to a set of static concepts. In this sense everything is sacramental and the rites of worship are enacted daily simply so that when I wake the world awaits me in the form of the explosion of light over the sea. The life force that is within me beats in unison with that tide that within me has taken the form of blood. My eyes invite the cascading waves and my ear rejoices in the plunge and whisper of the tides.

So what kind of writer does that make me? I hesitate to call myself a Catholic writer because I do not wish to confuse my own pronouncements with official Church teachings and practice for fear of leading others astray. My relations with Catholicism therefore are aspirational rather than conclusive. I am on my way back after a long period of exile but just how that way back is to be expressed I cannot say at the present time. I only desire that it should be sincere and not a reflex bred solely by the present crisis and the shortening path ahead of me as I age. I had budgeted for more time than is available to a single human life. As a result I feel that I am just reaching a point for commitments that others often make in their young adult years. I consider everything that I have done and thought as one great prolegomenon to existing as a single human being with a single destiny rather than one who endlessly reviews all options without ever taking a fixed position.

Some would say that to be a Catholic and simultaneously transgender is an oxymoron because these identities are incompatible. Both however have their roots sunk deep within me so that I have never been able to surrender one to the other. My participation as a writer in the Prompt Project requires a measure of identification however so I announce myself as both one and the other because both appellations are true of me to an extent. The process of realization of either is long and hard and I have not concluded them yet.

Turning then to writing as an activity proceeding from whatever inner qualities I possess; the question of why writers write is rather like asking why we breathe: we do so in order to live, not that most of us can live by writing in the pecuniary sense of the word but because writing is the path of our own vital impulses and thus inseparable for us from living at all. Art in all of its forms allows the life force to escape and to embody itself in a form that others can share. But even in the solitude of composition for the author alone it has value because it grounds us in language that like the force of gravity holds us to the earth. Writers do not exist though in solitude. To write is also to love reading what others have written and in this sense all writing is part of a long conversation between generations. I feel as close to many authors as if they were my own personal possession, as though the communication could reach upward through the text to the author and he or she would smile knowing that I understand them.

I first started writing in the seventh grade inspired by the writings of Edgar Allen Poe and my first reading of Bram Stoker's *Dracula.* Had I been more prescient and realized that Americans never tire of vampires I might have continued in that early strain of sensibility and created my own version of *Salem's Lot* or the *Twilight Series* and perhaps made a fortune. As a writer one takes one's chances with the public pulse and to anticipate a trend requires a gift of prophesy or at least a fortunate synchronicity.

Now and again it happens and the usual course of events is reversed so that publishers are found chasing writers rather than the usual case of writers chasing publishers. As for the reading public or rather publics, for they are both varied and integral, the writer drifts by temperament usually in a certain direction and if lucky finds an audience. I suggest however that to anticipate an audience and to write for it deliberately is to forfeit a higher calling that was once called being faithful to one's muse. In this sense a writer writes to please her own sense of excellence and if the public or a sector of it approves then all is well and good but first in the old cliché the writer must be true to herself.

This answers the question why I began writing and why I continue to do so. I began writing for the same reason that so many authors do: to discover in the process what I think about things and to use the medium of words as an artist. To this day I find that it is only in the process of writing that I discover my thoughts. I do not entertain a well-wrought and pre-conceived idea except in the most shadowy form and I am open to surprises as I channel as it were the voices of my inner being into print. If I use characters I let them speak and simply take dictation. Perhaps this is due to the fact that I began as a poet and poets listen before they speak because their very speech is meant to be overheard later by others though it was first an interior melody heard and transcribed. In this sense the *Ode to a Nightingale* by John Keats and his *Ode on a Grecian Urn* are the quintessential expressions of the creative process.

Once started writing I never stopped, although there were long periods of study when I was in pursuit of a facility and a voice that although fertilized by the efforts of other writers would be mine alone. Each new author brought me closer to that goal but like a mirage the goal itself always seemed to require something more before I could satisfy myself that I possessed the perfect tools for my task. I finally realized that I had been in pursuit of a mirage or a will-of-the wisp. Each writing effort is a discrete and insular endeavor and the work produced is similarly the fruit of its composition and in this sense a product of accident rather than design. There is no perfect preparation for this task nor is it ever complete; it simply is. At last I stopped waiting to be ready to write and began writing and all else has followed in due course.

The unasked question is why do writers keep writing? Some might say that it is only habit. Others would say that writing is now second nature to the writer. It may be a desire for a perfect object that has hitherto eluded the artist or it may be simply to do as well as one has done before even if our capacities diminish with time. To do so may bring pleasure or it may bring pain.   It may recall past ambitions only to see them disappointed once again. It may be simply one of life's inevitabilities that the rising of the sun each day that beckons us to return to the notebook or the keyboard and to dare again to reduce thought to words. In any case we do these things and in doing them often enough we find that we have become writers.

Moving from writing in general and reflecting specifically on the Prompt Anthology stories I would like to say something about writing from a transgender perspective. There is a natural assumption that the transgender experience is a univocal one when nothing could be further from the truth. Transgender people face similar issues and experience various levels of discrimination and oppression, but our ages and circumstances are such that radically different prospects and life courses emerge in front of us.

I lived my early transition years in a partially closeted suburbia rather than New York or San Francisco or Los Angeles. I also came up in an era where transgender existence was very dominated by the medical model and where any real communal structures existed more accessibly among the drag queen margins of gay society. Repercussions for being out were brutal, swift, and omni-present. Even movies depicted us as so freakish that our presence might trigger instant nausea if not violent assaults. Was it any wonder then that our lives were, if not nasty, brutish, and short, as Thomas Hobbes once said of human beings in a state of nature, they were at least marginal, risky, and solitary. We were pathetically grateful for simple tolerance and to be left alone. We were magnets for ridicule and the crudest possible references to our probable or supposed genitalia. So painful was this period that I write about it with difficulty so that only one of my stories deals at length with transgender characters.

Only one of my other books is entirely dedicated to transgender topics, *Transsexualism and its Discontents: A Political Profile.* Even the word, "transsexual," dates me because it traces its origins to 1966 and to Dr. Harry Benjamin who coined the term. As the tiny ripple of out transgender people has grown now to a wave through early diagnosis and treatment individuals find resources and degrees of enlightened response that were simply not present to early adult or mid-life transitioning trans-people of the 1980's and 1990's. All of which is to say that there is a sort of creaking of metaphorically speaking whalebone and crinolines in any memoir of that silent era.

Youth and beauty open many doors now that were not available to stars of the silent-era of transgender existence when we were often referred to with embarrassment at family get-togethers. Many of us watched as our prospective career prospects disappeared overnight when we began our transitions while the younger ones of us often survived by sex work and appeared all too predictably as victims of assault or even murder. These dreadful outcomes still continue today but they now at least merit some degree of investigation and prosecution.

As regards the aging transsexual, America has little reverence for dowagers unless they are colorful and well-heeled. A steamy memoir is unlikely to generate much heat if the author includes a more recent photograph that allows the reader to essay the damage that the years have wrought. We prefer that our close-ups should be artfully staged and dimly lighted. From the perspective granted by mature reflection on our lives a universal tone comes to predominate as we survey humanity and its many afflictions from the august if perilous position that age grants to us who have seen life from two opposed perspectives and can therefore provide extra depth beyond the usual proscenium wall. The mind is most expansive when the years in which to apply any wisdom gained have proportionately diminished. The powers once bestowed by charm, if we ever possessed them, now must rely upon persuasion alone and the naked power of connected words to draw a crowd and to achieve their effect.

All of which is to say that social and political recognition is the beginning for transgender people of the lives formerly denied to us. Instead a path from the cradle to the grave was dictated not so much by our biology but by the imposition of what is permissible for each gender in appearance, sexuality, and even how we are allowed to move. Imposed gender norms are an affected dance choreographed by an oppressive society that values focused violence in the male and automatic submission in the female. Each sex learns the tricks of the trade by selectively weeding out manners and behaviors that are deemed inappropriate to one's given gender. To be a gender rebel even if not dictated by profound Gender Dysphoria then is to make our own efforts at transition less extreme because the society itself is less rigid in its imposed definitions. If gender was not the political fulcrum that it is but rather a spectrum of identifications and behaviors then the systematic indoctrination that begins in childhood would not be necessary because each flower would bloom in its own time and season.

Education in America is largely dictated by the need to prepare young adults who are willing to take their assigned roles in our capitalist structure. The long lines on the freeways, the stifling office cubicles, the corporate hierarchies are the tribal norms of industrial capitalism. Gender constructed norms have shifted lately but not substantially changed. The violence that exists towards transgender people still exists because our very existence implies that these carefully wrought distinctions are not stable; but to shift them or to seek to call them into question or to supplant them, even by our tiny minority, is seen as open rebellion against religion, nature, and above all the economics of systemic repression that is necessary for an exploitive capitalist economy to grind up and expend the resources of the earth as quickly as possible so as to increase national wealth and power. This process ultimately leads to overconsumption by a few generations by imperiling the survival of future generations who will be starved to a degree that is a proportionate measure of our own self-indulgence. The trend in my present writing is to call out these processes that are leading to desolation so that they become more visible. Hopefully what I write will in some small measure turn the tide.

Which authors or books influenced you most as a writer?

Proceeding from the position that I take that writing is not a tangential activity to the writer but rather an extension of the thought processes of the writer combined with a commitment to develop her skills as a literary artist, I would to a degree conflate questions two and three by saying that development as a writer is simultaneously development of the writer as a person because she has found in literature a path to give testimony to the human community of truths and insights that proceed only through the discipline of literary creation.

If this seems to be an encomium that is not deserved when so few people actively attend to writers as sources of culture rather than other media figures I would point out that along with history, and philosophy, literary artists precede even science as the source of human knowledge in western culture from the age of Aristotle to our own. If the audience for serious literature has diminished because reading is a more demanding task than the passive enjoyment of other forms of media this is not a reflection upon the value of the literary artist but rather a comment on the way that reflection, creative silence, and critical thinking skills have diminished in the general body politic.

So in answer to this second question it would be easier to answer which authors or books have not influenced me than to specify a small selection of those that have done so. I point this out because I find something of value in every writer that I read but of course historically speaking I have had my favorites. I find that these favorites share a confessional attitude to existence and often write disguised autobiographies in their fiction. The closer that a writer remains to her key convictions the more authentic her testimony is likely to be. At the same time it is part of the imaginative faculty that it must be able to set out a hypothetical situation and then to allow the characters to speak for themselves without being mere puppets of the author the strings of which are visible and intrusive. The abiding final impression should be one of verisimilitude so that the imitation of life becomes not only life itself but life enhanced by the literary skill of the author.

The claims that I am making for authors are not to diminish the value of literature as a source of mere relaxation or entertainment. A skillful mystery or a novel of sentiment and romance is within its more limited sphere of equal value if it achieves what the author set out to do which is to please his audience from within the limits of the genre represented. Examples of these are science fiction, fantasy novels, and of course mysteries. I am very fond of Raymond Chandler for instance because of his ability to set a tone of weary discontent in his gritty stories and novels and I enjoy the thrills provided by H.P. Lovecraft and Algernon Blackwood the two greatest masters of the uncanny and the grotesque in the tradition of Edgar Allen Poe. I would also like to praise Shirley Jackson whose skill at setting a mood of anxiety and disconnection in her work shows an accuracy of judgment and a power of selection that makes her one of the greatest and most subtle writers of her era.

Having said all of this though I would like to list a few names here of writers of special importance, authors that I have used as personal models and as guides to good writing:

Thomas Wolfe, James Joyce, Virginia Woolf, William Faulkner, F. Scott Fitzgerald, John Steinbeck, Thomas Mann, Robert Musil, H.G. Wells, Thomas Browne, John Donne, Anton Chekov, Fyodor Dostoyevsky, Percy Shelley, William Wordsworth, Alfred Lord Tennyson, Thomas Carlyle, Matthew Arnold, Ernest Dowson, Robert Browning, William Butler Yeats, Robert Frost, Carl Sandburg, Amy Lowell, Georg Trakl, Tennessee Williams, Oscar Wilde, and William Inge.

The books that have most influenced me as a writer are:

Thomas Wolfe: *Look Homeward Angel; Of Time and the River*
James Joyce: *Ulysses; Portrait of the Artist as a Young Man; Finnegans Wake*
Herman Hesse: *Steppenwolf*
Romaine Rolland: *Jean-Christophe*
Boris Pasternak: *Dr. Zhivago*
Virginia Woolf: *To the Lighthouse; The Waves; The Years*
Arthur Conan Doyle: all of the Sherlock Holmes tales
Bram Stoker: *Dracula*
Sheridan Le Fanu: *Uncle Silas*
Charlotte Bronte: *Jane Eyre*
Emily Bronte: *Wuthering Heights*
Robert Burton: *The Anatomy of Melancholy*
Fyodor Dostoyevsky: *The Brothers Karamazov*
Herman Broch: *The Death of Virgil*
Herman Melville: *Moby Dick*
Shirley Jackson: *The Haunting of Hill House; We Have Always*

Lived in the Castle

Algernon Blackwood: *Supernatural Tales and Ghost Stories*

Joanne Greenberg: *I Never Promised You a Rose Garden*

Daphne du Maurier: Rebecca

Thomas Browne: *Urn-Burial*

Lawrence Durrell: *The Alexandria Quartet*

Andrew Holleran: *Dancer from the Dance*

William Styron: *The Confessions of Nat Turner*

William Faulkner: *The Sound and the Fury; As I Lay Dying; Absalom, Absalom*

C.P. Snow: The "*Strangers and Brothers*" Series of Novels

Eugene O'Neill: *Long Day's Journey into Night; The Iceman Cometh*

Tennessee Williams: *A Streetcar Named Desire*

Elizabeth Bowen: Her Novels and Short Stories

Edith Wharton: Her Novels and Short Stories

Robert Browning: Complete Poetry

Anton Chekov: All of his plays and short stories

William Inge: All of his plays

P.G. Wodehouse: Anything that he ever wrote

Ingmar Bergman: All of his Films

Alfred Hitchcock: All of his Films

David Lean: All of his Films

Such a long list demands an explanation and it is not hard for me to explain why these works were my models: because they and particularly some of their works answered something within me that was crying out for an answer. These authors and works like the Book of Ecclesiastes in the Bible seemed to confirm my own primary intuitions about the nature of the human dilemma and at precisely the time when I read them. I wanted to write books in order to answer essential human questions though not merely because they explored questions of interest to me but because their style of expression matched my own sense that manner and substance are part of a larger whole in which there is no separation. How we tell the story is the story.

Writing, if it is considered to be an integral vocation whether published or unpublished, affects every aspect of a person's life because it is based upon a habit of critical reflection and expression. For a writer the books that are read are testaments to living and inseparable from her daily life. Writers live their books for the simple reason that the act of writing consumes massive amounts of time and energy that otherwise might be devoted to more mundane activities and pursuits. To the true writer any time spent reading, reflecting on, discussing, and absorbing them into one's own repertoire of verbal and narrative skills is not time wasted but rather the very substance of life. Writers feel in connection with the long chain of prior aspirants who as artists are so caught up in life that they assume the role of re-creators in artistic form of the world that encases them but does not imprison them. Writing is an act of superlative freedom, a primary human endeavor that serves both a personal and a social imperative. It is personal in that it roots the individual in an identity and a position toward existence and it is social in that it is an act of communication that is potentially available to others through the act of reading. The author and the reader are joined in a single act of cognition and feeling, a celebration of the primal character of humanity occurs and the world is thereby enriched by a new creation.

Who can say why a certain book can affect us so deeply? I suggest that there is a synchronicity between the book and the particular sensibility of a person particularly at times of crisis. Adolescence and young adulthood are one long series of crises and for this reason young people are subject to being swayed into extravagant enthusiasm by what they read. This was doubly true for me because as a transgender person I was often in search of role models to help me to navigate an essentially chameleon identity structure. I looked to literature for the community structure and affirmation that was lacking to me in my everyday life. I used the written word to channel feelings that received no mirroring voice from my culture. Trans-people were essentially invisible. Their struggles were not celebrated but instead rendered unacceptable and therefore invisible. Part of being invisible is being gifted with an objectivity that would be impossible to a person who manages to neatly fit as just another card in the gender deck.

To transcend categories is the definition of freedom, not that gender is a mere choice, but rather that outcasts are allowed to find alliances wherever they can find them. I chose the classic authors to be my friends and to attune my own search to the vocabulary and the rhythm of their poetry and prose. This is a process of internalization. The paths of literature are as progressive in insight as those of scientists; each generation of practitioners builds upon what has gone before.

Which authors or books had the biggest impact on you as a person?

This question brings to the fore the responsibility of the author and further raises the question of whether writing is a moral or on occasion an immoral act. The fact that books have often been censored by governments and that the Catholic Church at one time, in its desire to protect the faithful from books that would harm faith or morals, kept an Index of Forbidden Books that required a dispensation or very good reason to read, shows the importance afforded to the written word. Examples abound from Baruch Spinoza to James Joyce of writers whose works were confiscated by religious or by civil authorities.

There is also the question of the vulnerable reader: what one person may read with impunity may have a bad effect on a different temperament. Still, a general disclaimer may seem somewhat affected or absurd. This element of personal responsibility as a writer has often troubled me, particularly on the vexed question of gender conflict and the legitimacy of gender transition. The spectrum of human freedom until recently has been curtailed by what for most cultures is a divinely ordained binary that runs through the human species and radically conditions our available options in form and in affective alliances.

That the body itself transitions from youth to age does not surprise us, but that the very seed-ground of sex roles may appear to yield to inner feelings and convictions is more problematic and even threatening. I will say here that the task of the writer demands an objectivity that in the writer's private life and personal decisions may not be interchangeable. Complete consistency surrounding subjects of great importance may prove impossible if one is to write at all. The best that I can do is to insert a cautionary note and leave it to the reader to consult alternate resources before assuming an authority in me that I do not possess. My own impressionist character and the nature of writing in general is tangential and evanescent.

I realize the power of influence however. The two writers who have touched me most deeply and personally have been the novelist Thomas Wolfe and the poet Conrad Aiken. Each has probed the primary terror and anxiety that exist beneath the placid surface of life. Each wrestled in his own way with the dark forces of destruction that Melville embodied in Captain Ahab's great white whale, Moby Dick. Each knew the knife-edged pain of a loneliness that has assumed almost metaphysical dimensions within him.

In a similar way I enjoy the way that Virginia Woolf manages to capture the fleeting immediacy of perception in her work. I respect Malcolm Lowry and James Baldwin also because they reveal the underside of life, the treacherous abyss of feelings and alienation that lie in wait for the unfortunate and the unwary, the addictive side of existence. Andre Gide and Albert Camus probe the nature of human sympathy and the problematic requirement of making human choices in a universe without a consistent vision of faith and an underlying girding in morality existing apart from our own inner feelings and compulsions.

The erosion of faith in the course of the 18th century enlightenment period and in the 19th century, when the Bible was first submitted to formal criticism and textual analysis and when science bore down heavily on various former presumptions of literal truth in elements of scripture, was followed by the repeated wars and existential crises of the 20th century. Literature has mirrored this erosion and the resulting anxiety and discontents. Thomas Hardy suggests that we should face our demons by looking at them directly and fully. I am not sure however that we are always prepared for the aspect of the head of the Gorgon and innocence once lost is with difficulty regained and restored. Still, I love Hardy's poetry for their irony but I find his inveterate depressive stance cloying over time. The same is true of writers like the Comte de Lautreamont, Louis-Ferdinand Celine, Emil Cioran, and other representatives of what I call the dead-end school of literature. Franz Kafka might also be listed in this school if his works were less accurate descriptions of the true horror of the middle years of the 20th century.

Depressive literature can deaden the heart and oppress the spirits. For this reason I recommend that those with a tendency to anomie or melancholy should instead read the books of a sustained optimist like Thornton Wilder or P.G. Wodehouse. This is preferable to wallowing in dark representations and I especially recommend

Theophilus North and *Heaven's My Destination* as helpful anodynes to human disillusionment and despair. I also think that the two books: *Cannery Row* and its sequel *Sweet Thursday* are must reads for every student of humanity.

My favorite authors are not necessarily the best craftspeople with elaborate plots but rather authors who describe life as fundamentally vague and inconclusive. It is often complained of that Chekov wrote plays where nothing ever happens; the characters are simply trapped in untenable situations from which they cannot extricate themselves. I find such visions to be true to life where our triumphs are often small and uncelebrated. This is why I adore books like Virginia Woolf's *To the Lighthouse* or Andre Gide's *The Counterfeiters* or Joyce's *Ulysses.* The vision granted is implicit, interior, and private.

My most recent novel is called *Pacific End: Notes for a Novel.* It is a work that questions the value of a meta-narrative for our lives asserting instead that life is for the most part a sum total of inconsequential moments. History can seek out grand patterns (Spengler, Toynbee) but the average individual is caught up like Humphrey Chimpden Earwicker and Anna Livia Plurabelle in a bar in Bristol dreaming universal history as portrayed in Joyce's magnificent verbal tapestry, *Finnegans Wake.*

My undergraduate studies were in the literature and philosophy. My degree is called a B. A. In Humanities. As an undergraduate my every instinct led me to adopt an interdisciplinary approach to my own education because I am fundamentally resistant to indoctrination. I compulsively see the flaws in virtually every system. This tendency led me eventually to legal study the very essence of which is to see the interconnection of precedents, specific fact patterns, and the rationale that directs appellate decision making. Lawyers are dedicated to a type of reasoning that is multifactorial in nature – policy must meet practice, method must meet content, and all must be both expressible and persuasive in an atmosphere of diversity and even conflict of opinions.

This mode of thinking has always been in me both natural and yet demanding of further refinement. My education has been a single-minded pursuit of what I might term significant truths leading to a vital engagement with reality. The writers that I admire share this characteristic: they are alive with a sense of intimate connection so that in reading them the spirit rejoices as precision meets beauty in accuracy of expression. There is a sense that the shadows of Plato's cave have been banished before a sudden access of divine light streaking out like lightening if only for a moment into total illumination of an aspect of experience. This is what I look for in my own writing and what I demand from life. Walter Pater in the conclusion of his book on the renaissance referred to it as a "hard gem-like flame." To have experienced it is to know what he was talking about.

The critic Matthew Arnold said that the goal of great literature was "to see life fully and see it whole." By this he meant a comprehensive view combined with accuracy in details. This goal presumed in the author a diversity of experience and careful observation. I used to imagine that my limited experience might be barring me from deep knowledge and variety in characterization, but then I reflected on Emily Bronte who from a girlhood spent in the isolation of a parsonage located on the West Riding of Yorkshire in the tiny village of Haworth managed to imagine Heathcliff and Catherine Earnshaw and their tempestuous romance.

Writers are not mere transcribers of reality but rather transformers of reality. Everything is filtered through the writer's unique sensibility and then reduced to words and these in turn may elevate experience to undreamed of intensity and insight. Behind the books that have meant the most to me as a person has always been the personality of the writer. I have always dreamed that these people must be fascinating. I have been surprised though when listening to author interviews to discover that the writer is not coextensive with her works; she may exceed it or she may fall short of our expectations.

In a sense the work of art is always a thing in itself to be judged independently. Often the sensitive reader co-creates the book by mixing it with her own experience. Often there is an ideal time to read a book when we bring to the reading a throbbing expectation that it will tell us something that we desperately need to know. I read Thomas Wolfe for instance at that time of life when everything was still before me and I could feel the poignancy of his own infinite longing for experience. Similarly when I read Voltaire today I find his saturnine reflections on human life and folly mirrors my own gently humorous tolerance for human frailty.

I have always enjoyed the 1960's song by Melanie where she speaks of looking for a good book to live in. Many books have been like that for me. I read *Dr. Zhivago* in college and it made even Stalin's Russia warm with the love of Zhivago and Lara. Movies can do the same thing for me. I carry the movie out of theater with me and only come floating down to earth hours later. This is more than "the willing suspension of disbelief" it is permeability to impressions.

The films of Ingmar Bergman haunt me in a way that nothing else can. I have to be careful because this very sensitivity can make experience like the long screech of feedback to a microphone. I have found ways to select environments so as to avoid falling into vicariously induced moods by sheer proximity to a source that creates an answering resonance within me. This tendency to take on the hue and shape of what surrounds me means that I can absorb too easily what I admire and lose something of myself in the process. To combine sensitivity to influences with a gradually evolving sense of personal convictions is the task of the writer. It means that we are open to experience but still able to sustain a central core of ideas and values out of which our literary works proceed.

I should also mention here several non-fiction books that made a decisive change in my view of the world. The first of these was *Walden* by Henry David Thoreau and his economic essay, *Life without Principle.* I was also influenced by *The Greening of America* and less popular book *The Sorcerer of Bolinas Reef* by Charles Reich. These last two were early manifestos that argued for an economy based upon a vision free of corporate control and for more tolerance for homosexual persons respectively. The book that completed by radicalization was *America is Hard to Find* by the Jesuit priest and activist Daniel Berrigan. These books in turn led me to books by alienated minority figures like James Baldwin and Edmund White and to books displaying a general attitude of rebellion particularly *The Rebel* by Albert Camus.

I developed a great respect and love for union organizers and worker movements that now extends to my ideological support for more open immigration and refugee policies. I favor liberation theology and the Zapatista movement in Mexico. The common features in all of these are simple: recognition of the basic dignity of all people, a standard of living and education that make a decent income possible to support all of the human, plant, and animal life on earth, an end to oppressive systems that benefit the few over the many, and the wisdom that each culture has to offer. Above all else I oppose systems that rely on fear rather than upon affirmation and promise as the primary motivators for human progress and salvation. I oppose a theology that uses an apocalyptic vision of history to justify depleting and destroying the earth and by crowding other species into extinction.

My current interest in post-modernist social theories require a critical reading of key texts in our civilization in the light of current needs and diversity while still retaining respect and reverence for the Western literary canon and its perpetual relevance. I believe though that the course of world history will no longer be Eurocentric. The future of the planet and of human life will be largely determined by Asia, particularly China and India. I am fascinated by geo-politics because history is largely determined by geological constraints and by ethnic loyalties.

I believe in the goal of a global sense of equity between nations while being skeptical of the human capacity for general empathy and goodwill. Absolutist claims to truth invite persecution and wars between contending groups so that peace on earth is more likely to proceed from a balance of mistrust than by perfect mutual understanding. I believe that social progress is slow and subject to reversal and that only by combination in the cause of justice does any human progress exist at all.

For this reason I despise dictatorships and ideologies of conversion by force or by the selective application of economic privation. I believe that the twin forces of leisure and culture do more to advance the happiness of humankind than mere superfluity of goods and the indulgence of material wants. Above all else I value actual freedom which means the ability to turn aside from exterior forces whether economic, political, or ideational structures that indoctrinate us, steal our precious time, and reduce us to serving others not through love but by artificially created scarcity and necessity.

I believe further that education as it has been traditionally practiced has been training in attitudes of subservience rather than a liberating force driven by curiosity and the simple joy of expanded cultural and scientific awareness. Each quadrant of life has its special tasks and abilities and there is neither time nor substance to be wasted on vanity and mental or moral slavery.

Which of your original twelve Prompt stories are you most pleased with?

I don't really have a favorite because each short story is a world unto itself and therefore not to be compared with the others. Having said that however I will attempt to square the circle and say that *Triptych* and *Ligeia* are the most personal to me while *Love and Death* is the longest and best exploration of character. As in *Triptych* I was able in *Love and Death* to use characters drawn from the LGBT community. This allowed me a degree of sympathy and intimate understanding that made these pleasant stories for me to write.

I like *Triptych* because I am in a very real sense all three characters. I also like the image of a three-paneled work of art. To borrow metaphors from allied art forms fascinates me in the same way that Thomas Mann thought of *The Magic Mountain* as verbal music in both composition and style, a sort of paean to illness and its effects upon love. My story *Love and Death* draws from that trend in German literature that traces how we often love in others dissociated fragments of ourselves seeking to heal in them what we cannot face or heal within ourselves.

It is often said that a short story should leave behind its own distinctive flavor or impact so that the reader is haunted for a time as if by a dream. Prose is allowed a certain poetic flavor. The reader enters unaware of who she will meet and must gradually acclimatize herself to the ambience of the narrative and to the person or persons she will encounter there. This means that as in reading poetry it is often helpful to read a short story twice or even three times because with each successive reading various structural elements and foreshadowing events appear and the story emerges as an integral and involved structure.

Novels may be written, poems may be composed but short stories are sculpted. Each genre has its own proper techniques and alliances with other art forms whether graphic or musical. Some vibrate around a central theme while others are discursive in nature and some manage to transcend all categories and are true to some organizing insight that may be particular to that single work. Some evoke a long tradition while others are their own genus or species. The fun of being a writer is to write with an awareness of the tradition and the main exemplars of it while being simultaneously free to challenge the form and to extend its parameters. My own two models for excellent short story writing are Elizabeth Bowen and Flannery O'Connor although they are very different is style and choice of subject matter.

The relationship between character and situation in the short story is bilateral. The best short stories probe a situation through the lens of a central character or a dyad of opposing personalities. I have always loved the ancient Greek philosopher Heraclitus who felt that all of reality is based on change which is paradoxically the only constant. He might be called the father of dialectical thinking that finds truth to be a function of the tension between opposing forces. It is not essential that a short story go anywhere or that it have an obvious termination or to reach a solution as long as the existing relations of the situation in all of its parameters are explored so that the reader herself is raised to a higher level of comprehension.

Chekov understood that to explore states of quiet desperation and unresolved conflict may be the best mirror of the average condition of many people. American culture thrives on the illusion of progress and ultimate resolution, a particularly naïve proclivity in the face of the long history of the world. My intention in the Prompt collection was to explore the form of the short story genre by allowing a degree of freedom to my expression rather simply telling a story in an A to Z fashion. Instead my goal was revelation, to let the story tell itself in whatever guise it chose so that no two stories would be alike. The Prompt Anthology is unique in the openness and diversity of viewpoints and styles of expression represented as well as the diversity of the authors that it has brought together.

Which of your original twelve Prompt stories did you find most difficult to write?

If I write at all I find that the stories just come. What I mean by this is that the words are not pulled out of me but rather ride on their own internal impetus so that I am in a sense merely transcribing them in real time. I have something to say and I say it. I may entertain an initial idea but the actual writing is as immediate as speech. This part of writing is therefore easy for me but what is not easy is for me to decide to let the writing go out into the world because the response is not something that I can determine. I take seriously the Socratic oath that physicians take, although I am not a physician but a writer, "First of all do no harm." In order however to tell a story I am obliged to honor the integrity of the story and its own inner dynamic. This is particularly necessary when the intent of the story is to write of something disturbing or unpleasant or confrontational.

The very title of my contributions to this anthology when gathered together, *Auguries of Desolation,* is hardly an invitation to a genial reading experience. They are rather an invitation to contemplate a year of anxiety that was prophetic of what was to come and has now arrived in the garb of the covid-19 pandemic that of course I could not have foreseen but rather felt along that delicate membrane of sensibility that writers often possess. Many cultures consider that transgender people display by their very marginality abilities that make them sensitive to collective influences in their environment. Whether that is actually true in a metaphysical sense is not for me to say. It would be flattering however if I might claim this to be true because it would mean that insight and feeling can produce a public augury to help us through dark times.

I do not approve of many of my characters or condone their actions or opinions. Some of them are nasty or misled in their thoughts and actions but as a result they are indicative of social forces in the difficult times that we are living through. Often their hopes may be vain although they may be the best response that they can muster from within their limited world view and experience of life.

This is also how I feel about specifically transgender topics. I know the price that is exacted by coming out as transgender and the price that I have paid for it and I still carry with me a sense that I forfeited a parallel life by the choices that I have made. On the other hand any suppositions that I might make about the course that such a parallel life might have taken is mere supposition just as it is supposition for me to imagine that if I had gone to New York rather than remaining in a small town in Washington I might have been part of the increasing visibility of transgender people in this comparatively open era of our collective existence. A final gloss on this topic of "what ifs" is supplied by the narratives that transgender people find layered upon them by various sources of disapprobation and condemnation. It is not easy to be an artifact of cultural anxiety and loathing.

There is much talk of the danger of what has been called "gender ideology" which would tend to destroy (according to those who find our very existence threatening) all differences between men and women, weaken or destroy the family, and turn humanity into a soup of various body parts interchangeable at will. My answer to these fears has always been that transgender people would not run the risks that we run if we found gender markers to be insignificant and changeable at a whim. The search for "realness" and the desire to find intimacy and family undergirds much of our lives even when we are rejected or exiled from our biological families.

The ready slot of gender conformity that is assumed to be simply waiting there for us to claim and take up simply ignores the fact that many transgender kids and adolescents spent every possible effort to assume a standard gender role in their growing-up years only to be rejected by their straight peers anyway for being somehow queer or different. Very few had the support and opportunity to live a gender role other than that assigned at birth. That our lives can so easily be co-opted to serve the collective agenda and allay the anxieties of larger societal groups whether religious or social or political ignores the fact of our individuality. We are painted as subversive to the same gender normative canons that never served us. The people who hate us most have never met us and realized that we are human just like them and need love, respect, and an opportunity to thrive.

The dilemma then for the transgender writer when she deals with transgender topics is to retain a neutral stance among whatever joint loyalties she may have from her past life. If she is overly sympathetic to her cause or her people she is said to be engaged in special pleading and if she is critical of her own community she is a traitor or a sell-out. This means that to take up such a thankless task is costly. It isn't fun for me to write too close to the bone and I am even surprised to find myself doing so here but since honesty is the primary purpose of writing at all I am doing so. I do not desire to promote the transgender experience or to get others to adopt it. I will say that to confront the fact that gender discomfort exists is the first act of acceptance that we owe each other and that to reduce the quality of life of transgender persons by ridicule or condemnation is a violation of our basic common humanity. I will now take a moment to focus on the specific question here by profiling a single story and the difficulty that writing it presented.

Bats was my most difficult story in many ways because in writing it I was feeling my way and asking myself what the short story is all about as a form and a genre. This story was an experiment in a free-flowing narrative modality as I sought to find a style and format for what I would have to say as the process of my contributions to the Prompt Anthology continued. As such this story is a bridge to the later stories, a blend of drama and exposition as I felt about for a voice and a format.

A careful reading of *Bats* will reveal that the central character is not at all clear about who she is and whether writing isn't some sort of witchcraft. Perhaps she is possessed after all. She believes that her inner anger can influence events. There is more than a touch of Shirley Jackson here; writers as sorcerers. They bend the world to their own conceptions and they invite us into haunted groves to discover ourselves. My general intent in each of the stories was to mirror the mood of a dark era in American history under the Trump Presidency by exploring characters that hover along the borders of dissolution in their pursuit of a stable identity and life-course.

As the first of my wounded and discontented characters Tiffany Amorth is in search of a stable identity and direction in life. She lives in an isolated home under the shadow of a father who sees the shadow side of her personality and cannot affirm her. He concludes in consequence that she is possessed by an evil spirit, a position that justifies the continuous low pressure rejection that he communicates to her. This rejection awakens great anger within her and that anger seeks an outlet in her writing. She comes to believe finally that she can write people's fates into her stories and in doing so she can make things happen in real life.

Her sense of vicarious power relieves her sense of victimhood and discharges the energy of her over-whelming anger that would otherwise be internalized against herself. The question raised therefore is whether this method of coping with her interior states is by its very operation a kind of witchcraft that invites whatever dark spirits may exist about us to take residence within us (a key way to look at the phenomenon of demonic possession). In the literature of exorcism a specific environmental entry point can provide a pre-condition for preternatural activity in a person's life.

There is a bleed-over effect between persons so that her father's inability to deal with his own emotions has made Tiffany a culture medium for his own repressed feelings. She feels that her trust expressed toward both her father and the world that surrounds her has been compromised and in her loneliness she has turned to the shadow realm for defense and companionship. She seeks power over others just as people have always had power over her and she processes her own sense of betrayal and insignificance by an assumed air of omnipotence. This raises the question as the story ends of whether Tiffany Amorth is in fact indeed possessed. In a paired story that follows *Bats* she resolves this tension as she dreams of escape to Denmark.

As I continued to write for this anthology I found that the writing came easier. Another function of the short story format is to explore the way that stories are like those Russian dolls that contain ever smaller versions of the same thing. Stories are like cascading levels of reality. We assemble our life-scripts from the remnants of those lives in the generations that have preceded us. Our memories can provide fixed anchors for later dysfunctional behaviors that are replicated generation after generation. This is one of the causes of mental illness as many psychologists have affirmed.

My approach to short story writing includes the improvisational. I believe that short stories are essay-like in that they attempt to portray essential aspects of life through transient events. There is neither time nor space to elaborate on character as it is formed over time. Instead what is revealed are those lightening-like moments of perception when what was already present is revealed or where a substantial change takes place due to an overwhelming alteration of experience. These were the moments that James Joyce referred to as "an epiphany" as exemplified in his first book, *Dubliners.* The later career of James Joyce is the story of his successive efforts to perfect a literary form before moving on to the next challenge. Only his play *Exiles* is flawed.

James Joyce ended his career with the seventeen year project of writing *Finnegans Wake,* a vast compendium of everything and everyone. HCE or Humphrey Chimpden Earwicker means "Here Comes Everybody." HCE is a universal figure of the human condition, flawed but noble even in defeat. His wife ALP or Anna Livia Plurabelle represents the feminine life-force that winds through time incarnating various versions of the human form in her children: Shem, Shawn, and Issy or Isabel, a younger version of herself. The subject of *Finnegans Wake* is the life process itself as it appears in history, in religion, and in all of the scrambled words of the world as they are brought together in a molten magma-like state under the hands of the great artificer who Icarus-like dares to soar above the human spectacle taking note of all things and writing them down in a single volume. If short stories are cameo presentations, *Finnegans Wake* is a panorama or pageant. The two forms stand at opposite ends of the literary rainbow.

Which book of writing do you recommend?

I believe that writing is best learned by a process of absorption. Just as in figure skating individual skills can be practiced but flow and rhythm are only attained by free-skating and letting the motion carry the skater on and into the jumps and spins. Style precedes substance and is often completely individual and almost innate. Most writers develop their own signature sound and style so that simply to hear a passage read is to recognize the author. Ideas are something else again; these require reflection and a critical sense. The good writer is always aware of her reader but not so as to become self-conscious and mannered.

A critical sense guides construction but far more it makes possible the smoothing process that occurs in the second or third drafts. Some writers require the skill of a sensitive editor who can provide a third dimension to the two dimensional text. Writers know best how a text should mean and sound but an editor if she is sufficiently skilled can reveal latent ambiguities that the author may have missed because her underlying idea has not been sufficiently embodied in the text as written. Good editors are rare. Maxwell Perkins edited Hemingway, Wolfe, and Fitzgerald each of whom had a unique style and a personality structure that did not suffer criticism gladly. Perkins knew this and took on the role of a literary midwife rather than a voice from above telling these great authors how to write; his role was to pare and trim not to constrict or to construct. A good marriage of author and editor is rare. Authors are a prickly lot; it is part of their charm. This is also why authors seldom get along when they appear together on talk shows; there is room for only one diva at a time onstage.

Ideas and themes are another matter still. When people say, "I would like to write but I don't know what to write about," they are displaying the aspect of writing that requires knowledge and experience. These are only acquired through much experience of life: careful observation, imaginative reconstruction, and reflection. A good dramatist also adds the faculty of dissociation that allows her to speak realistically from diverse characters; otherwise they would all sound the same. The appreciation of plot and story, careful timing of effects, adequate foreshadowing, and some degree of reconciliation at the end of the various strands of the story require a sense of construction and timing. This skill set may be the most difficult to acquire.

Not that every short story or novel should read with the neat probability of a television show with its carefully demarcated mini-climaxes before each commercial to sustain interest. A form that is too predictable is always boring. Good literature should be story-based but ultimately tied to life and life is nothing if it is not unpredictable. Stories emerge out of a general Weltanschauung or world-view. How does one acquire such a general sense of the way the world is?

The book, *Recovering Your Story*, by Arnold Weinstein is a good place to begin. There is a therapeutic value in reading great works of literature because they enable us to discover ourselves by seeing our own lives in the wider context of a civilization largely forged by literature. Writing requires that one take a stance towards what has already been written. Works of literature do not emerge from the head of Zeus fully grown. I believe that writing can only be learned through absorbing the works of other writers until they are part of us. Writing is not like following a recipe. The only exception to this is technical writing and perhaps writing non-fiction where topical development and clarity of expression are helpful, even essential. In fiction however the key is to master a genre through wide acquaintance with the masters in the field until they awaken an answering voice within us.

Having said this however I would recommend reading as much as you can about favored authors: their criticism, their biographies, their letters if published, and their autobiographies or journals. Writers write about writing and it pays to listen to them. Realize though that their witness is personal. Seldom do two writers agree about anything, so be prepared to take a position and run with it. A good starting point is *The Summing Up* by Somerset Maugham which describes his own evolution as a writer.

Most writers cannot adequately explain what they do; they may be as surprised at the dynamics of their own creations as their readers are. Good writers follow a craft tradition but in doing so they advance that very tradition by breaking prior norms. There is an oscillation between romanticism and classicism in most literary traditions. Northrop Frye for example has created an entire taxonomy of literary works. There is a motion within most literary works so that in the end there is a change of fortune in the main characters as they meet challenges. In the characters the standards of the community are either affirmed or called into question. In this sense literary works are social products the value of which is often disputed as Sir Philip Sidney discussed in his extended essay, *An Apology for Poetry.*

I confess that my critical preferences follow Edward Young in his *Conjectures on Original Composition* and Edgar Allen Poe's *The Poetic Principle.* I would also recommend the critical writings of Murray Krieger in a more modern vein. I am fond of 17th century prose and am never dismayed by the convoluted phrase. I think that the mindset and faculties of our present age are diminished by the bare declarative statement without texture or nuance and it is my hope that a better embroidered prose may soon supplant the present style of discourse with something displaying more meat and flavor. We will never realize what we have lost until we spend time with the baroque masters and attune our ear to their diction and rhythms. I agree with Thomas Mann that literature is like music. Good writers hear the words that they write and are never in advance of them. Thoughts form organically and are not the mere aftereffects of foregone conclusions. Writers are not puppets of some exterior master but seekers on voyages of discovery.

To read the published letters of great authors provides unparalleled access to the writer's mind and preoccupations. The collections of the journals and the letters of Virginia Woolf are a great place to start, and to finish since she is inexhaustible and encyclopedic in her scope of acquaintance and reflections on various writers. Writers tend to form *ad hoc* communities. These communities are not always friendly because writers read other writers in the same way that people engaged in the same sport follow the competition. The grounds for engagement may be critical reception, sales volume, or attention from a publisher. The end result though can be positive because technique is honed by encounter with difference. Writers both admire and distain other writers sometimes because of differences in their creative philosophy. It takes confidence to be a writer and to resist the pull of contradictory influences. To stand forth boldly as one's solitary self takes courage and sometimes bullheadedness. Posterity rewards persistence. Innovation in the arts as in so much else may be a lonely pursuit. Herman Melville's relatives thought that the poor man was mad. Each book that he wrote had proportionately smaller sales. Thomas Hardy gave up novels after the public response given to *Jude the Obscure.* Henry James reached a sort of peak in his refined and convoluted narrations with his novels, *The Golden Bowl* and *The Ambassadors.* Some writers' peak early and some are prevented from achieving their full promise by dying too young like Thomas Wolfe.

Then there are a tiny few like James Joyce whose genius is so great that he leaves his readership behind. I am a virtual apostle of his final achievement, *Finnegans Wake,* which is a virtual love letter to the human race. In it Joyce turned humor and even a rascally sense of the obscene into a history of the entire human race. Reading it is like learning to play a musical instrument; it takes time and repeated efforts. Joyce appreciated that on the other end of original sin there exists the drama of successive failures; even our saints are flawed. Complexity hides an overarching simplicity and the value of love. Joyce was more Catholic that he knew.

The value of criticism is not to judge and to degrade but rather to illuminate excellence so that we can better appreciate how the great writers manage to achieve their effects. Criticism exists to illuminate and to explicate in other terms what the writer achieves in the first instance by her text. This activity is similar to the study of the Jewish Talmud where each successive reading of the Mishnah results in greater depth and understanding, the Gemara. A Yeshiva school teaches a discipline of approach so that the Torah becomes a living rather than a dead historical text.

At its most basic level criticism is a guide book. So for what might be called a more accessible criticism I would suggest the writings of Alfred Kazin and of Malcolm Cowley. It is often helpful to filter our own personal responses to individual works through the sensibility of a sensitive spirit. For this same reason I recommend the book *Cultural Amnesia: Necessary Memories from History and the Arts* by Clive James, an Australian literary critic of immense scope and erudition. Another work that is of primary importance as a summary of world culture is by John Ralston Saul and entitled: *Voltaire's Bastards.* I also recommend the classic book *Mimesis: The Representation of Reality in Western Literature.* Finally, as a unique attempt at a synthesis of the western literary canon I recommend: Harold Bloom's *Genius: A Mosaic of One Hundred Exemplary Creative Minds.*

What advice would you give an unpublished writer?

I have already expounded on much of my philosophy of writing. The function of the writer is to write, the function of the editor is to edit, and the function of the publisher is to create a marketable product and to ensure distribution. Each plays a key role in mediating between the author and the reader. Each role has its proper boundaries. The writer comes first in point of origin but the temptation to never let go of the work and to realize that it is finished can prevent the actors and the director from staging a play and it can prevent an editor from eliminating ambiguities and the publisher from reducing the text to a saleable product. An overbearing influence by an editor can frustrate an author's desire to completely realize his or her vision while a good editor can help an author to fully realize his or her intent by clarifying key themes and by smoothing the edges of a text through careful trimming away of confusing or non-essential elements.

The publisher can provide encouragement at key moments when an author succumbs to self-doubt or exhaustion. At least in the past publishers were often an essential buffer between penurious or unstable writers and the folly of their own intemperate habits. Talent needs a home and appreciation as well as a market for our creations and the best publishers can provide these. Of course such delicate handling is often reserved for treasured authors and the young writer who brings such temperamental demands to the publisher will be disappointed.

The days of the family-owned publishing houses are no more. Book publishers were gobbled up by corporate conglomerates with a bottom-line mentality in most cases. Fortunately the advent of print-on-demand and smaller private niche publishing has given more voices a chance to be heard than in the old days. Good work will find a place and much of the run-around has been eliminated.

My overall advice then to writers is to do the writing job well because that is the task of the writer. Avoid publishers that are in the business of teaching writers how to write. Look for a publisher that spares the writer superfluous tasks but be prepared for a key truth: very few books have what may be called general appeal; writers have a target audience and all fiction is finally genre dominated. Decide who you want to reach and how and then trust your instincts and continue to write.

Many recent books have been written about self-promotion and marketing for budding authors. To say that they leave a nasty taste in the mouth is obvious because there are many items from detergents to toothpaste that are easier to sell than books. It is a sad fact but after high school and college fewer and fewer people read anything beyond a smattering of self-help books and predictable romances and thrillers.

On occasion a supposedly sexy read will vault a novel into the category of a must-read for those whose fantasy and visualization skills demand hypnotically suggestive passages. Certain other works slated to an age group of children or female adolescents will create cycles of books to fuel a micro-addiction to witches or vampires or what have you. There may be a central figure that one can identify with; many men once could imagine that there was a slumbering secret agent inside them and that they could alternate defeating improbable foes with nightly bedroom antics drawing on an endless supply of available females, fatal or otherwise.

Then there are various university presses on the other end of the publishing world that publish scholarly books that may sell a few thousand copies to the scholarly community that find such matters interesting or professionally required. There are few captive audiences anymore and to presume to gage the national or the international pulse with a breakthrough insight is unlikely to occur. The occasional bestseller does not alter this situation. All of which is to say that the writer must accept that the time spent writing, if exercised for expected pecuniary rewards, is time ill-spent. The good news is that this very fact frees the writer to create the best work that she can in order to live up to her own standard of excellence and then to begin the long and piece-meal search for those who can appreciate what she has done. It is here that publishers can help the solitary writer.

I hear much of book tours and book-signings but even these presume some degree of predictable author name recognition and a following have been achieved. Publicity tours demand larger publishing houses to finance them or available private funds and time. Small initial print runs have long since made an author's second book to be at least as critical as the first. The time allotted to achieve success in major bookstores is limited. To be listed on an online store is in many ways to be located somewhere as a drop in a vast ocean where a theoretical presence is in fact virtual invisibility.

Financed expeditions to find the author where she is lost in a jungle of towering trees are unlikely to exist. In the world of publishing as in so much else it is success that breeds further success. The public's memory is fickle and sustained loyalty even rarer. The net result is that authors often find themselves in the position of Norma Desmond waiting for Hollywood to call. Sustained labor can achieve results of course but time spent in other pursuits limits the time for writing and meanwhile one must still manage to exist.

Copyright grants protection that extends long past the shelf-life and appeal of most books. Look up any best-seller of two years ago and see whether a current edition is available. Printing on demand makes it possible of course for a trickle of life to be sustained in the desert and this has been the salvation of many writers. Micro-publishing allows for more freedom and intimacy to exist between an author and her readers. One can no longer repair to Cannes or Biarritz and send a novel off to New York every two years when funds are running scarce.

After these discouraging remarks however I would like to point out that quality never dies and I have personally been delighted to find a treasure of delights preserved by the Gutenberg Project of books long since in the public domain that exceed in quality and relevance most of what is published today to an avid readership hungry for trifles written by dullards who have no idea or concern for the general decline of literacy in America. As John Keats said, "A thing of beauty is a joy forever." So I urge all would-be authors to value their writing as they value themselves, not for celebrity but for that group of people who love them. There is no greater joy than to stand back from whatever one creates and to say, "There it is!"

Virginia Woolf solved many of these problems by creating with her husband Leonard Woolf the Hogarth Press. It was the Hogarth Press that published T.S. Eliot's great poem, *The Wasteland.* It was Sylvia Beach who published Joyce's magnificent and celebrated book, *Ulysses,* out of her Paris bookshop, Shakespeare and Company. Authors are in many ways a self-sustaining community. Now and again a publishing miracle will occur and entire schools of authors find a simultaneous voice. It is no accident that Shelley knew Byron, Wordsworth knew Coleridge, that the Sitwell brothers and sister were from a single family, or that the writers of the Beat Movement were all friends. Ezra Pound promoted James Joyce. Only Amy Lowell was a solitary apostolic voice as a poet, but then she had the money to do so. Above all then do not surrender hope for hope always finds a way.

Do you have a "dream project" as a writer? If so what would it be?

The copyright laws of the United States protect literary works for the lifetime of the author plus seventy years so it is natural that a writer for both artistic and commercial motives would hope that her books would be purchased and read for the full time allotted to her estate. After this period her works enter the public domain and may be reproduced without royalties to the author. I mention this because it is the hope of authors that their works will prove interesting and relevant so as to ensure a long period of readership. One of the dilemmas of the artist is that the more localized in time, place, or genre the book may be the more risk there is that changing times will diminish the appeal of that book except for those with antiquarian proclivities and tastes.

A classic work in contrast aspires to immortality or at least to a degree of longevity that exceeds the period in which it was first submitted to the public for approbation and recognition. Even many winners of the Nobel Prize for Literature are little read today. Some great works are discovered though at later dates and finally reach a readership that eluded them during the author's lifetime. Examples of this fate are Herman Melville, Franz Kafka, and F. Scott Fitzgerald. This observation is why I insist that writers must be true to their own vision and purposes, particularly if they aspire to lasting relevance. Many curious books have qualified as classics because in them is found something of perennial value while many celebrated works with great sales perish is short order as the public's fickle interest wanes.

The best creations like slow burning embers give off more heat than swiftly consumed kindling. The diminishing costs of reproduction and the Kindle revolution has made the concept of a beautiful leather-bound volume with gilt-edged pages seem somewhat absurd. Words today and phrases are of such brief duration and of so arbitrary a nature that the idea of long reflection and perennial relevance seems the height of vain aspiration. Even the speeches of key public figures scarcely stimulate recollection within a week of their puppet-like delivery since everyone knows that they were composed by teams of unacknowledged minions who will never appear for scrutiny by the public.

Literary history has its great names who have attempted encyclopedic assessments of human nature such as Shakespeare, Dickens, Balzac, and Joyce as well as writers who due to a single major work will be equally immortal such as Emily Bronte and Robert Musil. I say all of this as a prelude to explain that my dream project is to continue to reach that special group of readers who share my reverence for the classics. No one can directly intend to write a classic work and no fortune-teller can predict or even describe how or when anything will be considered to have reached that level of significance and appeal. Still for all of that I believe that certain writers believe that they are writing in the classical tradition, seeking to advance the long inquiry of art as it probes the human condition in its unfathomable complexity and variety. My dream project has been and continues to be to echo in some far off way the sound of a distant clarion from the writers, often long dead, who are for me living voices.

I do have another dream project however. Like many writers I would like to write specifically for films, not Hollywood blockbusters, which are usually farmed out to well known screen writers, but films that have the same expressionist sensitivity of the Ingmar Bergman films. To encounter his cinematic creations is to realize how European film-making differs from American films. The films of Bergman are both realistic and symbolic at the same time; they are films of moods and ideas that explore relationships. They take you inside the characters by the expressiveness of their highly talented cast members.

It is hard to pick a favorite, but I have always loved, *The Silence.* It explores the adult world from with a child's vision and point of view. The situation is only vaguely defined so that the elements cohere only by the fact that they are happening. There are few existing categories through which to interpret them and in this sense Bergman mirrors the way that reality impinges upon us in ways that are often dreadful and beyond our ability to find easy answers. There is no easy three act structure to provide resolution and because of this we are often left bewildered and anxious because we realize that Bergman has touched us in the places of uncertainty that exist for all of us. The dialogue is often less important than the visual scenes that develop an intensity and a significance that is more suggestive than it is literal.

I would like to write dramas and films like that because they are at once character specific and universal. They leave an impression that remains long after we leave the theater. Motion and facial expressions are no longer utilitarian but true windows to the soul as in Berman's film, *Cries and Whispers* or the suggestive but indeterminate relations between the nurse and her female patient in *Persona*. Some people are frustrated with Bergman because they expect an easy answer to what is going on in his films. This misreads Bergman's intent. His films are more like impressionist paintings, the painting is less a representation than an object that must be approached from within itself. There is no handy guide to offer outer testimony so that any two people might be affected by his films in different ways. The attention that Bergman devotes to minute details is not linear but three-dimensional so that meaning radiates outward in multiple directions. This type of art teaches us how it is to be apprehended; we have to step up to the challenges that it presents and by doing so we enlarge our own sensibilities.

Did the pandemic impact your writing? If so, how did it do so?

472

Before dealing with my personal response to the pandemic I would like to take note of the utter improbability in the minds of most people, particularly in America, that any such visitation was even possible. I had long since thought through the probabilities of the Cascadia Earthquake or even an eruption of Mount Rainer or perhaps a nuclear war with North Korea but like many Americans I trusted that the filter provided by the World Health Organization and the Centers for Disease Control would prevent any widespread plague of contagion in America. As the year 2020 progressed Americans began to divide around issues of freedom and the common good. The wearing of face masks became the insignia of the degree that Americans could be counted on to adhere to common-sense public health mandates. Long simmering resentments or suspicions of unwarranted government intrusion on private affairs and religious observances soon erupted into large scale resistance that has resulted in the exponential numbers of deaths and covid-19 cases of November/December 2020, as these lines are being written.

Loyalty to the President became identified with scorn for the virus and a displacement of its world-wide spread to its first country of manifestation, China. Donald Trump's trade war with China was now broadened to a general mistrust that mirrored the anti-Chinese sentiments of the late 19th century. The religiously motivated animosities of Americans began to shift towards a specific focus on Iran and China. The wall that had been in the process of construction along our southern border with Mexico had little effect on a virus. Instead of women and children from Honduras and Guatemala the virus arrived by air flights from Europe and from return flights from China to the U.S.A.

I wanted this year to get things off to a good and propitious start so I did not wait for May or June to head south to the Oregon coast. Within a week of my departure I was surprised to hear that my brother was the admitting physician for the patient identified at that time, February 29th 2020, as the first American to die from the virus. By then I was no longer in Washington. The pandemic began to take hold for me shortly after my arrival in Oregon. I left for the coast on impulse the weekend before Ash Wednesday. Two weeks later I just had time to visit a monastery for a short retreat and to pursue upon returning to the coast my usual activities of writing in coffee shops and haunting various buffets before the spread of the virus really became widespread and the state lockdown happened.

After that I simply adjusted to my present circumstances and I have remained here ever since. The county where I am situated has witnessed comparatively low virus spread to date. Here I have been able to do a great deal of reading and reflecting and to work on two new books: a sequel to my multi-volume, *The Confessions of Sherlock Holmes* and an extension of a book of political essays originally entitled *The Great Reset* that I first published in 2017.

The Sherlock Holmes sequel has been a multi-year project to understand the role of the individual in history in the light of the First World War. The book of essays explores current issues in American politics and also deals with various problematic issues in the Roman Catholic Church. These essays share in common a sense of helplessness and dissolution in two areas of life where many people seek guidance and stability, viz. in our political structures and in our religious institutions. When fundamental institutions seem not only divided in terms of policy but in the methodological norms that govern their procedures and essential underpinnings the result is a sense of confusion and anomie.

If there is one sense that human beings share in common at this critical juncture of history it is precisely this sense of things coming apart so that we are experiencing a simultaneous sense of crisis and of failure in critical institutional levels of support in our collective psychic infrastructure. Valid answers are not forthcoming because even their sources are perceived as biased by political factors, personal advantage, and even by epistemological collapse. This is more than a simple loss of trust because of a temporary set of aberrations. Instead, when I speak of epistemological collapse I am referring to a general sense that the truth function of a society is unattainable because the primary axioms and their corollaries are now in dispute.

It was precisely this problem that was explored in the writings of Michel Foucault. Like many post-modern thinkers Foucault was able to show that many of our social systems if not all of them rest upon a consensus that is social in origin and power related and not metaphysically grounded. As such these fundamental structures are subject to radical questioning and may collapse suddenly under stress. I believe that the coronavirus pandemic has nudged social institutions at all levels into a condition of recognizing their fundamental inadequacy under the present conditions of rapid change whether in politics, climate change, religion, or economics.

This was precisely what occurred at the time of the Black Death in the 14th century. Conceptions of reality can suffer their own earthquakes. The more fundamental and unquestioned these axioms and corollaries are the greater damage is inflicted on a sort of psychic scale, one that is exponential in nature. As we approach the most fundamental institutions and concepts the damage done and the disruption that occurs through their diminishing utility as coping mechanisms approaches the catastrophic. Under certain conditions whole civilizations can collapse.

It is my belief that the stories in the Prompt Anthology written last year as my contribution manifest a premonitory sense that something dreadful was coming. The clouds were gathering and each of the characters in my stories was dealing with changes that threatened their former precious but precarious sense of a stable existence and the ability to cope with new circumstances. Someone somewhere was presumed to be in charge, competent to the situation, and could guide us through the collective crisis and therefore deserved our loyalty and allegiance. He was not Donald J. Trump and his menagerie in residence at the White House.

As the year of 2020 draws to a close these assurances are ever more questionable. The very simultaneity of the corona crisis has made it a general human dilemma where life cannot go on as we have expected it would with only minor adjustments and accommodations as we sink deeper into the 21st century. The world is being asked to make swift and perhaps irreversible decisions that will affect the balance of world-trade, national sovereignties, fundamental rights, and basic individual security. The result is a potential for a degree of existential panic and violence as protests fill streets in nation after nation and as various oligarchs wonder if the systems that have ensured their economic primacy are about to collapse.

These are critical times, but the juncture of decisions is at hand. The biosphere has shown inordinate patience with our greed and folly; now is the time for a severe assessment followed by action on multiple fronts. From the bottom ascent in the only direction possible and I prefer to end on an upsweep, an optimistic and more salutary note. For these reasons I have chosen to copy the title of John Donne's famous poem, *A Valediction Forbidding Mourning*, as my final entry to the Prompt Project's last volume as a poetic farewell to a way of life and a degree of world consensus that is about to undergo unparalleled stress but perhaps finally to lead us all to a new assessment of what it means to be human and a better life.